MITZVAH STORIES
Seeds for Inspiration and Learning

MITZVAH STORIES: Seeds for Inspiration and Learning

Edited by GOLDIE MILGRAM AND ELLEN FRANKEL

WITH PENINNAH SCHRAM, CHERIE KARO SCHWARTZ, AND ARTHUR STRIMLING

Yossi Alfi
Noa Baum
Joel Ben Izzy
Yisroel Bernath
Renee Brachfeld
Roslyn Bresnick-Perry
Barry Bub
Phil Cohen
Anita Diamant
Helen Engelhardt
Ed Feinstein
Ellen Frankel
Mark S. Golub
James Stone Goodman
Dan Gordon
Janie Grackin
Eva Grayzel
Bonnie Greenberg
Tina Grimberg
Dan Grossman
Miriam Grossman
Fred Guttman
Jill Hammer
Sharona Halickman
Amichai Lau-Lavie
Benji Levene
Herb Levine
Syd Lieberman
Doug Lipman
Cindy Rivka Marshall
Melvin Metelits

Goldie Milgram
Lynnie Mirvis
Nadia Grosser Nagarajan
Steve Nathan
Caren Neile
Leon Olenick
Yoel Perez
Peter Pitzele
Jack Riemer
Carol and Neal Rose
Gail Rosen
Barbara Rush
Sandy Sasso
Zalman Schachter-Shalomi
Peninnah Schram
Rebecca Schram-Zafrany
Cherie Karo Schwartz
Howard Schwartz
Rami Shapiro
Danny Siegel
Laura Simms
Corinne Stavish
Naomi Steinberg
Arthur Strimling
Carla Vogel
Shohama Harris Wiener
Diane Wolkstein
Debra Gordon Zaslow
Steve Zeitlin
Jennifer Rudick Zunikoff

Reclaiming Judaism Press

MITZVAH STORIES: Seeds for Inspiration and Learning

For information about how to reprint material from this book, please download and e-mail a completed permissions form via website below. Reclaiming Judaism Press books may be purchased for educational, business, or sales promotional use. For information, please write: Rabbi Goldie Milgram, Editor-in-Chief, Reclaiming Judaism Press, publisher@reclaimingjudaism.org

Reclaiming Judaism Press site: http://www.reclaimingjudaism.org

Publisher's Cataloging-in-Publication data

Milgram, Goldie, 1955-.
   Mitzvah stories : seeds for inspiration and learning / Goldie Milgram and Ellen Frankel, eds.
   p.m.
   Includes index.
   ISBN: 978-1-4664155-3-9 (pbk, Library Binding)
   ISBN: 978-0-9848048-0-1 (pbk, Trade Edition)
   ISBN: 978-0-9848048-2-5 (Kindle/E-Book Version)

1. Jewish way of life --Fiction. 2. Short stories, Jewish. 3. Jews --Fiction. 4. Storytelling --Religious aspects --Judaism. 5. Jews --Social life and customs -- Fiction. I. Frankel, Ellen. II. Title.

PN6120.95.J6 M58 2011
808.83/935203924 --dc22
Cover design: Harwin Studios, Inc. & Taylor Rozek

Published by Reclaiming Judaism Press
17 Rodman Oval,
New Rochelle, NY 10805
Tel: 914-500-5696
http://www.reclaimingjudaism.org
Manufactured in the United States of America
      ISBN: 978-1-4664155-3-9 (pbk, Library Binding)
      ISBN: 978-0-9848048-0-1 (pbk, Trade Edition)
      ISBN: 978-0-9848048-2-5 (Kindle/E-Book Version)

"A teacher of Torah is like a pomegranate.
The seeds she plants bring *mitzvot* to life."

–Rabbi Goldie Milgram

This volume is dedicated in honor of Peninnah Schram

Please Note:

R. Baruch HaLevi cites: "R. Eleazar [who] further stated in the name of R. Hanina: Whoever reports a saying in the name of its originator brings deliverance to the world, as it says [Esther 2:22], 'And Esther told the king in the name of Mordecai' [*Megillah* 15a]."

http://rabbib.com/media/writings/RabbiB-Justice.Bshem_omro_and_Genevat_Daat.pdf

Accordingly, we encourage you to retell, and even reshape, this volume's *mitzvah stories*, so long as you attribute this volume and any given story's author as your source. Republication of stories and articles is also most welcome, so long as you secure written permission from Reclaiming Judaism Press and cite this volume as the first point of publication.

Table of Contents

Foreword
by Richard Joel, President, Yeshiva University

In her roles as teacher, author, and storyteller extraordinaire, Peninnah Schram has lit the fires of passion of her countless students, readers, and audiences. She has spread both her light and her warmth through her generosity of spirit. Peninnah uses the mysteries of story to convey the magic of life's possibilities while using the beauty of language to spur people to be all they can be. As professor of Speech and Drama at Yeshiva University's Stern College for Women, Peninnah shares and models her sense of joy, the rigor of her engagements with people, and the discipline of her teaching with the next generation of devoted Jewish storytellers. She lives fully and illustrates to her students and the world what "fully" means.

I can think of no better way to celebrate our remarkable raconteur than by contributing stories in her honor. Through this compilation of stories and memories, the work and ideals of Peninnah Schram gain a foundation to persist for people's enjoyment into the future.

Joan Didion titled a collection of her writing, "We Tell Ourselves Stories in Order to Live." As Jews we do not only tell stories in order to live, we tell stories to make lives worth living. Professor Schram's life and work has greatly contributed to the telling of the Jewish story, thereby enriching us all.

Mitzvot: Rights vs Obligations

As Americans, our foundational document, the Constitution, confers "rights." As Jews our foundational document, the Torah, mandates *mitzvot,* "obligations." Jews have always coveted the right to assume obligation. In fact, the Torah does not even have a word for "rights." Only in modern times did the Hebrew word *zechut* come to mean a right. I understand this hole in the Biblical lexicon as illustrating a profound truth about the foundations of Judaism. Certainly rights are a part of the gifts of a caring God. Clearly, the social compact is based on both rights and responsibilities. "Life, liberty, and the pursuit of happiness" is our American patrimony, but not necessarily the ultimate statement of God-given rights. In any event, rights are what are given to us; responsibility is what we should exercise. Rights alone can lead to a sense of entitlement. They force a person to look inward at what they deserve. Obligations, on the other hand, draw our gaze outward to what we must do for our loved ones, our communities and our Creator. The Torah bestows on us the gift of a mitzvah-focused life, thus granting us a life, liberty, and happiness no right ever could.

The *mitzvot* encompass every component of one's relationship with others, God, and self. Many do not require explanation, such as the prohibition of murder and caring for the orphan and widow. Others—like not coveting your neighbor's goods and respecting your parents—hold us to a high moral standard that requires a lifetime of dedication. Some exist to remind us of our place in the universe in relation to God, like honoring the Sabbath and thanking God after meals. And then some *mitzvot* do not seem to have any easy rationale—like attaining spiritual purity through the sprinkling of the ashes of a burnt red heifer—and yet we still subscribe to the idea of these obligations to illustrate, as Rabbi Joseph B. Soloveitchik posited, that all *mitzvot* emanate from God, whether we understand them or not.

Once we realize that the divine obligations of the Torah enrich our very being, we then have the potential to succeed. Just as in a game of bowling, we have parameters as to where the ball can and cannot go, but we control whether or not we roll a strike. It does not make us automatons; it simply delineates our boundaries.

One of my favorite stories perfectly describes the importance of accepting obligation. A watchman oversaw a railroad crossing. Whenever a train would come down the tracks he would take his lantern and swing it back and forth to warn pedestrians and cars. One dark night, a train collided with a car attempting to cross the tracks at the watchman's crossing, killing the passengers of the car. When the train company faced prosecution for their supposed negligence, they brought the watchman to testify. The prosecutor asked the watchman, "Please, tell me what happened on that fateful dark night that resulted in this terrible tragedy."

The watchman then recounted the events of that evening. "I saw the train speeding towards the crossing so I quickly ran out of my booth and began waving my lantern back and forth. All of a sudden a car came zooming down the road and I began wildly waving my lantern to signal it of the oncoming train. But the car never slowed down and the train collided with it on the tracks."

After hearing this testimony, the court found in favor of the railroad, acknowledging there had been no negligence. The railroad executives and their lawyers approached the watchman after the trial, congratulated him, and said, "You did a great job up there and you didn't even seem nervous." With that, the watchman began to shake and a tear descended down his cheek and he said, "Gentlemen, you say I wasn't nervous but I have to tell you that sitting on the witness stand after taking an oath to God Almighty, I do not know what I would have answered if asked if the lantern was lit."

Following our covenantal obligations ignites our fires and illuminates our world with the light of passion and purpose. Without this sacred glow, we can succumb to simply going through the motions of life without ever fulfilling our destiny.

Peninnah Schram: A Story of a Life - A Life of Stories

In Jewish tradition each person has three names: the name given to us, the name others give us, and the name we give or make for ourselves.[1] How did I make for myself the name, "Storyteller"? After all, I didn't dream of becoming a storyteller when I was growing up. While I grew up listening to stories told to me by my parents, being a storyteller was not a real 'profession' by which to make a living. However, what I did discover later on was that to be a storyteller was my life. How did it all happen?

During my teen-age years in New London, Connecticut, my dream was to become a movie star or go into the theater. In college, I majored in theater and starred in several productions at the University of Connecticut. When I came to Columbia University for graduate school, I began to realize the harsh reality of what becoming a stage actress

---

[1] Ecclesiastes Rabba 7:3, Tanhuma Vayakhel 1, and in Midrash Shmuel 23

meant: getting head shots with resumes printed up, competing with hundreds for the chance to audition or get a bit part or study at a professional school, such as Actor's Studio. No, that life was not for me. I was more of an academic theater person. Little did I realize that my talents and skills would lead me to a different performance art, namely, storytelling. Along the way, I began to teach in the Speech and Drama Department at Iona College in New Rochelle, NY (1967-1969), and then was invited to join the faculty of Stern College of Yeshiva University, NYC (1969 to the present).

In 1969, a friend invited me to take part in a group recording of Paddy Chayefsky's play *The Tenth Man* for the Jewish Braille Institute. After the recording session was completed, the director of the sound studio asked if I would be interested to volunteer to record books for the blind. I happily accepted this mitzvah-invitation.

One of the books I recorded was Isaac Bashevis Singer's first book of stories for children, *Zlateh the Goat*. I loved these stories, especially his versions of the folktales of Chelm. But when I would come into my classes at Stern College and ask if the students knew some of these tales, while all knew Biblical and Talmudic stories, very few knew Jewish folktales. I thought to myself, "Something is wrong here. Something has to be done about this."

Knowing the Director of Education at the 92nd Street Y, I made a proposal to begin a program of telling stories to elementary school age children. As it turned out, another young woman had made a similar proposal and, for the first time, I met another storyteller, Laura Simms. Together we created a weekly program of stories that we called, "Fire, Water, Stone & Air." We told stories from around the world and added creative dramatic activities, including movement, music, and art, in a participatory approach. In this way, I developed a repertoire of stories, including Jewish folktales—many that I knew from my childhood and others that I had read and told to my own two young children.

At one of these programs, I happened to tell a story from world folklore that the other storyteller also had in her repertoire. At the end of the program, she turned to me and said, "Why don't you tell just Jewish stories and leave the rest of the world to me!" I was stunned! It was as though someone had slapped my face so hard that it knocked the wind out of me! I don't remember if I replied or just burst into tears. However, because I respected and considered her a dear friend, I gave this remark great thought. After a time I realized that she had given me a gift for life, the push to fully become who I needed to become: a Jewish storyteller. We have remained good friends and I still thank her for that remark even though it was a painful experience at the moment. (I tell about this incident with her permission.)

From that time on, I researched and studied Jewish folktales more seriously and began to build my repertoire. It was at that time that more doors opened for me and I was invited to become the resident storyteller at The Jewish Museum in New York. Once a month, using one of their exhibits as a springboard, I would tell stories with themes related to the various objects and paintings. That led to my being invited to synagogues to present programs and workshops for educators and parents. I was being acknowledged as a Storyteller.

In 1974, the Dean of Stern College asked me to design a course in Jewish storytelling, the first of its kind. Together with my students, we then created a weekly program, in conjunction with the 92nd Street Y, to teach Jewish values to 8-12 year olds as an alternative to religious school. I called it "Kernels of a Pomegranate" based on the beautiful quote from *Shir HaShirim Rabba* 6:11: "Children sitting in a row studying Torah are compared to the kernels of a pomegranate."

One of my favorite experiences happened at one of these programs when I began to understand how powerful storytelling is. I had told the Biblical story of Joseph and his brothers. After the story, I passed around very large sheets of paper and placed a mound of crayons in the center of the floor, asking the young listeners to draw any scene or moment from the story they remembered. Afterwards the listeners would tell the story of their drawings. One young boy, about ten years old, held up his picture. The paper was completely filled with inverted V stripes (each one about 1 inch in width) and colored with vivid colors of the rainbow. He then explained that this was his drawing of Joseph's coat of many colors. Then he took a breath and added, "It's a close-up!" I still recall my amazed reaction. (The 1970's was years before zoom lenses and camcorders were easily available to children.) This young boy "saw" a different and fresh perspective while he was listening to the story. His visual imaginative interpretation was unique to him. Because of his vision, I continue to see his wonder-struck close-up every time I retell that Biblical story. No doubt he continues to remember the entire story in his very being. I often wish I could meet him again.

Throughout the years, from the time I began presenting storytelling programs and workshops at the 92nd Street Y and The Jewish Museum, my two children would accompany me. Rebecca was then about 7 years old and Mordechai was about 5 years old. They participated in the activities and listened well to the stories, frequently making requests and often giving me critiques on the way home since they had heard many of the stories from me at home or at other programs. It was joyous to share those programs with them. It was an additional way to nourish each *neshamah* with stories that I loved and found meaningful. Now grown up, they are both magnificent storytellers. Rebecca is a teacher of high school English and a master teacher of teachers in Israel. Mordy is a 4th generation Hazzan. They both use stories in their teaching, and Mordy also tells stories when he is called upon to give a presentation or a dvar Torah in the synagogue.

I have been fortunate and blessed to have many storytelling opportunities and, also, so many good listeners and students, some whom have become storytellers themselves. One of the main ideas I convey is that storytelling creates an extraordinary opportunity to "feel" the sounds of the words with all their connotations and to tell with images, not just words. Telling sets the story in the heart. In the oral tradition, it is through the voice, a person's exquisite musical instrument, that the words create internal technicolor worlds with an appeal to the senses. All of this, without a doubt, came through directly from my listening to my father, Hazzan Samuel E. Manchester, who *davenned* in such a way that the words of prayer were infused with phrasing, pause, rhythm, articulation and gesture, conveying the full meaning behind the words.

I have been blessed with knowing incredibly good and generous people who have reached out to me in so many ways and inspired me. They have been 'Elijahs-in-reverse' who have opened doors for me, and created new paths for me to follow. I am deeply grateful to these magnificent people, more than I can ever say. I also recognize my gratitude for the many storytelling students I have been able to meet and mentor in various ways, as well as the many extraordinary storytellers I have met and with whom I have formed friendships, especially during the over 30 years of attending the annual CAJE conferences and now the NewCAJE conferences. I *kvell* when I hear them tell stories and also when someone wants to tell a story from one of my books. That's the way of storytelling—to get more stories out into the world. We need constantly to create and cultivate a vast array of stories and storytellers so we can teach values, traditions, history and faith in the most beautiful way—through the sharing of stories!

Acknowledgments

Suppose you aspire to help unify the Jewish people in healthy and holy ways. You also desire to show why Judaism is a vital, meaningful lens for living. You want to reveal how Judaism, when understood and undertaken with respect and integrity across the entire spectrum of Jewish practice, yields a healthy, transformative spirituality necessary to the human future. You yearn to get this message out, to help more of your people appreciate and reclaim Judaism as their spiritual practice in deep and inclusive ways. You seek to empower them to shine a light of vibrant ethical hope to the nations. To whom would you turn? To a great Talmudist? A head of state? A famous novelist? A prominent social justice activist? A Jewish movie star? A corporate sponsor?

The answer came to me in a crystal-clear burst of consciousness: you would, of course, turn to Peninnah Schram, the prominent Jewish storyteller and mentor of storytellers. Peninnah, who helped elaborate numerous ways for new Jewish stories to be created and told. Peninnah, whose generous and unconditional love makes it possible for storytellers to succeed and flourish. Peninnah, whose books of stories today grace tens of thousands of Jewish homes and libraries world-wide.

Because Jewish women's leadership is so rarely honored appropriately, we originally founded Reclaiming Judaism Press with several goals: first, to convene voices across the spectrum of Jewish practice to share this R&D towards the creation of new tools for Jewish learning and living, and second, to honor women leaders in the field of Jewish education and spirituality by means of engaging their students and colleagues in contributing to these volumes. Our first effort, *Seeking and Soaring: Jewish Approaches to Spiritual Direction*, has done beautifully, B"H. It was created in honor of the first woman to serve as president of a Jewish seminary, Rabbi Shohama Wiener, *Rosh Hashpa'ah*, Director of Spiritual Guidance and Development here at Reclaiming Judaism. We have even higher hopes for this second volume.

We are honoring Peninnah with this publication because she is a great teacher and mentor. To celebrate her extraordinary contributions to Jewish education, we are therefore producing, in addition to this printed volume, associated podcasts and parent and teacher trainings in how to use these stories in mitzvah-centered learning. Who better to inspire such teaching than a master-teacher such as Peninnah Schram? Furthermore, all book sale profits will be donated to a scholarship fund in Peninnah's honor, which will ensure that all who wish to benefit from these programs will be able to do so.

Not surprisingly, when Peninnah was first approached with the idea of being honored through a special volume, she was reluctant to accept, claiming that she didn't need any more honors, that she wanted to make room for others. It was only when she understood that her good name would be enlisted to further the teaching of *mitzvot* through storytelling that she pulled out every stop to help orchestrate this effort. Early on she had informed me that her favorite symbol is the pomegranate, which in Jewish tradition symbolizes how each person, no matter how distant he or she is from the specific dictates of Jewish practice, is nonetheless chock-full of *mitzvot*. Peninnah's empowering appreciation of the *mitzvot* as embodied within every person comes across clearly in her storytelling, numerous books and mentoring. In Peninnah, we are truly blessed.

Over the years, Peninnah's many Jewish storytelling students and colleagues have themselves become super-juicy fruit with seeds of their own, each student ripe with the Torah of living a mitzvah-centered life. All of the stories in this volume, written by Peninnah's students, friends and colleagues, have been donated as labors of love. On behalf of the Reclaiming Judaism board, I want to express profound gratitude to all the contributors to this volume whose generous, holy story offerings engage so creatively with so many *mitzvot*.

Of course, a pomegranate orchard needs to be tended. Several outstanding professionals volunteered their time and expertise as the jurors and volume advisors: Ellen Frankel, Cherie Karo Schwartz and Arthur Strimling reviewed and commented on every story; Ellen also edited each and every story. Peninnah herself gave attentive guidance every step of the way. These advisors also helped shape the evolving vision for the volume and volunteered their time to create the introductory sections that so powerfully illuminate the art and method of storytelling. We also applaud the work of our publishing intern Miriam Grossman for her creative and detail-oriented engagement with the manuscript. Rabbi Shohama Wiener and Chazzan Micha'el Esformes contributed substantially to the manuscript proofreading, and Rabbi Samuel Barth weighed in on the mitzvah list—all with very helpful guidance for which we are also most appreciative.

Harwin Studios (www.harwinstudios.com) created and donated the magnificent volume cover created by Taylor Rozek. The lovely Pasuk Art piece that accompanies Peninnah Schram's biographical statement was created by her daughter-in-law, Judaica calligrapher-artist Sonia Gordon-Walinsky (www.pasukart.com). And the talented publicist Marion Gans volunteered professional support essential to this effort.

Our gratitude flows to Terri Schuster, founder of Makor Ha Lev Foundation for generously supporting the evolution of Reclaiming Judaism's Mitzvah-Centered Life Initiatives. Volunteers have undertaken every aspect of *Mitzvah Stories*, save for the important work of our publishing intern and the book designer.

One needs visionary board members for a well intentioned non-profit to thrive. I am so grateful for the support and guidance of Reclaiming Judaism Board Members: Sharon Ufberg, Janice Rubin, Sara Harwin, Lynn Hazan, and Gary Cohen, Esq. Reclaiming Judaism Press, founded in 2009, has evolved so rapidly in large measure because of our senior advisors Ellen Frankel and Arthur Kurzweil, whose guidance regarding effective and meaningful publishing is literally priceless.

Last and not at all least, profound love and appreciation to my hubbatzin, Barry Bub, for advising and driving thousands of miles while I sat beside him between speaking engagements, working on this volume as a labor of love.

Rabbi Goldie Milgram, Editor-in-Chief
Reclaiming Judaism Press

PS. The pomegranate is our symbol for this volume. It is Peninnah Schram's favorite image and appears throughout Jewish religious art. Rabbinic tradition imagines a perfect pomegranate having 613 seeds, equal to the number of *mitzvot* that the Rambam (Maimonides) enumerates as derived from the Torah. Pomegranates appear in the Torah as one of the seven species with which Israel is blessed [Deuteronomy 8:8]. Shimmering gold bells alternate with embroidered pomegranates on the hem of the high priest's robe [Exodus 28: 33-34]. In Solomon's Temple, they are said to appear on its front pillars [Kings 7:13-22]. The Song of Songs twice uses pomegranate imagery [4:3, 6:7]; and Song of Songs Rabba 6:11 compares students in their seats to pomegranate seeds. The Talmudic sages use it as a metaphor: "Even those who are empty are as full of *mitzvot* as a pomegranate" [BT Sanhedrin 37a]; in other volumes, the sinners among Israel, even so, are described to be as full of *mitzvot* as a pomegranate. [BT Eruvin 19a; B. Hagiga 27a].

Introduction: Appreciating Mitzvah as the Core of Jewish Practice
by Goldie Milgram

Mitzvah is the primary Jewish lens for living. *Mitzvot* (pl) are ethical and life-shaping ritual actions and so need to be birthed from the womb of learning into living. If we are honest and modest, we are probably not even aware of this fact, that a lot of *mitzvot* lie latent within us, still in a potential state. That's why mitzvah mentoring is at the heart of this volume's intent. We are all just as Jewish tradition describes us—as full of *mitzvot* as a pomegranate is full of seeds.

The practice and relevance of mitzvah goes far beyond "being a good person," and beyond its dictionary definition of "commandment," and even beyond how a given mitzvah is detailed in *halachah*, Jewish law. Mitzvah study and practice help us develop as individuals and as a people. Each mitzvah constitutes a category of Jewish spiritual practice that provides us ways of texturing our lives with meaningful actions.

I am blessed with a *maggid*, a teacher's voice that sometimes comes to me in waking visions and dreams.[2] This *maggid* explained to me, perhaps a decade ago, that Jewish life is ideally a process of steady re-alignment, *teshuvah*, a returning to the intention of living a mitzvah-centered life, rather than a self-centered life. The *maggid*'s teaching seeded this volume. It is important to understand that many *mitzvot* are practices of self-care, which is not at all the same as being self-centered. Rather, most *mitzvot* offer profoundly healing and healthy approaches to relationships.

The more typical use of the term *maggid* is in the original meaning of the word "preacher," a skillful, passionate teacher of a religious tradition's values and practices through stories. *Maggidim* (pl) are sometimes ordained, often not. While traditionally *maggidim* were

---

[2]   An extended discussion of this form of *maggid*, described by several Kabbalists, can be found in Hayyim Vital, "The Gate of the Holy Spirit," in *The Eight Gates*, translated by Aryeh Kaplan in *Meditation and Kabbalah* (York Beach, Maine: Samuel Weiser, 1982), pp 223-224. Also see the translation of the writing of Luzzatto's disciple Yequtiel Gordon in *Joseph Karo: Lawyer and Mystic* (Philadelphia: Jewish Publication Society, 1977), p. 23. Also see Louis Jacobs' translation in *The Schocken Book of Jewish Mystical Testimonies* (New York: Schocken Books, 1977; reprint edition, 1998), p. 24; a topic summary can be found at http://jhom.com/topics/voice/magid.htm#1.

accorded the title informally through the love and appreciation of their communities, today a number of *maggid* training programs exist. (See www.ReclaimingJudaism.org for a list and links). *Maggidim* craft their stories for telling and may derive them from a wide variety of sources: personal experience with a teacher or practice, the Torah, and/or oral vignettes provided in Torah commentaries and the Talmud, known as the *aggadah*. *Maggidim* also utilize traditional tales both by and about *Chassidic* dynastic rebbes, starting with the first acclaimed *maggid*, the Baal Shem Tov. *Maggidic* stories can also be about and by rabbis such as well as about the "mitzvatic" lives of individuals such as Viktor Frankl, Hannah Senesh, and Anat Hoffman. In *Mitzvah Stories* you will find all such story sources reflected in the light of contemporary Jewish values.

Maimonides, a thirteenth century sage, identified a total of 613 *mitzvot d'oraita*, *mitzvot* "derived from the Torah," in accord with the Talmudic counting of Rav Simlai [Makkot 23b]. The Chofetz Chayim, a nineteenth century sage, identified 271 *mitzvot* which apply in our time. These are divided into 194 *mitzvot assei*—actions in which to engage, and 77 *mitzvot lo ta'aseh*—actions from which to refrain.[3] Twenty-six *mitzvot* apply only in the Land of Israel. A few of the *mitzvot* are reserved for *kohanim* or *levi'im*, descendants of the Biblical priesthood. And a few dozen *mitzvot* are no longer practiced because they related to the sacrificial system, which ended with the 70 C.E. destruction of the Second Temple.

Just over two centuries ago, Reb Nachman of Breslov proposed that the greatest mitzvah is achieving sustained happiness—*mitzvah gedolah lihiyot b'simchah tamid*—which can be understood as his articulation of what it is like to fully realize the mitzvah of *ahavat Hashem*, "loving God." After almost two years of working on this volume, I can attest that surrounding oneself with Jewish stories is at least one way to attain this state of being.

In addition to the *mitzvot d'oraita*, there are *mitzvot d'rabbanan*, those *mitzvot* developed by the rabbinic sages. Maimonides did not include these in his original 613. A rationale for *mitzvot d'rabbanan* is provided in the Gemara [circa 500 CE], which cites a verse from the Book of Esther: "The Jews kept and accepted (the laws of *Purim*)." Since the festival of *Purim* emerged long after the Biblical period, this verse is accounted as spiritual evidence for living as though all of the guidelines for Jewish

---

[3] Rabbi Yisroel Meir Kagan, the Chofetz Chayyim, *Sefer HaMitzvot HaKatzeir, The Concise Book of Mitzvoth: the Commandments Which Can Be Observed Today* (New York: Feldheim, 1990), pp 97 & 275.

tradition were given and received at Sinai.[4] Other familiar examples of *mitzvot d'rabbanan* would be the ritual handwashing before meals and lighting the *menorah*.

Mitzvot d'rabbanan are divided into three categories: *gezeirah*, *takkanah* and *minhag*. A *gezeirah* functions like a fence that puts something off-limits to help protect a mitzvah. So if your intention is to experience the divine gift of free time on *Shabbat*, then the *gezeirah* of not handling an implement used for work once *Shabbat* has begun is a *mitzvah d'rabbanan* that is very helpful, e.g., not keeping your computer on nor having the temptation of a writing implement in your pocket. A *takkanah* is a "repair" to the tradition, for example, the still-running Ashkenazi ban on polygamy, the mitzvah of lighting *Hanukkah* candles, and the practice of reading Torah on Monday and Thursday as well as on *Shabbat*.

The third category of *mitzvot d'rabbanan* is *minhagim*, customs. Within a given community, some customs come to be regarded as having the status of a mitzvah, even taking on the force of law. By way of example, at a Reform synagogue in Holland, the *gabbai* at a High Holiday service whispered to me to please remove my *kippah* because "a woman cannot wear a *kippah* in this synagogue, only a man." "And what about a prayer shawl, a *tallit*?" I inquired. And to my surprise she responded: "Well, of course, you can wear a *tallit*." In the next town, in the same country, the *gabbai* was just as insistent that it was fine for me to wear a *kippah*, but absolutely never would they tolerate a woman in a *tallit*. And in Germany, a woman asked the Chief Orthodox Rabbi, who had invited us for *Shabbat*, to call the police to remove me, because she viewed it as against even the civil law for a woman to wear a *kippah* in synagogue. He told her to find evidence of such a law before he could proceed with her concern.

Jewish culture—Sefardi, Ashkenazi and Mizrachi—has evolved many ways of approaching, beautifying and expanding each mitzvah, giving rise to a delicious diversity across the full range of Jewish practice. You will see this diversity reflected throughout *Mitzvah Stories*, representative of the important mitzvah of *klal yisrael*, manifesting the underlying unity of the Jewish people. Like the Jewish world in miniature, you will find between these covers each author's loving care and attention to our tradition.

The concept of embellishing or beautifying a mitzvah is called *hiddur mitzvah*. The two primary dimensions to this practice are beautifully expressed in the publisher's foreword to the *Sichos of the Lubavitcher*

---

[4]   Also see BT Shavuot 39a, Horayot 2b, and Shabbat 23a.

Rebbe: "Every holiday possesses 'a body,' the laws and customs associated with its observance, and 'a soul,' the breath of life infused by the spiritual message the holiday conveys."[5]

The *Rebbe*'s discourse explains that seeking out—and I would add, commissioning—a particularly beautiful *Hanukkah menorah* qualifies as *hiddur mitzvah*. This is not about materialism; it is about art and the spirit that comes from it. The original *menorah* described in the Torah [Exodus 25:31-37] was sculpted whole in the form of an almond tree and is associated with the Tree of Life by the Kabbalists. Metaphorically, each branch holds and shines forth the light of Torah, the essence of the divine. In Ashkenazi homes, to increase the pleasure and glory of the light, *mehadrin min hamehadrin*, each person present brings or receives a *menorah* of his or her own for kindling that day's number of lights. In traditional Sefardi homes, the head of household lights one *menorah* for all.

Judaism is one of the world's longest continually evolving world wisdom traditions. History has shown the Jewish people to be highly resilient, surviving every challenge sent our way to date. Our strength lies in our inheritance and our diversity. So it is with the created world—nature is filled with great variety—many types of roses, butterflies, and Jews. Yet, despite this wonderful Jewish diversity, we still function, often unconsciously, as one people. One way to understand this is to appreciate that we share a commitment to <u>mitzvah-centered living</u>, even as we understand and express the *mitzvot* somewhat differently according to our talents, life experiences, and perspectives within the spectrum—from Jewish humanism through Orthodoxy. Through this shared commitment, we continually stretch each other in ways that help Judaism remain vital and valuable in the face of ever-changing times. Inevitably, we stress each other with our differences. This is mostly constructive stress, which our sages might describe as derech ha-teva, "the way of nature."

For example, the practice of organ donation was long eschewed as a Jewish practice because of low rates of success and concerns about resurrection traditions that implied one needed to be buried whole. Today organ donation is widely practiced, even within traditional Jewish circles, because it has come to be regarded as fulfilling the mitzvah of *pikuach nefesh*, saving a life. Blessedly, medical advances have greatly increased the rates of successful organ transplants. (Ask your rabbi for details and visit www.hods.org for Jewish organ donation documents.)

---

[5]   http://www.sichosinenglish.org/cgi-bin/calendar?holiday=chanuka25212

Another example of changing attitudes toward *mitzvot* concerns the roles of women in the Jewish community. In recent times, extensive Jewish learning and some form of *bat mitzvah* for women and girls have established their presence from one end of the spectrum of Jewish practice to the other. The notion of eco-kosher—the consideration of ethical treatment of workers and animals, the use of pesticides and other agricultural concerns—as well as related environmental issues, such as carbon footprints and ecological packing, are all receiving serious consideration across the spectrum of Jewish life. These changes reflect the rabbinic principle of loving God, *ahavat Hashem*, which is delineated in the Talmud as "pious audacity": *chutzpah afilu klapei shemaya mehanei.*[6] Even *chutzpah* in relationship to Heaven is permitted (for holy purposes). Loving our tradition while wrestling with it through changing times is how the Jewish people has continually functioned—as a research and development team on behalf of the Jewish and human future in every generation.

Stories not only give us insight into how *mitzvot* and Jewish practices evolve; they especially teach us how a mitzvah can look, sound and feel in action. *Mitzvot* would probably "lie like a lox" when read on a page of classical text if not for the *aggadah*, the "telling" of how they have come alive that is preserved along with the legal discussion. So it is that the sages and teachers in every generation cultivate great stories in order to transmit the meaning, power and practice of Judaism. *Mitzvah stories* also reveal consequences, for while acting from love, *ahavat Hashem*, is the higher consciousness in our tradition, we also act from *yirat Hashem*, awareness of the awesome/fearsomeness of the way creation works.

In the Book of Exodus, Moses asks the Voice he hears at the Burning Bush how to name the source of his experience. The answer he receives is: *"Ehyeh asher Ehyeh"*—"I Am Becoming What I Am Becoming," or "I Will Be What I Will Be" [Exodus 3:14]. Shaping a meaningful Jewish life similarly involves "becoming what we are becoming," that is, taking on a conscious relationship with the *mitzvot*. As above, so below, teach our sages. Just as God is always becoming, so we, too, evolve as we grow and change within our mitzvah-centered lives. And there is no need to do this changing all at once, to swallow the whole river in one gulp. Doing one mitzvah at a time is awesome enough, as we, too, are becoming what we are becoming.

After reading each story and, hopefully, studying *Mitzvah Stories* in *chevruta* (with a study friend), in a book group or class, consider exploring which *mitzvot* were addressed in each story, or perhaps tell/

---

[6]   BT Sanhedrin 105a.

write/share your own experience through stories with your friends that highlight one of these *mitzvot*. A bibliography to further your mitzvah studies is located immediately after the glossary.

Shema b'ni mussar avicha v'al titosh torat imecha

"Listen my child to the discipline of your father
and do not forsake the Torah (teachings) of your mother."

—Proverbs 1:8

This principle has been reinterpreted for our times by my teacher Rabbi Zalman Schachter-Shalomi.[7] The "fathers," the male sages, have traditionally had the power to develop and oversee the details of Jewish practice. The list of *mitzvot* and their related spiritual practices that follows is written through the lens of *torat imechah*, a mother's way of sweetening the message in order to help us be *m'karev*, "drawn near," to realizing the goal of a mitzvah-centered life, the manifestation and experience of the divine.

---

[7]   Rabbi Zalman Schachter-Shalomi and Rabbi Daniel Siegel. *Integral Halachah, Transcending and Including.* Victoria, BC: Trafford Publishing, 2007.

Upon reading each mitzvah story, you can return to the following list of *mitzvot* in order contemplate and discuss which of them have been incorporated into the story by the author.

Forty-Five Mitzvah-Centered Practices[8]

ahavat Hashem
Live in Love
Do what you do out of an expansive love of the world and all creatures. A love that comes from being out in nature and deeply aware of the divine beauty and intricacy of all that is.

yirat Hashem
Live in Awe
Be attentive to the power and laws of nature and the consequences of ethical marks missed, so much so that, virtually trembling in awe, you focus your speech and actions with care.

shalom bayit
Co-Create Peace
Undertake conscious acts of self-restraint, love and generosity that may yield greater peace at home.

geneivat da'at
Avoid Deception
Exercise truth when promoting self and others, products, programs and services.

shamor et yom ha-Shabbat
Savor and Secure Sacred Time
Re-soul on the seventh day of each week—away from money, media and materialism—through practices that deepen your connection to Torah, family and community, sustained by Judaism as a spiritual path.

---

[8] Reclaiming Judaism Press offers *Mitzvah Cards,* an attractive set of fifty-two cards including the Hebrew name of selected *mitzvot,* the modern meaning of the *mitzvah,* and its Biblical reference. Order through ReclaimingJudaism.org or Amazon.com; school and trade discounts available.

bal tashchit
Avoid Damage to Nature
Refrain from damaging the environment, on earth and beyond; protect life forms and habitats, and conserve resources.

kibud av v'em
Honor Loved Ones
Ensure your parents' well-being. Cause them no shame. Hakarat ha-tov, acknowledge the good they have done. Fulfill healthy requests. Say *kaddish*.

kol yisrael areivim zeh la-zeh
Be Counted and Accountable
Show up for others and appreciate those who show up for you in order to ensure supportive communities of prayer and care.

lo tikom
Take No Revenge
Address loss and anger carefully without taking revenge or multiplying wrongs.

lo tachmod
Restrain Dangerous Desires
Recognize jealousy and inappropriate attractions and practice non-attachment to that which is not ethically yours to have or to hold.

lo titeyn mikshol
Create No Stumbling Blocks
Resist setting up environments and situations in ways that trip others literally and/or ethically.

shema
Listen with Understanding
Connect, love and listen through the daily and bedtime *shema* as you pause and prayerfully reflect at the doorposts of your day, your dreams, and, one day, your life.

v'hadarta p'nai zaken
Honor Elders
Receive elders with respectful attention to their experience, capabilities and needs.

bishul kasher
Eat Consciously
Separate milk—the mammals' life-giving force, from meat—life taken away; then *hiddur*—"embellish" the mitzvah of keeping kosher with blessing and attention to ethical agriculture, slaughter, transport, labor and packaging.

sh'mirat ha-guf
Live Healthy
Take good physical care of your body, the precious instrument upon which your soul plays life for God.

hachnassat orchim
Welcome Guests
Host in your home and out in the world as though all people—in the markets, schools, buses, streets—are your honored guests.

chatunah
Cleave and Commit
Ritually braid your soul with your beloved into a state of committed relationship under the symbol for your Jewish home, a *chuppah*, the Jewish wedding canopy, in the presence of family, friends and community.

u'v'chol l'vavkha
Find the Prayer of Your Heart
Empty yourself of stress and refill with healing and connection through communal services and daily personal prayer which incorporate the arousing of love, awe, and awareness with the expression of gratitude and yearning.

pidyon sh'vu'im
Free Captives
Advocate, donate and strive to liberate those who are being immorally held in slavery or in prisons, by governments or captors.

batei tamhui
Feed the Hungry
Organize and assist in providing those-in-need a safe place to eat where they are given nourishing meals.

teshuvah
Heal Relationships
Work through issues with those whom you have hurt, and feel hurt by (when safe to do so), so that wholeness and holiness can return to your relationships. Forgiveness is a process that heals the heart and liberates the soul.

tza'ar ba'alei chayyim
Prevent Pain
Act to end unnecessary pain and suffering of animals in slaughterhouses, medical research centers, puppy farms, cosmetic production, and more.

ahavat tzi'on
Loving Israel
Take action to ensure a safe, just, beautiful State of Israel.

t'keeyat shofar
Wake Up
Heed the *shofar*'s call of a year's time passing and the need for healing of relationships within, between, and Beyond.

talmud Torah
Study and Teach Torah
Teach the children and immerse yourself in regular study and teaching of Jewish sacred texts, stories and practices as a lens for individual and collective awareness and growth.

v'halachta b'derachav
Walk the Talk
Engage each aspect of human nature—your own and others—in ways that make you a source of blessing.

tzedakah
Be Generous
Achieve an equitable distribution of your personal resources with care for those in need, and for worthy programs that develop and provide healthcare, education and tradition.

zeicher yetziyat mitzrayim
Remember the Exodus
Remember our people's story of leaving slavery for freedom as a faithful inspiration for living and loving, within the *kiddush* on *Shabbat*, through a Passover *seder*, and more.

asu lachem tzitzit
Wrap Yourself in Mitzvah
Move *mitzvot* from the fringes of consciousness toward your sacred center, as your prayer garment, your *tallit*, helps focus and shelter your spirit.

g'millut chassadim
Give of Your Time
Enrich many with your deeds of uncompensated loving kindness and services as a volunteer.

piku'ach nefesh
Save Lives
Sign on as an organ, tissue and blood donor, lobby for traffic lights and speed limits, report suspicious persons and objects, obtain fire extinguishers, and much more.

bikkur cholim
Visit the Sick
Support the spirit and healing of those who are physically or emotionally unwell with visits and calls; listen to and affirm their feelings; organize, as needed, any necessary transportation, supplies, meals, etc. Support research.

lo ta'aneh
Witness Honestly
Take exquisite care to report truthfully what was said or done lest justice be miscarried.

dina d'malchuta dina
Be an Active Citizen
Cultivate a healthier society by adding your vision, voice, views, values, vote, taxes, service, concerns, and attention to the laws of the land.

pirsum ha-nes
Spread the Light
Kindle the *menorah*'s increasing flames for each of *Hanukkah*'s eight
nights, contemplating and sharing the meaning of the miracle of the
Light.

tzedek tzedek tirdof
Pursue Justice
Work relentlessly for all and for each to live in dignity, with equal opportunity for and access to safety, food, education, healthcare, religion, and
culture.

leishev ba-sukkah
Sit in a Sukkah
Put together your fragile harvest home, then build life's inner circle.
Invite friends and neighbors for meals, ritual, study and contemplation
as awe of Nature filters in.

aliyah la-aretz
Go to Israel
Visit or live in Israel. Only experience can convey the meaning of this
mitzvah.

v'ahavta l'reyacha
Love Your Neighbor
Love others as you might best love yourself, including the many varieties
of Jews and all the world's peoples.

al mezuzot beitecha
Create Sacred Space
Place a mezuzah on all non-bathroom doorways at home, throughout
the Jewish community and, when feasible, at work, to mark each room
as sacred space for listening, understanding and loving.

Rosh Chodesh & kiddush levanah
Bless "Moon"thly
Gather, bless and share about life in rhythm with the new and full
moon.

brit bat and brit milah
Accept the Covenant
Take on the rituals to enter yourself and your children into membership in the Jewish people—a Jewish sacred name, male circumcision, immersion in living waters, and more—based on your parentage and denominational practices.

hadlakat neirot
Bring in the Light
Create the hearth of the Jewish home by lighting *Shabbat* and holy day candles to frame sacred times together.

mikveh
Immerse and Clear
Transition spiritually into marriage, covenant, holy days, healing and "monthly renewal," through the mitzvah of taharah, reflective immersion in the living waters of a river, ocean, lake or indoor pool facility.

brachot
Bless and Know You are Blessed
Bless in appreciation before and after eating. Say the *shehecheyanu* to express gratitude when wearing new clothes, for fruits eaten anew each year, the joy of lifecycle attainments, and more.

The Mitzvah Stories Driver's Manual

The Golden Chain of Jewish Stories

The Craft of Storytelling

Creative Ways to Use *Mitzvah Stories*

The Golden Chain of Jewish Stories
by Ellen Frankel

Jewish tradition teaches that at Sinai God's teachings were revealed in two forms—*Torah sheh-b'chtav*, the Written Torah (specifically, the Five Books of Moses), and *Torah sheh--b'al peh*, the Oral Law (the *Mishna*, Talmud, and later rabbinic commentaries, teachings, responsa and codes). In the eyes of the tradition, both of these Torahs embody the voice of God. To this day, Orthodox Jews hold that both Torahs, written and oral, derive incontrovertible authority from that ancient encounter at Sinai.

Jewish tradition also includes a third Torah, which dates back to the earliest days of the formation of the Jewish people. This Torah, though not always revered by formal rabbinic authorities, is as beloved to the Jewish people as the other two Torahs, and comprises some of Judaism's holiest teachings. This is *Torah sheh-ba-lev*, the Folk Torah, which long ago accompanied Abraham and Sarah on their first journey from Ur and has kept company with the wandering Jews ever since.

The Folk Torah is what is commonly referred to as *"aggadah,"* usually translated as "legend," but more accurately rendered as "telling," like the *Haggadah* recited at the Passover *seder*. This orally transmitted trove of material, consisting of stories, songs, customs, ceremonies, symbols and traditions practiced and revered by Jews in diverse communities around the world, has evolved over time, and has become integral to normative Jewish culture.

In the centuries-long enterprise known as the Talmud (200-600 C.E.), the ancient rabbis did not differentiate between these various forms of Torah, but freely mixed the serious business of formalizing rules, known collectively as the *halachah*, literally, "the Way"—with imaginative play, known as *aggadah*. However, as the stresses of exile progressively destabilized community cohesion, the rabbis' initially liberal approach gave way to more conservative forces. Rabbinic authorities increasingly drew hierarchical distinctions between law and custom, between sacred story and popular folktale, between bottom-up and top-down Judaism. The Folk Torah—two thousand years of stories, folk practices, proverbs and songs, preserved and transmitted in vernacular languages such as Aramaic, Yiddish, Ladino, and other Jewish languages used in the Ashkenazi, Sefardi and Mizrachi diasporas— steadily depreciated into the cast-off inheritance of *amcha* (the Jewish folk), of *am ha-aretz* (the salt of the earth). Jewish scholars and religious leaders safeguarded the authoritative rules and national epic in the holy tongue of Hebrew.

But now the pendulum of history seems to be swinging back. The forces of post-Enlightenment, post-Holocaust, post-modern Jewish culture are challenging the hierarchies of rabbinic authority. The melting pot of a multi-ethnic Israeli society boils over with a rich broth of Jewish folk traditions. Like the ancient Talmudic academies, the Internet fosters a riotous conversation among a thousand Jewish voices. Classic texts, halachic processes, and diverse folkways regularly meet each other in the midst of this conversation. The late Reform scholar Jakob Petuchowski described this ongoing process of expanding inclusiveness in Judaism as "the ever-widening holiness franchise."[9] It's an exhilarating and unstable moment, another uncharted journey of our people in the wilderness...

And Jewish stories can help us find our bearings on this journey, as they always have. As in other traditions, Jews are a storytelling people, using narrative to teach and exemplify values and norms. Within Jewish folktales can be found ethical teachings, role models, cautionary tales, and collective memory. Unlike halachic texts, which are prescriptive, or rabbinic *midrashim*, which are anchored in proof-texts (scriptural citations), folktales and personal stories assert their authority through the personality of the storyteller and the magic of narrative, which seizes hold of listeners' imaginations and prods their conscience.

The figure of the Jewish storyteller, *maggid* in Hebrew—initially referring to a supernatural presence, and later an itinerant preacher and sage—is as old as Judaism itself. Until the Hebrew Bible was written down and canonized—a process begun after the destruction of the First Temple in 586 B.C.E. and completed around the beginning of the Common Era—its stories and teachings were committed to memory and transmitted orally. In addition to Scripture, storytellers also recounted *midrash*im, legends, animal tales (called "fox fables"), parables, and stories borrowed from neighboring cultures. The Talmud reports that great rabbis such as Rabbi Meir would whet the appetite of Talmudic scholars by beginning their collective deliberations with a forshpeiz (appetizer) of such tales.

The *maggid* became a familiar figure throughout the Jewish disapora, providing unlettered Jews with summaries and explanations of the

---

[9] Jakob Petuchowski, "The Everwidening Holiness Franchise," *Moment Magazine*, May 1985, pp 60-62.

weekly Torah portion, teachings about musar (ethical behavior), entertaining tales about Jewish heroes, and inspiring tales about the Messiah. In the late 18th through early 20th centuries, the *maggid* became the voice and soul of the *Chassidic* movement, replacing the esoteric and formalistic style of Eastern European scholasticism with heart-warming parables and stories spun by charismatic rebbes and their storytelling emissaries.

In our own time, the figure of the *maggid* has been expanded beyond the tradition of males with the dramatic expertise to entrance and teach with tales from the Talmud, *midrash* and *Chassidic* masters. *Maggidim* have emerged across the spectrum of Jewish practice who both recount and invent stories that convey both the tradition and our people's developing history and practices. More than any other person, Peninnah Schram has championed this Jewish storytelling renewal, especially in the broader Jewish and even general community, raising up several generations of new *maggidim* to add links to the age-old chain.

What kinds of stories will the reader find here? Academic folklorists are usually fond of classifying tales into defined categories. In fact, the Finnish folklorist, Antti Aarne, developed an elaborate folklore motif system, which the American folklorist, Stith Thompson, then translated and expanded, ultimately cataloguing 2500 basic plots represented in European and Near Eastern folklore.

This volume is far less systematic and representative. Most of the tales here fall into a few broad categories:

Memoir—a lesson from the storyteller's life;

Teaching tale—an object lesson, known as a mashal in rabbinic tradition;

Dramatic monologue and dialogue—a soliloquy or an imagined conversation;

Midrash—the interpretation of a sacred text, usually Biblical;

Folktale—a fairy tale, animal fable, or other familiar "once upon a time" tale;

Legend—a story based on a well-known historical or popular character.

Though these stories take different forms, what they share in common is a mission to teach Jewish values through *mitzvot*, broadly defined as acting ethically in the world. However, unlike the traditional 613 *mitzvot* formally prescribed by rabbinic tradition, the notion of mitzvah is here expanded to cover any action that brings an added measure of godliness into the world or honors the divine image in another human being. And since all the storytellers in the volume are Jews, the deeds recounted speak with a Jewish accent.

So, we now invite you to listen, to learn, and to repeat what you hear in these pages, retelling these tales in your own distinct voice. And we urge you to credit the source of each tale you tell. By passing on these stories, you are adding your own link to the sacred chain.

The Craft of Storytelling
by Arthur Strimling

Introduction

Stories exist to be told. Just as a meal is not a meal until it is tasted, a story isn't a story until it is told and heard. Laid out before you is a fabulous feast of *mitzvah stories*. So please, read, enjoy, learn, and then... tell!

This Driver's Manual section is a short practical introduction to the underline telling part of storytelling: non-prescriptive suggestions and hints from someone who has been at it for a while. In that spirit, I suggest that you try them out, as you might try on a dress or a suit, or drive a car around the block and kick the tires. If a suggestion works for you, great! If it doesn't, let it go, as easily as you would put an unsuitable dress back on the rack, or return the car to the lot. But even if a suggestion doesn't work for you, you will have learned something in the process of trying it out. And that is crucial. Because storytelling, like all art, is personal: you have to look and look for the stories, styles, genres and audiences that work for you. The main thing is to keep looking. As Samuel Beckett, one of my Rebbes, says: "Fail again. Try again. Fail better."[10]

But First, a Sort of Manifesto

For me, telling Jewish stories is a form of prayer. Which suggests a lot, but this being a manual, the focus is on presentation. In prayer, *kavannah* (intention) and *keva* (form) weave together to open our *neshamah* (soul). This essay focuses on *keva*, form, but always, each element is shot through with the others, and they all weave together in our quest for the ideal. Our central prayers are never improvised in form or language. And they are spoken with deep attention to *keva*. The *shema* and its blessings, the *amidah*, the *kaddish*, prayers of thanks and mourning and celebration, prayers dealing with every aspect of life, are uttered in established language, developed over centuries. And we know when to bow, when to take three steps forward and back; we know the *nusach* or prayer modes that accompany our prayers. And most of all we care so much about getting the words right that we read them from the

---

[10] Samuel Beckett, *Worstward Ho.* NY: Grove Press, 1984.

book every time, even though we often know them by heart already. Yes, *kavannah* and *neshamah* are important, but first we have to get it right. And so it is with storytelling.

Of course, the difference is that in most prayers we inherit the form, whereas in storytelling we are usually creating a form for a story, and sometimes we are creating the story itself. But still, I believe that storytelling is like prayer in that **for each storyteller there is an ideal form for each story we tell**—the right words, the right voice or voices, the right gestures and rhythms. Which means that if you and I tell the same story, your finished version will be different from mine. But we each can find our own 'right' way of telling the story. And it is our sacred duty as storytellers to search passionately and ceaselessly for the right form.

The great dancer/choreographer Martha Graham wrote: "No artist is pleased…There is a queer, divine dissatisfaction, a blessed unrest that keeps us marching…"[11] I love this quote for its bridging of art and religion. Our imperative as storytellers is first to connect to that prayer-like passion for the ideal. If you tune into your own blessed unrest, you will undertake the quest for the craft and self-knowledge necessary to choose your direction, know where you are on the road, and when you get there. In the end, you may never find your ideal form, but the quest really matters.

So this manual is an invitation to a quest, and a set of suggestions toward finding your own process by which you can turn each story you tell into a prayer.

The Third Voice

For the audience, hearing a story is an entirely different experience from reading it; as an oral storyteller you need to be sensitive to that difference on many levels. The reader of a written tale can go at her own rhythm; stop, go back and reread a paragraph; get up and grab a snack from the 'fridge, and then return to the story. But the hearer of a story has to listen at the teller's rhythm, <u>your</u> rhythm; if she leaves to get a snack, she'll miss something. As a live teller, you have advantages over a book. You have voice, gesture, melody, rhythm; you can create characters, use costume or music if you like. In other words, you have the power to create a unique multi-level experience that happens in

---

[11]   Agnes de Mille, *Martha: The Life and Work of Martha Graham* (NY: Random House, 1991), p. 264.

the moment between you and your audience. You can evoke what anthropologist Barbara Myerhoff called "the third voice": In addition to your own voice and the "voice" of the listener, there is a third voice that hovers between you and your listeners, which makes each telling unique.[12]

How to Choose a Story

Choose a story that draws you, that makes you want to tell it to someone, anyone. Sometimes you know right away why you want to tell a particular story; sometimes you have no idea except that it draws you. Don't worry—at this point it doesn't matter why. Just accept that the story is calling to you and you need to share it—often the deepest meanings of a story don't reveal themselves until you have told it many times. All storytelling needs to emerge from an urgency to be heard, from an almost childlike place that shouts, "Listen, listen, I have a great story to tell you!"

Many stories in this collection reveal the impact of mitzvah on the one who performs it. Over and over, the message is 'Yes, a mitzvah helps the one on whose behalf it is done, but the impact may be even deeper on the one who performs it.' And the same is true of stories. We tell stories because we want to nourish the lives of others, but how much more deeply might a story affect the teller, the one who learns it 'by heart,' who tells it over and over? You can't say something over and over without being affected by it. So choose wisely; many stories may call to you, but be careful to choose ones that you will want to live with. Because they will change you.

Practice

Once a story has chosen me, I start with what master storyteller Laura Simms calls "mapping the story." Where does it start? Where does it go? How does it get there? My maps can get complicated because they include not only geography and time, but the emotional/spiritual trajectory as well. A good story is always in motion. Even if it digresses or is broken into many little stories, still, if it's a good story, it has a trajectory. Always keep that journey, that 'and then...and then...and then' element, urgently in your awareness.

---

[12] I heard Professor Myerhoff say this many times in conversation.

Tell the story to yourself over and over, until you know in your *kishkes* how it works. I am lucky to live near Brooklyn's glorious Prospect Park, which has wonderful paths through woods, where I wander with my dog, Easy, loudly telling him stories. Easy is the perfect listener at this stage; as long as there are interesting scents to investigate and plenty of treats, he is very patient. I have also discovered that the cell phone can be a great rehearsal device, because I can walk down Manhattan streets rehearsing animatedly, and everyone just thinks I'm talking to my mother or something.

And when I feel ready, when I know the story well, I tell it in public, usually first to my congregation, where I am *Maggid HaMakom* (storyteller in residence). We know each other, my congregation and I, and I trust the feedback I get from telling to them. Not so much what they say afterwards, but how it feels moment to moment as I tell it. Then I can move on to less familiar settings. It's important to have individuals and audiences whose feedback you understand and trust.

Often, as I rehearse, and in early performances, I know that certain moments in the telling of my story aren't right. The language or the rhythm or the voice or gesture or something just is not working. I haven't "found" it yet, and that "blessed unrest" is still making her demands. And sometimes, I have a performance scheduled tonight or tomorrow, so there is no way out; I have to tell the story. This happens a lot. My solution, suggested by a great director/mentor, Joseph Chaikin, is to do the best I can at the moment, knowing that this version is a "stand-in," not yet the "right" thing. Sometimes I find a better "stand-in," so I do that, without dropping the quest for the right thing. Eventually, in rehearsal or performance, or walking down the street or practicing yoga, the right thing does drop in. But until that magic moment, the key is to keep doing the best thing, and trying new "best things" until the right one comes along.

Persona and Voice

A storyteller has to have a persona! Call it attitude, presence, style, shtick, or whatever; it is not the same as how you are with your mother, your lover, your children, your boss or your friends. It is a stage presence, an essence, and it has to be developed and refined. Start from what you know about yourself and what you want to share. Are you a fast or slow talker; are you serious, sacred, antic, romantic, a clown, a dancer, a shapeshifter, a diva, a teacher...? All these and infinite other possibilities exist and work for different people. The important thing is to discover and refine your own style. Listen to teachers; observe storytellers and other performers whom you admire; try out different styles. Steal ruthlessly, by which I mean, if you see a gesture, a walk, or hear a voice or vocal effect that you like and think could work for you, copy it, use it, and eventually it will either become yours and unrecognizable from the source or it will disappear. (This emphatically does not apply to the actual text or substance of stories—see the discussion of *b'shem omro* below.) For example, in addition to learning from many of the masters included in this volume, as well as great actors, rabbis and other teachers, I admit to watching stand-up comics on Comedy Central. The material is often awful, but many of them have created amazing personae, and are good storytellers, and I draw inspiration from that. In the end, though, listen more carefully to audiences than to teachers, directors or other experts. If the audience responds, then whatever you are doing is working for you. Refine what works.

The keystone is your voice. The poet Ted Hughes said that when you meet someone for the first time, before you hear their words, you hear the music of their voice, which is the music of the soul. So do not hesitate to find a good teacher of speaking voice (training the singing voice uses different techniques), one who can teach you the mechanics of the mechanism, but who does not try to impose a particular sound on you. The goal, unlike singing training, is not to produce beautiful sound, but rather to free the voice so the unfettered soul can come through it.

b'shem omro

Stories yearn to be told and retold. You may need to adapt a story to the varying needs of your congregation or audience, and to your own style. You can respectfully adapt other people's stories in a wide variety of ways, as long as you are conscientious about naming your source. *B'shem omro*, "[acknowledging a source] in the name of the one who said it," is not merely a courtesy or even a legality: it is a mitzvah.[13]

---

[13] My thanks to Rabbis Goldie Milgram and Fred Dobb for the following citation: From Pirkei Avot (6:6; cf BT Hullin 104b, etc): *"kol ha'omer davar b'shem omro, mevi geula l'olam* - whoever says something in the name of the one who said it [first], brings redemption to the world (or, gains eternal life). Why redemption, for properly attributing source material?! The Talmud (BT *Megillah* 15) cites Esther 2:22–'Queen Esther told the King *in the name of Mordecai*' of the plot against him. This extraneous positive mention later surfaced, leading the King to put Mordecai above Haman, leading to the redemption of Shushan's Jews."

Even if you adapt a story extensively, it is incumbent upon you to cite the original source or sources. Judaism deeply values respect for the ancestors, and storytellers show that respect by naming them.

Some stories in this volume you can tell similarly as written. For example, Cherie Karo Schwartz's "A Single Seed of a Pomegranate," Jill Hammer's "The Wooden Axle," and numerous others are told in the narrative voice of the classic folktale form that anyone can use. If these stories appeal to you, then your challenge will be to make this traditional style and language your own, and to feel so comfortable with it that you can bring the story to life.

Some stories, on the other hand, demand a different approach. For instance, Ellen Frankel's personal story, "Saved by the Evil Eye," is told in the first person. Although I could quote her and tell it in the first person, I would not make that choice. Rather, I would tell it in the third person as "something that happened to my friend Ellen Frankel," making adjustments in the language and diction to suit that form, perhaps adding something from my own experience (not nearly so dramatic), and then inviting the audience to tell their own stories. This is a great workshop story, an invitation to dialogue, and I plan to use it that way.

"The God of Curried Fish," Goldie Milgram's wonderful tale of ordering take-out in a sketchy neighborhood, offers another kind of challenge. In this case, there is no way I could plausibly tell this story in the first person, because the story turns on the fact that Goldie is a small woman given to wearing fabulous hats. I don't know if she was wearing a fabulous hat at the diner, but nonetheless, she is about as non-threatening a presence as you could imagine. I am nothing like that–I am a solidly built man, given to wearing New York artist black. My presence in that diner would be a whole different thing. So if I were to tell that story, I would have to begin by evoking Goldie, coming back again and again to that sense of a friendly, *chutzpadik* Jewish lady in a precarious situation. I would have to find ways to help you see Goldie in that world, even though I am telling the story. Which brings us to the question of how to evoke characters in storytelling.

Be a Character

Storytelling is acting, but without the illusion of a 'fourth wall' through which the audience 'suspends disbelief' and sees characters behaving as they would if the audience weren't there watching. Storytellers talk straight to the audience. Without asking anyone to suspend anything, they freely evoke the most outrageous situations, worlds, creatures, and times. And unlike watching a movie, which shows us everything down to the smallest detail, so we can sit back passively and let it wash over us, listening to a storyteller requires an active kind of listening, a genuine collaboration between teller and audience. Our job as storytellers is not to embody every character, but rather to help the audience fully imagine them.

Laura Simms' story, "Words and Leaves," encompasses real and imagined times and worlds, people and creatures, kings, queens, bad princes, good princesses, a heroic commoner, a man-eating giant, and lots of other threatening creatures. So how can the teller help the audience imagine all these and still keep up the pace of the story? Many characters and situations pass by quickly and the language itself does enough to keep the story going. But every so often there is a character who demands to be felt more deeply, make an impact on the audience commensurate with her or his impact on the story. In Laura's story there is just such a character that demands a dive into imagination and space. Here is the moment:

The young man reached a house as high as a mountain. When the giant's wife saw it was a man, she urged him to leave. "Your life is in danger," she warned. "My husband will want to devour you." The youth convinced her that he would continue his quest without hesitation, regardless of the dangers, and told his story.

As soon as the giant returned home, his wife fed her ravenous husband. "I smell a man," roared the giant. His wife told him about the courageous visitor, whom she had hid beneath her bed. The giant was astonished at the young man's lack of fear and his dedication. And since he had already eaten, he gave him the necessary instructions.

Isn't the giant's wife amazing? I am riveted by this unnamed woman, who pops into the story, does what has to be done, and then disappears. Peninnah would call her an "Elijah figure." I want to know this woman: who she is, how she ended up being the wife of a monster, how she got so wise. I want stories about her. But we don't have time to linger over the giant's wife; this story has to move on. So the challenge is to find something in my voice and body, which, even though you only see and hear them for a moment, might pierce right through to your heart and make you see and remember this *lamed vavnik*,[14] this one who quietly, unobtrusively keeps the world going.

---

[14] The Hebrew letters, *lamed* and *vav*, have the numerical value of 36. According to Jewish legend, there are always thirty-six righteous people in the world, *lamed vavniks*, whose good deeds ensure the survival of the world.

The Essential Gesture

Here I turn to an idea developed by the great actor/teacher Michael Chekov called the "essential gesture."[15] Chekov taught that every character contains an essential gesture that can reveal her entire history and personality. The gesture can be a pose or an attitude; it can include movement, voice, and sometimes words. But the goal is to pare the gesture down to an absolute essence. Although in a literal sense this is a quixotic quest, I find it invaluable as an exercise, an approach to character in storytelling, because it encourages me to go for what is essential. For the essential gesture to characterize the giant's wife, I will look for voice and form that efficiently and powerfully evoke her intelligence, wisdom, compassion, quick wittedness, practicality and courage. The story needs to keep moving, but time needs to slow down enough to allow us to see the giant's wife for all she is and does—the whole story pivots on her action.

In Peninnah Schram's soaring "Serach Bat Asher," the main character, Serach, speaks through Peninnah, the story's author. If you choose to tell that story, Serach will be speaking through you. So you have the opportunity to assume a character in much more depth and detail than the giant's wife. But I would still maintain that as the storyteller, you are not trying to make the audience believe you actually are Serach Bat Asher, but rather that you are her vehicle, that she is speaking through you, and that through you, the audience can feel her, see her, believe in her. Begin with the language itself; there is a rhythm here that will tell you a lot about how she speaks. She exudes an energy that is at once ancient and ageless, creating a contrast between her bodily presence—perhaps she is sitting—and the acuteness of her mind.

Next consider to whom she is speaking. Is she still addressing those students in Rabbi Yohanan's class, and thereby the eager student in each of us? Or is she perhaps speaking to one special person, maybe her own granddaughter, the two of them alone in a tent in some eternal desert sharing tea and some little sweets she loves? The first choice of audience, the rabbi's students, will make her persona more presentational; the second, more intimate. Both are valid; the choice has to do with your own sensibility and what works for you. And why is she telling all this <u>now</u>? Although the frame of the story centers on how she came to be ageless and eternal, clearly so much more is going on in this tale. Serach is teaching us about courage and wisdom and the need

---

[15]   *To the Actor.* Oxford: Routledge, 1953.

to seize the moment. She is telling us that one individual can change history; she is passing on the legacy of memory and storytelling her grandfather gave to her. And so much more. As you find your way into the story, telling it over and over to your dog, the trees, your cell phone... you will discover your way of communicating all these levels and still keep the story moving.

When two characters are in conversation, the essential gesture becomes especially useful. If each character is represented by a clear and compelling gesture, the storyteller can drop the literary "he said/she said" repetition and just switch from gesture to gesture. This can be both very entertaining for the audience, and can also help enhance the rhythm and immediacy of the story. In Benji Levene's beautiful story "The Escort," one man shows another the way to his destination in Jerusalem, and the following bit of conversation ensues:

I brought him to the street—to the house—and said: "Here it is! *Shalom!*"

"Just a minute," he said. "Why did you stop and ask me if I'm looking for something? Why did you escort me? Young people don't do these things today." (I was young then.)

"Well, I probably wouldn't have done this," I said, "but my grandfather used to do this."

"Who was your grandfather?"

"Oh, you wouldn't know," I said.

"What was his name?"

"Levin," I said.

"Which Levin?"

"Areyh Levin."

"The famous *tzaddik*, Reb Aryeh Levin?" he asked.

"Yes," I replied.

On the page, the "I said's" and "he said's" orient the reader, and in the skilled hands of this writer, lend rhythm to the reading. But a storyteller can replace "he said" or "I said" with simple changes of voice and body shape, perhaps just a slight angle of the head. Look to the text for clues to the physical and vocal life of these two men: one is young, American, a student; the other, elderly, Israeli, a journalist; later in the text it says that the old man "looked up" at the student, so he is shorter. One is lost; the other knows the way and is fulfilling a mitzvah. There is no need to be elaborate or theatrical, but all these are clues to help the storyteller find subtle shifts of voice and posture that will open the audience's imaginations to the moment. Try reading this conversation aloud without the "he said's" and "I said's"; see what you find. Even better, read the whole story and then read the conversation without the speaker references and see if you can begin to let their different voices come through you.

***

To end where we began: storytelling is a sacred art. We are *maggidim*, griots, shamans. We are mediators between worlds: between the sacred and the profane, the seen and unseen, the mystic and the material, memory and imagination, past and present. We are what a famous book of my youth called "Technicians of the Sacred,"[16] which suggests that the storyteller's magic, like all magic, is a craft. This essay is a small introduction to the practical aspects of a profound art. I hope these thoughts and suggestions are useful and that they inspire you to pursue the sacred through the art and craft of storytelling. It is an endless pursuit, driven by a "blessed unrest," which is why in the end we storytellers have always said, "To be continued..."

---

[16]   Jerome Rothenberg. *Technicians of the Sacred.* Berkeley: University of California Press, 1969.

Creative Ways to Use *Mitzvah Stories*
compiled by Peninnah Schram & Cherie Karo Schwartz, with Goldie Milgram

The Jewish people are known as the People of the Book. However, Jews are also the People of the Story. Judaism has always revered and honored its oral tradition alongside its tradition of formal written texts. From the time of the Torah to the present day, Judaism has dynamically intertwined sacred written texts and oral transmission. Indeed, stories have often served as guides to the wisdom of the Jewish People, making the elaborate world of rabbinic tradition and law accessible to all.

Our Jewish stories are the mirror and the memory of who we are as the People of the Book. They provide enlivening, engaging entrée into the world of Judaism: its worldwide peoples, values, history, holidays, customs, rituals, and life cycle events. This guide is designed for use with this collection of stories that focus on *mitzvot*, stories spanning various genres, including autobiographical stories, re-visioned folktales, original stories, and *midrashim*. Each story opens the door for creative questions and discussions—and for learning more of Jewish values and wisdom. Reading and telling stories aloud, whether from sacred literature or from literary and folk sources, continues to help us transmit our oral tradition.

Stories themselves are essential to our human experience. Especially at this time when we are becoming increasingly dependent upon technology, we need more than ever to make time for and create events centered around this most human activity: sharing stories by telling them aloud. Telling stories is a way to befriend and bond with others as together we listen to their stories and they listen to ours. Built into our Jewish calendar are *Shabbat* and holidays, special moments when we set aside time to spend with friends and family. These are perfect times to share stories with each other. And the year is filled with other such moments: times of celebration and sorrow, of personal reminiscence and collective memory.

The authors represented in *Mitzvah Stories* have generously contributed stories that exemplify *mitzvot*. The stories give life to these *mitzvot*, showing them in action in our world so they can be felt and taken in deeply, resonating with our own lives. The power of story, after all, lies in its innate connection to ourselves. We, as readers, can vicariously experience these life lessons and then, by extension, can connect them to our own world and deeds. The beauty of story is in its sharing.

There are many ways to share stories; they travel easily! Stories easily fit into established curricula for classes and workshops for all ages and for any subject. They can also be shared informally around a table or living room. They can be offered at synagogue, organizational events or among friends. Stories can be used during regularly scheduled sessions or at special events. A synagogue or a group of individuals might create a storytelling *havurah* to get to know each other on a more personal level. Besides helping participants explore their identities and develop new friendships, these shared conversations about Jewish stories will also teach them about Jewish history, traditions, and values and, especially, the role of *mitzvot* in Jewish life. And, too, the stories can also be read and savored at any time by oneself.

Where to Find Stories and Storytellers

You may wish to use storytellers to facilitate story-sharing sessions. There are formal and informal storytellers in every community, treasured individuals who can be called upon for performances and workshops, and for help to find, create and share stories. *Mitzvah Stories'* contributing author websites are included here in their biographical statements. To help locate storytellers in your region, ask in your synagogue, organizations, and community; look in community directories and newspapers; and look online. You may also find helpful connections through the Jewish Storytelling Coalition's website and directory: www.jewishstorytelling.org.

On this same site, you can also access an annotated bibliography of current Jewish story collections, which was compiled by Peninnah Schram. Check for these books in your synagogue or public library. Books can be ordered through inter-library loan.

Model Story Exchange Events

There are endless possibilities for using *Mitzvah Stories* to enhance meetings, classes, and events. Here are a few examples to help spark ideas.

Cherie Karo Schwartz: I helped organize an interfaith telling event, where two storytellers sounded a bell and lit a candle to open the circle. After an introduction about how the two hours would unfold, each of us shared a brief story from our own tradition. Following that, there was silence to take the story in; and then anyone in the circle who felt so moved by what she had heard, in resonance, rose to share a story of her own. There were personal, folk, and sacred stories. Each was prefaced with its provenance and source. At the end of each telling, there was again silent time for someone else to hear the connection and to share his own story. The effect of this exchange was profound.

Goldie Milgram: One year at the National Havurah Summer Institute, the evening program involved many rings of chairs inside of a large room. Each room had a member present who had created a story she wished to share with the community. After hearing the story, the audience moved on to the next open story circle in the room, and so on. You might invite one of the storytellers in this volume to come and share his story, offer a workshop on story craft and storytelling, and in a few weeks, when those who have attended have completed their stories, hold just such a story exchange!

Peninnah Schram: During a weekend when I was the Storyteller/ Scholar-in-Residence at a synagogue, I was invited as the "catalyst" to a Saturday evening gathering of members of the synagogue's Board of Directors, along with the clergy, administrators and teachers. Everyone invited had been asked to bring a story of meeting "Elijah the Prophet" or being an "Elijah" for someone else. They had been hearing Elijah folktales throughout the *Shabbat* in my various presentations. After an informal dessert reception, we gathered in the living room of our hosts, and I began to tell a personal story of gratitude when I had been in need of help and along came "Elijah" to help me. This story served as a trigger, and people started sharing their stories—perhaps stories they had planned to tell or perhaps different ones that came spontaneously to mind in response to my story. People listened to each other's stories with awe and respect, discovering that they had a new relationship to the people they had known for years—because they had not known of these experiences and revelations. This story exchange opened up questions and curiosity to know more about each other. They decided to meet on holidays to continue this story-sharing experience that deepens friendships.

Using Stories and Storytellers

Shabbat/Holiday D'var Torah or Torah Discussion:

Find stories that speak to the themes of the *parshat ha-shavua* (the Torah portion of the week), using the thematic guide to these stories. Use the story as a springboard for group discussion or leader-led discussion. Or you may choose a story that resonates with a current event.

Many congregations host informal learning discussions after services. Story-sharing is a particularly appropriate, meaningful activity on *Shabbat* and other holidays. The stories in this book are indexed by themes, holidays and *mitzvot*. Choose stories that will provide relevant, meaningful story experiences.

Using stories, such as some of the midrashic retellings in this volume to bring Torah into the lives of your community is one of the most ancient forms of giving a *d'var Torah* or stimulating a discussion.

Jewish Holidays

Hanukkah, *Pesach*, or *Sukkot* week and dates like *Yom HaShoah* and *Yom Ha-Atzma'ut* are natural times for sharing stories. Deepen Jewish connections when you bring these stories to life through storytelling, discussion groups, guest storytellers, and perhaps even a Jewish storytelling festival!

Intergenerational Storytelling

Kinship and friendships develop when the generations meet and tell personal Jewish stories. Starting with tales from this volume, choose a story that addresses generations as an opener for the group, and then have all join in a conversation about the mitzvah illustrated in the story. Use the theme as a springboard for the generations to share personal stories with each other. In this way, elders and the young are linked in the ageless power of story.

Congregational and Organizational Meetings

Meetings are wonderful places to include stories. Telling, relating, or reading a mitzvah-themed story helps set the *kavannah*, the intention, of the meeting and can become part of the discussion for the day.

Story Swaps

Gather a group together and have each participant choose a story from this book which speaks to them. The stories can be read aloud with participants taking turns reading, or the stories can be read silently and then discussed. Have the person who chose the story share what drew them to that story. Once the story is read, give time for feedback and conversation about the story, its themes, and personal connections.

Or, once the story is read, participants may swap personal or known stories on the theme of the mitzvah story.

Stories Shared by Clergy

Rabbis and cantors search for stories to use in their divrei Torah (sermons), holiday, life cycle events and other presentations. Stories are powerful tools for giving lessons. Stories can also illuminate specific prayers and other parts of a service in meaningful, long-lasting ways. Story swaps at Rabbinic Council meetings, conferences and retreats can offer the opportunity for creating story connections and sharing resources. Clergy can exchange appropriate stories that have worked to inspire and teach for specific occasions and lessons, thereby increasing each other's repertoire of stories.

Family Gatherings at Holidays and Celebrations

Family gatherings are a perfect time to share stories. If you are planning a reunion, life cycle event, or holiday celebration, contact the group and offer suggestions of topics that may prompt memories for the family members to bring to the occasion. Memories can be of food, early days, generations, joyful times, school, missed opportunities, losses, triumphs, connections, play, scars, jokes and jokesters, riches, kindnesses, and of course, *mitzvot!* Find a story within this volume that can be used as an opener for the sharing of stories.

In the past, a special addition to a wedding, holiday or *bar mitzvah* was hiring a *badchan*, a humorous raconteur. In modern times (and now with the addition of *bat mitzvah*), this tradition can continue with the use of a professional storyteller to enhance the occasion. *Mitzvah stories* work beautifully for life cycle events, and can lead, with the storyteller's guidance, into sharing personal stories of the celebrants.

When there is a family gathering, there is an opportunity to learn from each other, to further complete the family "portrait": Who is in your family? What values have they held throughout the years? What were the favorite sayings or proverbs often repeated in the home? What blessings were recited at various occasions or moments?—and so on. In Judaism there is the tradition of an ethical will that focuses on the advice, values, Torah *pasukim* (verses) or lessons the person wants to transmit to the next generation—in other words, that person's ethical legacy. At a family wedding, for example, this type of advice can be written down for the bride and groom to use as guides in their new life together. At a *brit* (*bris*) or baby naming, this advice can become part of the family history, retold at *bar* or *bat mitzvah*, or perhaps entered into a book for the baby to have in later years. At the time of welcoming a new child, the parents and grandparents can share why the baby was given a particular name and who the baby was named after, including a biography of the characteristics of that person and their guiding *mitzvot*. These family stories become part of the baby's personal story.

Community Mitzvah Day Celebrations

Many synagogues and communities celebrate a special Mitzvah Day when participants are encouraged to actively engage in performing *mitzvot*. It's a type of "a taste of mitzvah" time. Later, when participants gather to exchange some of their experiences, it would be timely also to share a mitzvah story from this volume as an extension of the mitzvah celebration.

At venues where participants take Judaism classes, considered to be a mitzvah in itself, class leaders can take the opportunity to integrate and discuss some of the stories in this volume. For example, for adult life-long learning and family *b'nei mitzvah* classes, the discussion could focus on a specific mitzvah story and deepen the mitzvah practice in everyone's life. In addition to the publication of this book, podcasts are being made available for each story recorded by the authors. These podcasts are available at www.ReclaimingJudaism.org.

Either in preparation for or following the event, have people share personal stories of *mitzvot* they have either seen, been the recipient of, or have done themselves. They may also be encouraged to tell of *mitzvot* that occurred as they were participating in the Mitzvah Days in the past. These personal stories will be reinforced by the participation in the Mitzvah Day and may well offer stories for future events.

Women's *Rosh Chodesh* or Men's *Kiddush Levanah* Gatherings

Mitzvah Stories includes many gender-specific and provocative stories. Along with the rituals, prayers, and activities used at this sacred time, the telling and studying of stories can add special meaning to the celebration of the new moon.

Sharing Stories in a Group Setting

A group may wish, without a special occasion, to share stories and have a conversation about their meanings and connections. In order for there to be a productive and focused discussion, all members of the group must read the same story. Perhaps one member can be assigned in advance to choose the story to be discussed. Before the meeting, or at the meeting itself, participants should be given enough time to read and think about the story individually before the group discussion begins.

The session should begin either with a public reading or telling of the story. If read aloud, participants should take turns reading a single paragraph, or one or two expressive readers could read the entire story out loud. Alternatively, a member of the group could retell the story in an expanded summary so that the story comes alive to the others.

Stories are meant to be heard. Reading aloud and storytelling are two different but equally valid spoken arts. Even when one reads "silently," there is always interaction with the text and with one's inner voice. Whether read aloud or told directly without a formal text, the voice serves as the special tool for transmitting words, ideas, emotions, and experiences.

Questions for Exploring a Story

Starting the Discussion:

It's useful to seed a discussion about a story with some evocative opening questions, like:

What do you like about the story? What holds your interest?

What about the story line? The characters? The setting? The time?

Is anything disturbing about the story?

Is the resolution satisfying?

Does the story trigger a strong emotion?

Has anything similar ever happened to you or someone you know?

Has this mitzvah ever been done by or for you?

Does this story lead you to hope to fulfill this mitzvah yourself?

Why is this mitzvah so important in our lives and in our world?

How does this mitzvah contribute to our quality of life?

Is there a parallel or similar story about a mitzvah that you have experienced in your own life?

Making Story Connections

There are many approaches to choosing a story for discussion. To help readers identify the various *mitzvot* exemplified in the stories, this book lists stories by mitzvah, theme or occasion in the index.

If the Biblical *parasha* concerns a birth (of Isaac or Jacob, or Moses, or Samuel) or if there has been a recent birth in the community/family, then you might consider discussing Yossi Alfi's "Burga Baby."

If you want to focus on *Shabbat*, select Arthur Strimling's "The Shabbat Story I Want to Tell" or Sandy Sasso's "Shabbos Candles."

If the discussion centers on superstitions, look at Ellen Frankel's "Saved by the Evil Eye."

If you choose to feature a place, such as Israel, then you may read "The Dead Sea" by Howard Schwartz, or "The Escort" by Benji Levene.

Where to Go with These Stories

As you delve into the world of these *Mitzvah Stories*, you may well find connections with the *mitzvot*, characters, and situations. *Mitzvot* can lead to further *mitzvot*, just as stories lead to more and more stories. Read, hear, interact with, and breathe these stories into your spirit; share them and create new tales from your own life experiences and imagination. Become a teller of tales in your own right. Whatever your background, age, or practice, may your life be enriched by these encounters, adding new stories to the wellspring of our unfolding story.

I

Coming to Wholeness
Mitzvot of Love and Healing

The Burga Baby
by Yossi Alfi

Translated from the Hebrew by Evan Fallenberg

My mother moaned with labor pains for three days. At every opportunity she would recount the story of those pains to me, saying, "Ay, Yosef...with you it was the most difficult, *abdallak*.[17] It took so long for you to come out..."

She lay in the room at the top of the stairway that was known as the *tarar*, where the breeze from the roof met the coolness of the house as it rose from the cellar. Mosquito netting hung over her to protect her from all manner of pests, and a mat was spread beneath her to support her back. The Christian midwife's name was Atisha; it was Atisha who was called upon to birth the "pampered ones" from among the young Jewish women. She was a certified midwife and so knowledgeable that all the other women in confinement were jealous of those assisted by her.

> Mother told me of ancient woes,
> Among them, me!
> A yellowing mat
> A Christian midwife.
> Lengthy days.
> I was supposed to be born
> But was apparently not interested.
> I could have been born in Israel
> Thus avoiding yet another complex.
> But for whatever reason,
> When my mother wished to cross the border
> With me in her belly,
> I wished to be born in Iraq
> And I reminded her she was—pregnant.
> With me
> Inside her.
> Thus it was, a worn mat.

---

[17] Iraqi-Jewish term of affection, half Hebrew–half Arabic, meaning "may I be your sacrifice," or "I would die for you," expressing a mother's absolute love of her offspring.

I was born Yosef
I was given life
I said *Shalom*
And no one answered.
I was born.[18]

Then the Christian midwife Atisha said, "*Subhan Allah*. May God be blessed." And my mother was taken aback.

"What happened?" she asked. "What happened? Is the child all right?"

"Not only is he fine, he is special, a special child!" Atisha cried out, her bellowing voice an immediate summons to the first row of women positioned just outside the netting, among them my older sisters, who had provided assistance to the midwife throughout the birth. Behind them stood the expectant aunts, and behind them, my father entered the *tarar* in a rush, his face pale with fear and worry.

"A special child has been born to you, with Allah's help and that of the prophets. Women, ululate!"

"What? What's happened?" my father responded with a parched tongue, on the verge of fainting on the midwife Atisha's bosom.

"The boy has been born with a *burga*," Atisha exclaimed from between pursed lips.

"A *burga*?" my father asked, gathering the pieces of himself that had shattered in every direction: the frightened piece, the astonished piece, the blessed piece, the sanctified piece, the honored piece, the curious piece...

"A *burga*? I've never seen a child with a *burga*," my father said as he approached my mother, who was holding the baby in her arms. The baby's face was still covered with the caul that was attached at the corners of his forehead, two breathing holes open beneath the nose. My father took a look and once again nearly fainted. The midwife held him up and seated him on the low stool that had until only a moment earlier been supporting her. He sat down, wiping the sweat from his broad brow. He thrust his fingers into his mouth and bit them like a babe seeking a pacifier.

He muttered, "*Burga, burga*, we have a child with a *burga*..."

---

[18] From *How To Make an Iraqi: Poems by Yossi Alfi*. Sifriyat Poalim, 1981.
(Hebrew)

Throughout my life I had been searching for the proper Hebrew word for a *burga* but had come up with only an approximation. Then one day I was reading a book in which the author told of being born with a *burga*, which he translated to English using the word "caul"– and I learned that this term was a familiar one, and the matter well known.

Not much time passed before the early-rising synagogue congregants received the news of my *burga*-birth, and the rabbi was led with great ceremony to our house, where he ascended the stairs in the direction of the *tarar*. The room was now filled with all the members of the household, who had been awakened by my sisters' ululating cries, the gurgling praises made by the tongue at the top of the open pharynx.

The house contained a number of families, since we lived, as was the custom in those days, in a large home as one extended family– the uncle with his family, the aunt with hers, the grandmothers.

"A child born with a *burga* is not just special; he is one who heralds the coming of the messiah," said the rabbi quietly, privately, to my father, his pleasant words fluttering from his beard to my father's ears.

The midwife hastened to remove the caul from the baby's face, my face, tugging lightly at the corners of my forehead and gently tearing it. She folded it and placed it in the embroidered kerchief that had been on my mother's head through the long hours of the birth, and she placed it in the hands of the rabbi.

The rabbi opened the kerchief and gazed at the thin caul, then passed it to my father, who handled it with much anxiety, as though it were a precious diamond that might fall from his hands.

The kerchief was then passed among the men, then the women, and the rabbi said, "It must not be touched, must not be touched. This is God's handiwork, it must not be touched."

And the eyes of one and all at the top of the stairs were peeled wide, their necks stretched forward, in order to catch sight of the contents of the kerchief.

"*Burga*."

"*Burga*."

"*Burga*."

The *burga*, which was a part of my body, from fetus to the birth that had taken place only moments earlier, became public property and was brought ceremoniously to the synagogue for the morning prayers, and there the folded *burga* was placed inside a lump of silver that was then smelted closed and turned into an amulet.

I was raised on this story, a blond child from Basra about whom all who approached were warned, "Take care with that little 'Englishman'; he was born with a caul."

"English" because of my blondness, and the caul because of its holiness.

Right after reading about the term "caul," I went online, and it turned out that this phenomenon is well known, and that babies—one per several hundred thousand—are born with them. There are people—not just in Iraq where I happened to be born, but in other places like Europe and the rest of the world—who perceive cauls to be a symbol of holiness, and there are people who take part in caul cults for preserving cauls and sanctifying their lives through them in one way or another. I even saw dried cauls—go figure...

I remember, in my early childhood in Iraq, when I was three years old, and later in Israel that people would come to me for a blessing. I would place my tiny hand on the person's head and say, 'Bah-bah-bah' just as I saw my father do when he would bless me with the verse:

"May God give you of the dew of heaven and the fatness of the earth..."

Most surprising of all was that they, the adults, would come to me in awe and reverence and my mother would ask me—always humorously, with laughter, so that "the child will not be startled, *abdallak*," to bless them, and she would take my hand and place it on the person's forehead. In Israel, where I had already been living for more than a year with my grandmother but without the rest of the family, people would come to our tent in the transit camp for new immigrants and declare to my grandmother:

"Is this the boy with the caul? Tell him to bless me!"

And my grandmother would stroke my hand and place it on the head of the supplicant and tell me to say, 'Bah-bah-bah,' and I would hasten to do as she told me.

Once I had grown older and become Israeli in every way, "and not as we expected him to be," as my uncles would say, they would remind me: "Do you remember how you would bless us with 'Bah-bah-bah?'"

That is the story with which I grew up: the boy born with a caul, a *burga*. I know that word, *burga*, since it has been with me my whole life, so often repeated. "What are you talking about? Do you know who this boy is? He's the one born with a *burga*." I fought it, always; from the time I was a child, then a youth, an adolescent, an adult, I fought against such superstitions. Till this very day there are old people still alive who give me that look—do you remember that you used to do 'Bah-bah-bah' for me? I would bless them. It is now a kind of a joke, but for them it was a serious matter. For me, I was certain it was some sort of child's play.

The *burga* became an amulet that my mother wore her entire life on a chain around her neck and used to heal one thing or another. She told me that when my father was in the throes of death and in terrible pain she placed the *burga* on his chest and it calmed him. In other cases of using the *burga*, I employed my powers of logic to fight all those concepts, and I ran away from all those old-time beliefs, seeking new answers in the Israeliness I had created as a means of protecting myself from my past.

Mother fell ill and suffered excruciating pain from cancer and other maladies. In our tradition, there is no such thing as sending a parent to an old age home, so my mother lived on at home though she spent a lot of time at my sister's house. One night the heavy amulet that was always hanging around her neck was apparently keeping her from breathing easily, so she slipped it off and laid it on the headboard. The amulet fell behind the bed where no one could see it and even she did not notice its absence although she had worn it her entire adult life, had made *aliyah* to Israel with it after many hardships and lived with it for years upon years, from a tent in an immigrant camp to homes in Petah Tikva and Ramat Gan.

When she died a number of years ago, everyone went looking for the amulet, though no one ever mentioned it to me. Then recently my sister moved apartments, and one Friday evening she told me:

"Yossi, listen. We found something that belongs to you. I have to return it to you. Just don't get upset about it."

She gave me this thing wrapped in an old cloth of Iraqi linen that had been specially tailored to fit the heavy amulet.

I looked at it and told her, "I recognize this...this is what Mother would wear hanging...it's..."

My sister said, "It's your *burga*."

And the *burga* took me, a man in his fifties, straight back to childhood. At that time I had been unaware that my mother had been wearing it all the time; I had thought it was hidden somewhere. I knew they had used it in the synagogue, that it was brought to sick people and placed on their bodies. Before my uncle died, my mother took my father aside and told him: "Put the *burga* on him and he will be at peace."

They put it on him and he passed away tranquilly.

My sister placed the wrapped *burga* in my hand. I sniffed it, and it had my mother's scent, a delicate soap smell, the smell of a pampered daughter of rich parents, the smell I grew up with as a shoot, a bud, a flower of a brand-new Israeli life. That scent of my mother lives on and is preserved in this *burga*, and I simply burst into terrible sobs that I could not contain inside me, the sobs of a child separated from his caul, which has returned and now seeks a place in his life.

So shocked and dismayed were they that my sister, my son, my daughter and the family members who were hosting us did not know what to do with themselves.

"I'm sorry, perhaps I shouldn't have given this to you..." my sister mumbled.

"No, no, no," I said. "It's good that you gave this to me and I'll save it. I really did wonder what had happened to it."

I placed the amulet in my wife's hands, and she tucked it inside a velvet bag and put that into a safe, where it remains until today.

I do not know why I am telling this story that I have never told before, but this is yet another birth, another separation from knowing myself. A different self to an individuality that I will apparently never understand among all the screens and masks I have used to cover my face and my personality.

Provenance: In recent years there seem to be more frauds and charlatans, who present themselves as ones who possess higher powers and use false claims, in order to enrich nothing but their own pockets. My hope is that this story will inspire people to believe in their own power and strength because one's own mind is stronger than any other.

Yossi Alfi's unique life is reflected in his stories, beginning with his 1949 voyage as a three-year-old, fleeing to Israel from Iraq with his grandmother. A performer from a young age, by age 16 he directed and taught theater for schools. His studies at LAMDA–The London Academy of Music and Dramatic Arts, led to a career as a prominent Israeli author, actor, theater director and storyteller. Yossi's storytelling television shows are broadcast in Israel and the US. Yossi has published over 20 books of non-fiction, poetry, prose and children's books and is a writer of stories, plays and screenplays.

A Father's Gift
by Noa Baum

Bilal grew up in Lahore, in the Punjab province of Pakistan. When he was a young boy there was a war between India and Pakistan, and Bilal asked his father:

"Baba, why do the Muslims and Hindus hate each other? Why is there all this war?"

His father said, "When you're older, we'll talk about it."

A few years later, Bilal turned thirteen, and his family traveled to visit his uncle up north. Bilal loved those visits! His uncle's house had a courtyard with a large fountain in the center. Along the walls surrounding the courtyard were all the rooms, with the kitchen on one side and an open stairway leading to the second floor on the other. He loved the house. He loved eating outside, sitting on low stools near the fountain, but most of all he loved playing with all his cousins around the great banyan tree in the back of the house. He and his cousins were about to go climb the great banyan tree when his father called him.

"Come, Bilal, it's time to answer your question."

"What question?"

But instead of answering, his father took him by the hand and led him up the stairs to the second floor, walking along the balcony corridor above the courtyard below until he stopped in front of the last door. Bilal could not believe it: his father was taking him to the attic room! The only room in the house that was ever locked—The *Jinn* Room—the ghost room that his cousins told spooky stories about!

"Baba, I...I don't want to go in there. I want to go play!"

"You'll play later," his father replied. "Come, there's something I need to show you."

His father unlocked the door, and Bilal followed him into the dim room. A few rays of sunlight filtered through the slits of the closed wooden shutters. It looked like a storage room. Everything was covered with dust: old cots and chairs, his grandfather's helmet and old musket from the British army, boxes and a large wooden trunk. Outside the window he could hear his cousins playing under the big banyan tree. He really did not want to be in this dusty place that smelled of old things. But his father opened the trunk and brought out a large leather-bound book.

"Come closer, Bilal," he said. "Look, this is our Bahi—the book of our family's history. It passes down from the oldest to the oldest sons—that is why it is here, in your uncle's house, my oldest brother. You need to know what's in it. Open it, but be very gentle."

Bilal had never seen anything so old. It had about 200 pages. Carefully and slowly he opened it. On the first page, written in ink, were 10 names, and there he saw his own name, **Bilal Ahmed Sahi**, right above his brother Jamal and sister Sarah! And there was his father's name, **Ghulam Sahi**, and his mother, **Naeema Cheema Sahi**. There were the names of his uncles and aunts and cousins. He turned the pages, and on each page were 10 names, the names of more uncles, aunts and cousins, his grandparents, and their parents. Everyone that he knew or ever heard about was written in there.

"Hey, that's us!" he said. "All our family is here!"

His father smiled. "Yes, all our family is here. Turn the page."

Bilal turned the page. Once again there were 10 names, but the names were different. He read: **Singh Gurmeet Singh Sahi**. That was not a Muslim name! He looked at his father.

"These are not Muslims. They are Sikh names—they can't be our family!"

His father said: "Yes, they are your family, too. Keep looking. Turn the pages."

Once again Bilal turned the pages, and soon the paper was very brittle. And the names...**Anil Sahi.**

"Anil!? What kind of a name is this?"

"That's a Hindu name," said his father.

"Hindus?" he cried.

"Yes," replied his father. "They are your family, too. Keep going."

The paper was almost disintegrating now as he kept turning the pages and reading the names. Then the paper became parchment, and after several pages the names were not even Hindu. He had no idea what kind of names these were, and after a few more pages, the script was so strange he could no longer read it.

He looked up at his father. "I don't understand. What does this mean?"

Bilal's father always encouraged his children to come to their own conclusions.

Whenever they would ask, "What does that mean?" His father would say, "Well, that's for you to think about."

But this time his father said, "You asked about the hate, remember? Now you can see yourself that we're all the same. God lives in everything. Don't you let anyone ever tell you to hate another because you know now that they are all here, in this book: Muslims, Sikhs, Hindus, Christians, Jews. They are all your family."

Bilal was only thirteen and couldn't wait to get away from his father's serious musings and that stuffy attic room, so he said, "Can I go now?"

Off he ran to play with his cousins and soon forgot all about that conversation. Many years passed. Bilal became a doctor, moved to the US and now lives in Rochester, NY, with his wife and three children.

One day after his father passed away, Bilal heard about The National Geographic's Genome Project through which, according to your DNA, they can map your family's travels throughout the world and you can also find out your genetic ancestral origin. According to the DNA, there are specific markers for specific population groups; if your markers match the markers of someone else, you're genetically most closely related to that person, and they give that person your e-mail. Like his father, Bilal was interested in history and genealogy and decided to find out his genetic heritage. He ordered the kit from The National Geographic's Genome Project, and sent in a cheek swab in a little vial with preservative solution. A little vial with a number. No name. No name at all.

After a few weeks, the results came back. There was a map of the world tracing where his ancestors had been: like all of us, they, too, came from Africa, moved to central Asia and spent around 5000 years in Ukraine, then in Poland and Denmark. Then about 5000 years ago, they started moving to India and ended up in northern India 1000 years ago. Soon the e-mails from his genetic relations began to arrive.

He received an e-mail from **L. Frieberg**. Another arrived from **David Barry Baum**, and others from **Maurice Krasnow, Clayton Schultz, Ed Leviten, Jack Salzstein**. It seemed that according to the DNA results, the most recent genetic relatives of Dr. Bilal Ahmed, the Pakistani Muslim, were Ashkenazi Jews from Poland...

It was then that Bilal remembered. He looked at his thirteen year-old daughter and said, "You know, when I was about your age, my father gave me a very special gift. He took me up to the attic of my uncle's house and showed me our Bahi, the family book..."

And he told her the story. Bilal has been telling that story to his children ever since. He tells it at every opportunity so that they will never forget his father's words: "Don't you let anyone ever tell you to hate another, because you can see —they are all your family."

Provenance: I grew up in Jerusalem, Israel. I grew up in a perpetual state of fear, conflict, and wars. I grew up longing for peace, but not knowing what it feels like. Here in the openness of America I tasted it. Today I use storytelling to help heal divides of identity and build bridges of dialogue and peace between Israelis and Palestinians, within the Jewish community and between people of all faiths. I often lead interfaith workshops between Jews, Muslims and Christians. At such an interfaith workshop, in Rochester, NY, one of the participants was a Pakistani Muslim, Dr. Bilal Ahmed, who shared a story about a special gift he received in his life. He offered his story to me to shape and tell, and wanted me to pass on his father's gift. I offer it here to you.

Noa Baum was born and raised in Jerusalem; she is trained in theater and education. Noa is an award-winning storyteller who focuses on her craft's power to heal across the divides of identity. Her show, *A Land Twice Promised*, relives her heartfelt dialogue with a Palestinian woman, illuminating the complex and contradictory history and emotions surrounding Jerusalem for Israelis and Palestinians alike. Since 1982, Noa's performances and interactive workshops have captivated and inspired audiences internationally. Noa studied with Uta Hagen in New York and received an MA in Educational Theater from NYU.

One Day at Stone Mountain
a friend's experience, reframed by Renée Brachfeld

Over the course of two years, our eldest son has struggled mightily with debilitating, life-threatening illness. The small non-malignant tumor located in his brain has caused overwhelming headaches and incredible sensitivity to light and sound, making normal everyday functioning almost impossible. There have been three surgeries to remove the tumor and repair the damage, and then, almost worse, surgeries to correct problems caused by the first operation. Not only is Ariel exhausted from the experience; the family itself is tired. The constant strain of fear and anxiety, as well as the actual work of caring for an ill child, has taken a toll on everyone. Most days, everyone is going in different directions. No one's connecting. Family members are out of synch.

Rafi, the youngest, has certainly been left to his own devices far more than appropriate for an eight year old. Somehow he's come through it still full of joy and laughter, and ever attentive to the small details that most people miss. Malka, serious and studious at 12, is in the habit of being very helpful, and then fleeing to her room at the first opportunity to lose herself in books or her own imaginary world. Ariel, almost healthy now at 14, is making some progress towards reclaiming a normal life. Even so, he is still fearful that the debilitating pain might return, and is reluctant to fully engage with the world.

Lying in bed one Sunday morning, I go through my list – everyone healthy? Check. No doctor visits or therapy appointments? Check. No plans or obligations? Check. Weather? A rare, spring-like day for the region, neither hot nor cold, no chance of rain. With rising excitement, I realize it is a day when we could all do something together. What might we do? If we stay at home, being really "together" never happens. Charlie, my rabbi-husband, will go off to study or work. The kids all have their own rooms and their own projects. For the past two years, family together-time has mostly been about coping, about making sure everyone is at least fed and minimally cared for in the face of the intense needs of caring for Ariel. Sure, there have been good moments in the midst of it, bouts of fun or laughter or the kind of dark humor that emerges when a loved one is critically ill for so long. Now that Ariel is healthy, how to fashion a "normal" life together again? The two younger kids tend to disappear as soon as they can; they're so tired of needing to be reliable and supportive. What can be done to bring everyone together?

Of course—a picnic! Get out of the house. Hike. Enjoy nature and the beautiful day. We can go to Stone Mountain! Stone Mountain is just a short drive northeast of Atlanta, where we live. It is, depending on your point of view, a kitschy theme park, the Mount Rushmore of the South, with a giant carving that celebrates the Confederacy—Stonewall Jackson, Robert E. Lee, and Jefferson Davis, or an amazing geological formation and great place for a hike. Perfect—the theme park, a hike, a great view from the mountaintop, and then the leisure to loll in the grassy plain below and picnic together.

It might take some time to convince everyone else this is a great idea. One will want to watch a movie; another has homework.

Oy, no one seems thrilled by the beautiful day or the promise of mild weather. We are unused to heading outside. All the illness has led us to learn how to cope with being at home to care for Ariel. So I plead, cajole, badger, and beg. At last—universal, albeit grudging, agreement! Now to prepare.

A picnic for a family of kids and parents with food allergies and sensitivities and likes and dislikes (not to mention kashrut and the debate over whether we are bringing a picnic that is milk or meat) is not a simple thing to assemble. The whole idea is to have a good time. Can't have anyone feeling deprived by not having food they want to eat.

Almost ready. Oh, right, of course, the dogs have to be walked. They are not allowed on the trail up the mountain. And we can't lock them inside on such a beautiful day without at least a short walk. Can't anyone help with this? All right, all right—I'll take them.

Finally, just when despair is setting in, I realize—the food is packed, the dogs have been walked, the children and husband have been sent back inside (twice, in some cases) to put on footwear suitable for a hike. Everyone has a small daypack and a water bottle as their share of the carrying. Finally, finally—everyone is in the van.

It's a miracle! It is as if the script for today has been memorized by all. Everyone seems buoyant and cheerful. The children are being kind and gentle with one another in the van. Charlie seems energized and excited, rather than grudgingly giving up a free afternoon at home.

Remarkably, despite the lovely weather, the park does not seem crowded. Look, a parking place! Everyone ties their shoes, daypacks are slung over shoulders, no one complains about the burden, and we begin to hike up the mountain—a huge exposed rock. From a distance, it looks like a smooth pebble that a giant has dropped, a single mountain-sized stone sitting in relatively flat surroundings. But once one starts walking, there are ups and downs, small trees growing in bits of soil, puddles that have collected in small indentations, and bugs and animals to observe. We walk together at first, and then scatter a bit. The kids run ahead in excitement.

"Birds, *Ima*!!"

Rafi, ever exuberant, and deeply attentive, is the first to spot a mother bird in a tree. His siblings race over, transfixed as the bird tends to its young, flying back and forth to a nest in the tree, returning each time with food to distribute to eager, peeping beaks. By the time Charlie comes over the rise, they are excitedly calling him to watch nature's drama unfold.

We all watch for a while, then head up the weaving trail again. We fall into an easy rhythm. I walk with Malka for a while; the boys run ahead with Charlie. We walk slowly, watching, listening.

"Look, *Ima*," Malka observes: "When we walk fast, it seems like there's just rock and trees. But when we stand still by the trees and listen and watch—we can see so much more!"

How true! What a joy, to stand here with her, admiring the sight of so many different shades and shapes of leaves. We touch the rough bark of a tree. We count...five, six, at least seven different kinds of insects, three birds, and a chipmunk in this grove. We walk on slowly, trying to look and listen, and really see as we go. The world has become richer. And then—she's off and running.

Ah. There are the boys. They are gathered over a shrivelled worm. "Look, *Ima*," they say, "it needs water." Probably not. Still it is touching that, rather than leaving the creature to die, they carefully lift it onto a supporting leaf, and then gently move it to a puddle in the shade. Oh my, the worm is wiggling, reviving. Amazing!

There they go racing off again, but not Ariel, who is slowing, his stamina ebbing. Years of illness and inactivity have left him out of shape. "Come, honey, let's take a break." We sit on a rock, have a snack, some water, enjoy the sunshine.

Revived, we walk on together, slowly.

Finally, we are all at the top of Stone Mountain. The view is incredible. We can see for miles in every direction. Not that long of a hike, in fact, but we saw a lot, and we're all ready to set up the picnic and settle down. So happy to be together, to be in this little sea of calm. We polish off every morsel of food. Charlie and I lean back and relax against the warm rocks. Ariel stretches out and appears to be dozing. Rafi and Malka are exploring nearby, examining bits of rock, trying to locate our house in the distance. Perfect.

"It's getting late—let's pack up."

The walk down is quieter. Everyone is tired. Going down is faster, but still makes us work to keep our footing. Out of shape legs are tired and wobbly. By the time we reach bottom, we're exhausted, but happy with the day. It's late when we reach the parking lot; few cars remain besides our own.

The kids rush to the car to throw their packs in the back of the van. Good, we'll have an easy departure. A door slams shut. What's that? Why is Charlie screaming at the top of his lungs?! I can't tell what's going on. The kids are confused, freaked. What's happening? What's wrong? Oh, my God, Charlie's hand is somehow slammed in the rear door. In a moment of panic, time stands still. I stumble around the side of the van, but the kids are in my way. I can't get to him.

Suddenly, a man appears beside me, seemingly out of nowhere. He radiates calm. He turns the keys, which are still protruding from the door, and opens it. I'm so upset; I don't know what to do. The stranger produces a clean cloth, and wraps Charlie's bleeding hand. Ice is produced from a cooler in his car and wrapped around the throbbing hand. He lifts the injured hand in the air, and shows Ariel how to keep it elevated and apply pressure.

I'm fighting my own hysteria. Where is the nearest hospital?

"I'll drive you," says the man, and gently guides us back toward our van. He climbs into the driver's seat, cool and competent, and drives us to the hospital. Charlie is clearly in shock, his face white and drawn in pain. The stranger has tucked a sweater around him. We're not clear yet what the full nature of the injury is. No one wants to look at the mangled hand. Silence reigns. The kids are too upset to speak.

The kind stranger escorts us from the car into the emergency room, finds a nurse, and now he's going to park the car.

A nurse is assessing Charlie's hand. "He will be fine," the stranger assures me, placing the car keys back in my hand. He is so calm, so sure. I study my beloved Charlie, who does not look at all fine.

Oh my, have to thank the stranger, find out his name. "I'm sorry, we don't know your name, after all you've...done for us." He's not there, gone. I only turned my back for a minute.

Doctors arrive, x-rays are taken. In the end, the stranger was right. Charlie is fine, some stitches needed, a splint, some physical therapy, and no permanent damage anticipated. The kind stranger has not reappeared; the children don't know his name either.

"I wish I'd at least asked his name. Ariel? Malka? Do you know our angel's name? How can we thank him?"

Malka looks at me, surprised. "But *Ima*, of course we know his name."

"What do you mean? Did you ask him?"

"I didn't need to ask," says Malka "It must have been Eliyahu Hanavi, Elijah the Prophet."

Provenance: This story is a composite of 2 different stories told to me, one of which was about a family hike, and the other about a chance meeting with Elijah the Prophet at Stone Mountain, Georgia. Stone Mountain is one of my favorite places, and Elijah the Prophet is one of Peninnah Schram's favorite characters, so I thought the two went well together. Surely, you've experienced, or observed from up close, a family coping with critical illness. Doesn't matter who it is—parent, spouse, child, grandparent, even an aunt or uncle—coping with critical illness takes a toll on everyone in the family. Schedules are thrown off; attention is all on the one with the illness. It can be very hard for families coping with illness or its aftermath to maintain their equilibrium. Even for families not in crisis, dealing with multiple growing children and their needs can make it hard for everyone to do something together.

Renée Brachfeld, a professional storyteller, has been delighting audiences since 1985 with her unique combination of storytelling and juggling skills. She has been featured on NPR and at storytelling festivals around the world. Her unique teaching methods empower people of all ages to tell their own stories. Together with her husband, Mark Novak, Renée has served as Scholar in Residence at over 130 congregations throughout North America. Their acclaimed recording, *King Solomon's Daughter*, received the Parents' Choice Gold Award. Renée homeschools her fourteen-year-old daughter Kaziah, bakes a lot of *challah*, and has lots of stories to tell about that.

Mr. Kharrubi and Me
by Helen Englehardt

Part One

In 1980, my husband and I moved into our new home in the Midwood neighborhood of Brooklyn. On the other side of a green wall of hedge growing on the boundary line between our properties, a gentleman from Cairo, Egypt, lived with his Jamaican wife. Tall, thin, soft-spoken, very courtly in his manners, Mr. Kharrubi usually met me when I was taking out my garbage pails to the sidewalk and he was warming up his four-door-maroon-sofa-on-wheels in his driveway.

"Good morning, Miss Helen. How are you today?"

Mr. Kharrubi was always traveling. He imported and exported foodstuffs to and from the Middle East. The Kharrubi family comes from the Kharrub Valley, north of Palestine. Kharrub means carob, that brown leathery pod also known as St. John's Bread or bokser. For 1400 years the Kharrubi family has lived in Palestine, Egypt, Libya, Tunisia, and Algeria. Carob is tough but sweet. Just like Mr. Kharrubi.

I began doing a lot of traveling, too. In 1988, returning from visiting his family in England, my husband was killed on Pan Am Flight 103. Within one month of the disaster, the families had formed an organization to fight for justice for their loved ones, to improve aviation safety and security, and to provide emotional support for one another. Our family group met every month somewhere between Boston and Washington, D.C.

In the weeks, months, and years that followed my husband's death, Mr. Kharrubi did anything he could to help me.

"You don't tell me what I can do for you!"

He made himself into my chauffeur. As soon as he saw me stepping out my front door, he asked where I was going, and drove me there, even if it were only to the subway station.

Because my husband had been killed by a bomb planted by people who came from the Middle East, I felt it was very important for me to get to know people of good will from that part of the world. So I joined the Dialogue Project when it began in Park Slope in the spring of 2001, becoming part of a circle of Jews, Muslims, Christians, Israelis and Palestinians meeting one afternoon every month to talk about the conflict in Israel and Palestine and to get to know one another as individuals, to listen to one another's life stories.

After two years, I helped organize a dialogue circle in my own neighborhood. I invited Mr. Kharrubi to join us.

It was a warm night, so everyone sat outdoors on the front porch. I introduced him to the group. And so it was there, in front of people he didn't know, that I learned, after twenty-three years living next door to him, who he really was, where he really came from.

Part Two

I was born in Jerusalem in 1928. I went to school in Rumama, in the village called Lifta, which is part of Jerusalem. After I finish the 7th grade, I transfer to a school in Br'chameya, on Salach'idin Street in Jerusalem. I graduate the 13th grade, in 1947, '48. I attend to Damascus University in Arabic Language and Literature, get my master in 1955.

Let me tell you first how we became refugees. Our home in Rumama is on the Jaffa Road outside the walls of Jerusalem. My father has a house with four apartments. My father rent the first floor, stores, apartments. When we were in our home in Rumama, we are living, Arabs, Jews together. I have a friend named Moishe. When English mandate finish in 1947 from that area, we start to fight, Israelis, Arabs together.

The man who lives in my father's house is Cohan, and we are very, very close. We eat together, the children play together, and he and my father work together. He said to my father, "Abu Achmad—means 'Father of Achmad'—leave, take your children and go from here. They are planning to attack. I don't want your children to be killed, so leave."

My father, he took it serious. After we had dinner we left around 11 o'clock that night. It's in '47. I think it's June, no rain and not cold. And we walk. We don't pack anything.

Cohan said to us, "Leave, and you will be back. I will take care of your things." We took our key only for the house we live in. We left the rest of the keys with him.

He said, "Go to Ramallah."

We walk 16 kilometers [around 10 miles] that night, through the mountains. There is no way to go by streets; they surround the area, the Shtern gang. Anybody go there, they kill. We have food, we have water. I carry my child. My mother, my father, my two sisters, my brother, myself and my wife, and my aunt and my uncle. We arrive at Al Bira [Al Bira and Ramallah are almost one city] at 8 o'clock in the morning. We have friends of us over there. They feed us, we relax. My uncle's wife is from a village called Duralcara between Ramallah and Nablus. So we went there.

The refugees come from the west, that is Jaffa and Lydda. The Red Cross make a camp in Duralcara. They ask, "Who is educated here? We want to open a school." They call me. They know I finish high school so then I start a school with a tent, and the boys sit on stones. They give me two dinars and ten pounds of one ration, ten pounds of sugar, and rice and lentils. In 1950 the United Nations they came and move refugees to a camp, Jelazone Camp. This is not far from Duralcara. I was responsible for the food center from 4 o'clock in the morning until 8. From 8-12–school. From 5 til 9 o'clock in the evening as a camp manager. I work three jobs almost one year, 1949, '50.

The war start and they do not come to Ramallah, to West Bank. They occupy the area where our old house is, and you cannot go back. No telephones, no communication, no nothing. Except my father, one day, he went to Jerusalem, to Al Aqsa Mosque and he told us, "I saw Cohan today! He was at the Wailing Wall and I pass inside and we face to face and we hug each other. He said, "Your house is the same. Don't worry about it. When you come back you will find it the same." From that time, '49–67, the Six Day War, there is no further contact.

We learned after 1967 that Mr. Cohan had died and the government had sold our house to an Israeli soldier and his family for $5,000 to pay back in 20 years. Almost 200 years our family in that area, more than 100 years the age of that house. I play basketball in the back garden.

We have walnut trees, apricot and fig trees.

I stay in Jelazone Camp almost 20 years. The United Nations decide to build a school—a boy's school, a girl's school. I had 25 teachers in the school. In 1969 they transfer me from the education department to the welfare department because I was active in sports, youth activities centers. They gave me three villages from Jerusalem to Tel Aviv along the Jaffa Road. The army demolished them 100%. They gave me responsibility to take care of the refugees from these three villages plus the youth activity centers on West Bank.

1 o'clock in morning my aunt knocked on door of my room and she said: "Achmad, there is a police!" So I am in pajama and there are two with machine guns.

"Are you Achmad Kharrubi? Put on your clothes. Come with us. The commissioner wants to see you." My wife starts to cry. I said, "I'll be back."

When I went to the Commissioner's office at the police station, there was nobody like me over there, just soldiers. They ask me some questions about my activities. I tell them. They ask me who is your boss? I told them his name. Then after that, I tell you the truth; they put something on my face. They take me one hour, one day, one week I don't remember. But I was in a place, I remember it is small place, you cannot sleep, there is one blanket over you, under you, it is cold, no bed, it is concrete. The bathroom over there it smells. I can't see the sun.

When I came back to the station I saw same person and he said, "You are away for 40 days. You can go home now."

I heard later that they thought I work with the youth to train them to make

Molotov cocktails to throw at soldiers. It is not true. Two days later they came 2 am in the morning.

"If you don't leave within 24 hours, you go back to jail."

That time I had a visa to the US which was valuable for six months. Before I left, I came to my supervisor at the United Nations. He let me resign to give me my benefits.

Part Three

How you feel? You leave your family, you leave your job, you leave your friends, you leave your land, you leave everything behind you. I came here, believe me, with $50, with my passport, with my suit. Even a piece of chocolate in my pocket, none.

My family stay over there. Nobody can go anywhere. That's why I have to divorce. It is a forced divorce. So I can marry here and stay. My visa only for few months. I never see my children again for 7 years. Two sons, two daughters. It is a big story!

When I come here, I start to work for my brother-in-law. He recommended work for exporters to Saudi Arabia, to Kuwait. I have a brother in Oregon, brother in Jerusalem, a sister in Saudi Arabia, a sister in San Jose, California, a sister in Chicago, a brother in London, brother in Italy, a brother in Sao Paulo in Brazil, a brother in Frankfort, Germany. All born in Palestine. My brother in London, got his Ph.D. there. What is he going to do with Ph.D. in West Bank?

One of my relatives in Oman asked me if I want to go back to Palestine. I said, "With this occupation—who would go there? It would be a big prison for me. If there is any peace settlement, of course, I would like to go back to stay among my people, family, friends."

The group was speechless. Only two of us had ever even been to the Middle East. Our life stories had all been along the lines of where we grew up, our family backgrounds, how long we had lived in Brooklyn, why we were interested in the Middle East. They were speechless, and I was stunned.

"Why did you let me believe you were Egyptian all these years?"

"You see, Miss Helen, we have no deep connection." We say, 'Good morning, how are you.'

"We don't know each other deep. Because you are Jewish, afraid that you say, 'Oh, my neighbor is Palestinian,' and people come to harm me. I hide from you that time. And then I just let everything stay the same. My situation is the Israelis took my land, they put my brothers in jail, they put me in jail. I left my family, my job. I left everything. I was not happy person to the Jews.

"But you change me. When your husband died, they accused Arabs. Instead of hate, you become a peacemaker. You don't show your anger, even to me who you think is Egyptian. I see what you are doing with your meetings, your activities, your telling me, 'Come to this meeting we are having.' I see that you are a different person than I thought before.

"I said to myself, "Well, nobody killed from my family. This lady, her husband died, and she is now peacemaker. Why to stay angry? You turn the page in my situation. Your husband in a plane that was bombed and you don't say, 'Kill the Arabs, push them out.' This I can read from your eyes, not your words.

"Now, I'm sorry, I have to leave, my wife is sick. I have to go home to her."

Sister Celia, who belongs to the Sisters of Sion, whose mission is to foster understanding between Christians and Jews, looked at me and said quietly, "Where I come from, we call that 'grace.' "

Provenance: Last summer, at the National *Havurah* Summer Institute, I attended Dr. Ellen Frankel's presentation on *The Golem Psalms*, a cantata composed by Andrea Clearfield for which she had written the libretto. And so my continuing interest in the *Golem* now led me to meet a delightful and creative woman. It was she who told me about this project and encouraged me to contribute to it. The story, "Mr. Kharrubi and Me," is one that grew out of long friendship with my "best neighbor" and my deep involvement and active support of individuals and groups who are listening to each other's stories and working for justice and human rights in Israel and Palestine.

Helen Engelhardt is a poet, writer, storyteller and independent audio performing artist and producer. She has been performing traditional and personal stories before audiences since 1997. Her first story, a personal variation inspired by *The Golem*, led to a First Prize at the Hemingway Days Storytelling Contest in Key West in 1999, and inevitably, to study with Peninnah Schram at the 92nd St Y in the spring of 2003. Since 2007, Helen has been producing a series of audio documentaries and has published two audio books, which can be found at www.midsummersoundcompany.com. She is a member of The Dialogue Project and Kolot Chayeinu, New York City.

Saved by the Evil Eye
by Ellen Frankel

Rabbi Hisda said: [If a] daughter [is born] first, it is a good sign for the children. Some say, because she rears her brothers; and others say, because the evil eye has no influence over them.
    —BT Baba Batra 141a

Buffalo, New York, March 2000.

My topic was Jewish customs and beliefs about the Evil Eye, ayin ha-ra in Hebrew but better known by the Yiddish phrase used to ward it off: *kayna hora* or *kenayna hora*. After making some brief remarks about Jewish folklore and superstition, I invited those gathered in the living room to share personal stories from their own families. I've learned over the years that no matter how assimilated the group—fourth generation Reform Jews from the South, Israelis who grew up as secular Zionists, professors, scientists and doctors—everyone has stories from a *bubbe* or mother or great-aunt about how to avoid the power of the Evil Eye.

Don't step over bodies lying on the ground. Never place a pair of shoes on the bed. Plunge a knife into the ground if you're pregnant. Sew red threads into the crib bumpers. Never marry a woman with the same name as your mother.

The way they talked about it revealed a reverence for its power. Even though most of them laughed as they shared their *bubbe mayses*, you could hear in their voices a nervousness, a fear of offending.

On this particular night, one man immediately piqued my curiosity. He looked to be in his early sixties. Not American, by his accent and mannerisms. Most likely from Eastern Europe. Too young to be a survivor, but maybe a child of survivors.

He listened to my presentation and to the others' comments with rapt attention. At one point, I thought his dark eyes filled with tears. But I was too intent on listening to someone else's story to know for sure.

When the program ended, I wandered into the dining room for cake and coffee. The man was standing in the corner, waiting for me, his eyes still slightly moist, his expression melancholy, almost brooding.

"Where are you from?" I asked him. "I hear an accent."

"Italy," he told me. "My parents moved there from Romania after the war." Then he fell silent. I waited for him to continue but he seemed reluctant.

"Why did tonight's discussion affect you so much?" I asked.

"I never understood until tonight why my mother used to tell me that she wasn't my real mother."

I was dumbstruck by his words. What he was sharing with me seemed altogether too intimate. After all, I had just met him, didn't even know his name. How could he trust me with this confidence? And what did it mean?

Now that he had begun, he seemed unable to stop.

"When I was small, my mother used to tell me all the time, 'I'm not your mother. I sold you to the lady next door. Go visit her. Bring her a nice present.' I knew that my mother had lost two sons before I was born but I never saw a connection between the deaths of her babies and her telling me that she'd sold me to the neighbor. I now realize that she had been protecting me from the Evil Eye. She thought she was fooling it by declaring that I wasn't really hers. I guess she was hoping that I wouldn't die like my baby brothers before me."

He paused and smiled. "But I always felt she didn't love me. Now I understand that she was doing it *because* she loved me. But she never told me why she had decided to sell me. So I always thought she was rejecting me, that I just wasn't good enough to be her son."

His sad eyes again filled with tears, which he quickly wiped away. I knew I was in the presence of a powerful *tikkun*, a repair of some deep brokenness in this man's soul. The evil eye—activated, according to Jewish custom, by its envy of others' good fortune—had finally been banished, leaving behind his mother's blessing in its place.

Provenance: This was the third program in a scholar-in-residence weekend that took place in a congregant's home on a bitter-cold Saturday night at the end of winter.

Ellen Frankel is the former CEO and Editor in Chief of The Jewish Publication Society, and now serves as its first Editor Emerita. She currently works as a freelance writer, editor, and lecturer. She is the author of nine published books, including *The Classic Tales, The Encyclopedia of Jewish Symbols, The Five Books of Miriam, The Jewish Spirit,* and *The JPS Illustrated Children's Bible,* which won a National Jewish Book Award. In addition to her books, Ellen has written libretti for several choral works, and is now working on a commissioned opera, *Slaying the Dragon,* premiering in June 2012 in Philadelphia. (www.ellenfrankel.net)

The Clubhouse Turn
by Leon Olenick

I was on my rounds, visiting a nursing home, and was asked by a staff member to speak with Max[19], one of the residents. I entered the room and found him in a chair reading the sports page of a local paper. A frail man, his six foot frame was filled out to only around one hundred pounds. His drawn cheeks revealed his bony face and toothless mouth. His legs were skeletal, unable to support his body.

He introduced himself to me by saying, "You have to lose some weight. You're too damn fat."

"You're right. I wish I could give some to you."

We laughed. I sat down and asked him how he was.

"How should I be doing? I'm stuck here in this cage." He went on to tell me about his life.

"You know, I was a street guy. I gambled, whored, took drugs—I was one of the wise guys. I was respected. My friends were loan sharks, bookies, con artists and number writers. Those were the days." He went into many stories. As he spoke he gained energy and became animated. We visited for a long time as the stories flowed.

"So, tell me, Max, you are a hospice patient and you are aware you are approaching the end of your life. Is there anything I can offer you at this time?" He looked into my eyes.

"I used to hang out at the track every day. I met my friends there. I knew the horses and jockeys. That was my home. I have no family—the track people were my family. I'll tell you what I need: one more day at the track, a pack of cigarettes, and some gambling money." I did not respond. I told him I would stop and see him again next week.

"This was good. I like you," he said.

I left his room, his stories dominating my thoughts. What could I do for this character? I called the local racetrack and told them Max's story. The public relations woman was touched. She said, "Why don't you bring him here as our guest? We will make sure he has a seat in the clubhouse and treat him to lunch." I told her I would try and arrange it. I then contacted the nursing home to see if this was feasible. They were excited and said they would provide transportation and an aide. All was

---

[19]   This name has been changed for privacy purposes.

set. I confirmed a date and went to tell Max. He could not believe it. I thought he was going to hug me. Excitement enveloped his entire being.

"Hey, Leon, don't forget the cigs!"

I laughed as I left the room.

The big day was upon us. I picked my wife up at home. She had never been to a racetrack, and I wanted to share this day with her. On the way to the nursing home, we stopped at a convenience store to purchase a pack of Marlboro 100's, his cigs of choice.

The CEO of the nursing home decided to join us and bring four other patients who she knew would appreciate the day. It was a very unusual scene as the patients filed into the van, schlepping their oxygen tanks, wheel chairs and canes. We followed the medivan in our car. When we arrived at the track, we were directed to VIP parking, and a representative from the public relations department met us. She introduced herself and told us she would be our escort for the day. When we entered the track she escorted us to the clubhouse. Max said this would not work for him. He told her that his home is down by the midway where he is close to the action.

"That's my hangout." We proceeded there.

She handed Max a program and said, "Look at the fourth race." He opened it. In large print it read, "The Max Schwartz Handicap." His eyes became bright in disbelief. She also told him he would be escorted to the winner's circle after the fourth race to present the trophy to the jockey. His smile was larger than his face. We had all chipped in some money so he would be able to place a bet on the races. He was too weak to walk to the window, so he picked the horses and we bet and brought him the ticket. He stared at the ticket to make sure it was correct, the ash from the cigarette hanging from his mouth dropping on the ticket. He brushed it away. After losing the first three races he smiled and said, "It's like old times. I lose every race." The pari-mutuel board lit up for the fourth race. The top of the board read in giant letters:

THE MAX SCHWARTZ HANDICAP

He stared at it with utter joy, a toothless smile encompassing his entire face. No words were necessary. The bugler stepped out to blow the horn for the race. He was dressed in the colorful attire of the track. A red formal jacket with black pants tucked into his high boots. The announcer said, "Welcome to the Max Schwartz Handicap—four furlongs." Max leaned back in his wheelchair. His Marlboro was hanging off the side of his mouth. The contentment on his face told his story.

"And they're off!"

Max hung on every call from the announcer.

When the race was over he was wheeled to the winner's circle. He presented the trophy to the jockey and had his picture taken with the horse, the jockey and owner.

We stayed for one more race. Max began to lose his energy. It was time to leave. We thanked the track representative for all her planning, work, compassion and presence. The van was waiting, and all the patients from the nursing home piled in. It was a grand day.

The next day I went to the nursing home to bring the pictures my wife had taken. Max's bed was empty. His soul remained at the track.

Leon Olenick is a hospital and hospice chaplain in South Florida and also active in leading bereavement and support groups. He has earned both *Maggid* and *Ba'al Ha-Bracha* ordination from Rabbi Zalman Schachter-Shalomi, as well as ordination as a Rabbinic Pastor. Some of Leon's stories have been published in *The National Jewish Post and Opinion,* and he is presently completing his book of stories, *Encounters with the Last Dance.*

Joe the Butler
by Danny Siegel

Years ago I read a story in a newspaper about a certain Joe Lejman who used to dress up as a butler and serve food in a local shelter for victims of domestic violence. I thought it was a brilliant idea. The article was only a short blurb, so there was only one "incident-moment" that the reporter chose to relate. Fascinated by the reporter's story, I had hoped for more detail, but in retrospect, and with years to reflect, I understand the reporter's wisdom. The incident he related was The Incident, the one that would teach us almost everything we needed to know about Joe Lejman and his marvelous mitzvah.

One day, after Joe had finished serving a meal at the shelter, he went around pouring coffee for the residents. He poured for one woman, and then lit her cigarette. And she began to cry. She told Joe she was crying because this was the first time she could remember that anyone had done something nice for her.

Now, years after reading this story, my mind is wandering and I am beginning to wonder: Is it possible that this woman regained every shred of her lost self-respect because of Joe Lejman's single act of unadulterated caring and radiant goodness? It's possible.

Did she then tell the social workers at the shelter that she had emerged from her despair, regained her energy, and wanted to go job-hunting the next day? She might have.

Did she then get a job, give the appropriate portion of her first and every subsequent paycheck to *tzedakah*, do homework with her kids at night, and help get them through high school and into college? Perhaps.

Did the children then go to college, graduate, get jobs, give the appropriate percentage of their first and every subsequent paycheck to *tzedakah*, and raise their own families to do the same? Maybe they did.

Were the other women in that shelter so inspired by what she did that they did the same—start life all over again because of Joe Lejman? Maybe they did, too.

How many more heartbeats were added to the world's total? Billions upon billions. How far out into the entire population of Planet Earth did the concentric circles reach because one man, Joe Lejman, got this crazy idea to be a butler in a shelter for women, who, by all measures of reasonableness, should have sunk into lifelong oblivion?

How much did Joe spend on a butler's outfit?

You save one life, you save the world.

Danny Siegel is a poet, author, and lecturer, who has written several books on *tzedakah* and *tikkun olam* as well as a number of books of poetry. He lectures frequently throughout North America on Jewish values and *tikkun olam*. He founded Ziv Tzedakah Fund in 1981, which during its 27-year history distributed nearly $14,000,000 to little-known *tzedakah* programs in Israel, the Former Soviet Union, and the United States.

Flowering Words
by Laura Simms

I dreamed once that I was on a road going somewhere, when I heard voices chanting prayers in Hebrew. I entered a very old stone synagogue and immediately descended steps that were suspended in mid-air. Way below in the distance, I saw my grandma and grandpa seated side by side in a small forest. It seemed impossible to reach them without stepping off the stone steps onto what was no road at all. Yet I knew I would reach them.

When I awoke, I had the vivid memory of my father's parents, Ida and David, seated together at the end of the *Pesach* table set up in our living room in Brooklyn. Their eyes were half closed and they were leaning towards each other, reciting the *haggadah* in Hebrew by heart. They made this ritual journey each year with their three children and their families. However, I never knew what secret borders their memories crossed as they incanted prayers and stories, sang songs and whispered to one another. Their life stories were never fully told, and because it was not considered polite to pry, I never asked the question: why are these people different than all others?

Ida was four foot nine. She was born in Poland, the third daughter in a rabbinical family, and spoke six languages. She never learned English well enough to converse. I didn't know about her intelligence or her capacity to dream up answers to questions until her funeral. Grandpa Dave was a burly six foot one. He drove a trolley down Broadway at night and worked in the meat market during the day. He was uneducated and the only child of a Russian immigrant. His father sold tin pans from a pack he carried on his shoulder from town to town near Hudson, New York. His mother was a mystery. In the evenings, on weekends, his pant legs rolled up, grandpa Dave watched phony fights on television in the Bronx while Ida cooked in their tiny kitchen.

I draw a circle around these fragments of remembered image and dream and call it a story. How do I explain what this means to me? I am reminded of another story told by Peninnah. Her arrows hit the mark each time. The story is about a rabbi who told stories. His congregation increased in size every Sabbath. A learned man from the community asked him when was he going to teach like a real rabbi.

"All you do is tell stories?!" the learned man said. The rabbi was silent and then said, "I will explain. Let me tell you a story...

There was once a king and a queen, Jews, in Kurdistan who had three daughters. The king wanted his daughters to marry wealthy princes, and his first two daughters did. But the youngest princess fell in love with a poor man. She married for love against her parents' wishes and her father banished her. So she lived outside the kingdom.

Soon afterwards, the king awoke blind. Of course, he awoke blind— he had banished his daughter. Doctors could not heal him. Until a doctor, who knew magic and medicine, described a tree, which had healing leaves that would restore his sight. The tree grew in a distant land from which no one had ever returned.

The king commanded his two sons-in-laws to make the perilous journey. He told them that if the leaves were retrieved and his blindness healed, they would receive part of his wealth and power. But if they did not bring back the leaves, they would be killed. The princes set off with strong horses, gold, and food. They had no choice. The king's banished daughter heard about her father's illness. She begged her mother to let her husband make the journey as well even though they had been banished. She wanted to help heal her father. So the poor husband willingly set out on an old horse with no gold. He carried with him the desire to heal his wife's father. He agreed to the same conditions as the others.

The two princes arrived at the border of the Land of No Return, where a guard described the awful things they would face and the gruesome dangers that lay ahead. The princes were terrified. They did not want to risk their lives. Knowing they could not return to their homes empty-handed, they opened up an inn not far from the border and remained there.

The third husband came to the same border. He stopped at the inn to rest. Instantly he recognized the princes, but they did not know him because they were blind to anyone that was not as great as they thought they were. He inquired about the Land of No Return. Hearing his inquiry, the two princes assured the stranger that he would be back at the inn within a few hours. But the young man, despite hearing the same dire warnings from the same guard, nevertheless insisted on making the journey. His motivation to heal the king was greater than his fear. The guard told him that the only one who knew the way to the magical tree was a fierce giant who lived in a house in a nearby valley.

The young man reached the house, which was as high as a mountain. When the giant's wife saw the man, she urged him to leave.

"Your life is in danger," she warned. "My husband will want to devour you."

The youth insisted that he would continue his quest regardless of the dangers, and he then told his story.

As soon as the ravenous giant returned home, his wife fed him.

"I smell a man," roared the giant.

His wife told him about the courageous visitor whom she had hidden beneath her bed. The giant was astonished at the young man's lack of fear and his dedication. And since he had already eaten his fill, he gave the young stranger the necessary instructions to reach the tree and harvest its miraculous leaves.

"You are the first human being I have met who is not a coward!" said the giant.

The giant told him: "You will ride for seven days until you come to a crossroads. In one direction it is written, 'Take this road and find safety and happiness.' In the other direction it is written, 'Do not take this road. Whoever follows this road will not return.' Don't hesitate. Take the Road of No Return. Travel until the road ends and there is nowhere to go. Then say out loud, 'What a beautiful path!' Then the road will continue on.

"Next there is a valley filled with poisonous snakes. No human being can survive its passage unassisted, so you must call out, 'What a beautiful valley filled with honey!' The snakes will disappear, and you will be able to travel onwards.

"After a while you will come to a valley filled with blood, vipers and awful beasts. Announce joyfully, 'What sweet butter!' The valley will empty out, and you will be able to continue."

The giant went on: "Pay attention. When you come to a palace guarded by a dragon and a viper, you have arrived. If the creatures' eyes are open, they are sleeping. If their eyes are closed, they are awake. Wait until their eyes are open, and move past them. Enter the palace and walk until you come to a door. It is guarded by four lions. If their eyes are open, they are sleeping. If their eyes are closed, they are awake. The door is made of bells. I will give you cotton cloths with which to muffle the bells so when the door opens you can enter silently.

"Inside, you will find a queen asleep on her bed. When she sleeps, all the creatures sleep with their eyes open. Beside her bed grows the tree with healing leaves. Fill a bag with these leaves. Do not forget to place leaves also in your pockets. Carefully exchange rings with her. Then without hesitation, return just as you entered."

The young man did all that he was told, retrieved the leaves, exchanged rings with the sleeping queen, and completed the entire journey. But when he crossed the border, he decided to spend the night at the inn before continuing to the palace.

The two princes saw the heavy sack he was carrying and asked about his adventure. The youth told them everything except for the details about the ring and the leaves in his pocket. Needless to say, that night they fed him poison, threw acid into his eyes, blinding him, and locked him in a closet. Then they stole his sack and made their way back to the palace to claim their wealth.

In the inn the next morning, the young man awoke, blind and imprisoned. He remembered the leaves in his pocket and healed himself. Then he broke open the closet doors and made his way back to his wife on his slow mare.

He showed her the leaves he had, but she said, "My sisters' husbands have healed my father. You are too late."

Meanwhile in the Land of No Return, the queen awoke. She saw the unfamiliar ring on her finger and noticed leaves missing from the tree. She had a carpet beneath her bed on which she could soar through the sky and beyond the border into our world. She mounted her magic carpet in search of whoever it was who had stolen the leaves and awakened her from sleep.

She inquired everywhere without success until she heard about the two princes, now prime ministers, who had healed the king. She travelled to the palace and asked for their story. They told her what little they recalled but in the end said that they had found the tree in a forest and picked the leaves.

She said, "That is not true!"

The third princess's husband rode to the palace that same day. He recognized the queen. He showed her her ring, and she asked him for his story. He agreed to tell the story, but not only for her, for the king and his wife, their three daughters, and the two prime ministers as well. He told them all in exact detail what had occurred.

Satisfied, the queen took back her ring and returned to her land. The two prime ministers were banished from the kingdom. It is my hope that on their journey they learned to tell the truth and will be admitted back into the kingdom at a later time.

When the king heard the third husband's story, he understood what had taken place, perhaps even understood the cause of his own blindness. The third daughter's husband became a trusted advisor, and they all lived happily ever after in the palace.

As for the queen in the Land of No Return, I have no idea if the way to her palace is still fraught with danger or if she remains asleep. But because the story is true, I do know that she exists and that each time the story is retold, she comes to life within each listener. And therein is the secret of the healing leaves and the art of drawing circles.

Provenance: Peninnah Schram tells a Dubner Maggid story about a man who was considered a perfect archer. When asked about his accuracy, he revealed that he shot the arrow first and then drew a circle around it. I have come to see that this is the way of love and wisdom. It is also the skillful means of the storyteller today. In a world where understanding is mistaken for revelation, and intellectual analysis is disguised as wisdom, storytelling is an alternative: it is direct experience during which the events and characters of the unfolding tale come alive within the heart and mind of the listener/reader in the moment. The journey itself makes meaning manifest as the voice of the teller opens the heart. The sequence of dream, memory and story came to my mind when I set about finding a story for this collection. I am extremely grateful to Howard Schwartz for his brilliant literary telling of this story. I have retold it in my own words, since once having heard storyteller Naomi Steinberg tell it, I could not resist the adventure. To read Schwartz' text and commentary, obtain his marvelous collection of tales, *Elijah's Violin & Other Jewish Fairy Tales*.

I first retold this story to a fifth grade class in an elementary school on the Lower East Side of Manhattan where children were struggling with bullies. Then I emphasized the betrayal perpetrated by the two princes. Another time I told it as an example of how a story is uncovered and told with truth and meaning. It also became the narrative template for compassionate leadership trainings, and a tale that has helped drama therapists access the healing power of fairytales. I personally feel that storytelling is one way that we can awaken the sleeping feminine, too long ignored or abused, in order to further peace in our world.

Laura Simms premiered her one-woman show *Mercy into the World* in London, Oslo and Winnipeg. A three-time artist for Lincoln Center's Aesthetic Arts Institute, she is a member of the Therapeutic Arts Alliance of Manhattan, teaches Shambhala Buddhist meditation, and is a Senior Research Associate at Rutgers University. Laura recently received the Brimstone Award for Engaged Storytelling. Mother of best-selling author, Ishmael Beah, Laura works in Haiti with Mercy Corps, consults to ETSU's Cancer Stories Project, serves as co-faculty at Terry Tempest Williams' New Generation Environmental Project, and as storyteller in residence for the New Alternative Arts High School in Portland, Oregon. (www.laurasimms.com)

II

Expanding the Heart
Mitzvot of Joy and Generosity

The Mitzvah House
by Roslyn Bresnick-Perry

"Let me live in a house by the side of the road and be a friend to man," wrote the American poet Sam Walter Floss in 1897. That sentiment was also the philosophy of my Aunt Esther, my father's sister, who often told us that she wanted to buy a bungalow on the road in the country and help people who had no other place to go.

My Aunt Esther had never heard of that poem. When she quoted her version of wanting to buy "a bungalow on the road," I told her she didn't have to bother to buy that bungalow. Her house had always been a Mitzvah House, even though it was on Colgate Avenue in the Bronx.

The next time I saw my aunt, I brought the poem and read it to her. "This is a very nice poem," she said. "That man is a real *mentsch*, even though he is not Jewish. If I could read and write English, I could have written about all the people who lived in my house. Oy, did they need help! It was terrible during the depression. Oy, would I have sad poems."

My Aunt Esther had a heart that stretched across continents. She was the one who continually urged my father to leave the *shtetl* and join her in America. She sent him money, which she could ill afford, to buy a ticket for passage. He stayed in her house until he earned enough money to support himself. If not for my Aunt Esther, my mother and I would have joined all our family and townspeople in the unmarked graves of the Holocaust or the ashes of the crematorium. She enabled my father to send for us, and she tried to help us adjust to America.

My aunt would say in Yiddish, "*Oyb es is do an ort in hartsen iz do a bet in shtib*," which translates into: "If there is a place in your heart there is a bed in the house."

And she meant what she said. I had no idea who lived with her before she married my Uncle Sam, but I do know that as soon as she married him, his young sister moved in with them. Gladys was her name. She was, I was told, a very unhappy young girl who had lost her mother when she was still a child. She acted out her unhappiness by being wild and unmanageable, and was taken in by an organization called the "Big Sisters," which was rumored to be very formidable and no place for a Jewish girl to be raised. My aunt, a young bride herself, now had to deal with this rebellious teenager. As far as I know, she must have done a remarkable job, because when we met Gladys, she was married and had two children. She always had a special affection for my aunt.

And she wasn't the only one.

Mr. and Mrs. Levine, who had previously lived in South Carolina, migrated north when Mr. Levine, a truck driver, lost his hand during a driving accident. It was almost impossible for him to find work where they lived, as no one was interested in a one-handed Jewish truck driver. I don't know how they found my aunt, but having found her, she immediately had them living with her in her one extra bedroom. She encouraged Mr. Levine to think about buying his own taxicab. In those days being hired to drive with his disability was out of the question. She offered to invest in his cab and become his partner until he could pay back her investment and buy her out. Eventually, he did. The Levines moved out on their own, and they were forever grateful to her. Her extra room was now available to shelter the next person in need.

I never understood how my Uncle Sam put up with all of my aunt's generous impulses. He was a silent, intense man who was not too social, but who had a deep commitment to a socialist ideology. When he voiced an objection, my aunt would put him to task,

"Where is your love for the 'people' that you are always worrying about?" she would ask him.

He always submitted to her wishes. Another mystery was figuring out where all of my cousins slept. There were three of them. When I asked them where they slept, as there was only one extra bedroom, they said: Everywhere around the house, wherever their mother put them.

As fate would have it, my own family was the next recipient of Tanta Esther's Mitzvah House hospitality. It was the summer of 1931. My father had closed his butcher shop when he could not afford to keep it going. It was constantly losing money. He put the fixtures of the store and our home furniture in storage and moved us to Rockaway Beach, where he had a job in a large butcher shop for the summer. We lived in what was then called a "cokh-a-lane," a rather large rooming house near the beach, which consisted of many one-room, subdivided apartments where a family slept, cooked, and ate. The toilet was in the hall and used by all who lived on that floor. It was a wooden structure, three stories high, and inhabited by working class people who could not afford anything better to escape the summer heat.

But summers have a way of ending, and with fall just around the corner, people began to leave for home. Little by little the large house emptied out.

The only ones left were the mice, roaches, and my family. I was nine and my little brother a year and a half. My father did not have enough money to retrieve his fixtures from storage to open another store, or even to take out our furniture so we could move into another apartment. My mother was beside herself. I had to go to school, and the house had no heat. My father had contacted all the people he knew for help, but no one had any extra money those days, including my aunt.

But when there is room in the heart, there is room in the house. My Aunt Esther made room in her home for our family to stay in her one extra bedroom that had helped so many people before us. We lived with her for six months, which enabled my father to get on his feet again.

My memory of that long ago time is my aunt with her smiling face and cheery manner. She was a delight to be with all of her life. If you ask me, not only was her house a Mitzvah House, but also she herself was a blessing to all who knew her.

Provenance: Thinking about writing a story about *mitzvot*, the one person who stood out above all others was my Aunt Esther. Her giving was so natural, so much a part of her life it never occurred to her that she was doing a mitzvah, and isn't that the greatest giving? Her saying that "When there is room in the heart, there is a bed in the house" has always left me feeling a little wanting, living as we do in our own personal worlds.

Roslyn Bresnick-Perry is an award-winning storyteller, author, recording artist, lecturer and translator. Among her many honors is the National Storytelling Network Lifetime Achievement Award and the Premio a Mejor Contadora Extrajera as the outstanding foreign storyteller of the International Story Festival in Havana, Cuba. Her books include *I Loved My Mother on Saturdays*, which won the Anne Izard Storytellers' Choice Award, and the children's book, *Leaving for America*. She has represented New York City at the Smithsonian Folklife Festival, told stories at the Library of Congress, and participated in many storytelling events at venues throughout the U.S. and Canada.

The Hitchhiker
by Joel ben Izzy

One day I pulled into a supermarket down the street from the temple and made my way to the fish department.

"What have you got that's not fresh?"

The butcher, who looked as tired as I felt, didn't seem to understand.

"Maybe something that didn't sell yesterday. Or the day before that. It's for a project," I explained, not wanting to go into detail. "I'm an artist."

That seemed to register. He nodded, then went into the back room and emerged a moment later holding a very dead-looking trout by the tail.

"It's been stinking up the back for awhile," he said. "You can have it."

He wrapped it in butcher paper, and I put it in my storytelling bag and went off to teach my class. When it came time for my story, I began by reciting the words, "If you give someone a fish, they eat for a day." I then pulled out the package and unwrapped it. "But if you teach someone how to fish..."

That's as far as I got.

"Oooh, gross!" someone shouted. "It's a dead fish!"

"...and it stinks!"

"Where'd you get that thing?"

"Yuck!"

Later that afternoon, as I drove back toward the Bay Bridge, it struck me that whatever half-baked idea I had in mind had not worked. What's more, my students were right—the fish did stink, more so each minute as the car heated up. Driving through Berkeley, I spotted a trashcan near the underpass leading to the freeway. I pulled over, got out, and threw the fish away.

Walking back to the car, I saw a man standing on the corner, his thumb outstretched. He looked a few years older than me, and a good deal scruffier.

"Where to?" I asked.

"San Francisco," he said.

"Hop in."

He introduced himself as Tom, and as soon as we got on the freeway, he reached into a shoulder bag and pulled out a Polaroid camera.

"Here," he said. "This is for you."

"Why?"

"Well, you're giving me a ride to San Francisco, which I appreciate, but I don't expect something for nothing. So I'm giving you my camera."

"Thanks," I said, giving it some thought. "But I don't need a camera. My business is stories. If you tell me yours, we'll call it even."

He gave it some thought, then agreed. He told me how he had recently come out from Chicago, where he had been a construction worker. A few years earlier he had fallen in love with and married a woman by the name of Ellen. They had made a down payment on a house and had plans for a family. But then she got sick, very sick, with what turned out to be a brain tumor. They had no health insurance, and spent everything they had saved on her medical care. When that was gone, they sold their house to pay the medical bills. Finally, he stopped working to take care of her. Three months later she died.

Estranged from his own parents, he turned to her family in Oakland. With no money and no place to live, he had hitched out from Chicago, hoping her family might help him start anew.

"But when I showed up at their house," he said, "they just shook their heads and shut the door. I think they blame me for Ellen's death, though I don't know why."

That had been six months ago. Since then he had been looking for work, but with no home and no phone, and only the clothes on his back, it hadn't been easy. He had been sleeping in the overpass where I had found him. It was there, hidden in a corner, that he kept the few possessions he had brought with him from Chicago, including the camera.

"So where are you going now?" I asked.

"Saint Anthony's," he said. "They have a free meal on Sundays at five."

"But now it's just one," I said. "What will you do until it opens?"

He shrugged. "I don't know. I usually have to wait three or four hours to get a ride, but you picked me up right away. I guess I'll wait."

In the silence that followed, I thought about that morning's failed lesson, and the fish, now stinking up the trashcan in Berkeley. To be honest, Tom didn't smell a whole lot better than the fish. I thought about my home in San Francisco, which I shared with a group of friends. We had a refrigerator full of food, left over from a *Shabbat* dinner, and a shower.

"Have you eaten today?" I asked.

He shook his head.

"So come to my house," I said, "for a meal, and a shower, if you want."

"That would be great," he said.

He ate, and then showered. While he was in the bathroom, I looked through my closet. I had far more clothes than I needed, and figured he might be able to use some of them, and brought out a couple pairs of jeans and some button-down shirts, along with an old duffel bag. I gave him a new razor and he shaved, and then tried on the clothes. He looked like a new man.

"Hey, look!" he said, standing before the mirror. "A perfect fit!"

Seeing him there, I was flooded with thoughts—about how he just happened to be my size, about what my housemates would say if they were home, about teaching someone how to fish and, finally, about my brother. He had a small business refinishing floors, and had just landed a big job for a restaurant in Berkeley. It wasn't construction work exactly, but was close. I asked Tom if he would be interested in working for a time at refinishing floors.

"Are you kidding? That would be great!"

I called my brother, Lee, and told him about Tom. Yes, it turned out, he needed help for the next few days. I put Tom on the phone, and they worked out an hourly rate and plans for a time and place to meet the next morning.

I drove him back to St. Anthony's, giving him bus fare for work the next day—and another twenty dollars besides. As I did so, his eyes welled up.

"I've got to tell you," he said. "This is the first kind thing anyone has done for me since I came here."

That was the story I told my seventh-graders at Hebrew School the following Sunday, starting with the fish—which they well remembered—and ending at St. Anthony's. After the story there was a long silence—which was unusual for seventh graders—and in that silence I could hear the question on all of their minds: Did he show up?

But I didn't let them ask their question. Instead, I posed a question of my own, one that had been on my mind for several days: Was I a fool?

Provenance: Some years ago, when I was just out of college and living in San Francisco, I found a job teaching at a religious school in Lafayette, a well-heeled suburb in the East Bay. My challenge each Sunday morning was to face an audience of seventh graders who were every bit as jaded as they were sleep-deprived, telling them stories to impart Jewish values.

I've shared this story several times over the years since that morning, and I like to end it just this way, with the two questions floating in the air. It tends to lead to a discussion much like the one I had with my students that morning. They did not want to say whether or not I was a fool until they knew how the story ended. But I would not tell, until they answered my question. I wanted them to learn that we do *mitzvot* because they are the right thing to do, not for what they may bring back to us.

It was only when they got this idea that I told them what happened. When I called my brother I learned that Tom had never shown up. Though I was disappointed, I did not feel cheated. I had been given a chance to do a mitzvah and, in the bargain, had been given a story as well. As it says in *Pirkei Avot 2:12,* "Though we may not be able to finish the task, neither are we free to refrain from beginning it."

Joel ben Izzy has gathered and told stories in the United States, Europe, Israel, Asia and South America. Based in Berkeley, California, he has produced six award-winning recordings and written the highly acclaimed memoir, "The Beggar King and the Secret of Happiness," which recounts the strange true story that began when Joel awoke from a surgical procedure to discover he could no longer speak. Joel works as a story consultant for numerous community-based organizations doing good work, helping them to craft stories that shape the world. (www.storypage.com)

My Mama's "Elijah"
by Lynnie Mirvis

"And Elijah was disguised as a beggar...to see
how people acted toward each other."
—Peninnah Schram

*I'll never forget the time I was playing outside on that hot summer day
way back when I guess I was about nine years old. We lived on York Street—our
houses were close together and they all had front porches. That's when I first saw
him. Why wasn't I afraid? When he came, it turned out to be a blessing for me,
a blessing—my Mama muses in her soft southern lilt...*

Memphis, TN 1935

The sweat beads glistened on Dotty's neck as she jumped to the
rhythm of her neighbor's beat...her dark curls bouncing up and down
with each jump. Double Dutch jump rope, as it was called then. Her
two neighborhood girlfriends swung the ropes high over their heads—
each one a point-counter-point to the other, and Dotty ran in.

"Grace, Grace, dressed in lace-went upstairs to powder her face-
how many powder puffs did she use? One, two, three..."

Dotty, her skinny legs and arms flying upward, jumped high and
quick and was on number 36. She had made it to 200 the day before
and was named the Jump Rope Champion of Peabody Park. On this
scorching day, Dotty only jumped to 55, and she and the girls finally
stopped playing and threw themselves on the clover under the shade of
a large elm, white heat blanketing a cloudless sky. The only sound—the
mournful sigh of a passing train rumbling on the nearby tracks.

"The sidewalk is hot enough to fry an egg!" one of her girlfriends
lamented.

"Let's try it!" Dotty laughed mischievously.

The night before the girls had played outside till a multitude of stars
scattered overhead; they caught lightning bugs in a jar—and Dotty had
let hers go free, while the others grabbed them from the jars and wore
them proudly as sparkling jewels. They made fun of her and called her
scaredy cat! She didn't mind their teasing. She was strong for her age
and could take care of herself. She really didn't want to harm those
lightning bugs—they were so wondrous with their glowing lights that

blinked on and off like tiny sparks of green flames. She just had to see them fly once more.

Now, in the heat of the day, before anyone could take up the egg challenge, a stranger suddenly appeared in front of them with a frayed white bandana tied around his forehead, raggedy overalls, a torn shirt and stubble on his face that looked like it had been there forever. With his head bent, he mumbled, "Could you spare some food?" His weary eyes pleaded though he spoke in a monotone.

At first the threesome were speechless, and finally Dotty's neighbor, the oldest of the three by 6 months, placed her hands on her hips and hissed, "You just get on—we don't have nothing for you!"

Well, my Mama just looked at that man— and his skinny ribs were just poking out of his shirt—and with one backward glance at her neighbors, she says to the grown man with all the authority her nine-year-old voice could muster, "You come with me. I'll get you some food."

And off they went—he like a meek, raggedy giant following behind a little nine-year-old girl with dark curly hair, down the tree-lined street of small white houses, each with its own front porch.

Dotty ran into the house while the bedraggled man waited by the screened back door. In the kitchen, she moved a chair to the pantry and carefully found the jar of peanut butter and the homemade apple jelly that Little Grandma always shared with them. Little Grandma always fed strangers and those down and out with their luck. They would gather at her back door and would sit around her kitchen table for a quick bowl of chicken soup, hot biscuits and fried chicken left over from Friday night dinner before they wandered back out to the tracks to hop the next freight train.

Climbing from the chair with her treasures, Dotty spread the peanut butter and jelly on left-over slices of *challah* bread, wrapped them in waxed paper and took a banana from the table. Then she poured a large glass of lemonade, opened the back door, and handed the glass to the stranger. He drank it down in a hurry, gave the glass back to her, and then took the sandwich and the banana from her. With a quick look at Dotty before he turned on his way, he quietly murmured, "God bless you child, God bless you!"

Dotty stood in the doorway, and as she watched he seemed to disappear, walking slowly down the street toward the railroad tracks—a small white dot with his bandana shining in the sunlight among the still green trees.

When my Mama finished that story, she would close her eyes and nod her head: and from then on, she would say, yes, I knew I was blessed. And she would recount the names of all of her children and grandchildren and great-grandchildren and wonder once more: I don't know what made me think I could help him, when the others didn't. I just knew, that's what you do, that's just what you do.

2010 Memphis, Tennessee

I am late for a haircut appointment, my cell is ringing, the radio is blaring the latest crime statistics of muggings and robberies, and I am remembering how the doors to my house used to be unlocked just like in the days when my Mama was a little girl. And now things are different. People lock their doors with chains and alarms and build fences around their properties.

Out of the corner of my eye, as I begin to make a right turn, I see a man with raggedy clothes and a stubble of growth on his face sitting precariously on the edge of the curb. The man is beginning to stand, and he looks a little wobbly and his ribs are sticking out of his thin shirt. He seems to be holding something in his hand. In this neighborhood of well-manicured lawns and imposing brick houses with large circular driveways, he is out of place.

"Does he need help?" I wonder.

Then all at once, my Mama's story floats into my mind. I hear her say: "I was only nine years old. How did I know to help him when the others didn't?" And then she adds, "I just knew, that's what you do. That's just what you do."

Slowly I back into a driveway and turn the car around. I unroll my window next to the man and ask him if he needs help. Then I see what is in his hand: it's a sign that reads, "I am hungry—will work for food."

Quickly I take the two braided *challah* loaves out of the bags on the seat beside me and hand them to him. His watery eyes look into mine and he quietly murmurs:

"God bless you child, God bless you!"

I watch as he walks up the street, pulling out a white bandana and wiping the sweat from his brow—slowly, slowly. And as a train whistles in the distance, he suddenly disappears, a white dot sparkling in the sunlight among the still green trees.

Provenance: Sometimes there are moments in our lives when the storytellers and sages tell us Elijah appears—we just don't know it. We have choices to make. We decide to do something good or not. And the blessings follow. My Mama was always sure of those moments and saw the hand of the Divine even as a little girl, growing up Jewish in the Bible Belt in Memphis, Tennessee. This is one of those stories she likes to tell. I've always been fascinated with Elijah—he always drank the wine at our *seder* table or so I thought until I saw my father shaking the table leg, but I could never be sure. And then my Hebrew name is *Elya*, a version of *Eliyahu* (Elijah for my grandfather.) Although my mother didn't tell me any Elijah stories, she loved to share her childhood memories of growing up in Memphis during the Depression, and I grew up on those stories; to this day she still shares those times, yet it is only over the last few years that her memories have taken on new meaning for me. Peninnah Schram's collection of Elijah tales opened the door for me to find those Elijah moments—those seemingly ordinary moments in life when a decision must be made, seemingly small but resonating for a lifetime—to understand how my mother was able to see the Divine in the ordinary—to take small moments and make a difference. Small moments can make a story. Small moments can connect generations.

Lynnie Mirvis, community storyteller and educator, hosts GHS TV's "Story Time" and is a Storyteller-in-Residence at Pinocchio's Bookstore. A native Memphian, she has been a Wolf Trap Artist for the Performing Arts with Head Start and a teacher with the Florence Melton Adult Mini-School. Lynnie has a B.A. in Education from Stern College of Yeshiva University and a Masters in Library Science from the University of Memphis. She lives with her husband in Memphis, and when not storytelling, travels to Boston, New York, and Israel to visit their children and grandchildren where she shares and learns new stories.

The Melody
by Nadia Grosser Nagarajan

Along a stone-paved road in Cochin, facing the Arabian Sea, a small, lean girl was leading a skinny, white cow with black spots home from pasture. Priya, which was the little girl's name, led the cow home from pasture every day, and despite its pitiful thinness, the animal had large udders that provided a substantial amount of milk needed for the family's survival. It was shortly after dawn and the sun rose slowly on the horizon, spreading its subtle light on the small cluster of houses that stood in the center of Cochin, the ancient town that was Priya's birthplace in the state of Kerala in India. The sun seemed to touch gently the roofs of the modest white-washed homes where Jewish families had found refuge from persecution and fled from ill-wishers in the distant past.

Priya walked slowly along Jewtown Road, lined on both sides with stores that were still closed since it was so very early in the morning. The Jews' street had always fascinated her—the many objects that were displayed inside and outside, the colorful candle holders, other religious items, the mats, postcards and different kinds of jewelry, necklaces, bracelets and earrings that glittered and shimmered as the advancing rays of the sun touched and embraced them. Most of the owners of the stores had been Jewish, but many had died or left Cochin; yet most of the road had been left untouched. Some of the empty stores were closed or had been bought by non-Jewish merchants who also made their living selling trinkets to the tourists. The street still led straight to the Paradesi Synagogue. Priya had learned at school that this was not the original Jewish house of prayer built in the fourth century under the protection of the rule of Raja Ravi Baskar. He had seen the benefit of the mercantile talent of the Jews and allowed them to pursue business along the Malabar Coast, which is now also called Kerala. In 1524, Priya remembered from her history books, the Portuguese had destroyed the synagogue, and a second one, carrying the same name, was constructed at the identical location under Dutch patronage in 1568 and had stood there ever since.

Priya approached the shop of Leah the embroideress, who had become her friend. It was the smallest shop at the very end of the street, and Priya had to pull the cow gently since she was tired and had trouble following Priya. When they reached the store, the cow lay down on the cool stones and did not move; she seemed to know that Priya was going to take some time visiting her friend and that she could rest.

"There, there, Pashu," said Priya in her lovely, soft voice. "Rest, rest. I will bring you some water right away, my poor, tired cow."

The little girl knocked three times on the wooden door that was decorated with embroidered yarmulkes and colorful hamsas. It opened at once, giving way to an elderly, white-haired woman whose face lit up when she saw Priya. She invited the girl into the shop, and when Priya ascended the three steps, Leah embraced her lovingly and looked at her as if she had not seen her for a long time. And indeed it had been almost six months since Leah had left South India with her husband Isaiah to visit Israel, which had always been their dream.

Priya asked for water for her tired Pashu, and Leah promptly brought the red plastic container she kept exclusively for the cow. It was filled with clean, cold water, and the cow gratefully drank the cool liquid quickly in gulps, then closed her eyes and fell asleep. Priya enjoyed a glass of sweet lemonade Leah brought for her from the small kitchen in the back of the store. They just sat silently facing each other; no words were needed to express the love that was so obviously inscribed on their faces.

Nevertheless, after a short pause, Leah told Priya about her sorrowful trip to Israel, how she and her husband Isaiah had reached the shores of the Holy Land, grateful to *Hashem* for allowing them to fulfill the dream of their life. They had proceeded towards Jerusalem where, within a few days, at age eighty Isaiah had fallen very ill with a viral disease, and the doctors could not save him, no matter how hard they tried. He had passed away in a small house in Meah Shearim where a gentle widow had let them stay while visiting the city.

The last words Isaiah had whispered to Leah were: "I am happy."

She buried him in a small, distant lot of Har Hazeitim, the Mount of Olives. She spent all the money she had to purchase the plot but wanted her husband to be buried not far from where the kings of Israel had been interred in the distant past. That eased her pain. She knew Isaiah would have wanted it; after all, he was her king. She had stayed in Jerusalem for three months and earned some money working in an eatery, Tnuva, an old establishment that sold only milk products.

Leah enjoyed working there since she preferred a vegetarian diet, as did many of the Indian people with whom she had spent most of her life. Within three months she was able to save enough money for her passage back to Cochin. She wanted to come back to Jerusalem to die and be buried next to her husband, but in the meantime she still had a shop to attend to in Cochin and still needed to care for her little

Priya. She made up her mind to call the little girl "Ahuvah," beloved, in Hebrew, from then on, since she had found out from a university professor in Israel that the name Priya meant "beloved" in Sanskrit, and beloved indeed she was. Also, Leah missed the company of the few friends who still lived in what was left of the small Jewish community in Cochin.

Only a few elderly Jews still lived in dilapidated, faded homes in the Jewish quarter of the city. They were old and without families, since the young people had left for the big cities in search of a better life, only visiting on rare occasions and sending home money when they could. There was no rabbi, the *mohel* had been Isaiah, and one old man filled in as cantor and rabbi. That was where Priya had learned the *zemirot* and Sabbath songs. Her Uncle Vishu had a job in the synagogue as the janitor and Priya used to help him polish the silver and pewter objects. That was where she saw Leah one Friday evening for the first time. Leah and Isaiah were enchanted when Priya sang a few *zemirot* she had learned from the cantor who had passed on since then. He had been amazed by her unusual musical talent and had taught her all the *zemirot* he knew. And so she became a permanent member of the Friday night and holiday services. The congregation of Cochin missed their cantor. When Priya sang for them, they knew that *Hashem* must have sent them a nightingale whose voice was a marvel to be heard and admired.

Isaiah and Leah had been together for a very long time. Their parents had matched them. She belonged to the Ashkenazi group of wealthy, educated Jews who had arrived from Europe to escape pogroms. He came from a family in the Middle East where his forefathers had been spice merchants for many generations, sailing the oceans in search of business. It had been a very happy marriage, marred only by the fact that they were childless. Thus when Leah heard Priya singing one day at the synagogue and later saw her at the steps of the shop bringing her a *challah* that the synagogue distributed to its members, Leah felt as if the child was God-sent and as if she were her own. Isaiah did not say a word when Leah expressed her feelings to him, but when he heard Priya's crystalline voice as she sang a zmirah, his heart opened up and he also loved the little girl as if she were his own.

Priya had a most beautiful voice, clear, high-pitched but mellow at the same time. She was the pride of her mother, since she could remember any melody she heard and could sing it right away without making a mistake. Priya's mother worked very hard and had not much joy in her life, since her husband, a fisherman, and their only son had both perished in the high seas. The only family she had left were her own brother and her precious daughter.

Priya's Uncle Vishu lived with them in their tiny, white-washed house that consisted of two rooms where they slept, a kitchen, and a bathroom, a recent addition which was the envy of the neighborhood and the pride of the small family. The cow slept in a small hut that Vishu had built for her. Vishu was very gifted. His hands were blessed, Priya's grandma used to say, since he could build and fix anything, and all he touched would turn out for the very best. Thus he worked and provided for his aging parents as long as they lived, then helped his widowed sister and niece. He never contemplated marriage since he was too busy to think of himself.

That day, after Leah told Priya about Isaiah's death, Priya led the cow home, feeling sad and thinking of the best way to help Leah. She knew that there was nothing that could make up for the loss of a loved one; she herself had been very small when her father had perished in the ocean with her brother, and she never forgot her mother's heart-breaking laments, which lasted many long days.

When she reached her home, she tied Pashu to the pole inside the hut, making sure she had enough water, and then left to look for her mother, who worked those days in the flower market in nearby Ernakulam. Priya loved the flowers and the beautiful wreaths her mother made and sold, and sometimes even got a banana from one of the friendly vendors who had a stand close to her mother's. It was a very hot day, and the enticing scent of the flowers was overwhelming in the heat; still it was much more welcome than the stench of the fish displayed on chunks of melting ice that were sold on the other side of the fence.

The day passed quickly. After helping her mother to clean up, they both collected what was left of the merchandise and headed home. While her mother was fixing something to eat, Priya immersed the flowers in buckets of cold water, hoping they would last till the next day. Very early next morning, mother and daughter headed back to the market, pushing the cart Vishu had made to transport the merchandise. It was summer and the schools were closed, so Priya could help her mother before taking Pashu out to pasture.

Priya asked her mother if she could make a small wreath for Leah. Her mother encouraged her to do so. Leah had once given her a lovely embroidered shawl, which she cherished. Priya was very dexterous and artistic, and quickly created a beautiful wreath with colorful, fragrant flowers that she knew Leah would like. She reached Leah's shop by noon and found it open with a few customers buying her lovely embroidered artifacts. She went to the synagogue in order not to distract Leah and sat on the steps there. It was not as hot as on the previous day, and a light breeze caressed Priya's face. A couple of young girls, tourists no doubt, were approaching the synagogue, singing the most marvelous song Priya had ever heard. When they approached the synagogue, they smiled at her and sat down on the steps to rest. Priya knew they had sung in Hebrew and wanted them to sing again.

She said, "*Lashir shuv, todah*," smiling and trying to pronounce properly the little Hebrew she knew.

The phrase meant: "Please sing again, thanks."

And they did, not once but twice, and Priya joined them, their voices rising to the heavens. Whoever happened to be there paused in awe. The two girls hugged Priya and said in Hebrew, "*Yerushalayim shel zahav* (Jerusalem of Gold)." She understood it was the name of the song. After the girls left, Priya crossed the street and knocked on Leah's closed door. When Leah opened the door, Priya handed her the wreath, somewhat wilted but beautiful nevertheless, and started singing the song she had just learned. She did not know the words, so she just sang the melody. It sounded as if a hundred crystalline bells had joined together in perfect harmony. Leah was speechless. Sitting on her stairs, she put the wreath around her neck and hugged Priya when she finished the song. It was the song Isaiah had loved while in Jerusalem, one that she had heard many times before he passed away.

Tears started rolling down Leah's face. Priya wiped them away gently with the palm of her small hand till Leah stopped crying, and only one big tear was left resting in Priya's palm.

"Look," said the girl, "look how beautiful your tear is, like a pearl! It does not melt—it is a miracle!"

"No, my sweet Ahuvah," said Leah, "it is just a tear. It comes from my heart. But the miracle is your voice, and I will be forever grateful to Adonai for granting me such a precious gift!"

Provenance: Visiting my husband's native land, I was fascinated by the magic it emitted. Cochin, in southern India, is one of those places where the past takes over and the present seems to dissipate slowly. There we saw a little girl, leading a cow, and she smiled at me. Her eyes shone and there was much grace in her posture. We followed the little girl down a narrow road and saw a sign that advertised handmade embroidery of a woman, who was no doubt Jewish since her store window was decorated with Jewish paraphernalia. We heard the low humming of an old Jewish melody. The door opened and the elderly owner of the shop, Sara Cohen (whose name has been changed to Leah in the story), invited us in. She smiled and waved to the little girl as she watched her and the cow disappear around the corner. I could feel the unspoken deep bond between them and thus my story was born. Maybe one day we will go back to Cochin and visit again the lonely elderly woman, hoping she will still be there, attending to her shop and continuing to hum ancient Jewish melodies.

Nadia Grosser Nagarajan, Ph.D., was born in Czechoslovakia, and educated in Israel and the United Sates where she received a Ph.D. in Comparative Literature from the University of California at Berkeley. Nadia has lectured on Jewish culture as well as 19th century European literature. She has two published books: *Jewish Tales from Eastern Europe* and *Pomegranate Seeds – Latin American Jewish Tales*. *Pomegranate Seeds* was honored in 2005 as a runner-up for the The National Jewish Book Award For Sephardic Culture. Nadia resides in Virginia with her husband, and they have two sons and two grandchildren.

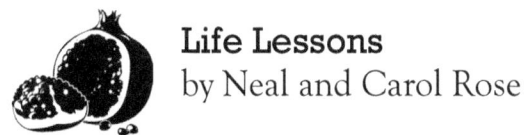

Life Lessons
by Neal and Carol Rose

Neal and I were just newly married when he accepted his first High Holiday gig for a youth community in Chevy Chase, Maryland. The community, of course, was quite willing to pay for the young rabbi's expenses, but not so for his nineteen-year-old wife (even though Neal and I had already prepared study materials for the *chagim* together). This meant that I was to remain behind in New York during that first *Rosh Hashannah*.

Shortly before the holidays, Neal and I went for dinner to a nearby kosher eatery, which used to serve students attending the Jewish Theological Seminary and Yeshiva University students, as well as local residents who lived on the upper West Side. During dinner, the proprietor, Mr. Golding, came over to chat with us. He had heard that we were recently married and wanted to congratulate us. Then he asked us where we would be for *Rosh Hashannah*, perhaps intending to invite us to his table for one of the festival meals.

When we told him that Neal was taking a pulpit for the holidays, he asked, "And your wife?" We explained that the hosting community had sent only one train ticket. Without batting an eyelash, Mr. Golding took out his checkbook and asked us how much a round trip ticket would cost. Quite embarrassed, I said, "Thank you so much for your kindness, but we really don't need charity."

Mr. Golding looked at me and said, "This is not charity at all. It is a mitzvah. You are giving me an opportunity to fulfill the mitzvah of *g'millut* chassadim (acts of lovingkindness). Would you deny me that? You see," he continued, "according to *halachah* (Jewish Law), a bride and groom are not permitted to be apart during the first year of their marriage. Most likely, the *ba'alabatim* (leaders of the congregation) in Chevy Chase have forgotten this, so now I have an opportunity to correct the oversight."

A bit taken aback, we both said, "Thank you! This is such a kindness. How will we ever pay you back?"

With a great, big smile, he said, "Oh, that's easy. You will pay me back many times. Each time someone is in need, you will offer to assist them. Thus, my mitzvah will continue throughout your lifetime. I will benefit from this over and over again."

And we like to think that we have honored that compassionate act.

Carol Rose is a writer, educator and spiritual counselor. She holds an MA in Theology, and degrees in both Religious Studies and Cross-Cultural Education. She also has certification as "Mashpiya/Minister, Spiritual Director, *Maggid* and Preacher" from Rabbi Zalman Schachter-Shalomi. Creator of *Walking the Motherpath* cards, her books in print include *A Free Hand; Behind the Blue Gate and Spider Women: A Tapestry of Creativity & Healing* (co-editor). Her poetry and essays appear in journals in the United States, Canada and Israel.

Neal Rose, a family therapist, also serves as Director of Spiritual Care at The Sharon Home and Professor of Near Eastern & Judaic Studies & member of the Department of Religion at the University of Manitoba. Ordained as a rabbi through JTS, he also holds a doctorate from HUC/JIR and teaches for the Aurora Family Therapy Institute of the University of Winnipeg.

Neal and his wife Carol have five grown children and ten grandchildren, and are founding members of P'nai Or. They have led the High Holiday Alternative *Minyan* at Congregation Etz Chayyim for more than 35 yrs.

The Demon of Dubrovna
by Gail Rosen

Once, in the small *shtetl* of Dubrovna, a tiny village in Eastern Europe, there lived an old woman. Actually, she didn't live in the center of the *shtetl*. The rabbi, the merchants, the important people lived there, near the *shul*, the synagogue. The old woman lived on the edge of the *shtetl*, in a tiny house, with old and mismatched furniture that others had discarded. But she had a bit of a garden, and she would help out her neighbors. The people of the *shtetl* would call on the old woman whenever a new child was about to come into the world, for her hands were cool and calm, and she knew about herbs. They would call on her, too, whenever an old one was about to leave this world for *olam ha-ba*, the world to come. For her hands were cool and calm, and her words were comforting. But even more comforting was the quality of her silence. The people who could afford it would give her a few coins for her trouble. The ones who couldn't, would share whatever they had. And so the old woman lived contentedly.

Always, the women of the *shtetl* would make sure that the old woman headed back to her little house before nightfall, because, you see, the *shtetl* had long been plagued by a terrible demon, a monster known as the Demon of Dubrovna. The Demon of Dubrovna could change its shape! Demons, you see, were created by God at twilight on the sixth day of Creation. It was close to the end of the day, close to the Sabbath, the day of rest, even for God. God didn't have time to make bodies for them. So demons remain spirits and can change their shape and appearance. The Demon of Dubrovna would take on the form of all kinds of monstrous creatures. It would squeal and roar and whinny. It tricked and surprised and frightened men, women and children alike, and sent them scurrying for the safety of their homes. And often, behind them, they would hear the Demon laughing.

One night, the old woman had been called to the side of an old, old man who was about to die. For hours she sat by his bedside, helping him to settle old quarrels and to make peace with those he truly loved. And when, as dusk began to fall, the man's soul left his body, it did so as gently and quietly as the last flicker of a candle flares and then goes dark. The *chevra kaddisha*, the burial society, was there to care for the body. There was family gathered to comfort one another, and so the old woman took up her shawl and prepared to leave.

But the other women said, "No! You mustn't go out in the dark. It's just a few hours 'til dawn. Stay with us! On the road alone, who knows who you might meet, maybe even the terrible Demon of Dubrovna!"

But the old woman said, "Demons! Demons want the very young and the beautiful. They like newborn babies and brides on their wedding night. With my white hair and stooped back, what would a demon want with me? I'll be fine." And she wrapped her shawl about her shoulders and set out.

It was early in spring, a week before *Pesach*, the Passover holiday, and there was half a round moon and so the old woman could see her way easily. She walked along enjoying the dark and the quiet. She hadn't walked far when on the side of the road she saw a cooking pot, a sturdy metal pot with a lid.

"Now why would someone leave a cooking pot on the side of the road," she thought, "unless it had a hole in it?"

Well, never mind, even with a hole she could make good use of it. She would plant her herbs in it to keep by her kitchen door. She walked over and lifted the lid to look inside. There was no hole in that pot! The pot was filled with gold coins! Those coins shone in the moonlight like the golden *schmaltz* on a pot of good chicken soup.

"What a *bisl mazl* (a bit of luck)!" she said. "I shall be an important lady now! No, not me! I'll give this gold to the rabbi. That's what I'll do. There are so many in the *shtetl* who are in need of help, and the *shul* needs a new roof. The rabbi will know what to do. This is a *bisl mazl*! But how shall I get it home?"

It was far too heavy to lift, so she took off her shawl and wrapped it 'round the pot and began to walk, dragging the pot behind her. It was heavy and after just a little way the old woman grew tired and stopped to rest. She turned to admire that gold gleaming in the moonlight— but when she unwrapped her shawl and lifted the lid, there was no gold there at all! The pot was filled with silver pennies, gleaming in the moonlight like the scales on the freshest fish you ever bought for *Shabbos*.

"Oy! Isn't this a *bisl mazl*!" she said. "A rare *bisl mazl*! That gold would have been no end of trouble. The peasants would have wondered, 'Where would a Jew find gold?' They might have accused me of stealing it! And at the *shul*, well, they would argue over who should get how much, and there would be trouble. Silver pennies are much better! I know what to do with silver pennies! The woodcutter's daughter is getting married. I will be able to give the happy couple a warm featherbed, and I'll hide the rest beneath that loose stone behind the stove and spend a few this week, a few next. This is a *bisl mazl*!"

She wrapped her shawl around that pot and again began to drag it behind her. It was heavy and after a little while the old woman grew tired and stopped to rest. She turned to admire those silver pennies shining in the moonlight - but when she unwrapped her shawl and lifted the lid, there were no silver pennies there at all, and no gold either! Now there was nothing in the pot but a great lump of iron!

"Oy! Isn't this a *bisl mazl*! A rare *bisl mazl*! A fine *bisl mazl*! Those silver pennies would have kept me up at night. I would have worried and fretted about how many to spend and how many to save and what if they ran out. A lump of iron is much better! I'll take it to the blacksmith. He will give me a few copper *groschen*, and I will have milk and eggs for my table this week. This is a *bisl mazl*!"

And she began to drag that pot with the lump of iron. She had almost reached her gate when she grew tired. She stopped to rest. She turned and unwrapped her shawl—and now there was no gold, no silver, no lump of iron and no pot either! There was just a great, round stone!

"Oy! Isn't this a *bisl mazl*! A rare *bisl mazl*! A fine *bisl mazl*! A lovely *bisl mazl*! How did it know that I was in need of just such a great, round stone to prop open my door on a lovely spring day!" She reached down to roll that stone to her door, and just as she did, the stone rose up into the air, grew to the size of a horse, four great legs sprang out and two heads with huge spinning eyes and a great flourish of a tail. The thing reared back and whinnied and screeched. It cackled and roared. The old woman stood, with her hands planted on her hips and watched.

"Oy! Isn't this a *bisl mazl*! To see the Demon of Dubrovna, and me so close!"

The thing squealed and bellowed, and changed again. It was a huge, slobbering wolf, then a roaring lion, then a giant, hissing serpent. Finally, standing in front of the old woman was an odd, little man. He had a long, gray wisp of a beard, a wrinkled face and odd, furry, pointed ears, rather like a cat, and he was kicking his toe in the dirt.

"Aren't you frightened then, old woman?" said the Demon of Dubrovna.

"Why should I be frightened?"

"The changes," he said. "Men, women and children alike run screaming when I change."

"Ahh," said the old woman. "Nothing compared to the changes I see—babies being born and people dying, souls coming into this world and souls going out. I've seen far too many changes in my long life to be frightened by yours."

He looked quite disappointed.

She worried that she had hurt his feelings, poor thing. "I'm just about to fix something to eat," she said. "Would you like to join me? I don't have much, just dark bread and herring, but what I have you're welcome to share."

He brightened. "Don't mind if I do," said the Demon of Dubrovna. And he followed the old woman into her house, sat at her table and she reached to the cupboard to put out bread and herring. And when she turned, there on the table were a bowl of fine boiled eggs and a pitcher of fresh milk, too.

The old woman said the *bracha*, the blessing for the food, and the Demon answered, "Amen." She was surprised, but she thought, "After all, he, too, is one of God's creations."

They ate, and the Demon of Dubrovna regaled the old woman with tales of his mischief, how he had changed his shape, tricked and surprised and frightened men, women and children. And she laughed 'til tears ran down her face. And then she told him about the changes she had seen, helping people into this world and out, until a tear or two came to his eye. And they both declared they hadn't spent such a pleasant time in many a year.

Now, on occasion, the Demon of Dubrovna comes to sup with that old woman, and she notices that her cupboard is never empty and her woodpile is always stacked high.

And if she hears the people in the shetl talking in hushed tones about the terrible Demon of Dubrovna, she laughs and says, "Ah, the Demon of Dubrovna, he's just doing the work God made him to do in the world. And besides, if you can look those changes square on, frightened or not, you might find in them for yourself a *bisl mazl*—a rare *bisl mazl*, a fine *bisl mazl*, a lovely *bisl mazl*."

Provenance: Based on "The Headly Kow," a Celtic folktale, I came across this story as I was preparing a story presentation on change. It happened to be at a time in my life when things were changing rapidly for me—career, marriage, and family. This story reminded me of Rabbi Nachman of Breslov's words, "All the world is a narrow bridge, and the main thing is not to be afraid." Peninnah Schram once presented a talk, based on the theory of Dov Noy, about what makes a Jewish story Jewish. She said that the components to consider are Jewish time, Jewish places, Jewish characters, and especially Jewish values—as well as Jewish storytellers! So what was a Celtic story became a Jewish one.

Gail Rosen uses storytelling to support and inform the experience of grieving. Gail founded the Healing Story Alliance, a special interest group of the National Storytelling Network. She performs and leads workshops on storytelling, story-eliciting, and burnout prevention in retirement communities, hospitals, hospices, synagogues, churches, and schools, and has presented at national conferences. She has travelled the U.S., Germany, Israel, Poland, Austria, Japan, and Canada, telling the story of a Holocaust survivor, and personal stories and folktales that explore the unpredictable, unexpected journeys of our lives and how we draw meaning from them. (www.gailrosen.com)

Elijah's Yellow Balloon
by Rebecca Schram-Zafrany

My four-year-old daughter, Dorielle, loved shiny, black patent leather Mary Jane shoes. She had already outgrown the pair I had bought her only six months earlier and had been asking for a new pair for quite a few weeks. In fact, she was becoming very vocal about it. Every morning she asked, "Mommy, can we go shopping for my new Mary Janes today?"

And every night she asked, "Mommy, can we *please* go shopping for my new Mary Janes tomorrow?"

When I answered that I didn't have time that day or that she was going to be busy all the next day, she said, "Don't forget, Mommy, I really need them soon."

Over time the questions got even louder and more frequent.

I knew she wanted them and needed them for her best friend's birthday party, which was coming up soon. So, one sunny summer afternoon, we both were free to go to the shoe store. Dorielle loved going to the shoe store, and she especially loved getting the balloon that the 'shoe-store man' always gave children after their parents bought them shoes. Dorielle always waited for the shoe-store man to ask her if she wanted a balloon and she always chose yellow, her favorite color. I had also promised her that afterward we were going to buy her a new book at the bookstore just down the street.

As we approached the shoe store, Dorielle turned to me and asked me for perhaps the tenth time that day, "Mommy, will I get a balloon from the store if we buy shoes today?" I assured her again that we would.

"Mommy, are you sure I can get a yellow balloon?" Again, I told her that she could get her usual yellow balloon after we bought the shoes she wanted.

As soon as we entered the store, Dorielle and I went directly to the children's section in the back and immediately spied the shelf with all the black, shiny Mary Jane shoes lined up in neat, sparkling rows. After examining all the shoes, Dorielle picked out a nice pair she was sure was the shiniest of them all. Dorielle tried them on, felt them on her feet while walking around the store twice, examined them from every angle in the mirror, and finally decided that this was the pair she wanted. After Dorielle put her sandals back on, we both went up to the front counter and watched as the sales lady put the new, very shiny Mary Jane shoes neatly into their bright pink box, and I paid for them.

Now came the moment that Dorielle had been waiting for with such anticipation—the balloon. The shoe salesman approached her and asked her whether she wanted a balloon.

Dorielle answered, "Yes," as she gave him a look as if to say—"*Are you crazy? Of course I want a balloon!*"

"OK," said the shoe salesman. "What color?"

Dorielle didn't have to think very long.

"Yellow," she answered, "my favorite color."

The shoe salesman went down a flight of stairs and came back two minutes later, carrying a bright yellow helium balloon floating above us at the end of a thin, white string. The shoe salesman handed the balloon to Dorielle with great ceremony and said, "Don't let it go. If you do, it will float right up to the sky."

I then turned to Dorielle and added, "Why don't you let me tie it around your wrist so that it won't fly up to the sky?"

Dorielle looked up at me with a very determined expression and said, "No, Mommy, I can hold it all by myself. I won't let it go. I'm a big girl."

"OK," I said.

Just as we were about to leave, Dorielle turned to the shoe salesman with her sweetest smile and said, "Thank you, Mr. Shoe-Store Man."

He smiled back, waved at us, and we walked out of the shoe store. Dorielle was looking up proudly at her yellow balloon, holding its thin string, and I was walking beside her, holding her other hand and holding the plastic bag with her new shoes in their pink shoebox.

No sooner had we gotten five steps out of the store, than the white string slipped out of her little hand, and she watched her yellow balloon float gracefully up into the blue summer sky.

"Oh, noooooo!" she wailed. "Mommy...look...my balloon...in the sky!"

I looked up and saw, as she did, the balloon flying away, dancing gracefully in the breeze high above the trees and the buildings around us.

Dorielle's face crumpled, and she began to cry, tears streaming down her cheeks. Without another word, we turned around and walked back into the shoe store. I immediately saw the same shoe salesman who had given us the balloon not two minutes earlier.

"Could you give us another one?" I asked. "My daughter accidentally let her balloon go, and it floated away."

"No problem," said the shoe salesman with a smile. "This happens all the time."

He promptly went down the flight of stairs again, and came back a minute later with another yellow helium balloon floating at the end of a thin, white string.

As the shoe salesman knelt down to give this second balloon to Dorielle, he said, "Don't let this one go, too, or it will float away, right up to the sky."

Dorielle nodded as I wiped away her tears, and we began to walk out of the store.

Again, she thanked 'Mr. Shoe-Store Man,' and then I turned to her and said, "Why don't you let me tie it around your wrist so that this one won't fly up to the sky?"

Dorielle looked up at me with an even more determined expression and said, "No, Mommy, I can hold it all by myself. I'm a big girl. I promise I won't let it go."

"Are you absolutely sure?" I asked.

"Yes," Dorielle answered quite boldly.

"OK," I said warily, "but I won't come back into the store and get you another balloon if this one floats away, too."

Dorielle nodded, and we walked out of the shoe store. She was holding the string attached to her yellow balloon very tightly, looking up at it as she walked, holding my hand. I knew that I needed to be more assertive with her and set boundaries about tying the string to her wrist, but I didn't want to make a fuss in the store, so I let her have her way.

This time we had gotten halfway to the bookstore when suddenly Dorielle wailed, "Mommmmyyyyyyy!"

I knew instinctively what had happened. This balloon had escaped from Dorielle's hand a second time.

"Dorielle," I said, "we can't go back into the store and get another balloon. You didn't want me to tie the string around your wrist the first time or the second time, and both times the balloon floated away. I told you I was not going back to get another one, and I meant it. I will not go back to the shoe store to get another balloon."

"But Mommmyyyyy!" she wailed very loudly again with more tears streaming down her cheeks.

This time people were beginning to look at us on the street, and I was beginning to feel embarrassed and greatly frustrated. I absolutely didn't want to go back into the store and bother the shoe salesman for a third balloon—but then I looked at my daughter. She was utterly devastated at having lost her yellow balloon yet again. Even though I knew that Judaism teaches us to be kind to those who staff our lives, I felt I had no choice but to bother the shoe salesman again. I just couldn't let my daughter be without this balloon she had waited for, for so long. So I turned around and walked back into the shoe store, trying to muster as much courage as possible before facing the shoe salesman again, and trying not to show how embarrassed I really was.

As I walked into the shoe store, I immediately saw the same shoe salesman who had helped us twice before. I looked down at the floor, not able to look him in the eye.

Very meekly and with an embarrassed smile on my face, I said, "Excuse me, sir. My daughter let her balloon go again. Could you possibly get us another one?"

This time, the shoe salesman was not amused.

"Another one??" he asked, disbelieving.

Without a word and with an annoyed expression on his face as if to say, '*Why can't these parents and children just learn to hold on to a simple balloon?*' He went back down those same stairs and came back two minutes later with another yellow balloon floating at the end of a thin, white string. This time he said, rather gruffly, as he handed Dorielle the balloon, "Little girl, let your Mommy tie the string around your wrist this time so the balloon won't float away."

I could tell he was controlling his frustration with a great deal of effort.

"No," Dorielle answered with a sniffle, but very strongly. "I promise I won't let it go this time. I will hold on really tight!"

"No, Dorielle," I said. "You must let me tie the string around your wrist this time. We are not leaving the store with you just holding the balloon string."

Dorielle stood up as straight as she could and said in her strongest, most defiant voice, "I really won't let it go this time, you'll see. It won't fly away this time—it won't!!"

"All right then," I answered with a sigh, feeling slightly defeated. Then I continued, in a voice that was a lot louder than usual, so that most of the people around us could hear, "but if this one floats away, I won't come back to get another one. DO YOU UNDERSTAND??"

"Yes, Mommy," Dorielle answered happily.

Once again, we walked out of the shoe store. I thanked the shoe salesman profusely and watched Dorielle smiling up at her new yellow balloon, her third. I was still holding the bag with the shoebox and watching her hand tightly wound around the thin, white string, praying that the string would not slip out of her hand this time, and that disaster would be averted.

We made it all the way to the entrance of the bookstore, the balloon still with us. I was about to breathe a sigh of relief, thinking that even if she let it go inside the bookstore, a worker could get it down from the ceiling. But just as we were about to step through the outside doors of the bookstore, I heard that all-too-familiar wail.

"Mommmyyyyyyy, my balloooon!"

That was it, I was through. "DORIELLE," I said in loud, very angry voice, "I WILL NOT GO BACK TO THE SHOE STORE AGAIN. YOU DIDN'T LISTEN TO ME OR TO THE SHOE-STORE MAN. YOU DIDN'T LET ME TIE IT AROUND YOUR WRIST, AND YOU WILL NOT GET ANOTHER BALLOON!!!"

All I got in return was a piercingly loud scream.

I didn't care. I dragged her into the bookstore and up the escalator toward the children's section. Everyone was looking at an angry, frustrated mother with a child who was crying and screaming something about a yellow balloon. When we got to the children's section, all the other parents who were reading quietly to their children stopped and watched the tantrum, which was in full swing by this time. Dorielle was getting louder by the second, and I was feeling more and more humiliated.

Suddenly, my daughter stopped crying. I felt a slight tap on my shoulder and turned around to see who it was, certain that it was a security guard coming to ask us politely but firmly to leave the quiet bookstore. But there standing behind me was a woman, a total stranger, holding a yellow helium balloon floating at the end of a thin, white string. She silently handed the balloon to Dorielle, who was staring at her in amazement, as was I.

"I was sitting outside the shoe store in my car," she told me, "and I saw the whole balloon episode. When I saw that your daughter lost her balloon for the third time and that you didn't go back to the shoe store to get another one, I decided to go back into the shoe store myself and get it for her. I saw you go into the bookstore so I assumed you would be in the children's section. I simply couldn't bear to see her without her balloon."

She then turned again to Dorielle.

"Now, little girl, your Mommy is going to tie the string around your wrist. OK?"

Dorielle looked up at the woman and nodded silently, her cheeks still stained with tears. Then she held out her hand and let me tie the string around her wrist. *Finally.*

"What's your name?" I asked when I could finally get some words out.

She told me, though I have since forgotten it. I began to cry, then the woman began to cry, and we hugged each other. Dorielle joined the hug, her yellow balloon floating above us. The three of us stood there, hugging and crying in the middle of the bookstore. I turned my head to look at my daughter and saw her staring up at her yellow balloon, smiling. I was sure we were truly in the presence of Elijah, whose good deed had saved the day.

Provenance: This is a story that really happened. As I remember this Elijah incident in our lives, I wonder, whether I should have been stronger in imposing boundaries on my daughter, or was I just too new to this motherhood experience, not sure how far to go regarding my daughter's need to assert herself and her independence? (I put this lesson to good use later with my younger children.)

Rebecca Schram-Zafrany is a high school English teacher and storyteller. She holds a BA in English Literature from Hebrew University and an MA in Applied Linguistics from Tel Aviv University. Rebecca performs and leads workshops in the United States and Israel. She served as cultural coordinator for UJA Federation summer day camps and Jewish programming coordinator at the JCC of Manhattan Summer Day Camp. Her story, "The Miracle of the Black Pepper," was published in Peninnah Schram's *Chosen Tales: Stories Told by Jewish Storytellers*. Rebecca resides in *Moshav* Shdema, Israel, with her husband and three children, Dorielle, Aaron, and Ilan.

A Single Seed of a Pomegranate
retold by Cherie Karo Schwartz

Kavannah (setting the intention):

Upon the anointing by Moses of Aaron as high priest, to make him holy, Moses is to take some of the life blood of the sacrifice and put it on the ridge of Aaron's right ear and that of his sons; upon Aaron's right thumb and that of his sons; and upon his right big toe and that of his sons [Exodus 29:20]. We may understand this as a sign: that we are holy as we listen with our ears, and act holy as we extend our hands to another and move forward with our feet, helping to bring holiness into the world. It is up to us, through the generations, to help restore life.

Once upon a time, long, long ago and far, far away in the land of the Sultans, there lived a man named Shlomo who was so poor that he could not even feed his family. Every day he set out with hope in his heart that he could perform enough small tasks to be paid enough so that he and his family could survive, but every day those hopes were dashed. And why? You see, the Sultan was a cruel, hard-hearted ruler who hated the Jews. He created rules that made life in his lands almost impossible for any Jews living there. And any breach of his inhumanly strict laws was an excuse for cruel punishment.

One day this poor man could stand it no longer. Out of extreme hunger, and with grief over the plight of his tiny family, Shlomo brazenly stole a single loaf of bread from the baker in the market.

Immediately, the Sultan's guards grabbed Shlomo, dragged him to the dungeons and threw him into a dark, dank cell to await his punishment: death by hanging the next day.

Poor Shlomo sat on the ground of his filthy cell and wept for his sad life and for the plight of his family. He rose and began pacing like a caged animal. And then, remembering himself, he called from his place of grief to the Holy One of Blessing, pouring out his heart in tears.

As he stood there, Shlomo absent-mindly placed his hand in his pocket. There he felt something small and hard. He pulled it out and gazed at it in the dim light. A seed: a pomegranate seed. How long had it been there? A seed—of hope? Shlomo's heart began to race. A seed! Yes, of course, a seed!

Shlomo's voice rang out through the long, dark hallway of the dungeon. "Guards! Guards!" The guards came running down the hall, their footsteps reverberating against the stone walls.

"What is it, prisoner? How dare you disturb our rest!"

By this time, Shlomo was slowly pacing back and forth, rocking on his heels, holding the pomegranate seed, at peace, a smile playing on his face in the shadows. As he stood there in the cell, he was humming a *niggun*, a little, wordless melody.

"Well, what is it, Jew?"

Shlomo held up the seed for them to see. "I was just seeing this tiny seed and remembering something. It is too bad that the secret will die with me...."

"What secret, Jew? All things are known or will be known by the Sultan! Speak! Tell us!"

"Oh, I could not possibly tell you. This secret is for the ears of the Sultan."

The guards held up their spears, their eyes flashing with anger. "Tell us, Jew, or you will now die right here!"

Silence fell in the dungeon. Shlomo the Jew pondered his fate.

"It's only a seed. There's nothing more to it."

Silence again.

Then, "Tell us. Tell us now!"

"Slowly he began, "Really? Well, I suppose I could tell you part of the story. You see..." The guards bent closer, listening intensely. Now here was something that could allay the boredom of their lives.

"This is no ordinary seed. It is a pomegranate seed, a magic pomegranate seed. If it is planted, by the next day a full pomegranate tree will have grown in its place, covered with ripe fruit."

The guards laughed, their coarse voices reverberating through the passageways of the dungeon.

"That is ridiculous, Jew! Why did we waste our time with you? Come, let us torture other prisoners. This one is pitiful." And they began walking away.

Shlomo waited until they had turned on their heels to go. Then softly he said, "This secret was taught to me from my father, who heard it from his father, and so on for generations of our family. It is true, as I stand here...."

The guards stopped in their tracks. Surely they had heard the tales of how the Jews were possessed, how they knew magic and dark arts. What if it were true? Wouldn't the Sultan grant them a grand reward if the story were really true? Should they miss this opportunity?

Off went the guards, disappearing into the darkness. Not knowing what they were doing, Shlomo collapsed onto the filthy floor of his cell. With a heavy heart, he fell into a restless sleep.

Shlomo awoke to the sound of quick, heavy footsteps, the clanking of keys, the creaking open of the rusty barred door of his tiny cell.

"Up! On your feet, Jew! Up now! Walk on your miserable legs. Prepare to meet your destiny!"

Shlomo was led through the maze of the dungeon, up, up the worn rock steps, and out into the blessed light of the courtyard. Then, across the courtyard he was dragged, straight to the royal palace, down hallways and into the sumptuous room of the Sultan himself. The Sultan was propped upon silk pillows of all colors; his richly brocaded robe swirled about him. Tapestries danced upon the walls, and intricate rugs rested upon the marble floors. The Sultan was surrounded by well-dressed and well-armed guards who were fanning him gently. Fruits and other delicacies of every kind and color were artfully displayed upon golden trays. Shlomo's mouth watered in hunger.

Shlomo's eyes were surely deceiving him, but yes! This was the Sultan himself before him, gazing down at him cruelly.

When the Sultan spoke, it was with a voice of gravelly disdain, tinted with just a hint of curiosity.

"So, Jew! Jew thief, Jew liar. What have you told my guards? Speak, Jew!"

Shlomo stood, weak but proud, before the potentate. He paused.

"Speak, Jew! Speak now, for soon we shall hang you." A smile played about the Sultan's face.

Taking a deep breath, lightly touching the pomegranate seed in the pocket of his tattered pants, and offering a pleading prayer—"Please forgive me, Holy One, for telling this tale!"—Shlomo began.

"Sire, Sire, there is a tradition in my family." Shlomo's voice grew in strength as he quickly continued.

"In every generation in my poor family, which used to be wealthy and well-known, there has been a secret passed down to the eldest alone, a secret which has been preserved for centuries."

The Sultan leaned forward as he bit into a ripe apricot, the juice running down his beard as he spoke.

"This secret—tell me! Tell me now!"

Shlomo nodded, sighed, and continued,

"This secret concerns a seed, a magic seed, from antiquity. And I, being the eldest in this generation, have always held it close. Here it is."

And Shlomo extended his hand, briefly displaying the single pomegranate seed to the Sultan, then replacing it safely in his pocket.

The Sultan growled, amused but impatient.

"So, what is this to me, who has everything, who knows everything?"

"Sire, this is a magic pomegranate seed. When this seed is planted, by the next day a full mature pomegranate tree grows in that spot, laden with sweet, ripe, deep red fruit."

"And you really expect me to believe your lie, Jew? What do you take me for, a fool?" Around him came the cruel laughter of his many simple guards.

"O, great Sultan, this is truth, I tell you. And there is only one way to find out for yourself. With me there, for I must be present, plant this seed tomorrow in your own courtyard, and observe for yourself what will happen."

There was a long silence as the Sultan pondered his move. Then the words thundered out, "So be it! Tomorrow at dawn let the Jew be brought into the courtyard. There we shall see what we shall see. I have spoken. Now, take him away!"

And so, Shlomo was dragged from the royal presence and marched away, back down the heavy steps to the dank, dark dungeon, whose cell now seemed safe, since he had secured for himself at least another day of life.

All that day and night, Shlomo swayed in prayer, hovering between life and death, waking and sleep, wrapped in the Presence of the Holy One.

All too soon, dawn crept into the sky. Shlomo again heard the guards' footsteps, again he was dragged from his cell and marched roughly to the courtyard, where he felt the warmth of the sun, the whisper of the wind, and the promise of day, as he looked into the expectant eyes of all who gathered there.

The Sultan roared, "This Jew says he has a miracle to show us, for our pleasure. By tomorrow we shall have a tree full of pomegranates, right, Jew? Hah! So, Jew, plant the pomegranate seed!"

No one moved.

"What is the matter, Jew? Is this a lie? Another lie?"

Shlomo paused, breathing a prayer for redemption. Then he spoke: "O, Sire, the tale is true. But I forgot to mention one part. Please forgive me. This is truly a magic pomegranate seed, but it is an honest pomegranate seed. It may only be planted by someone who is completely honest. You yourself, Sire, established the rule that no one may steal. I am not honest; I am a thief, who was caught, and I am worthy to die under your law. I cannot plant the seed."

The Sultan stroked his beard. "Then you, my Minister of Affairs, plant this seed!"

The minister looked down at the ground.

"Well, go ahead—plant the seed!" prompted the Sultan.

"I am sorry, Sire; I cannot do this. For once, actually far more than once, I let others' desires and money influence how I scheduled your appointments."

"What?!" roared the Sultan. Turning quickly to his Minister of Commerce, he issued the same royal order: "Plant this pomegranate seed!"

And all heard his reply, "Please, Sultan, do not make me do this, for I cannot plant it. More back-handed deals have been struck for the sake of influence than I can even remember. I am, sadly, dishonest, too."

"So you, my Minister of Finances: you must be honest. Plant this pomegranate seed."

"Alas, Sultan! I have always tried to be honest in all my bookkeeping. Yet, do you remember the great and beauteous pearl that you were given through a foreign emissary? Well, I began to place it in your royal treasury, but then I thought of what a loss it would be to have such luster shut into a dark vault. I deeply regret it; I took it home, where it is safe. I promise upon my life that I will return it to the treasury, but I remain your dishonest servant."

Looking directly at the ruler, Shlomo continued:

"It appears, O Sultan, that there may be no one else who can plant this seed, does it not?"

All eyes turned toward the Sultan. His face was flushed. He stammered. Then he stood in silence, facing the condemned man.

The Sultan's eyes grew misty. He began to speak, slowly forming the words.

"When I was a young boy, I would sit at my mother's feet as she sewed, embroidering upon a white background all manner of designs: flowers and birds and butterflies of every shape and hue. I was fascinated, sitting there for minutes on end, gazing at the life she drew out of the threads and upon the fabric. The sunlight filtered through the windows and played about the room. And the sun struck the golden needle she sewed with, catching my eye. When, at the end of the day, she happened to drop that golden needle, I did not say a word, but waited until she slipped from the room, and then took the needle for my own. I have kept that golden needle, lo these many years. I still have it hidden. I, too, am dishonest."

Silence overwhelmed the courtyard.

Then, after a time, the Sultan once again spoke: "None of us can plant this honest pomegranate seed, and neither can I, myself. Yet you, Shlomo the Jew, you have indeed planted a seed. You have planted a seed of Mercy within us all. All is not lost, though.

"First, before we set this seed free to become the tree it was meant to become, let us set free the one who brought this wisdom here to this court. Guard! Unshackle this prisoner!"

And Shlomo was freed.

The Sultan gazed from Shlomo to the hole in the dirt before him. Then he drew a deep breath.

"Now, let us plant a seed: this seed of Justice...filled with the infinite seeds of promise for the future. If we each call forth the most honest part of ourselves, then together we can plant this seed, water it, and set it on its journey toward becoming perhaps one whole pomegranate tree, all in its own good time. And as we watch it grow and help nurture it over the years, we will remember. So may it be."

One seed.

Provenance: A Jewish story from the time of the Sultanates, recorded in such sources as *The Exempla of the Rabbis*, #433 (M. Gaster), and the Israel Folktale Archives (from Morocco and from Iraqi Kurdistan). I first told this story at the 92nd Street Y in New York City in a program for Peninnah Schram's story series there, two decades ago. Peninnah and I both tell the pomegranate story. In honor of our three decades of story/heart connection, I created this heartfelt *tikkun* at the end of my retelling of this.

Cherie Karo Schwartz, MA in Developmental Theater, is a storyteller, author, and educator living in Denver. She has shared stories with audiences of all ages throughout America and abroad for forty years. She shares a kaleidoscope of spirit-filled tales of wishes, wisdom, and wit drawn from worldwide Jewish folklore, sacred texts, family folklore, original stories, and modern *midrashim.* Cherie offers storytelling performances, master classes, workshops and keynotes for conferences, organizations, museums, storytellers, schools, and libraries worldwide. She was co-founding coordinator of the international Jewish Storytelling Network of CAJE. Cherie has authored three books and many articles, and recorded numerous tapes and CDs. (schwartzstory@earthlink.net; www.hamsapubs.com)

Grandma and Mr. Pushke
by Corinne Stavish

When I was a little girl, I loved to bake with my Grandma. She was an artist—no paint-by-number creations for her. She was an original. She used no recipe and measured nothing. In Yiddish, it's called a *shitenrein* cook. She'd scoop up handfuls of flour, followed by sugar, pinch in some salt, sprinkle liquids, crack eggs, and whoosh...dough would elasticize into a translucent wonder.

My mother and older sister tried in vain to repeat her no-recipe wonders. Once, my sister stood next to her, and each time my grandmother filled her hand, my sister would have her dump the contents in a bowl; then she'd measure. She added up all the measurements of each ingredient and wrote out the recipe. But it did not come close to resembling my grandmother's strudel dough.

"Grandma," my sister implored, "tell me what I missed."

"Oy, Dollenu, I don't know. I just put in a *bisl* (a little) of this, and a *bisl* of that, and your cups don't measure in *bisls*."

After the dough gathered itself into a ball, I watched with saucer eyes as miracles happened. Grandma would roll the dough thinner than the waxed paper on which it unfolded, then dip her hands in oil and smooth the wrinkles of the dough, sprinkle cinnamon sugar that resembled fairy dust, followed by nuts that she allowed me to chop with a magical chopper that screwed into a glass jar. She'd adorn that with chopped apples, cut so precisely that a machine could have done it, and golden raisins.

Then, she cautioned, "Tightly, *Mamela*" (an endearment which translates roughly to "little mother," because in my tradition your destination and expectations were declared early on)—"you must roll it tight so that the apples don't spill out."

She'd start at the wide end and roll and roll, until magically, there was a cylinder, without holes. She'd transfer that to a baking sheet and without setting a timer, know when to bring this golden perfection from the oven. When the dough cooled, she would sprinkle it with confectioners' sugar and cut the pieces with the precision of the machines at the bakery. She artfully arranged pieces on a plate for our dessert. I devoured the crumbs that remained.

What she did not place on the dessert plate, she would wrap in little waxed paper pockets and bring to neighbors as tokens of good will. When I was nine, I lived with her the entire summer. It was what she'd asked for when my parents had asked a few months before when my grandfather had died, "What can we do?" She wanted me to come from Oklahoma and spend the summer. I became her assistant cook, which consisted of helping to chop the nuts in the bottle, measure out the waxed paper, and lick the bowl.

That summer, she wrapped up more and more pockets of baked goods to distribute to the neighbors.

"They were so kind and generous when Grandpa died. This is the least I can do."

She baked and gave away; baked and gave away. Grandma was great at giving things away. She gave away old clothes to organizations, fresh baked goods to neighbors, along with unsolicited advice, and coins to the beggars who came to the door.

"Don't call them beggars, *Mamela*. They're just people down on their luck. There but for the grace of God..."

She never finished the sentence, but I knew that it meant that anyone could have the same bad luck. She took the coins from her *pushke*, a small jar with pennies and nickels where she put her change at the end of the week. One man in particular seemed to come to the door more than anyone else, so I started to call him Mr. Pushke.

If I opened the door to the knock, I'd call in: "Grandma, it's Mr. Pushke," and she'd come scurrying and bring some coins.

Grandma went into baking overload that summer and was giving away so many pockets of baked goods that the neighbors began to refuse them.

"You can sell them to us. That's the only way we'll accept them."

"Please, Mrs. Borim," the ladies on our floor would argue. "You have to buy ingredients and spend so much time."

Grandma finally agreed, with the condition that no one told my uncle what she was doing. I was enlisted into the conspiracy, and I understood why without explanation.

My Uncle Max, her youngest child, who was the one who lived with her and took care of her, could be a harsh man. He was not inclined to "give charity." His exact phrase when someone came to the door to ask for a handout was: "We don't take charity; we don't give charity."

I knew better than to tell Uncle Max about Mr. Pushke—we don't give charity. I knew better than to tell Uncle Max about Grandma selling baked goods—we don't TAKE charity. For him, getting money for those pastries would have been charity. My lips were sealed. In case I forgot, Grandma would hold her finger to her lips to remind me — *Sha!* Don't tell! The neighbors seemed to know to come to the door only during the week when my uncle was at work, and Mr. Pushke seemed to have the same radar.

I don't know if my uncle was home from work one day because he was sick or because it was some sort of mid-week holiday. He was sitting in the living room, reading the paper, noticing that there were continuous knocks on the door, which sent my grandmother scurrying into the kitchen, returning with little packages, and exchanging whispers. I watched as Grandma pushed the coins into her apron and then transferred them to the *pushke* that stood in the hallways at the crossroads of the door, the living room, and the kitchen. Each time Grandma passed, she held her finger up to her lips, indicating that I was to say nothing.

Maybe it was all the unusual activity that made my uncle finally get up and answer the door himself when there was a knock. It was not a neighbor; it was Mr. Pushke. My uncle understood immediately as the hand extended toward him.

He said: "We don't take charity; we don't give charity," and started to close the door.

My grandmother emerged from the kitchen into the foyer. I was right behind her.

"Max, don't close the door." My grandmother's tone could not be disobeyed.

I watched my otherwise fearless uncle pause with his hand on the doorknob. My grandmother walked to the *pushke* jar, shook out some coins, walked to the door, and deposited them into Mr. Pushke's dirty, shaking hand. I swear my uncle was growling. Then she held up a finger to Mr. Pushke, indicating that he should wait. She marched into the kitchen and took all of the strudel on OUR dessert plate and wrapped it in waxed paper. Then she walked back and deposited it in Mr. Pushke's dirty hands. I realized that he was going to get to eat my dessert without having to wash his hands.

My uncle closed the door. Grandma stepped away, and I got between them.

My uncle almost barked: "Mama, I don't want you to ever do that again. I work hard for that money, and I don't want you giving it away."

I turned sideways so that I could get a good view of both of them as I ping-ponged my head. My grandmother faced him as he stood with his arms folded.

I then whined a question not worth voicing: "Did you give away our dessert?"

I mean, some coins were one thing, but my dessert? My grandmother did not even bother to turn around toward me and answer. She continued to stare at my uncle.

"It's not your money," she declared. "I earned that money. I bake for the neighbor ladies, and they pay me."

Steam was escaping from my uncle's ears, making him resemble a little teapot. I was thinking that my uncle could counter her statement with the fact that his salary paid for the ingredients of those baked goods. I was too young to understand that the value of an artist's work is measured not by the ingredients but by the labor and result. Besides, I couldn't say anything because my mouth was still in the shape of a whine.

Then, my grandmother stretched herself to her full height, about 4' 10." In her sternest voice, one that my uncle must have remembered from his childhood, using his Jewish name, she said:

"Mottel, it's not charity—I earned that money by baking for the neighbors. And that man earned my giving it to him through his hard luck."

After that, she turned me toward her, and answering my previous whine, she bent to kiss the top of my head and said, "*Mamela*, we'll bake again in the morning."

There was a long silence. Next, I felt my uncle embrace my grandmother and me, heard him whisper, "Yes, you'll bake again in the morning," and I raised my eyes in time to see him kiss the top of my grandmother's head as she kissed the top of mine.

Corinne Stavish specializes in personal narratives and *midrashim* that are witty, powerful and poignant, enhanced by a varied and lively performing style. She has been featured at the National Storytelling Festival; presented workshops nationwide; was a keynote speaker at the 2005 National Storytelling Conference; guest-edited Storytelling Magazine; was a Detroit Jewish Woman Artist of the Year 2001; produced award-winning recordings; and contributed to *Chicken Soup for the Jewish Soul* and *The Storyteller's Companion to the Bible*. She is a College Professor in Humanities at Lawrence Tech University, where she was honored as Professor of the Year.

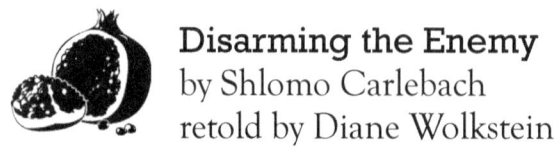

Disarming the Enemy
by Shlomo Carlebach
retold by Diane Wolkstein

Shlomo Carlebach's father, Naftali Carlebach, was the rabbi of a large synagogue in Berlin in the 1930's. This was a very intolerant time, even among the Jews. In Naftali's synagogue, a German Jew stood by the entrance, and if any Jews came from Poland, he would tell them that they had to sit in the last two rows of the synagogue. At that time in Germany, Polish Jews were not allowed to stand at the pulpit to give the blessings of the *kohanim* during the high holidays. Shlomo's father began the custom of allowing Polish Jews to join German Jews at the pulpit at *Yom Kippur* to offer blessings. After one holiday, a German Jew who was a multi-millionaire found himself standing next to a Polish Jew whose socks were torn and who smelled terrible. The next day he sent a letter to Shlomo's father. The letter said:

Dear Rabbi Carlebach:

Yesterday in synagogue, I stood next to a Jew whose socks were not only torn but he smelled so horrible that I could not pray. Either you end this new custom of allowing Polish Jews to stand as kohanim or I quit.

Max Kugelman

Shlomo's father wrote back to him:

Dear Mr. Kugelman:

Thank you for your letter. I was expecting a letter from you. But the letter I had hoped you would write said: "Dear Rabbi: Yesterday in shul, my heart opened as I noticed my neighbor who was standing next to me. He must have been so poor he could not afford to bathe or buy new socks for the holiday. I thought I have so much. How can I help this man? If his socks are torn, maybe his heart it also aches. Tell me, Rabbi, what can I do?

Rabbi Naftali Carlebach

When Mr. Kugelman received this letter, he wept. Then he went to the rabbi with a check and said, "Forgive me. Thank you for teaching me to be a Jew."

Provenance: Peninnah Schram made contact in the late eighties with a conference center in northern Westchester, NY, where the New York Storytelling Community held a conference called *Stories: The Voice of Peace.* It took place October 14-16, 1988. I told this story at that time. I first heard Shlomo Carlebach tell this story about his father three months earlier on July 1, 1988.

Diane Wolkstein was a member of Shlomo Carlebach's *shul* from 1968 to 1994. She wrote *Treasures of the Heart: Holiday Stories that Reveal the Soul of Judaism* after Shlomo's death and dedicated the volume to him. Another of her Jewish books is *Esther's Story.* A performance of stories and songs that Shlomo and Diane did together at the American Museum of Natural History in 1994 was made into the DVD: *Celebrating Our Mistakes.* Diane tells stories of both *Chassidic* and Biblical origin. (www.dianewolkstein.com)

The Girl Who Told Stories
by Steve Zeitlin

"What remains of a story after it is finished?"
—Elie Wiesel, "Another Story," Sages and Dreamers

Once there was a girl who told stories. She told stories in the village squares, in the town halls, and around the kitchen table. She gathered tales from women with withered faces, from old men, and from ancient manuscripts with yellowing pages. When the girl who told stories was a small child, her mother, listening to her tales, called them fibs, but the young girl would not desist. In fact, many of her tales were passed on from her father, a cantor, and from her grandmother, a boundless source of proverbs and folktales.

As she grew up, the girl who told stories spread the news, arranged marriages, and even healed the sick with stories. She became known far and wide for her tales. Even her parents—who might have wished her to marry a wealthy man—came to believe that she was doing God's work. They came to realize that those "lies" she told were the truth.

Tale-telling paid very little in her time, and often she earned only enough to sustain her fragile frame. But she learned to live on stories, even to thrive on them.

As the young woman came of age, a pall fell over the land. People in the towns and villages began to talk of the "modern world."

"Your stories are old-fashioned," they told her. New forms of entertainment were introduced each year, until no one listened to stories any more. The girl who told stories often waited hours for a crowd to gather. Each year she traveled further into the countryside in search of villages still untouched by this so-called modernity. But soon, she encountered the same indifference in every village and town.

Even worse, the girl who told stories could find no one who could tell her a story she hadn't already heard. Without new stories to tell, her tale-telling dwindled. Most of the villagers had heard all of her tales, some more than a dozen times. She searched for new stories among the rabbis and priests, and for folktales from the fishermen, cobblers, seamstresses, and tailors.

"I have heard that tale before," she found herself saying, time and again.

The girl who told stories returned to the land of her father. In her home village, sadness fell over the town. Even the old stories failed to engage the children. The market was crowded with villagers bargaining for lower prices, but rarely sharing the tales that had once been the staple of the town. The spirit of storytelling was dying.

At last, the girl who told stories lay in her bed, pale as a ghost, and frightfully thin in her small house adjoining the village square. She was surrounded by friends and family and well-wishers. They were despondent, not having a single story with which to comfort her.

In the woods above her village, there lived an old woman from the hills. She did not worship or socialize with the townspeople. She had a wizened face and tattered clothes. Many thought her a witch. She had not visited the town for more than 30 years, and her appearance that day at the bedside of the girl who told stories frightened the townspeople. She carried with her a walking stick, carved with faces of cobblers and tailors, brides and grooms, undertakers and mothers—all talking to one another with animated expressions.

"It's a curse," exclaimed the fish-seller.

"It's the sign of death," called the peddler.

"She's a witch," cried another.

But the girl who told stories quieted them all.

"No," she said. "Give her a chance."

Then the old woman from the hills began to speak.

"Take this walking stick," she said. "It is a gift from me. With it, you will find the strength to travel one more time. Go down to the river, and there, in a small cove, you will find a wood canoe. Sail to where the river meets the sea. On the horizon you will see an island. On that island is a lake, and at the center of the lake is a tiny isle, like a tale within a tale. On that isle is an ancient oak. Within that oak, there is a duck, and beneath the duck there is an egg. Break the egg, and you shall find all the tales you seek."

"Insanity!" cried the fish-seller.

But the girl's cheeks began to blossom as she took the walking stick in her hand. Suddenly, she had her strength back. The girl who told stories set forth for that island, and then for the lake, and then for the isle. With her last ounce of strength, she hobbled to the oak tree. Reaching into an opening in the tree, she grasped the duck, and beneath the duck, she found the egg. Exhausted, she broke the egg. And inside the egg she found…nothing. Not even a yoke. Nothing.

She collapsed onto the grass. Just then the face of old woman from the hills appeared before her.

"I have found nothing," said the girl.

"I have followed you here," said the woman from the hills, "over the sea to the island and the lake. I needed to make sure you would be safe."

"But I have found nothing."

"You must hold the shell up to the light," said the old woman from the hills. As the sun rose on the isle, the girl held a piece of shell up to the light and found on engraved on it a few words written in small letters.

She read aloud, "Once there was a girl who told stories."

"That is my story," she told the woman from the hills, repeating again, "Once there was girl who told stories."

And so her story began again. For life itself is a tale that is told, from generation to generation.

Provenance: Peninnah Schram wrote a book called *Stories within Stories*, and we have spoken on a number of occasions about tales within tales. As a teller of tales myself, I also didn't hesitate to incorporate a favorite folktale image that I gleaned from Joseph Campbell, who, in turn, gleaned it from Sir James George Frazer's *The Golden Bough.* It's about the search for a secret hidden within an egg within a duck within an oak. In the words of Roald Dahl, "Watch with glittering eyes the whole world around you because the greatest secrets are always hidden in the most unlikely places."

Steve Zeitlin is a folklorist, filmmaker, writer, and cultural activist. He is the founding director of City Lore, which fosters New York City's and America's living cultural heritage. Steve received his Ph.D. in Folklore and Folklife from the University of Pennsylvania. He is a commentator for public radio, and the author of many books on America's folk culture, among them *Because God Loves Stories: An Anthology of Jewish Storytelling,* and *City Play, A Celebration of American Family Folklore.* Steve has documented, recorded and fallen in love with carnival pitches, children's rhymes, family stories, subway stories, ancient cosmologies, and oral poetry traditions from around the world.

III

Celebrating Sacred Time
Mitzvot of *Shabbat* and Holidays

Light
by Yisroel Bernath

It was the summer of 2001, and I was finding my seat on an Egged bus headed to Tzefat. To my left sat an elderly Ethiopian gentleman; the morning sun protruding from the window cast shadows on his face. His cane leaned against his leg, and a broad smile welcomed me for the next three or so hours. I returned the smile.

"So," which seemed like a good way to make conversation, "maybe you have a story you can share with me?"

"A story?" He was clearly puzzled, unsure how to stereotype the young, red-bearded, black-hat-wearing rabbi sitting beside him.

"You must have a story to share with the next generation."

Like an enlightened philosopher, his eyes lit up and his words began to flow:

There was once a king who was growing older in years, and he couldn't figure out which one of his three children would be the one to assume the throne and rule the kingdom.

His eldest son was strong and brave, a warrior and leader. His middle son was brilliant, quick and witty; he could outsmart just about anyone. His youngest child, his daughter, was young, very young. He loved them all equally and wanted each of them to take over the throne.

He thought and thought and finally came up with an idea. In the middle of the picturesque royal garden, there sat a small shack.

"Whoever can fill the shack to capacity," the king exclaimed, "will take over my throne." Each child would have seven days to fill the shack with anything they chose.

The oldest child decided to go first. His siblings watched as he lugged stones and rocks of all shapes and sizes and tossed them into the shack. Day after day he carried the heavy loads. When there was no room left, he filled the cracks and crevices with small pebbles, to fill the room to capacity. At the end of the week, the king walked down the winding, narrow path that led into the garden and reached out to open the door of the shack.

"My son," the king said as he smiled, "you have filled the shack to capacity; you may be the next king." He then ordered his servants to empty the shack.

The middle son, the smartest and fastest, took his turn to try to outwit his brother. The others watched as he ran back and forth from the chicken coop to the shack, carrying bags and bags full of feathers, dumping the feathers into the shack, time after time. When there was no room in the shack, he jumped on the feathers to make room for more. Before long, the entire shack was filled to capacity with feathers and so was the rest of the garden.

At the end of the week, the king came walking down the winding, narrow path that led into the garden. The entire garden looked white as snow. The king reached out his hand and opened the door.

"You have surpassed your brother," the king exclaimed. "With the rocks there were still little holes left over in the crevices. With the feathers, however, you have managed to fill the room to capacity. You may be the next king." Once again he ordered his servants to empty the shack.

It was now the youngest child's turn. The brothers pleaded with their father not to let her compete or at least to wait until she was older.

"She doesn't understand, father. This is the whole kingdom on her shoulders," they declared.

The king would not hear of it.

"You each got your turn; now it's hers."

The first day passed, and the shack was empty. The second day, the shack was still empty. The third day, still nothing had changed. By now the townspeople had heard of the competition and began crowding around the palace, wondering what the princess had planned.

The fourth day passed, and the shack was still empty. The brothers continued to plead with their father.

"She is making a mockery of the throne."

The king just waited.

The fifth and sixth days passed and the shack remained empty. On the seventh day, the king slowly walked down the winding, narrow path that led into the scenic garden. Only this time he was not alone. Scores and scores of people followed behind him, wondering and waiting for what would be.

The king reached out his hand to open the shack. People pushed and shoved to try to get a view. A stillness passed over the crowd. The door opened...and the shack was empty. Yet before a word could be uttered, the young princess passed under the arm of her father the king and headed straight into the shack. She knelt down, reached into the folds of her robes and revealed a small candlestick. She reached back into the folds of her robes and pulled out a candle. She proceeded to light the candle, and the entire shack was filled to capacity with light.

The king smiled. "You, my child, will take over my throne."

The crowd cheered. The brothers also cheered. They all lived happily ever after.

As the sun sets on Friday evening and I watch my wife light the *Shabbat* candles and utter the *brachot*, I think of that bus ride and this story. The *Shabbat* candles–they fill our homes, our lives, our souls with light. The *Shabbat* candles–they fill the world with light.

Provenance: This is a traditional tale told by the Jews and non-Jews of Ethiopia.

Yisroel Bernath is a graduate of Central Yeshivas Tomchei Temimim and a Hadassah-WISO diplomat in Structural Cognitive Modifiability. Rabbi, Jewish educator and author of three titles, he has entertained worldwide. He was the liaison responsible for Jewish Cultural Programming in Montreal public schools. His hands-on *Hanukkah* experience, *Maccabees*, was visited by over 10,000 children. Yisroel creates quality Jewish children's entertainment, thus far with Shazak, Inc, Big Bang Animation, Realtime Jewish Media and Young Avraham. Spiritual Director of the Jewish Monkland Centre-Chabad NDG and Loyola Campus. He lives in Montreal with his wife, Sara, and children Chaya, Zalmy and Leiba.

It's Crowded in My Kitchen
by Janie Grackin

My friend Ellen describes my kitchen as "the size of a postage stamp," and she might be exaggerating. It might be smaller. And cluttered. And every holiday, it's crowded in my kitchen.

I always tell my students that the place to be before any festival meal is in the kitchen. Not so that they can get any goodies before they hit the floor or are given to the dog, but because it is **there** that family happens, and memories survive, and stories are told.

From the time that I was very small and permitted to join the women in my Bubbe's kitchen, I understood that what happened there was like Las Vegas—whatever happens there, stays there. The conversations, gossip, even the foods that were eaten, never appeared at the dining room table.

And so, the kitchen became a sacred space.

And so it is in my home. Before each holiday, birthday, or festival, as the food is prepared, there is sharing and caring, laughter and tears.

We mark time by the passing of holidays and also by the empty chairs at our tables. This year Aunt Joanie is gone. Last *Rosh Hashannah*, Uncle Len was here.

My father died at *Purim*, and as we dress in costumes and read the *megillah*, we will always remember that the last time he saw my daughter, she was dressed as Queen Esther. And a few weeks later, we gathered together for the first Passover without Daddy, who always chopped the *charoset*.

And it got crowded in my kitchen.

All day long, as we peeled and prepped each item of holiday food, we remembered seasons past. Enter the memory of Bubbe, and her stories of growing up in Palestine, as she rolled each *matzah* ball between her palms and dropped them in the boiling water. And as my mother reached into the fridge, she came across the dark chocolate-covered orange peel, my father's favorite, and she began to cry as we passed the agridulce (bittersweet) candy around the kitchen. As we chewed each piece, we remembered stories of the things my father loved, and we talked of how we would miss him this year. And, of course, we ate all the candy, so our guests never saw any of it. We talked and we cried.

And we laughed! We laughed about how my father would never accept the use of the food processor machine for making anything as sacred as chopped liver or *charoset*. It always had to be done by hand, in the wooden bowl, with the round-edged chopping blade.

Who does that anymore? And who will make the *charoset* this year?

And so, a new tradition was born in our family as we passed on the secret recipe for our sefardic *charoset* to the new "man" in the house, an ex-husband, a high school friend, an out-of-town visitor.

And the kitchen got more crowded.

Last year, my daughter brought the love of her life home from London to join us for Passover, and he learned much about slavery and redemption in the time we had to prepare for the cast of thousands about to descend upon our dining room. It got more crowded in the kitchen as he learned about the "miracle" of pareve (non-dairy) whipped cream (you mean it doesn't come in a can?), the mystery of *matzah* balls, and the history of *charoset*. And, of course, stories were told, people were remembered, tears were shed, and we laughed. How we laughed! The relatives came; friends filled the room, as did flowers, candlelight, wine, music, food and the *hagaddah*.

And it was crowded in my kitchen.

So, this year, as you prepare to celebrate the holidays, invite some people into your kitchen. Bring in the neighbors to help cook and taste. Tell stories and share memories.

And always invite a stranger.

Provenance: I studied storytelling intently for many years before I went "public." One of the most impressive workshops was taught by Peninnah Schram in which she told a story about a piece of string. A piece of string! The story reminded me of my Grandmother's arriving by train for family visits with shopping bags and packages tied up with string. From this lesson, I learned the value of gathering a morsel of memory, turning it over and over, and tasting its sweetness—and then sharing it.

Janie Grackin uses the art of storytelling to inspire and educate. Janie creates programs for intergenerational populations in synagogues and schools in the United States, England and Israel, including *Being Torah Alive!*, her unique approach to teaching Torah. In 1997, she was inducted into the National Women's Hall of Fame for her commitment to AIDS education and was awarded the Solomon Schechter Gold Award for Family Education. Janie has served as national co-chair of the CAJE Jewish Storytelling Network. She was recently ordained as a rabbi. (www.janiegrackin.com)

The Wooden Axle
by Jill Hammer

One Saturday night, during the festival of *Hanukkah,* an old Jewish carpenter was trudging home from synagogue to his house up in the hills. He had lingered at *shul* to recite the *havdalah* prayers and watch the lighting of the *shul's menorah.* Then he had taken his tools from where he'd left them in a barn Friday afternoon, and gone out into the village to work for several of the evening hours, chopping firewood, repairing wooden shutters, and fixing broken toys so rich families could have a warm and happy holiday on this snowy night.

The carpenter had spent the last of his money to buy bread and wine for the Sabbath. He had no more coins to buy candles or treats for his family. He lingered at the homes of the rich folk, but none of them paid him. He had been able to beg a candle-end from the rabbi so he would at least have some light to celebrate *Hanukkah.* He knew that when he came home he would find his wife and their three little children waiting for him in the dark. They would be disappointed, but tomorrow perhaps he would be paid. Then he could buy fine candles and holiday food for them.

The carpenter passed a well. He was thirsty, but he did not draw any water because that *Hanukkah,* evening had fallen on the winter solstice. It was the custom of the Jews not to draw water on the solstice. This was because when the seasons changed, the angels changed shifts. For a moment the world was unprotected and could go any which way. If the water of the solstice tasted sweet, it was said, the coming season would be sweet, but if the water of the solstice tasted bitter, well, the coming season would hold nothing good. It was better not to drink at all. So he did not draw any water, but he did stop to rest for a moment and look at the stars.

As he stood there in the starry night, he heard the whinnying of horses. He peered into the darkness, and there was a wagon coming toward him. A woman dressed all in white was driving the wagon up the rocky path. Her hair was thick and black as the night, flecked with white from the snow. Her fine strong horse was as gray as a raincloud. Inside the wagon were many small children. They were all wide-awake, laughing and singing and crying and poking one another. She was singing too. He had never seen such a joyous sight.

As he watched, he heard a loud snap, and the wagon came to an abrupt stop. The woman jumped out and knelt down by the wagon, which now tilted to one side. The children all peered over the side of the wagon, asking questions and jostling one another for a better look. The gray horse neighed as if to ask what the problem was.

The carpenter hiked up toward the wagon. "Madam, you shouldn't be out driving on a night like this," he said to the woman. "What's happened to your wagon?"

"My children and I have been visiting dear friends," said the woman, "and now we are on our way home. But look! My wagon has broken an axle. We can't go any further. What are we going to do? I don't want my little ones to spend the night in the snow on this cold mountain."

The carpenter was eager to get home to his own family, and very reluctant to get involved with this strange wild-haired woman in the middle of the night. "If you walk down the hill, you'll find a village. The rabbi of the village is a very kind person. I'm sure he would give you and your young ones a place to stay until morning. Tomorrow I can come and fix your wagon."

"Oh, no," said the woman. "I have many, many children. Your rabbi could never find a bed for all of them. And in any case, they are tired. They could never walk the long way back to the town. Isn't there some way you could help us tonight?"

The carpenter fell silent. He noticed a log lying by the side of the road, a bough from an apple tree that had fallen last spring. It would probably do for an axle if he trimmed it, and chipped it into a cylinder shape.

"Perhaps I could help you tonight," said the carpenter. Giving a quiet sigh, he took out of his pocket the candle-end that he had meant to light for *Hanukkah.* He took a long match from another pocket and lit the candle. He handed it to the woman. She held it near him, sheltering it from the wind with her body.

The carpenter rolled the log into the path, and went to work with his knife, his axe, and his rasp, chipping away at the log until he had a smooth column shape. He propped up the wagon with stones, took away the broken axle and removed the muddy wheels, measured the wheel sockets, then rasped away at the log a bit more until the axle was finished. He fitted the rough axle to the wagon and attached the wheels. The work took him a long while. The children buzzed around him, interrupting him with their questions. The horse whinnied and complained as the snow fell harder.

Finally, he was finished. His back ached, and his hands had a few new blisters. He turned to the woman. "It's not perfect, but you should make it to wherever you are going tonight."

"I'm afraid I have no money to pay you," said the woman. "But here, please take the two pieces of the broken axle, and all the wood chips." Quickly the children scrambled around, gathered up all the wood chips and stuffed them in the pockets of the astonished carpenter. The woman lifted the two pieces of the broken axle and balanced them on his shoulder. He was too startled to reply.

"Thank you for your help," the woman called as she reharnessed her horse. Then she drove off into the falling snow, the gray horse clip-clopping briskly into the darkness. The children began to sing songs and play and laugh and shove one another.

The carpenter was stiff and sore. The woman must have been crazy, and who knew where she'd stolen those children from? The carpenter stomped home, angry and tired. It was close to midnight. He dropped the pieces of broken axle in his yard; maybe they'd do for firewood. He went into the dark house, where his wife and children and his old mother were drowsing by the coals of their small fire. They wished him a *gut vokh* and asked him: "Did you bring any light for *Hanukkah?*"

"I had only a small candle, and now even that is gone," said the carpenter, and he told them the whole story. "And look, after all my trouble, all the woman paid me was woodchips." He reached into his pockets and pulled out their contents.

To his astonishment, the chips of the old log had turned to gold coins. His family couldn't believe their good fortune. They danced in a circle around the table. "A *Hanukkah* miracle!" cried the children.

"If only it weren't too late to go into the village and buy a few candles," the carpenter's wife said.

As she spoke, the farmer remembered he'd thrown the broken pieces of the axle into the yard. With a yell, he raced outside. In a dark corner he found a silver *menorah*, and a jar of olive oil to go with it. Sure he was dreaming, he carried these beautiful things into the house. The family put wicks into the oil, lit the *Hanukkah menorah*, and made *Hanukkah* together. They shredded their few potatoes and used some of the oil to make potato *latkes*.

His belly full, the carpenter sat by the fire and dreamed of what he'd do with his new wealth. His wife fell asleep while telling stories to the two dozing children. His old mother leaned forward to him and said: "Do you know who that woman was?"

"I have no idea," the carpenter said.

And this is what she told him: "On *Shabbat*, the *neshamot yeteirot*, the extra souls of all the Jews, come to visit us. On Saturday night after *havdalah*, the *Shechinah* takes our extra souls back to the Garden of

Eden to live with Her during the week. You must have seen them on their journey."

Whether that was true or whether it wasn't, the carpenter and his family never wanted for anything again. They always went out of their way to do deeds of lovingkindness, so as to deserve the miraculous gift they had received. They made especially sure always to be kind to small children, who might turn out to be souls in disguise. They never again saw the woman with her wagon, but whenever the carpenter or his family stopped to drink at the well in the woods, its water was as sweet and fresh as anyone could wish—even on the winter solstice.

Provenance: The story is based on an old German folktale. In the folktale, Perchta (a Teutonic goddess also known as Frau Holle) is driving a wagon full of children. These children are the *heimchen*, children who have died as infants. Their souls are in the care of Perchta, who watches over birth and death. Perchta's wagon breaks down, and a poor man helps her. He is rewarded with the wood-chips that resulted from his labor, but he only carries away a single wood-chip, which has turned to gold by the time he gets home:

Grimm's stories of Perchta and the heimchen captivated me. They reminded me of stories of Elijah, who often appears as a poor man in need, so that others may have the opportunity to do good deeds and be rewarded. I re-invented the story of the wooden axle to tell a tale of the *Shechinah*, the Divine Presence who dwells in exile with Her people, and the souls She watches over: the *neshamot yeteirot* or Sabbath souls. I imagined the *Shechinah* bringing the Sabbath souls to the Jewish people and then taking them home when *Shabbat* ends. The Zohar teaches that on *Shabbat*, the *Shechinah* gives new souls to all of Her people:

We ask the *sukkah* [*Shechinah*] to spread itself over us and rest upon us and protect us as a mother protects her children, so that we will feel safe on every side. When Israel...welcomes this *sukkah* of peace to their homes as a holy guest, the holy Divine presence comes down and spreads Her wings over Israel like a mother embracing her children. This *sukkah* of peace grants new souls to Her children, for all souls have their home in her. [Zohar I, 48a]

In my story, Perchta becomes the *Shechinah*, the *heimchen* are the Sabbath souls, and the countryman is a Jewish carpenter. Like Perchta, the *Shechinah* has a wagon, and the wagon breaks at just the right spot for a poor Jew to do a mitzvah. The carpenter meets the *Shechinah* on *Hanukkah*, on the day of the winter solstice, a time when the *Machzor*

Vitry tells us that one should not draw water from wells because spirits are around. The story takes place on *Hanukkah* and the solstice in order to remind us of how light comes out of darkness, and also because the winter solstice was Perchta's holiday, and this story was originally hers.

Rabbi Jill Hammer, PhD, is the Director of Spiritual Education at the Academy for Jewish Religion. She is also the co-director of the Kohenet Institute, a program in women's sacred leadership, and the founder of Tel Shemesh, a website and community celebrating Jewish traditions connected with the earth (www.telshemesh.org). Rabbi Hammer is the author of two books: *The Jewish Book of Days* (Jewish Publication Society, 2006) and *Sisters at Sinai: New Tales of Biblical Women* (Jewish Publication Society, 2001). She is an essayist, poet, and *midrashist.* Her poems, stories, and essays have been published in many journals, newspapers, websites, and anthologies, including *The Forward, Lilith, www.MyJewishLearning.com, The Women's Torah Commentary,* and *Zeek Magazine.*

The Dress: A Purim Fairy Tale
by Amichai Lau-Lavie

The dress, blue and billowing, appeared out of nowhere and vanished right back. Maybe it never really existed? The facts don't matter much. This is a different kind of knowing. The dress, a perfect fit, taught me the most unusual and subtle of Jewish commandments: Know yourself by transforming yourself: turn reality upside down, silly and sacred, for just one day a year. A mask of sorts, the dress transformed me into another, teaching me how to be my very self by being, briefly, not myself at all.

"On the holiday of *Purim*," instructs the Talmud, "one must be sufficiently intoxicated so as not to know the difference between the evil Haman and the righteous Mordechai" [BT Megillah 7b].

As far as the rigid system of Jewish laws goes, this is a wild card, obligating the pious to step beyond the safe and ordinary codes of conduct, endorsing chaos and the blurring of boundaries. The commandment originates in the Biblical scroll of Esther, echoing the moment in which the tables are turned and the Jewish would-be-victims seize control: "*ve'nahpoch hu*"—upside down, topsy-turvy, and transgression as a state of mind. *Purim* commemorates this mythic moment with an obligatory annual day of celebration, complete with drinking beyond capacity and dressing up. It's a complicated commandment, rarely fully obeyed.

It was always my favorite. From an early age—as young as five years old—I'd wait for *Purim*. As soon as *Yom ha-Kippurim* was over, I'd start planning my costumes. The masks and make-believe, the fabrics of fabrication, this carnival of imagination, gave me permission to play, to pretend, to paint outside the rigid lines of religious regulations.

Only many years later I would learn how deeply connected *Purim* and *Yom ha-Kippurim* are—each offering the human soul another attempt at change and transformation. But as a child I cared only for the shiny fabrications of self: a medieval troubadour in green velvet, Dr. Doolittle with stuffed animals pinned to my hat, a British Palace Guard, an astronaut. But mostly, and most often, I'd dress as a girl: my cousin Rachel, Mary Poppins, an old Russian *babushka*, a bride. There was that time I dressed as a princess, and went with mother and a basket of chocolate-covered strawberries to visit Tante Jenny in her nursing home nearby. She held court in her immaculate tiny lounge, barely seeing, wrapped in a floor-length evening gown, silvery and shining, from those days in Berlin, wrapped in a fur, dripping with diamonds. Her fragile friends, in jewels and ball gowns, sat around her, sipping cognac from crystal goblets, laughing a lot and loving my costume. That was her last *Purim*. And that was the last time I was permitted to wear a dress on *Purim*.

"You are a big boy now," mother explained as she drove us back home. I was nine. "Enough is enough."

There is another commandment, a religious law, prohibiting cross-dressing. It is perfectly clear: "A woman must not wear the garments of a man, nor may men wear the dress of a woman—these are abominations" [Deuteronomy 22:5].

But somehow, sometimes, the forbidden blurs, as commandments collide, crossing over the invisible boundaries of proscribed and prohibited, familiar and feared. And there, and then, in that no man's land of legal obscurity, the threshold of *Purim*, is when the dress appeared, twice in a lifetime, shaking things up.

It was blue, crisp cotton, with white polka dots, puffy short sleeves, and a full skirt, and it showed up in the costume box, just like that, on the day before *Purim*, a few months after Tante Jenny died. The costume box was a large trunk, stationed along the wall in our backyard, next to the plum tree. Lace curtains became veils inside that box, and ragged rags turned to magic cloaks. On Saturday mornings, after we came back from synagogue, the box would open and we would play: bull fights with Gypsy the dog, weddings under the grand piano.

I hadn't seen this dress before but somehow knew it once belonged to my mother. I vaguely remembered a black and white photograph of her as a very young woman, smiling, radiant, lit by a Mediterranean sun, a dark dress with white dots tight on her body.

Slippers appeared, too: Black, pointy, with low heels, open at the back. I slipped them on, and wore the dress, and trotted out into the street, one hand pinching the hem of the dress, the other clutching the black velvet skullcap, which I had taken off. It was mid-afternoon, and the streets were quiet and empty as I made my way, heels clicking on the pavement, off to meet my friends at a pre-*Purim* party. The walk was long, and I remember the heat and the quiet, an occasional glance from a passing driver slowing down, a figure in a window pulling curtains aside to get a better look. I remember the shame, and the sinking feeling in my stomach that something was terribly wrong and that nothing was the same as it used to be or would be again.

No other costumes were worn that day at my friend's house. One of the girls put on make-up; another one wore a large beret. None of the boys wore costumes. Except me. There's a photograph: we are all on the street, in front of Tami's house. One of the girls is holding two fingers behind some boy's head. Everyone is laughing. I'm sitting on the floor, slightly off to the side, legs stretched ahead, hands leaning back and tongue sticking out at the camera, black slippers off, but visible in the frame. Were there tears? Did I walk home alone? I don't remember. Mother was right. Enough was enough. It was the last time I put on a costume for *Purim*, of any sort at all. *Purim* became insignificant, minor, and somewhat tolerable. And with time, the same attitude took over my religious life: practiced, but not with fervor. Nothing was as it used to be.

And then, twenty years later, she returned.

It was the morning before *Purim*. I opened my closet, at home in downtown New York City, to get dressed for work. An unfamiliar shape and color caught my eye. A dress, blue, billowing, with white polka dots, was hanging, simply, among my suits.

I didn't question its existence or origin. It smelled faintly of familiar perfume. And it fit just right. That night I wore it to the synagogue, dressing up for the first time in all those years. There may have been shoes, too, or make-up, perhaps a wig. The scroll of Esther was chanted; the music started. I danced, carefully at first. We were laughing a lot, and sipping cognac from flasks and, later, crystal goblets. Free to be someone else, I was more myself than ever before. The dress was just a garment, but I wore it on the inside, too.

I wore it the next day too, visiting friends for *Purim* feasts, giggling, giddy, delivering little baskets of chocolate-covered strawberries, Hershey kisses, bottles of wine. She slowly emerged—a wise widow, teaching and preaching deep secrets I did not know I knew—yet all who listened loved and wanted more. *Purim* was back—a carnival of colors, a masquerade of myth and magic, permission to ponder and penetrate secrets, to peel off a mask and wear another, or perhaps, none at all. At some point I walked up a staircase, hearing the click-clack of high heels on marble, the familiar sound of my mother, aunts, grandmother, coming up to tuck me in and say goodnight. The heels were mine, but whose were the memories? I paused on the staircase, breathless with the knowledge that I was them, all of them, understood them for the first time, and knew who I was and why I loved them, and loved myself, just as I was, perhaps, again, for the very first time.

And then, at dusk, I took the dress off in the bathroom, hanging it up before changing back into the ordinary. It was left alone in the bathroom for just a moment when the fire began. Was it the candle that caught on cotton? Was there a candle at all? When I ran back, in stockings, smoke filled the bathroom and soon the apartment, and the alarm was wailing and the dress was gone.

No photographs were taken that day, and no tears spilled. But the singed smell lingered in the bathroom, like mystery, like loss. Fact or fiction? Was there really a dress at all? *Ad lo yada*—the commandment of *Purim* is to not know at all, and none of this is about real knowledge, hard facts. It doesn't really matter. *Purim* has never been the same again, nor have I. She wrapped me tightly, blue and perfect, reminding me to live and learn and laugh and love and care for the most complex of all commandments, Jewish, human, timeless: know yourself to know the other—become yourself, with all true colors of compassion, polka dots, permission, tears and fears and courage: at least one day a year.

Amichai Lau-Lavie, founding director of STorahtelling, Inc. is an Israeli-born teacher of Judaic Literature. He has studied at Har Etzion, the Shalom Hartman Institute and the Elul Center in Jerusalem. He has written and/or performed with the Theatre Company Jerusalem, The Acco Theatre Group and the Avodah Dance Ensemble. Amichai has served as Artist-in-Residence at Congregation B'nai Jeshurun and as a Jerusalem Fellow at the Mandel Leadership Institute, as consultant to the Reboot Network, and as a member of the Synagogue 3000 Leadership Network, the Advisory Council for the Six Points Fellowship, the Advisory Board for Faithhouse Manhattan, and the Board of Directors of Nehirim. (www.sTorahtelling.org)

The First Light
by Doug Lipman

Suddenly, they were coming.

I looked out into the square of our village and saw the dust rising above the wagon carrying the king's emissary. People ran in all directions looking for places to hide.

I heard someone say, "They will come door to door," and another, "They will make us pray in front of pigs!"

Some stood nervously by as though trying to decide, "Should I pray before the idols and unclean flesh, or be killed? What will the others do?"

But I felt strangely calm, as though I had somehow known that this moment was coming. Up to now, though, I had only thought, "We in our village will stay with the old, holy ways, even if those in the cities turn aside from the Law. They will surely be punished."

When the order came, first in Greek, then in Aramaic, to assemble in the square, I followed it. I watched them unload the altar from the wagon and erect it—not indoors, protected, as an altar should be, but in the open air. I watched Yannuh, son of Jacob, always the first to appease the powerful, walk up to the altar and begin to pronounce the heathen words. In my head I heard only, over and over again, words like a song: "This is the first turning point. Then comes the moment when it is your turn, and you refuse. Then you die."

A great shriek interrupted the words in my head. There stood Mattathias, his neck bulging with rage, his knife drawn. Suddenly Yannuh, son of Jacob, lay across that filthy altar, bleeding.

A cry of rage came from my throat, too. I willed Mattathias's knife into the chest of the king's envoy, and I danced with the others around his fallen body, stamping his blood into the earth, forcing it down beneath the clean, white sand.

Then we were on our way to the mountains, freed by our rage, stamping a new music with our sure, determined feet.

It was soon night in the mountains. The others were asleep, except for the watch. Around my goatskin shelter, the wind sang the commandments: "You shall not bow down to them or worship them."

The song was steady and proud.

"Whoever sacrifices to any god but the Lord shall be put to death."

But then the rocks themselves added a shrill accompaniment to the song: "You shall not commit murder."

A great trembling came over me.

The next night, we went further into the mountains. We were fugitives now.

That night I couldn't sleep. I climbed higher up into the mountains. I found myself standing at the highest place I had ever been.

I saw countless stars. With my eyes, I outlined the shape of the earth against the night sky. And then I saw a glow...as though a star had fallen and lay on the earth. Coming closer, I saw that the glow came from a cave.

In front of the cave sat a man, dressed as a simple nomad. Was he a spy? His eyes met mine. Something in his gaze drew me to him.

"One of you has come," he said. "Only one, out of so many, has been drawn to this holy light. Do you wish to know what light this is? Do you care? But I should not be harsh with you. It is the others, who have not come here, who deserve harshness. Do you wish to hear my story? Sit down."

I sat down before him. Was he a prophet or a fool?

"On the first day of creation, God created light. On the fourth day, God created the sun and the moon. So the light on the first day was not the light of the sun. What light was it? It was this light, this great, primal light, that glows from this cave. With this light, Adam could see from one end of the earth to the other.

"When Adam sinned, God knew that others would follow who would use the light for evil. So God took the light away. But whenever God destroys something, God keeps some portion of it hidden away, undefiled.

"This is the light that shone to honor Methuselah, who was so holy that God refused to let any sinners die while the world mourned him, lest the mourning for him be sullied. While this light shone during the first twenty-four hours after his death, no other person could die.

"The light shone again on the birth of Moses. But when Moses went to live in the house of the Pharaoh, the light could not follow him there. He only found the primal light again when he climbed Sinai.

"And this is the light that will shine at the end of all time. God will say to me, 'Elijah, blow the trumpet!' I will blow one blast on Michael's trumpet, and the light will be released throughout the world. At the second blast, the dead will awaken. At the third blast..."

For some reason, I believed him. I believed that he was Elijah. I listened to his stories through the night. Just when the night was darkest, he said to me, "You alone have come here. You alone have listened. I will grant you one use of the light. What do you want?"

I thought of how our little band would have to run from one hiding place to another, always pursued by the king's soldiers.

I said, "Let the light shine so that all things that have ever been lost on the surface of the earth will be visible. Let me see all the hiding places that have never been found."

Before I finished speaking, it came to pass. I saw them all. And so our fugitive band went from one hiding place to another, until we had no more need of them.

Four years passed. Things changed greatly. Old Mattathias died; his son, Judah, became the head of a great army, which defeated the armies unleashed by Antiochus and his successors.

Now it was no longer against the royal law to follow the Torah. But Judah had not stopped fighting. He said, "The rich Jews in the city have betrayed us. The pretenders to the priestly caste are our adversaries. Those who call themselves Jews but do not obey the Torah are traitors. We will seek them out and destroy them."

With Judah victorious, obeying the Torah was compulsory: those who did not follow it would be put to death. Our forces went from town to town, taking captives. We compelled those who had called themselves Jews but had abandoned the old ways, to obey the Law.

Many were the times when I held a baby, and someone else held back the protesting mother while the baby was circumcised, as the Law requires.

Our ranks swelled. We were no longer just a band of fugitives, but an armed force. On one foray, we camped near that same mountain where I had spent my first night as a fugitive. I climbed it again, looking for the cave. I found it. The old man was still there.

"You've come back. Now you have stories to tell me. And yes, I will grant you another use of the light."

I said to him only, "Let that primal light shine forth like lightning. Let it show where our enemies are among us, that we may find them and be avenged— and blot their memory from the earth."

Without looking at me, without smiling, the old man turned away. But it was so. We traveled from one place to another, destroying the threat inside our nation.

For we were a nation now. As the years passed, we became a force to be reckoned with in the world. We formed foreign alliances. But we learned that, having drawn and wielded the sword, we could not easily put it down. When our new allies made enemies, those nations became our enemies as well. So we were invaded from all sides and forced to fight back. We allied ourselves with the Romans, and three thousand of us went out to fight in their wars.

In the early years, we had taken only enough spoils for our needs. Now when we took a city, we plundered. We took booty for the pleasure of it.

One city refused to surrender to us, in spite of the authority granted to us by the Roman emperor. So we laid siege to the city and then put it to the torch, ignoring the screams of the dying. When the fires cooled, we poured into the charred city, looking for gold and jewels. I broke down the door to a house, and came upon a door to a hidden room!

When I forced the door open, I found not treasure but a living human face. I took out my knife, determined to end its life swiftly. But when I raised my hand to strike, I saw on that face a look, not of terror, but of calm. A strange sort of calm, as though to say, "This is the first turning point. Then comes the moment when I die."

The next thing I knew, I was running, my knife left behind, all the booty left behind. I tried to leave that face behind, too, but I could not. For three days I ran. All that time, the face followed me.

I found myself back at the mountain. I climbed, and there was the old man, still sitting in front of the glowing cave.

He spoke to me. "These stories are almost too painful to tell. Yet they must be heard. Tell them all."

I told him of the battles, the plunder, the burned cities. At last I told him about the face filled with calm.

I said, "I do not even know what I ask of you. Once, I nearly let enemies ravish the altar of my heart and steal my strength. I have run away. I have killed—in self-defense, but also for revenge and even for greed. I have allowed the altar of my heart to become impure with the blood of those I have killed."

When I had finished, Elijah looked at me. "This is the greatest use you have requested. And this, too, will be given to you.

"The greatest miracle of *Hanukkah*, then, will not be the victories, miraculous though they were; for a victory can be overturned.

"The greatest miracle of *Hanukkah* will not be that the Jews will survive, although that, too, will be a great miracle. For the Jews might survive but, over time, become ever more like Antiochus.

"The greatest miracle will be that, once a year throughout the ages, your spiritual descendants will light the smallest candles. And in those candles will shine the great primal light that shone on the first day of creation.

"If any of your descendants are drawn to that light, if they are open to it, then it will shine in through their eyes and onto the altars of their hearts, illuminating for them those parts of themselves that are still undefiled."

Provenance: I was alone in my office one night. I had a fever and knew I should go to bed, but I was struggling to create a story about the Maccabees' rebellion celebrated at *Hanukkah*. Without warning, a voice began to speak in my mind. For the next minutes, I "took dictation," typing frantically, trying not to miss a word. Surely, it was my fever talking. But I had the eerie feeling that I was actually hearing an eyewitness's voice, somehow translated through the intervening millennia.

Doug Lipman told his first story to emotionally disturbed adolescent boys in 1970. After a few seconds, they fell into a listening trance. Ever since, Doug has pursued connection through storytelling—as a performer, coach, and award-winning author and recording artist. His many CDs include his Jewish mystical epic, *The Soul of Hope*, (www.soulofhope.com). He has authored books, instructional videos, and multi-media toolkits like the *Storytelling Workshop in a Box* (www.storytellingworkshopinabox.com). His model for storytelling coaching has spread internationally and he offers a free email newsletter, *eTips from the Storytelling Coach*. (www.storydynamics.com)

The Moon's Garment
by Cindy Rivka Marshall

One evening, as *Shabbat* drew to a close, people gathered outdoors to look for the first stars to appear. To their amazement, they overheard this conversation between the Moon and the Sun.

"Will you look at all those people, gazing up at the sky," said the Moon. "It's an honor that they measure their months by my light, but they have no idea how cold I am up here in the night sky!"

"Oh, Moon! A little cool air sounds awfully good to me. I'm always so hot!" exclaimed the Sun.

"Yes," the Moon replied. "I appear now and then during the day, just to warm up. But Sun, you never visit me at night, so you just can't imagine. I'm shivering up here."

"Oh, Moon, I'm sorry you are so cold. Listen, I'm not the one who decided who should be where in the sky. God put us here, and made me the greater light. Nothing I can do about that," teased the Sun.

"Oh, Sun, let's not start that old argument again," the Moon complained.

"I must say, it is too bad you're feeling cold," the Sun said reassuringly. "Do you see how the people down there wear clothing to keep warm? Why don't you put something on already? Go get a sweater, a blanket, a coat."

"But Sun, I don't have a thing to wear!" the Moon said.

"Well, there are a lot of skilled tailors in the land below. Maybe in time for the next New Moon, they could make something for you to wear, to keep you warm," the Sun suggested.

"What an idea! I hope they will," the Moon called out.

Well, the very next morning the tailors all got together and talked about it.

"Did you hear that?" asked one. "Skilled tailors in the land below. That's us!"

"What, we don't have enough work to do already?" asked another. "Now we're taking orders from the Sun?"

A third tailor pointed out, "How would we measure? The moon is forever changing size. And what material would we use?"

The tailors concluded there was no way to fashion a garment for the moon, and looking skyward, they shook their heads and shrugged apologetically.

The seamstresses got together that morning, too. "Why didn't the Sun ask us to make clothing for the Moon?" asked one. "I think we should do it."

"I think we should, too, but I don't know how," said another.

"We know how to make clothing for people, but the tailors are right. There's no way to make clothing for the Moon," claimed a third.

But there was one seamstress, named Leiba, who did not give up so easily. At the beginning of each month, on *Rosh Chodesh*, when the moon was dark in the sky, there was a gathering just for women. This gave Leiba a special connection to the Moon, and she spoke up passionately. "If the Moon is too cold, then something is not right in the world, and it is up to us to do something about it. It seems to me that the Moon is like the Jewish people, except we have the Torah to protect us through the winters of our exile. But the Moon needs a garment to keep warm. I believe that if I search, I could find a way to make clothing for the Moon."

Leiba's friends, the seamstresses who worked in her shop, were impressed by her determination, and they assured her that if she found some kind of material that could somehow grow larger and smaller to fit any size, they would help her make a garment for the Moon.

The next day, after work, Leiba went walking out into the hills and came upon a farm where the sheep were being shorn, and the wool was being spun into yarn. Leiba thought, "If I wove that yarn very loosely, it would stretch into a big blanket." She worked on it that evening and then brought it back to the other seamstresses in her shop.

At first there was excitement. They said, "Yes, look at how it stretches. But will it get small enough?"

Leiba said, "If you put wool in hot water, it shrinks." She tried it, and sure enough, the blanket became much smaller. Her friends said, "Well, that's good, but what about when the moon gets big again?"

They pulled on either side, but the shrunken blanket did not grow any larger. That idea was not going to work.

The day after that, Leiba finished her work early and went walking down by the sea. She watched as the fishermen were tying knots in rope to make nets. When they cast out the nets on the water, the nets stretched out large. As they pulled them back in again, the nets looked smaller. Leiba went over and asked a fisherman, "Could I borrow one of your nets? I'd like to show it to my friends." He agreed, so she brought it back to the shop.

The seamstresses went outdoors and stood in a big circle, holding the net.

"Yes, yes, look how large it stretches." Then, when they walked towards each other, the net grew smaller. "But it is so heavy," they said. "How could we ever lift this up and toss it high enough into the sky to give to the moon?" They looked sadly at Leiba, and she said, "I know, this idea isn't going to work either."

Several days went by. Leiba sat in her shop and sewed clothing and did not have any more ideas about how to solve this problem. One evening, after she put her work down, she walked outside. On the horizon she could see a full moon, swollen and orange, rising in the sky. Without even thinking about where she was going, she walked towards the Moon, and at the edge of town, she kept walking, into the woods.

It was darker under the trees, and Leiba slowed down as she stepped through the undergrowth. Then she noticed a flicker of light dancing through the trees, and she followed it until she came to a clearing. There she saw a woman of breath-taking beauty, wearing a white dress. As Leiba watched, she saw the hem of the dress catch on a rock, and tear.

"Oh!" the woman cried. "The royal gown! This has never happened before! It's unraveling!"

"The royal gown? Who are you?" Leiba gasped.

"Oh! I am the princess. Who are you?"

"My name is Leiba. I live in the village. I know how to sew. Can I help you fix your dress?"

"I don't think a needle and thread will fix this. Here, take a look," said the princess. The princess held out the hem of her dress, and Leiba took it carefully in her hands. She pulled a loose thread on the hem, and it unraveled and seemed to dissolve into thin air. This was no ordinary fabric. It seemed to glow as if made of light.

Just at that moment, the Moon rose in the sky, illuminating the clearing in the woods. With eyes closed, the princess raised her face to the full moon. The moonbeam came streaming down and touched the gown. Leiba watched in wonder as the fabric glowed even brighter. As Leiba held out the end of the gown, the princess turned, and together, they held all surfaces of the gown in the moonlight. It seemed like the gown was growing, that the fabric was being repaired by the moonlight. They turned it and turned it again. And the gown was whole.

"Leiba! You helped me repair the royal gown, and you have helped to repair the world."

A bit of light caught Leiba's eye. There was a scrap of fabric stuck on the rock. She picked it up and held it in the moonbeam, and it, too, began to grow. "May I have this?" she asked. "I believe this is just what I have been looking for."

"Of course," the princess agreed.

"Would you hold this end?" Leiba asked again.

And once more, as the two women held the fabric from the gown in the moonbeam, it grew and grew into a large cloth.

Leiba closed her eyes, thinking, "With this I will make a garment for the moon."

The next thing Leiba knew, she was back home, opening her eyes, and it was morning. She had a moment of confusion, thinking it had been only a dream. But then, looking down, she saw the glowing material in her hands. She took it right away to show her friends at the shop.

The seamstresses all exclaimed, "It's so light and see how it grows larger and gets smaller!"

By the time of the next New Moon, the garment was ready. A group of women gathered under the stars for *Rosh Chodesh*. As the women sang, Leiba thought she glimpsed the princess in their midst. And then she understood. The princess was the *Shechinah*, the feminine aspect of God. The faces of the women glowed as if reflecting the light of the royal gown. Surely the princess was present among them.

Then Leiba and her friends, the seamstresses, stood in a circle, and they stretched out the clothing they had made to keep the moon warm. And they began to circle, and to spin and spin around. Lifting the cloth high above their heads, they offered up this garment to the Moon: and she tried it on. She was just a tiny sliver, but it fit her perfectly.

The Sun took one look and couldn't help exclaiming, "Moon, I must say, you look marvelous. It's you!"

"Thank you. It was an excellent suggestion, Sun. And those women did come through for me. I'm grateful they believed it was possible—with a little help from *Shechinah*."

All through that month, through each phase of the Moon, the women watched. She waxed large and full and then waned to a small crescent again, but each night her clothing fit her perfectly.

To this day, the Moon wears this garment. She is no longer cold in the night sky. She smiles down at the people below, wearing her garment with pride and joy, for, after all, it was fashioned out of her own light.

Provenance: The dialogue between the Sun and the Moon refers to their legendary competition over which one is the greater light. See the *BT Hullin 60b* for a rabbinic explanation of Genesis 1:16, which I recorded on the CD, *By the River: Women's Voices in Jewish Stories.* This approach to the story originated with Rabbi Nachman of Breslov (1772 -1810), a *Chassidic* rabbi known for his storytelling. However, only the beginning—a fragment of a story—was written down by his scribe, Rabbi Nathan of Nemirov. Howard Schwartz wove this fragment into whole cloth and published his story in *Miriam's Tambourine: Jewish Folk Tales from Around the World.*

For this story I am indebted to Howard Schwartz, although this version is a significant departure from his. I changed the protagonist from a tailor to a seamstress, and stitched into the tale the women's participation in the new moon ritual of *Rosh Chodesh.* I also embroidered it with the presence of *Shechinah*, the feminine aspect of God. Many of the symbol-laden fairy tales told by Rabbi Nachman of Breslov have the *Shechinah* represented by a princess character. As I created this story, I liked the idea of the Princess appearing to help Leiba, and Leiba helping the Princess, along with helping the Moon. I turned this story many times before this telling came to light, so to speak.

Cindy Rivka Marshall is a professional storyteller who performs Jewish folktales, legends, *Chassidic* stories and *midrashim* for all ages. She visits synagogues and schools across the US to share her stories and teach. Her workshops in storytelling techniques help children, parents and educators bring Jewish narratives to life. Her award-winning audio recordings include *Challah and Latkes: Stories for Shabbat and Hanukkah* and *By the River: Women's Voices in Jewish Stories.* Cindy co-chairs the Jewish Storytelling Coalition. She has an MA in Communications. A former filmmaker, her credits include *A Life of Song: A Portrait of Yiddish folksinger Ruth Rubin.* (www.cindymarshall.com)

A Story from My Teacher, Abraham Joshua Heschel
retold by Jack Riemer

Dr. Heschel grew up in Warsaw. His father was a *Chassidic rebbe* there. And when Dr. Heschel was ten years old, his father died.

The *chassid*im wanted to make him their *rebbe*, for he was a child prodigy. But he did not want to be a *rebbe*. He wanted to get to the outside world. How do you get to the outside world? By learning Polish. Jews had lived in Poland for centuries, and yet many of them barely knew the language.

He asked his mother for money with which to buy a Polish grammar book. She hesitated for two reasons. One was that they were very poor. And the other was that she understood what it meant to study Polish. She understood that it was the way into the secular world. So she was reluctant to give him money for the grammar. But she loved her child, and so she finally gave in and gave him the money.

He bought the book, and hid it under his Talmud. And within a day or two, he had learned it by heart. And so he came to her and asked if he could have money with which to buy volume two of the Polish grammar. This time she said no, not only because she could not spare the money but because she feared what might happen if he fully learned Polish.

The young boy was very upset. But then he remembered that he had one *chassid* in the *shteibel* who was very fond of him, and who was fairly wealthy. And so he ran to the synagogue in order to ask this *chassid* for the money with which to buy the second volume of the Polish grammar.

It was late Friday afternoon, and when he arrived at the *shteibel*, he found that the *chassid* had already started *Shabbos*. And yet, the young Heschel could not restrain himself. He asked this *chassid* for the money with which to buy the book that he craved.

The *chassid* said nothing. And the young Heschel said the Friday night prayers with the congregation. But his heart was not in the prayers. He was full of depression and frustration. The next morning he came to *shul*, and the same *chassid* came over to him, and handed him a book by the Kotsker Rebbe. And when the boy opened the book, money fell out.

Can you imagine the young Heschel's shock when this happened? He lived in a world in which no one handled money on *Shabbos*. He had never seen anyone touch money on *Shabbos* in his whole life! And so, of course, he did not pick up the money from the floor where it fell. In shock he said to the *chassid:* "How can you possibly give me money on *Shabbos?*"

The man, who was a Gerer *chassid*, which is a branch of Kotsk, answered:

"*Shabbos* is very important. But if a person is in *atsvus*—if a person is in depression—he cannot really observe *Shabbos*. And so I gave you the money on *Shabbos* so that you would know that you would have it after *Shabbos*. Now go enjoy the rest of the *Shabbos*."

Heschel told me that he never got over what that man did for him that day. He said to me: "This man taught me that there are priorities even within the law."

Provenance: This is a story that I heard from my teacher, Dr. Heschel, many years ago. It has stayed with me ever since I heard it, and I want to share it with you today.

Jack Riemer is a well-known rabbi, storyteller, sermon writer and essaysist. He is the co-editor of *So That Your Values Live On: A Treasury of Ethical Wills,* and the three volumes of *The World of the High Holy Days.* His prayers have frequently been set to music, and appear in the prayer books of the Conservative and Reform movements in the United States, Israel, England, and South America.

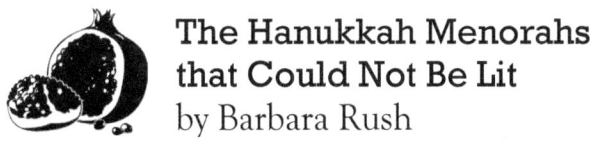

The Hanukkah Menorahs
that Could Not Be Lit
by Barbara Rush

The miracle of the oil must be proclaimed to the public. The sacred lights must be kindled in a specific order, first one light, ascending each night to eight. Lights must be separate from each other and in a row, so that no one night is more important than another.

—BT Shabbat 21b

About five years ago, in our local Jewish day school, I was teaching fourth and fifth graders how to tell stories. The tales were often written by the children themselves about something that related to class studies and/or to their lives as Jews.

At the time of this incident, the children were studying about the Holocaust, and so I invited them to bring an object from home that might relate to the subject, and to gather in my home on a Saturday night to share stories about their objects. Surprisingly, everyone brought something, and what followed was an outpouring of wonderful objects and tales. Some children brought yellowed photos of relatives, long gone, whom they and their parents had never known.

One girl proudly showed a box owned by her grandfather, who had been in the community of Shanghai Jews who had taken refuge from Eastern Europe in that city during the war. One boy clutched a teddy bear that his grandpa, then a small child, had taken out of Germany when he and his parents fled the Nazis.

All the stories were memorable and poignant. But one object, in particular, left an indelible mark on my heart. It was a *hanukkiah*, commonly called a *Hanukkah menorah*, the eight (plus-one)-branched candelabra which Jews, male and female alike, are obligated, according to Talmudic prescription, to light every year on *Hanukkah*.

And why? The lighting commemorates two events—the first, historical; the second, tied to legend. History tells us that, near Jerusalem, in the second century BCE, a small band of Jews gained religious freedom in a military victory over a mighty pagan tyrant who had defiled the Temple and forbidden the practice of Jewish life. Legend, created centuries later by the rabbis, tells us that after the victory, a divine miracle occurred: the small pitcher of oil containing only enough to last for one night lasted instead for eight, sufficient to cleanse the Temple and rededicate it to God.

Thus the eight branches—eight receptacles for light! In some times and places, these have been filled with oil and wicks; in some places, and especially in more modern times, they have been refashioned for wax candles. In addition to these eight lights, there must be one extra holder for the *shamash*, or "servant," which is detached from the body of the candelabra so that its wick can be used to light the eight others. Or, when wax candles are used, the servant candle is lit first, and then it lights the others.

The *Hanukkah menorah*, brought by my eleven-year-old student named Ben, was about seven inches high and equally as wide. Made of brass, now dulled, it certainly seemed quite old, belonging to another generation in another time and place. The metal *menorah* was shaped like the inverted concentric branches of a tree, each branch looking as fragile as a bone and as skinny as my pinky finger. The important thing was that it had eight cups, all in a row atop the eight branches, for eight wax candles. Yes, it was definitely a *hanukkiah*!

Yet something was wrong with it: there was no place for a *shamash*, for a servant candle that would light the others. Ben related its story, which I paraphrase here:

My Opa (grandfather in German) was a teenager in Germany in 1938. On November 9, the Nazis suddenly swept across the country, destroying everything Jewish. Synagogues and Jewish shops and Jewish homes were ruined. In fact, so much glass was broken on that night that it was called *Kristallnacht*, or Crystal Night, and that is what it is called today. I remember the name and the date because my grandparents, Opa and Oma, told the story so many times.

Fortunately, Opa and his family were away at the time, and so their lives were spared. But when they returned, they found almost everything gone. Sinks had been ripped from the walls, leaving a flood of water on the floor. Some things, like paintings, were just plain stolen.

But many things that the Nazis didn't want were just thrown out the window. So there in the street was a heap of rubble. Somewhere in there was the stamp collection Opa had received for his *bar mitzvah*; it was never found again. Somewhere in there was his beloved violin; it was broken beyond repair. Gone were so many family treasures!

In the days that followed, the family rummaged through the pile. They found *haggadot* that had been used at the family's *Pesach* seders for more than a century. They found love letters that Great-grandpa had written to Great-grandma in German words written in Hebrew letters.

And there, buried in the pile, was the *menorah*, which the family had used for generations to fulfill the mitzvah of lighting *Hanukkah* candles.

But something was wrong with it: the *menorah* had no *shamash*, the extra candle that lights the other eight. Where could that small piece be? Just like the stamps and the violin, it was gone forever.

Soon after that, Opa's family decided to leave Germany, and they took with them the family *haggadot*, and the love letters—and the *menorah* that they loved, even though it had no *shamash*. They could not bear to leave it behind.

That's how the *menorah* traveled through Europe, to Palestine/Israel, and eventually to America. But since that horrible night in 1938, the place for the *shamash* had remained empty.

And without a *shamash* the *menorah* could never be lit.

And so Ben ended his story.

Well, the moment Ben finished, I gave out a big *geshrai*, a loud shriek, and ran at once to my den, where I retrieved, from the hearth a small *Hanukkah menorah*, about four inches high and three inches wide, made of brass. I showed it to the class and told them this story:

My husband and I found this *menorah* in a junk shop in Krakow, Poland, in 1985. We knew at once that it was a *Hanukkah menorah*. On top, as decoration and fashioned out of brass, was the seven-branched *menorah* commanded by God to be created by Moses and carried by the Children of Israel throughout their desert wanderings. Such a *menorah* was used in the First Temple, the Temple of Solomon, and then in the Second Temple as well—a symbol of Jewish unity. This seven-branched lamp has since decorated many a *Hanukkah menorah*. Also on this little Polish *hanukkiah* were the lions of Judah, symbolizing the strength of the small Jewish army led by Judah Maccabee, a decoration which is also found on many *Hanukkah* menorahs. But, most important, there were the eight receptacles all in a row, as if on a bench, ready for the oil wicks, which would be filled and lit on *Hanukkah*. Yes, it certainly was a *hanukkiah*!

But something was wrong with it: the holder for the *shamash*, which had been screwed into the top of the *menorah*, held a tiny brass cup designed for a wax candle. Immediately, my husband and I understood that someone had made a mistake. Although the person who had affixed the holder knew that the *menorah* needed a separate place for the *shamash*, he or she did not know that a wax candle could not be used to light wicks meant for oil.

We approached the shopkeeper. "Do you know anything about this?" we asked.

"Well, it has something to do with the Jews," he replied. "That's all I know."

Who would have some information about the *menorah*? Who could help us? We decided to turn to Mr. Jacobovitz, the leader of the Jewish community who had lived in Krakow during the war, and who, only the day before, had taken us on a tour of Jewish Krakow: the corner from which Jews were taken to Auschwitz, the green grassy fields under which thousands of our people were buried, and the synagogue, now ghost-like, where thousands had prayed. Yes, surely it was Mr. Jacobovitz who would know about our little *hanukkiah*.

"Do you know anything about this *menorah*?" I asked him. "Do you know who owned it?"

"No, I don't know that," he replied. "There were so many families..."

We were disappointed but did not show it. "Mr. Jacobovitz," we said, "the *menorah* belonged to someone in your community. Surely you should have it."

The kind, elderly man thought for a moment. "No," he said emphatically, "there is a reason that you were drawn to it, so you must have it."

But what is the reason? I thought. For what purpose was I drawn to it?

Mr. Jacobovitz must have read my thoughts. "You don't know the reason now," he said, "but someday you will understand."

And so we thanked Mr. Jacobovitz and took the little *menorah*, carefully wrapped, back with us to America. For one year, then two, three, and many more, the *menorah* remained on the hearth in our den. From time to time I would dust it, and talk to it.

"Little *hanukkiah*," I would ask," for what reason was I drawn to you?"

But the *hanukkiah* never answered.

Thus nineteen years passed. And one day I said to my husband, "The *hanukkiah* cannot be lit, so we cannot use it for *Hanukkah*. And I still have not found out for what reason we are keeping it."

"You're right," my husband answered. "Let's keep it on the hearth for one more year. If then, after twenty years, we have not found out the purpose, let's just store it in the attic with our other no-longer-being-used possessions."

And with those words I finished my story.

Then an amazing thing happened. In one fleeting moment, I knew, at last, why I had kept that *menorah* for all those years. Had Ben guessed what I would do next?

Without wasting a minute, I unscrewed the brass *shamash*-holder from my *menorah* and handed it to Ben. (Yes, I remember that moment as if it took place just yesterday.)

Grinning from ear to ear, Ben thanked me (I even think he hugged me) and took it home. And the very next day, Opa affixed it to their family's *menorah*. And wonder of wonders, it was just the right size!

Can you imagine the joy in that family! On the very next *Hanukkah*, they would be able to use their precious *menorah*, after sixty-seven years, to perform the mitzvah of lighting candles on the Festival of Lights. And on that very next *Hanukkah*, Ben's family invited my husband and me to join them in the mitzvah, too.

And what happened to my own small *menorah*? It now stands, minus the *shamash*-holder with its tiny brass cup, in our kitchen, where I often look at it and speak to it. Whenever I do, I am reminded of the kindness of Mr. Jacobovitz, whose prophecy, after all, did come true. And whenever I look at it, it seems to me that my small *menorah* has grown just a bit in stature. That must be because its chest is puffed with pride at having helped another *menorah* to fulfill the mitzvah of casting light in the *Hanukkah* celebration.

Chances are that my little *menorah* will never be lit. But who knows? Perhaps there's another story waiting to be told.

Provenance: This is the story of two different sacred objects in two different families, in two different places, which came together by chance–or, perhaps, by destiny? –to help perform a mitzvah. It is a true story. It is my story.

Barbara Rush is a librarian, teacher, writer, and storyteller who resides in America and Israel. She holds an MA in Jewish Studies and has authored/co-authored 200 stories and 13 books, including *The Diamond Tree* (winner of the Sydney Taylor Book Award), *The Book of Jewish Women's Tales, The Kids' Catalog of Passover,* and three books on Jewish art. One of the first to bring Sefardic tales to American audiences, Barbara also helped develop the first course for professional storytellers in Israel. The U.S. government also sent her abroad, as an ALA Book Fellow, to teach storytelling and develop children's libraries.

Shabbos Candles
by Sandy Eisenberg Sasso

My grandmother died when I was still a toddler. I barely remember what she looked like, and try as I may, I can't recall at all the sound of her voice. But I do have the stories about her that my mother told me. Here is one of them.

Grandmother, you were a new bride, and it was your first *Shabbos* at home. Friday was spent in preparation. You were known even then for your love of cooking, and everyone loved what you cooked. That afternoon, chicken soup, into which you would later toss thin egg noodles, simmered on the stove. The gefilte fish was made earlier in the day, an arduous but loving task. The *challah* rose on the kitchen counter. Later you would brush egg whites over the twisted braid and sprinkle poppy seed. The house filled with the aromas of freshly baked bread and roasted chicken.

When the cooking was completed, you spread a white cloth, a wedding gift, on the dining room table. Cream-colored china plates, rimmed with a fine spray of pink roses, were carefully set for you and your groom. In the middle of the table sat the *challah*, still warm from the oven, covered with a large, white linen napkin. At either side were two bronze candlesticks. Into each holder you placed white tapers. Two glasses of wine stood ready for the *kiddush* prayer.

You must have heard Grandfather's footsteps on the stairs leading up to your apartment, and he had to have smelled the warm sweet aromas that poured from your kitchen into the hall. Grandfather was strong even into old age when I knew him, and his steps were steady and determined. I imagine you running a comb through your light brown wavy hair and straightening the blue floral print dress you wore. Grandfather opened the apartment door. He saw you standing there, his new bride. He saw the table set to receive the bride of *Shabbos*.

"I will not have this!" he yelled. With no further explanation, he turned his back and slammed shut the door.

I learned as I grew up that Grandfather was a proud Jew and an ardent Zionist. But religion was different. It was of the old world. He would have none of it. Oh, yes, there would be a *seder* filled with song, but no synagogue, no prayer, no *Shabbos*.

I still see you standing there in the dining room, tears reflected in the *Shabbos* candlelight. Grandfather's brother came to visit.

"Don't worry, Fannie," he said. "I'll eat with you."

Uncle Lou would always be there to relish your cooking. That night he said *kiddush*, and you said nothing.

Grandfather returned later that night when the dishes were put away, and the *Shabbos* candles had burned down. Neither of you spoke about what happened that evening. You never made *Shabbos* for Grandfather again, but you did make *Shabbos*. Every Friday night you placed white tapers in the freshly polished bronze candlesticks, placed them on the kitchen counter, covered your eyes, and said the blessing. When Grandfather would return from work on Friday evenings, he would pretend not to notice that the candles' flame made long shadows on the red Formica counter.

Years later when you had children, three sons and a daughter, you made certain that your sons were tutored in Hebrew, so each could become a *bar mitzvah*. Grandfather wouldn't hear of it. When the days came for each of them to read from the Torah, you went with Uncle Lou to the synagogue and sat behind the *mechitzah* alone. Everyone raved about the sponge cake and strudel Fannie had baked for the *kiddush*.

Grandfather was a strong man. He came from Teplik, a small town in Russia that is no more. He left as a teenager and traveled to America with a few coins in his pocket and not a word of English in his vocabulary. He was proud, determined, and successful. But Grandmother, you were a wise woman. You had a generous heart and a religious soul. You found a way to keep the peace and the faith. I am told that you died just a few days after my third birthday. I wish I could have known you longer.

I would like to believe that somehow you can hear me, your granddaughter, retelling this story. I hope you will look in my window on Friday evenings. There on the table are your bronze candlesticks, and the flickering white tapers welcome the Sabbath bride. Grandmother, the cooking is not as good, but I hope you are pleased.

Provenance: I grew up knowing my maternal grandfather as the strong patriarch of the family. He was a proud Jew but adamantly secular. Having left Byelorussia as a teenager, knowing no English and having just a few coins in his pocket, he marched for workers' rights and built a successful family business in America. An ardent supporter of Zionism and Jewish culture, he held a certain antipathy for religion that he passed on to most of the family. So I wondered from whence my own affection for religious thought and ritual came. It was in listening to stories of my grandmother that I learned of a gentle strength and a faith that was kneaded in the dough of extraordinary culinary skills and that nourished my mother and me. This story was one my mom told again and again.

Sandy Eisenberg Sasso is senior rabbi at Congregation Beth El Zedeck in Indianapolis, Indiana, where she has served since 1977. She is the author of eleven award-winning children's books including *God's Paintbrush, In God's Name, Noah's Wife, Cain and Abel: Finding the Fruits of Peace. God's Echo–Exploring Scripture with Midrash* is her first book for adults. Sandy teaches at Christian Theological Seminary and Butler University. She writes and lectures on *midrash*, women and spirituality, and nurturing the spiritual imagination of children.

Queen Esther's Joy
by Naomi Steinberg

There was once a poor man who lived only for *Purim*. No other holiday interested him. In springtime, as the snow melted and the housewives began scrubbing their kitchens for *Pesach*, the poor man was unconcerned. He lived alone in a dilapidated one-room cottage, which he readied for the festival by lackadaisically sweeping out some crumbs. As a guest at a neighbor's festive table, the poor man sat yawning. The *seder* did not hold his attention; the sips of wine brought him no delight. To him the whole experience was as dry as *matzah*.

After *Pesach* the villagers counted the omer each day and looked forward to Shavuos, but again, the poor man was indifferent. If it were the tenth day of the omer or the fortieth, what did it matter to him? Others meditated on combinations of the holy *sephiros*, the mystical emanations, but the poor man found it tedious and uninteresting. On Shavuos evening pious villagers gathered at the *shul* and studied all night until dawn, but the poor man slept soundly in his bed. Nor did he bother himself to walk into the village to partake of holiday blintzes.

When the summer sunburned down on the village, the community gathered for *Tisha B'av* to fast and bewail the destruction of the ancient Temple. The poor man fasted as was required, but he shed no tear. What was the ancient Temple to him that he should mourn its loss?

When the month of *elul* arrived, the *shofar* was sounded every morning. The villagers hung their heads and counted up their sins. Pious men rose long before dawn to pray, and even the *cheder* boys grew serious and pensive. But the poor man made no change in his demeanor. If he had sinned, those sins did not seem to hang heavy on his soul. On *Rosh Hashannah* the villagers dipped apple slices in honey and wished each other, "*l'shanah tovah*," a sweet New Year. But the poor man shrugged and said nothing, as if he gave no thought to the coming year.

On the holy day of *Yom Kippur* villagers beat their breasts and wept, but the poor man sat among them impassively. If the gates of Heaven opened or if they did not, what difference did it make to him? For the Sukkos festival the villagers decorated their *Sukkot* and sat singing and making merry, delighting in the harvest of their humble gardens and orchards. The poor man stepped inside his neighbor's *sukkah* and sat for an obligatory moment, but he would not stay long. He shivered in the autumn chill and hurried home. Nor did he rouse himself to joy on

Simchas Torah. As others eagerly vied for a chance to dance with the holy scroll, the poor man stood watching with a blank expression, as if the Torah celebration meant nothing to him.

In the dark of winter the villagers gathered around the soft glow of their menorahs, singing, spinning the *dreidl* and frying potato *latkes*. A goodhearted neighbor invited the poor man over, but he would only enter the house—he never entered the rejoicing. On *Tu b'Shevat* the villagers shared fruit and nuts lovingly dried and saved for the holiday, the food of the Garden of Eden. They made the blessing for the fruit of the tree and contemplated the mysteries of the supernal Tree of Life. The poor man murmured the blessing and tasted a bit of fruit, but he left the singing and contemplation to others. For him the New Year of the Trees was just a day like any other.

But as *Purim* approached something seemed to stir in the poor man's soul, and it was as if he suddenly came to life. His humble cottage held little more than a bed, a chair, and an old trunk, which served as his table for most of the year. A few weeks before *Purim* the poor man climbed on the chair and reached up to a nail in the rafters, where he kept hidden an old key. Then he climbed down with the key and unlocked the trunk, in which he kept stored all the items needed for the village *Purimshpiel*. First he took out the tattered scripts and carefully examined each one, copying out new pages where here or there one had been torn or smudged. He then trudged through the frozen streets seeking out the *Purim* players, delivering the scripts into their hands with the admonishment not to lose them and to diligently learn their lines and practice their gestures.

He then took out of the trunk all the old costumes, the robes, veils and turbans, carefully examining each one, looking for signs of wear or damage. He spent many hours making repairs, reinforcing the seams, pulling tight any hanging buttons. He went to the village peddlers and begged them for a piece of ribbon or a bit of lace, "for the joy of *Purim*." When the costumes were refurbished and hung out to air, the poor man reached into the trunk and took out all the wooden masks: King Ahashverosh and his counselors, wise Mordechai, evil Haman, and lovely Queen Esther. The poor man examined each mask carefully, looking for chips and scratches, and then went to the village artisans to beg a bit of paint "for the joy of *Purim*." Then he cleverly repaired and repainted the masks, darkening the furrows of the king's brow, or applying a fresh blush of red to Queen Esther's lips and cheeks.

The day before *Purim* the poor man gathered the players together at the *shul* and rehearsed them in their parts, exhorting them to speak loudly and clearly and to put passion into their voices and movements.

The poor man himself acted the part of Queen Esther, which he did with an uncommon gracefulness and a melodious voice.

Every year on the eve of *Purim*, the villagers crowded eagerly into the *shul*. Many *l'chaims* were made, and much schnapps was consumed. The villagers jeered and hissed at the evil Haman, drowning out the sound of his name with their noisy *groggers*. Whenever Queen Esther appeared, a surge of delight would pass through the crowd. And as Queen Esther spoke, all the people felt the worries and cares of their hard lives fall away as they reveled in a pure and precious experience of joy.

When the holiday was over, the poor man returned the costumes, masks and scripts to the trunk, locked it, hid away the key in the rafters, and returned to his old, indifferent ways. And so it went year after year, and no one thought that it would ever be otherwise. But one year, as *Purim* approached, the poor man climbed up on his chair to retrieve the key from its hiding place, and as he did so, he experienced a wave of dizziness. As he trudged through the village distributing the scripts, he shivered with chills. And as he sat repairing the masks and costumes, he felt himself falling ill. Each day he grew worse and worse, and, as the holiday drew near, he realized that he would not have the strength to discharge the part of Queen Esther. And so he trudged across the frozen streets and entrusted Queen Esther's script to a bright village lad. The day before the holiday, the poor man feebly made his way to the *shul* to deliver the costumes and masks and rehearse the players. Then, exhausted, he returned home and collapsed into his bed.

The next evening the villagers crowded into the *shul*, and many *l'chayims* were made, and much schnapps was consumed. The *Purimshpiel* began and the audience cheered and hooted and shook their *groggers*. The young lad performed the part of Queen Esther with youthful enthusiasm. His voice was pleasing, and his gestures not unlike those of a queen. Yet, despite the merriment, none of the villagers could feel that special surge of joy, that they had come to expect on *Purim*. The *Purimshpiel* progressed, the characters came and went, but the villagers took no pleasure in it. Hoping to raise their spirits, they consumed more and more schnapps. Becoming increasingly intoxicated they bellowed and hooted at the evil Haman with growing fervor, but they could not taste that wonderful joy that for so many years they had felt with the appearance of Queen Esther. Their cares still hung heavy on their hearts. The lad tried his best and declaimed Queen Esther's lines with passion, but the audience grumbled and shifted uneasily each time he spoke, growing restless and surly, until finally someone pulled the lad down from the stage and took the mask from his face.

In their drunkenness, the people moaned and cried out, "Queen Esther! Where is she? We must have Queen Esther!"

After much slurred complaining and confusion, someone remembered that Queen Esther's part had always been played by the poor man who lived on the edge of the village. But where was he? Why was he not playing his part? Then one of the actors recalled that the man was very ill; undoubtedly he lay in his bed, and, who knew, perhaps he had even died?

Hearing this, a roar of alarm went through the crowd. Someone grabbed the mask and costume, and with much jostling and cries of "Queen Esther! We must have Queen Esther!" the drunken crowd surged through the synagogue door and poured into the moonlit street.

Once outdoors the groggy villagers stood blinking and confused, made sober for a few moments by the chill of the night. Then, remembering their mission, the cry, "Queen Esther!" rang out again. They argued and shouted, debating in which direction the poor man lived. And then the crowd lurched forward, rolling along in the moonlight like one great, clumsy animal with dozens of heads and arms and legs. They made their way through the rutted, narrow streets of the village and came to an open field. The full moon shone down on a smooth expanse of snow, and in the distance, the villagers could see the poor man's cottage standing dark as a tomb, not a wisp of smoke coming from the chimney.

A cry of panic went through the crowd, and the throng charged across the snowy field. They tore open the cottage door and surged inside, people filling every inch of the tiny room while more pressed in the doorway. The light of the full moon streamed in through the small window, and everyone saw the poor man lying motionless on his bed. No one knew if he was alive or dead. People began to weep, moaning and crying, "Queen Esther! Queen Esther!" every heart pounding with hope and dread.

After a few minutes the poor man stirred, and the crowd let out a gasp of relief, and then a cry of excitement as he opened his eyes. His feeble glance took in the crowd of familiar faces, and a faint smile played across his parched lips. Plaintively, like children pleading with their parents, the villagers cried, "Queen Esther! Give us Queen Esther!" They draped Queen Esther's robe across the bed and pressed the mask into his hands. The poor man smiled again and slowly lifted the mask to his face. And as soon as he had done so, a wave of joy swept through the crowded room, and the villagers watched entranced as, lying there on the bed in the moonlight, the poor man declaimed Queen Esther's lines. And with every word, the people felt their burdens fall away and their spirits rise, until every heart in the room was overflowing with joy!

When the poor man finished all of Queen Esther's part, and as he slowly lowered the mask, the villagers saw that his face was lit up with radiance. All the people felt as if they were gazing at the face of Queen Esther herself. And when the poor man spoke, the people knew in their hearts that they were hearing the true voice of Esther the Queen, who addressed them with a passionate, joyful intensity, saying:

"In this world of good and evil, right and wrong, it is necessary for each one of us to wear a mask that conceals our true nature. But there will come a time when all the masks will fall away. The hidden will be revealed, and each of us will appear as we truly are–as pure, limitless souls, forever suspended in joy!"

Provenance: My stories come to me in an unpredictable flow of inspiration in which I hear the details of the tale unfolding in my mind. Sometimes the process is swift; sometimes the story emerges slowly. "Queen Esther's Joy" began as a powerful distraction while I was learning in a class taught by Rabbi Miles Krassen at the Aleph Kallah many years ago. I struggled to push the story out of my mind, but it continued unfolding, demanding my attention. I couldn't imagine how the story would end, nor what teaching it might contain, because at that time I felt very little connection to *Purim*. In the last few minutes of the class Reb Miles said with quiet excitement, "I want to give over another teaching that just came to me. It's not on your handouts. It's about *Purim*." He proceeded to share beautiful insights. As the class came to a close, the story came to its conclusion in my mind, and many of us in the room were weeping.

Naomi Steinberg lives on the Redwood Coast of California where she is active in efforts to protect and restore the forest ecosystem. She serves two congregations and teaches in the Religious Studies Department at Humboldt State University. She received rabbinic ordination from Rabbi Zalman Schachter-Shalomi and other mentors. She and her husband, Saul, are blessed with two children, Miriam, who is a physician, and Berel Alexander, who is a musician. A book of her mystical tales is forthcoming.

The Shabbat Story I Want to Tell
by Arthur Strimling

A little *Shabbat* story:

An artist sets out on a quest for the perfect subject to paint. He journeys until he comes upon a beautiful woman drawing water from a well. And she inspires him to paint perfect beauty. But the painting leaves him unsatisfied, and he journeys on until he encounters soldiers returning from the war. And they inspire him to paint perfect peace. But still he's unfulfilled and journeys on, and then he comes upon an old man praying, his face radiant with reverence and the wisdom that can come from a long, hard life well lived. So the artist paints perfect faith. But he is still unsatisfied. And then he realizes that his journey has brought him full circle, and it is Friday, and if he hurries, he can make it home in time for Shabbat. And as he runs toward his house, he sees framed in the window, his wife lighting the candles and blessing their children. So there it is: perfect beauty, perfect peace, perfect faith, all in one place—and that place is his own home. He never needed to leave.

Isn't that a lovely story? It's a little classic, in a genre of which there are thousands of examples. Who could dislike a story like that?

Well, me, for one. I hate it! It's too sweet; it's too pat. It's like a Hallmark card or a commercial for the phone company that brings a tear to the eye, and I hate myself for being sucked in.

You see, I can't help wondering, 'So, what happens to our artist now? He paints pretty pictures of his wife and kids? No chic SoHo gallery's going to show that. And the Jewish Museum? Forget about it. So he can't sell his art, and he has to support his family. So...he becomes a waiter, and tries to paint at night, but the only apartment they can afford is in the far reaches of Queens, and it's so small there's no room for a studio, and anyway, the kids are screaming and he's exhausted, so he stops painting, borrows some money from his father-in-law, goes into business, makes a pile, moves to the suburbs, and then starts buying paintings by edgy artists who never heard of *Shabbat*? Is that what happens?"

Well, that's not my story. I want *Shabbat*, and I want to keep my edge as an artist. Where's that story?

I mean, I love *Shabbat*. Abraham Joshua Heschel promises us "sacred time." And the rabbis of old go even farther; they call *Shabbat* a weekly taste of heaven. Wow! I want that!

So, it's Friday night; the table is beautiful. The candlesticks stand rampant; the wine seductive in its silver goblet. The *challah* waits modestly under its frilly cover. Delicious smells waft from the kitchen. The lights are turned down low. I hear the scratch of the match; I am standing at the gates of heaven...And I'm freaking!! Because behind me, all around me, are the glowering ghosts of my ancestors, generations of religion-hating, fire-breathing atheists.

I was raised to scorn religion. You know—opiate of the masses, a prop for the powerful, a crutch for the weak, the cause of all misery, ignorance and war. I grew up believing that once the yoke of ignorant superstition was lifted from the *shlumped* shoulders of the opiated masses, science and sweet reason would lift us to a just, democratic and healthy world where...well, I wasn't precisely sure what this utopia would look like, but in my kid-mind it seemed that in the perfect world to come, the strong workers and union leaders would defeat the bad bosses and capitalists; there would be no nukes and no smoking; Negro kids and white kids would go to school together. And there would be this big thing called "The Family of Man," which was this book of photographs that sat on our coffee table—when I looked at the pictures, it made me well up inside, like the story about the artist.

But...But...in my kid-mind I knew that even though there wasn't any God, the universe was still ruled by a mysterious and terrifying force. And this force was even scarier than God, because as far as I could tell, only my parents understood and controlled it. And this mysterious and terrifying force was called "Good Taste." Ahhh! Now in my daily kid-world Good Taste meant "TV bad/books good," and never ever smacking your lips, sucking your teeth or shlurping anything.

And for grown-ups, I knew that Danish modern furniture was very important. And sensible cars, with no fins. In my kid vision of the Good Taste Utopia to come, everyone, everywhere, would sit up straight in their Danish modern furniture and read *The New Yorker Magazine* and complete the *Sunday Times* crossword puzzle like my mom. Everybody would sing along at Pete Seeger concerts and go to Ingmar Bergman movies together. And we would all always vote for Adlai Stevenson!

So, here I am: it's Friday night. I'm trying to enter heaven and these ghosts, these secular rationalist ghosts of people who don't even believe in ghosts, are beckoning me toward their secular, lefty utopia.

Heaven?...Utopia?...Heaven?...Utopia? And I can't just leave them behind; I can't thumb my nose at them. No, that would violate *Shabbat*, because *Shabbat* includes respect for our ancestors' continuity, *l'dor va'dor* and all that. I have to find a way to include them, welcome them. I have to connect...

When my grandparents and great-grandparents left the old country, they left religion behind. But what they left wasn't your nice Park Slope progressive Judaism, no. It was rigid, mean-spirited, arid fundamentalism. That was their *mitzra'im*.

They had been told for centuries that "God will strike you dead or worse if you do not light the candles, perform the rituals, obey the laws, fulfill the obligations to the letter!"

So, imagine what it was like for them. Imagine choosing for the first time <u>not</u> to light the candles, or say the *shema*, or observe the High Holy Days or even *bar mitzvah* their sons. Imagine the first time they went to a Chinese restaurant and ordered shrimp chow mein—and paid for it on *Shabbat*. Whether you approve or not, imagine the courage that took!

And that's it; that's my continuity, my *l'dor va'dor*. I know, I know; I'm using their courage to reconstruct what they struggled so hard to shatter. And I love the irony; my *Shabbat* has to include irony.

Now that's the beginning of a *Shabbat* story I want to tell.

But I'm still not ready. They're here, my ancestors, but what about me? Well, I do have this sense memory of heaven—a sort of pintele *Shabbat*. Where does that come from?

And then I remember: when I was a boy, maybe eight or nine years old, we lived in a small town in Minnesota. And on Saturday afternoons, every kid in town went to the movies. There was only one movie house in town, and the owner must have made a deal with the parents, because for twelve cents, we got four or five hours of ecstatic entertainment: cartoons, serials, a double feature, and in between the two movies, a live show, maybe an accordion champion, or the rubber-jointed sisters, or even better, an audience participation event like a yo-yo contest with prizes.

So...we pay our twelve cents and enter the sanctuary. The lights go down, and the "service" begins with that beloved, traditional cinematic *niggun* [*sings the Warner Bros. theme, at first like a Jewish melody and then as the audience gets it, everyone joins the cartoon intro theme*]. And then we get Bugs Bunny, Daffy Duck, Road Runner—all that delicious, malevolent mayhem. And then the weekly installment of [*Calls like announcer*] "*Buck Rogers*"—these were old even then, with men in saggy tights, and special effects that were as clunky to us as the original Star Wars movies are to nine-year olds now. So we took the opportunity to create some spitball mayhem of our own. Then came the double feature, usually two westerns. We loved Roy Rogers and hated Gene Autry—even then we knew him for a phony drug store cowboy. And sometimes, something great like *High Noon* or [*Calls like the boy in the movie*] "Shane! Come back, Shane!"

There was beauty and faith and moral teaching in those movies. And they all ended in harmony and peace. In that dim sanctuary we kids experienced the security and joy of being in a safe place on our own with our friends. So that was it—Heschel's sacred time; the beauty, peace and faith of that little *Chassidishe* story made alive.

I know it's a stretch, but it was a separate, boundaried Saturday world that gave children hope that there could be order and justice and goodness and joy in the world, that life could be exciting and at peace all at once.

And then we would burst out of the darkness into the late afternoon sunlight, ricocheting off the low, brick buildings. We'd mount our bikes and ride like mad up into the hills just outside of town to the Horse Thief Caves, where, it was said, Jesse James and his gang hid out after robbing the Northfield Bank about twenty miles away. *Emmes:* this is true! There were actual horse stalls carved in the soft sandstone cave walls.

And if we got there in time, we could watch the sky darken, not from the sunset, but from millions of black bats that streamed up from the bowels of that cave. The sky really did turn black, and the sound! Millions of bats screeching and twice as many millions of bat wings flapping made a deafening, uncanny noise, like the whole universe was shattering. And we stood there, gripping our handlebars tight so our knees wouldn't buckle under us, screaming in terror and awe at the utterly mysterious and savage power of nature. And that was our *havdalah.*

So now, as I face the *Shabbat* candles, anxious, wired, a little giddy, I summon the courage of my forebears, and recall the sanctuary of my little Minnesota movie house, and I know something of what it means when we say that *Shabbat* is a weekly taste of heaven.

Arthur Strimling is *Maggid HaMakom* at Congregation Kolot Chayeinu in Park Slope, Brooklyn, where he lives with his love, Cantor Lisa B. Segal. Performer, writer, director, and author, he has appeared at venues including Lincoln Center Out-of-Doors, 92nd Street Y, Symphony Space, and across the US, Europe, and Latin America; and has been featured on NPR and the PBS series "In The Prime." He is the Founding Artistic Director of Roots&Branches Intergenerational Theater and author of *Roots & Branches: Creating Intergenerational Theater.* He has been in residence at MacDowell, Yaddo, and the Jewish Museum. (www.steadywork.blogspotcom)

The Magic Gourd: A Story for Sukkot
by Debra Gordon Zaslow

Once, long ago, there was a young couple who were truly in love. They decided to be married in the autumn under the canopy of the *sukkah* in the presence of their friends and relatives. When the time came, they invited the *ushpizin*, the ancestors, and said their vows with the full moon peeking through the *s'chach* that lined the *sukkah* roof.

After the ceremony, the guests came forth to offer gifts and blessings to the couple. Suddenly a stranger stepped forward. He had a long, full beard, a lined face, and rumpled clothes. Everyone was puzzled.

"He must be from another town," they murmured to each other. "Probably traveling through."

The man spoke to the bride and groom.

"Because your love is so true, I have a special gift for you."

He held out a smooth, round gourd that gleamed in the soft light.

"This gourd is magic," he said. "It contains a wish, but only one wish. So you must use it very wisely and carefully. Don't waste it." The guests stared at the strange man as he continued.

"The wish must be made in the autumn when the moon is full. Come into the *sukkah* and speak to the ancestors. Then together, agree on your wish before you make it."

The strange man handed them the gourd, and before they could thank him, he was gone. They hung the gourd in the center of the *sukkah* where the moonlight gave it a special glow.

It so happened that a greedy man among the guests overheard the story about the magic gourd. That night he snuck into the *sukkah* in the wee hours of the morning, stole the gourd, and replaced it with another that looked identical, but was as empty of wishes as the air.

On the way home in his wagon, he was so excited thinking about how the gourd would make him rich that he forgot to look where he was going. He drove his wagon off the road into a mud hole where its wheels became hopelessly stuck. The more he tried to get out, the deeper he sank.

Finally in desperation, he yelled, "I wish I was out of this mess!"

Instantly he was on dry land, and the single wish was wasted and gone forever. Meanwhile the young couple started their life together. When the winter rains came, they brought the gourd into their home to keep it protected throughout the year. In the autumn they hung it in the center of their *sukkah*, thinking, of course, that it still contained a wish.

Everything went well for them for a few years, but after awhile their business began to fail, and they had trouble making ends meet. That year, on the first day of *Sukkot*, the woman turned to her husband and said, "I think it's time to use our wish. If we could only get on our feet financially, I think everything would fall into place." Her husband agreed.

That evening they went into the *sukkah* and sat for a while in the stillness. Then they welcomed the ancestors, Sarah, Rachel, Rebecca, Leah, Avraham, Isaac, and Jacob. They invited the spirits of their grandparents, and all those who had come before them. When they felt their presence, they spoke to the ancestors silently. When it was time to make their wish, they placed their hands on the gourd.

The husband spoke. "I've been thinking. Maybe if we concentrate on our work and we work together a little harder, we can make a go of it without wasting this wish. We might really need it later."

His wife nodded. So that night they ate dinner in the *sukkah* under the stars, without using the wish.

From that moment on, they concentrated on working together and working harder, until business began to improve. After a time, they were earning plenty of money to get by.

A few years passed, and one day the husband said to his wife, "There is only one thing missing from our life."

She knew just what he meant—a baby. So again they entered the *sukkah* on the full autumn moon and sat in silence. They invited all the ancestors and waited until the *sukkah* filled with the holiness of those who came before them. When they put their hands on the gourd, ready to make the wish, the wife spoke.

"You know, I think we should be patient. Perhaps if we pray for a child, we may be blessed with one. Who knows? We might really need the wish another time." And her husband agreed.

And so they prayed for a child and waited patiently, and eventually they were blessed with a baby. A few years later another baby arrived, and then another. And the children grew up, and the man and woman grew old.

One day the wife turned to her husband and said, "I think it's time to use our wish."

He nodded, for he knew the only thing she would wish for—to be young again, to live forever.

So they went into the *sukkah* where the gourd hung in the glow of the moon. They invited the ancestors and sat quietly with them in the soft light. When they put their hands on the gourd and looked into each other's eyes, they both shook their heads and said, "Not yet." For in the moonlight they had realized that their love would live forever, just like the spirits of their ancestors.

"Who knows, maybe someday, we'll really need that wish."

They went back in the house, and grew older. Eventually the husband passed away and his wife followed soon after. Their children kept the gourd and then passed it on to their children, who passed it on to their children, through the generations.

Many years later, when their great-great-grandchildren were decorating the *sukkah*, one of them unearthed the gourd and called to her brother.

"Look at this old gourd. I think there was some kind of story to it." They passed it back and forth.

His sister said, "I remember Grandma told me it was a wedding present to her grandparents. She said it was magic, and it had a wish."

The great granddaughter shook the gourd and handed it to her brother.

"Feels empty now. They must have used it up." They laughed.

Then he held the gourd to his ear.

"This is strange...you can hear something inside," he said. "Kind of like a sea shell." He handed it to his sister.

She held it to her ear. " It sounds like the wind, or like whispering voices."

His eyes widened. "Maybe it still has magic."

They hung it carefully in the center of the *sukkah*, and that night when they invited in the *ushpizin*, the *sukkah* filled with the quiet voices of the ancestors as the gourd shone with the light of the moon.

Provenance: Stories drift in and out of cultures, shape-shifting as they migrate. Years ago I encountered the kernel of what became "the magic gourd" in "The Wish-Ring," by Martha Hollaway, in *Best-Loved Stories Told at the National Storytelling Festival* (1991). Martha credits Barbara Snow of Eugene, Oregon, for giving her the original story. In Martha's version, a magic ring is given to a farmer, who instead of wasting his wish, works hard alongside his wife to create what they want. I was intrigued by the idea of work, faith and hope being potent tools to build a life. I first adapted the story into a Jewish story for a wedding, using a basket as the magic object. Later, for a *Tu b'Shevat* story, I used a tree as the magic entity that grows through the generations. A few years ago, when I needed a story to tell in the *sukkah,* the object morphed into a magic gourd so that the *ushpizin* join forces with faith and hard work to weave the tapestry of the couple's life. As I told it in the full moon under the hanging gourds of our *sukkah,* we sang the refrain *"ufrose aleynu sukkat shalom,"* and felt the glow of our ancestors. As with most stories, I'm sure the theme of it has traveled in and out of various cultures. I invite you to use this Jewish version in your *sukkah,* or shape it into another form for a different storytelling occasion.

Debra Gordon Zaslow met Peninnah Schram at CAJE in 1988, and has been inspired to tell Jewish stories ever since. She received smichah as a *maggidah* from Reb Zalman Schachter-Shalomi in 2000. She teaches storytelling at Southern Oregon University and her CD, *Return Again,* contains Jewish stories of healing and transformation. Since completing her MFA in writing in 2004, she has published numerous stories and articles, including an excerpt from her memoir, *Bringing Bubbe Home,* in the 2010 edition of *Drash: Northwest Mosaic.* She and her husband, Rabbi David Zaslow, offer a *maggid* training program.

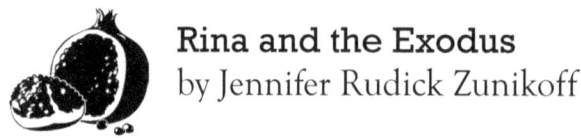

Rina and the Exodus
by Jennifer Rudick Zunikoff

Do you remember Rina?

I remember Rina.

When I think of Rina, I think of color. Rina's eyes were blue and green with flecks of gold.

When I was a little girl and Rina was a young woman, her hair was curly, chestnut brown, and streaked auburn from the sun. When I was a young woman and Rina was middle-aged, the streaks were gray, but she was just as beautiful.

In the desert, we wore simple dresses made from plain, brown fabric, but Rina sewed in threads of sapphire, ruby, and gold, the colors of the sunset.

When I think of Rina, I think of the color she brought to our world.

Rina was different from the rest of us. She did not see herself as a slave.

In the desert lands of Egypt, the Hebrew men were assigned to one area of the fields, and we, the women, to our own section. Rina and I were often stationed to work together. That was back when my daughters were little, and my husband was still alive.

Each day we had to build bricks for the Pharaoh's cities. I would grab some straw and mud and quickly construct a block, placing it on top of my pile. We were ever wary of the taskmasters standing behind us with their whips. Everyone felt tense; everyone except Rina.

Rina would collect a bit of mud and some straw, fashioning the materials into a brick as if she were creating a work of art.

Her pile of bricks was far smaller than anyone else's, but never in all my years did I see a taskmaster's whip strike Rina's back.

I think they were afraid of Rina because she was not frightened of them.

At the end of the day, the foremen tallied our bricks, set down their whips, and returned to their fine houses and their families.

I would run home to my husband and daughters. But not Rina.

Rina would stay.

She would stand in the empty field, selecting some mud and straw and forming yet another brick. And sometimes another and another. Rina did not stop working until *she* decided she was finished.

After the evening meal, I would bring my daughters to Rina, just like my mother had brought me to Rina when I was a child. Rina sat outside her tent and told many children her stories, drawing pictures of the scenes in the sand.

"The green leaves turned crimson and gold," Rina said in one story.

"In a distant land," Rina shared in another tale, "cold, white flakes gently fell to the ground."

She spoke of mountains that stretched toward the heavens and of deep valleys of green grass. She told of seas that spread toward the edge of the world.

Rina had lived in the desert her entire life, just as we all had. Yet when she told her stories, I believed that somehow she had seen these things.

"Girls, we must go home," I would often tell my daughters after Rina finished a tale. "It is late."

"No, *Ima*, please," they begged. "Let us hear one more story!"

After the children were asleep, Rina continued her work. She built instruments. Where she got the stamina, I do not know. In her hands, reeds from the Nile River became flutes. She transformed bits of wood and animal skins into drums.

Late at night, she would play these instruments. She sang—not the mournful songs of a slave, but songs of celebration, of joy. Especially in the days after my husband was gone, those songs brought me hope.

It was around this time when Moses returned. Moses. I could hardly believe he was real.

I had heard stories about him since I was a child. About the baby boy, a Hebrew, who had been raised as a prince by the Pharaoh's daughter. It was said that he had fled to a distant land. That one day he would return to us. That he would bring us out of this narrow place.

Suddenly, he was really there! I saw him with my eyes. I stood there among the crowd, listening to him.

We had to lean in to listen, for Moses sometimes spoke with a halting voice.

"God remembers you," he said, carefully enunciating each word. "God has seen your pain and will bring you out of Egypt, out of *mitzrayim*."

When he spoke, Rina was there, listening in the back of the crowd. She was smiling.

She had known Moses would return all along.

Pharaoh, our oppressor, would not listen to God. Pharaoh did not heed Moses's warnings. So the water of the Nile became a river of blood.

Frogs leapt from the sky, and lice crawled upon the Egyptians. Of course, we the Hebrews were safe. The plagues did not hurt us.

But I saw my neighbors in such misery. How does one describe such a thing?

The horror of it.

Their animals died, falling over onto the ground. Locusts ate their crops; fiery hail destroyed anything that was left.

But the darkness...

How do I explain the darkness? There was light inside our homes, but outside... I tried to walk outside, but the darkness was so thick, I couldn't move. I could not see my own hand in front of my face.

No one should know of such darkness.

And then, the final plague. It was the middle of the night. We were inside, protected. I heard the screams, the screams of the Egyptian women.

I will never forget those screams.

Just before dawn, Miriam came to our tent. My daughters were asleep and I was unable to settle myself enough to lie down. Instead, I was baking bread and doing chores.

"It is time to leave," Miriam said.

"What," I asked, stunned. "Now?"

"Yes, now."

"But I'm not ready! My daughters are asleep! I just put the bread into the oven."

Miriam picked up my hands and held them in her own. "I know you do not think you are ready," she said. "But you are."

She left.

I looked around my tent. What was I supposed to do? I grabbed a pot, some utensils, and cloth.

"Girls," I called. "Wake up! Wake up! We're leaving! We're going to Freedom!"

"*Ima*," my eldest daughter said. "*Ima*, now?" She smiled.

"Yes! Help your sister. We have to go." I opened the oven and pulled out the bread. It was flat. As we left, I put it on my back. I knew it would bake in the sun.

I held my little girl in my arms, and my older daughter walked beside me. We left our home; we left everything we had ever known.

We walked.

We passed Rina's tent. She was just leaving, too, dragging a sack behind her. Clink. Clank. Ding!

Rina was bringing her instruments.

I could not believe my eyes and ears. We were leaving Egypt, and she was bringing instruments.

"*Ima*, may we walk with Rina?" my daughters pleaded.

"No," I said. "Come here, girls. Let's walk this way." I pointed ahead.

All of us women gave Rina a wide berth. But we could not get away from the sound of her instruments.

Clink. Clank. Bam!

After many days of walking through the hot desert, we set up camp near the Sea of Reeds. We formed a makeshift tent. My daughters went inside and quickly fell asleep. They were exhausted from the journey. I sat at the mouth of the tent, looking out at the sea. I thought about my husband: how much I wished he was with us. The joy he would feel knowing that his wife and daughters were almost free.

My husband had been killed, murdered. Murdered by the whips of the Egyptian taskmasters. As I thought of him, I looked back at the sea.

There was Rina.

She stood there, her toes near the water, the sack of instruments at her feet. The bag was open, and one tambourine had fallen onto the sand.

Rina watched the sea. Her hair blew in the wind.

The wind was growing stronger. Even though I sat a distance from the sea, I could feel droplets of water falling on my feet and my arms. Within the wind, I heard a noise. It sounded like rain; but there was no rain. I looked away from the sea, turning toward the sound. I saw dust. Then there was a squeaking and a sound of hoofbeats.

It was the Pharaoh's army coming for us.

No, I thought. No! This couldn't be happening! I looked back at my daughters. They were asleep, dreaming of freedom. I would not allow my daughters to be taken. They would not be slaves like I had been!

The hoofbeats and squealing of the chariot wheels grew louder. The cloud of dust reached toward us.

I looked at Rina. She held her hair back from her face and calmly looked out to the sea.

The camp was in turmoil; everyone was screaming and yelling at Moses.

"Why did you bring us here? Was it for the want of graves in Egypt that you brought us here to die?"

I looked back at Rina. She was an island of calm amidst the chaos of the camp.

She seemed to be looking at something aside from the sea. I followed Rina's gaze. She was looking at Nachshon. I knew Nachshon. Everyone did. He was a leader of my tribe, the tribe of Judah.

Nachshon looked out toward the sea as well. Everyone else looked toward Egypt, but Nachshon and Rina faced the sea.

I could not see Nachshon's face, only his back, and his white beard, blowing in the wind.

I noticed another sound, a resonance calling from within the blustery wind. I heard music. I heard Rina's instruments singing in the wind. The wheels of the chariots squealed, and the horses' hooves pounded the ground. And the wind played Rina's instruments.

Nachshon must have heard the music, too, because suddenly, he spun around and looked at Rina. He looked down at the sack by her feet, seeing the tambourine on the sand. He looked back at her face and smiled.

Breathing deeply, Nachshon turned back toward the sea. Now Nachshon knew that someone believed that our people would be free.

He stepped into the water.

The water sloshed around his ankles. Nachshon took another step, descending into the sea. The water touched his knees. The wind pushed and pulled the sea, forming a wall of water beside him.

Rina walked toward him, dragging along her sack. The force of the wind pushed down the back of our tent. My daughters awoke and ran to me.

"*Ima*," my little daughter cried as my elder screamed, "*Ima*, no! The Egyptians!"

"Don't look at them," I commanded, hugging them close. "Look at Nachshon and Rina!"

By now the water had reached Nachshon's belly. Rina, holding her sack in the air, was stepping into the sea as well. The wall of water grew taller alongside them.

"Girls!" I cried. "We are going to follow them." I stood up, my little daughter in my arms, my older one beside me. We ran toward Nachshon and Rina.

The water splashed again Nachshon's chest. I held my little daughter, my older one grabbing my elbow. We stepped into the water.

Nachshon took another step, and the water covered his mouth.

Suddenly the water fell! In the midst of the sea, we were walking on land!

We began to run, Nachshon and Rina leading the way. We ran between walls of water toward freedom. All of the Hebrews were running with us.

We were on the other side of the sea. Each one of us was there. Moses was standing with us, holding out his arm as we finished crossing the sea, the Egyptian army close behind.

Moses dropped his arm.

God closed the sea.

The men formed a circle around Moses, and we, the women, encircled Miriam. Clink. Clunk. Bam.

We turned around. Rina was pulling her sack toward us. We opened our circle, welcoming her inside. She walked to the center, to Miriam. Rina reached into her sack and pulled out a tambourine. She handed it to Miriam, who held it close to her heart. She smiled warmly at Rina.

Miriam stretched her arms toward the heaven, shaking the tambourine. "We are free!" she cried out. "We are free!" Miriam began to sing, praising God.

During Miriam's song, Rina walked around the circle, handing each of us an instrument.

"Thank you, Rina," I whispered.

We began to dance. My little daughter was dancing in my arms as her older sister was dancing with her body and her heart.

"We are free! We are free!"

Of course, all this happened forty years ago. And now you, my children and grandchildren, my people, are about to enter the Promised Land. You have graciously listened to my stories these past forty years.

I have saved this story for last because I want you to remember Rina. As you step into our land, think of her. Remember how she made instruments because she believed we would have a future.

I cannot go with you. I am an old woman now, and my story is through; but the story of our people will continue forever.

There will be trying times ahead. There will be challenges and heartbreak that we cannot yet imagine. But as you walk into our land, the land of Israel, remember what Rina always knew: That no matter how difficult the challenges may be, for the Jewish people, there will always be a reason to celebrate.

Provenance: This story is based on Exodus 14:22, when God parts the Sea of Reeds. In the Talmud, BT Sota 37a, Rabbi Meir describes the tribes as striving with each other to be each the first to enter the sea, and Rabbi Judah envisions Nachshon the son of Aminadav, Prince of the Tribe of Judah, as the first to enter. And Exodus 15:20 reveals that: "Miriam the prophetess, Aaron's sister, took a tambourine in her hand, and all the women followed her, with tambourines and dancing." When I imagined Nachshon's story, I saw a woman there with her instruments and named her Rina, meaning "joyous song." She brought her instruments into the desert because she knew God would free the Hebrews and the women would dance.

Jennifer Rudick Zunikoff tells stories from the Torah and *Midrash* as well as contemporary tales. Jennifer facilitates the Student Immigrant Stories Project in Baltimore, sponsored by the Jewish Museum of Maryland. She also co-teaches the Oral History of the Holocaust course at Goucher College. Jennifer coaches students and teachers to use their intuition to transform mental images into powerful stories. She serves as a consultant with the Louise D. and Morton J. Macks Center for Jewish Education in Baltimore, where she creates and performs stories to help deepen the connections of local families to their Jewish community and Jewish traditions.

IV

Seasoning Our Lives
Mitzvot of Life Cycle and Learning

Honor
by Phil Cohen

As he walked from the foyer of the synagogue toward the sanctuary, a woman approached him.

"I was so sorry to hear about your father," she said. The sympathy in her voice was genuine."

"Thank you very much," he said.

"I'm here for you," she said.

He nodded, smiled in gratitude, and they hugged. The offer was a strange one, since he didn't even know the woman's name. He had seen her from time to time at the synagogue, but had never learned her name. Still, she had generously extended herself to him.

So it had been for the last month and a half since his father's death. He'd been deluged by such expressions of compassion. Cards, emails, contributions, warm expressions during personal encounters—all of these had come to him in abundance from friends as well as from people he barely knew. These proclamations were wonderful. He felt cared for. He felt part of a community.

"Grief comes in two hundred flavors," Rabbi Simon had told him when he came to visit the rabbi in his office ten days or so after the funeral. "You must simply allow your grief to follow its own path."

Wise words coming from a decent guy, but they didn't fit this context.

"Do you miss your grandfather?" he asked both of his adult children after the traditional month of mourning had passed.

"No," Ron told him.

"No," said Samantha.

"Why not?" he asked them.

And though he asked each separately and over the phone, both answered with nearly identical words.

"I didn't have a relationship with him."

He looked inside to find sadness. He tried to miss his father. He tried to find a hidden reservoir of love for him. But he could not. He simply could not. He worried that he had somehow caused the reaction his children had expressed, that he had somehow been the conduit through which they passed in order to get to their grandfather, and that the passageway had colored their perceptions.

Possibly. But they were adults, independent beings subject to their own feelings. If parental influence upon children is an inescapable constant, still, that influence doesn't have to be a prison. Children make their own decisions unfettered by their parents' junk—these two were quite capable of independent thought and emotion. Why, then, did they experience the absence of a relationship? Was it his fault? Perhaps. These things are complicated. But he believed their experience of their grandfather was mostly uncluttered by his own baggage. And if so, then his father had somehow failed to bring these two grandchildren into his orbit. He failed to earn the name, "Grandpa."

Grief comes in two hundred flavors, the rabbi had said. Maybe. But that was beside the point. His problem was that he felt no grief. He had shed no tears. He felt no longing to call his father on the phone to chat about things—only then to realize his father was gone. He felt no hole in his heart requiring mending—another phrase uttered by a friend in an expression of sympathy. He felt no spontaneous moments of sorrow that would suddenly pop into mind along with his father's face.

Then he worried if this emotional emptiness pointed toward some psychological problem, a shattered synapse perhaps, that hinted at a neurosis, or worse, a psychosis—in short, that something was wrong with him. And as always he was met with turmoil in his head when he contemplated the matter of his relationship with his father. There existed the possibility that he was an emotional *golem*, a lump of clay. And worse, that he had passed *golem*-ness on to his son and daughter. He worried anew that there now lived on this earth three people with fissures where healthy emotions should be.

But then he remembered how it had been when his grandmother had died, now almost thirty years ago. This memory eased his mind. For he recalled how badly he had missed her long after her death, how for so many years he wished he could hear her voice over the phone when he knew he no longer could. He *was* capable of grief, but not for his father. Not for his father.

He recalled a short story he had written called "My Father Speaks." In it, the narrator's father speaks at length to his son. It was out of character for the father in the story, but the father speaks to the son nevertheless. In the first part, the father spins a tale about how he had won more than fifteen hundred dollars at a neighborhood poker game, but as the consequence of the final bet, he has to take his son to Yellowstone National Park after his son's *bar mitzvah*. Then, in Yellowstone, the father tells another anecdote, a sad one about his childhood on the Lower East Side. This tale tells of how his younger brother had been murdered while attempting to make a drug delivery as a favor to his older brother. In the final scene of the story, the father, clad only in his boxers and an undershirt, courageously stares down a bear, which has invaded their campsite early in the morning to feast on their leftovers.

Now he realized, more than when he had originally written the piece, that the fictionalized father had served as a reconstructed substitute for the real one, a deep contrast in so many ways. The father in his story was his wish for the father he would never have. His real father had never told stories about his life. Not once. Not ever. His real father would have never taken him to the beach, much less camping in Yellowstone National Park.

He had sought father figures in his life, men whose character stood in contrast to his real father's. He had written about them in an essay called "My Four Fathers." The first father in the essay was his biological father. The second father taught history at his undergraduate college. The third was a philosopher he'd studied under as a graduate student. And the fourth was a well-known theologian who taught at the seminary he'd attended. All fathers had commonalities. All three fathers were intellectuals. All were demanding teachers. All were garrulous. All were Jewish to their core.

As he now entered the sanctuary of the synagogue, a man and woman approached him with words of sympathy. The man offered his hand and conveyed his condolences. The woman extended her hand, and he took it with both of his own; they kissed on the cheek. How strange. He'd thought this woman disliked him.

He wrapped himself in his *tallit* and said the blessing.

He believed he had some insight as to why his father had become the man he became, but the "why" of it seemed irrelevant now. His real father—not the fictional one, not the surrogate ones—was a closed book. He had been a wall of silence, a man whose powers to express emotion never grew, and frequently seemed nonexistent. What the man felt was virtually unknown. He had been unable to bring his interior life, whatever it consisted of, to the exterior.

This thought saddened him. He doubted his emotions could be completely non-existent. Everyone feels, doesn't he? Everyone has a heart, doesn't he? Everyone experiences fear, anger, love, happiness, joy—doesn't he? His father must have had an interior emotional life. And to be honest, he did remember laughter and anger punctuating the air from time to time throughout his life, occasional bad jokes at the dinner table. But not enough times. No. Nowhere near enough.

"Damn! What am I doing?" he thought. "What kind of demands am I making on my dead father? He was the man he was; why not just accept him and love him for the man he was? Miss him, mourn him, grieve for the loss of him. He was my father, after all. There was always food on the table, shelter, gifts. Support."

All true.

Then why didn't he feel anything? Why couldn't he grieve; why didn't he grieve? What lay in *his* interior? Why no tears in his eyes for the man who had supported him without complaint?

His *tallit* wrapped around his shoulders, he sat down, opened the prayer book to the proper page and joined the congregation in worship. As happened from time to time, he found himself absorbed in the prayers.

Well, here's the heart and soul of it. His father may have loved him; probably he did; unquestionably he did. But his father could not say it aloud, and more importantly, he could not show it in his acts. He had never shown love. That's it. He could not hug, much less kiss, his children. He never called on the phone, or answered an email, or in the old days, sent a letter. He was not the type to take his son to a ball game or fishing or to a library, or to sit and talk while taking a break on a hike, or to offer good advice in the face of a crisis. These things did not lie in his skill set.

He sat in prayer, reflecting on what compelled him to be in attendance that *Shabbat* morning. He had long known that his emotional reaction upon his father's death would be negligible. Even at the hospital, as his father literally expired before him, his brother, and his mother—an undeniably profound experience—he had felt no sorrow. As his father lay on the bed, he had recited the *vidui*, the traditional confessional prayer said by or on behalf of the dying. He did what he had to—what, in the case of his father, no one else could do and no one else felt the need to do.

Yes. Yes. As he sat in the synagogue that morning in prayer, two unrelated thoughts came to mind.

The absence of a relationship with his father hurt. When he focused on it, he could feel pain in the pit of his stomach. But now, there was no reason to assign blame. Perhaps in the past, when his father was still alive, when something still might have been done, but not now. Perhaps he had silently assigned blame in the past; regardless, that time had passed. He had heard innumerable friends speak of the quirks in their relationships with their fathers. Yet when the end finally came, inevitably there was grief. But not for him; and when he thought about it, he felt wounded.

The Jewish tradition, he knew, commanded duty, honor for one's father, not love. The Jewish tradition demanded action toward one's father, a set of tasks he knew he owed his father. But responsibility could not compensate for a lifetime of absence. Duty could not reconstruct a lifetime of emotional neglect. Duty could not build from the grave what had never existed.

But duty could insure that a memory would forever be preserved, and in that preserving, be honored. The Jewish tradition demanded honor. Not love. The tradition did not demand that the father do anything specific to earn honor from his son. Not fishing trips. Not library cards. Not a lifetime of good advice. A man who chose to become a father earned honor simply for making that choice. Not only did the Jewish tradition demand honor of the son, it created the means to express and maintain that honor.

He could not grieve. He could not feel sad. He could not dismiss the pain in his belly. But he could honor his dead father. He had an obligation to honor him, an obligation he accepted. That was in his skill set.

The service leader intoned, "If you have *yahrzeit* or if you're in mourning, please rise for the Mourner's Kaddish."

He rose, and in unison with perhaps fifteen others, he began, "*Yitgadal, v'yitkadash, shmei rabba...*" Words that remember and commemorate, words that create a bond, words that express honor. Together all those standing recited the *kaddish* to the final line, "May the One Who makes peace in the heights, may that One make peace among us, among all Israel, and let us say: Amen."

When the prayer concluded, he sat down with the others, inexplicably comforted as the service moved toward its conclusion.

Provenance: I lost my father in the summer of 2010. It was the end of the life of a man who grew up in poverty and built a life for himself and his family. Yet he and I had a difficult relationship. A very difficult relationship. This story is an attempt to describe my feelings in a fictionalized context. At the same time, I sought to work through some of my reactions to his dying.

Phil Cohen has served in many rabbinic capacities over the years—including teaching at college, serving pulpits, and directing schools. He is married to Beth Gamburg and is the proud father of Elly and Talia. He also holds a Ph.D. in Jewish thought from Brandeis University, and has developed a specialty in the intersection of Judaism and bioethics. One of the constants in his life has been his joy in writing and using stories as tools for opening up the world to himself and for his students.

Mikveh
by Anita Diamant

God divided the waters below from the waters above. And it was good. And it is water that nurtures and sustains the on-going miracles of creation, too. From the amniotic sac, to the invisible transport of blood and lymph, to the powerful energies of tides and clouds feeding the planet. All of it sacred: the shower, the kiss, the tear, the flow, the nearly-liquid body. Every drop sacred. At Mayyim Hayyim, storytelling is a primary method for teaching about the potential and power of mikveh. Anita Diamant and Janet Buchwald have written a series of plays called "The Mikveh Monologues," which are based on in-depth interviews with people who have immersed there. The following scene, "Niddah," is an excerpt.

I have a secret. I go to the *mikveh* every month for *niddah*, to immerse after my period. It's not something I've been very forthcoming about. Not even my best friends know this about me. I worry that they would think it's a weird thing to do. After all, I'm a Reform Jew, hardly the hat-and-long-skirt-type of woman that most people think of when they picture regular *mikveh*-goers. And yet, there's something about the idea of a monthly separation that seems right to me, and when I asked my husband if he'd be willing to give it a try, he said okay.

Judaism was a very big part of what had brought us together, and from the very beginning of our marriage, we've tried to bring it into our everyday lives in ways that work for us. So we always make a blessing before we eat anything. We sing the *shema* to our children every night as they snuggle in their beds. If we try to add Judaism to eating and loving our children, why would we exclude sex from this holiness-making?

Refraining from lovemaking for a certain length of time began for us as a trial, and then became completely integrated into the rhythm of our marriage.

Here's another secret. My observance of *niddah* never ended with an immersion in a *mikveh*. I took a bath or shower at home to mark the end of separation, because that was the only thing I could do that felt honest.

But when Mayyim Hayyim opened, I was <u>there</u>. The experience itself was–where to begin? A whole hour to spend on myself? When you have young kids? It's unheard of! I soaked in the tub uninterrupted, pumiced my feet, filed my nails. Heaven.

When I got into the water, I thanked God for the wonderful

husband who shares my life, our children who bring me so much joy and love. I thanked God that I was healthy, and have meaningful work.

Ever since, I have looked forward to my monthly immersion. Secretly. Let me be honest. Sometimes the experience is less than perfect. I forget to bring something to read for inspiration, or I have a stupid little argument with my husband on the way out the door.

But other times, it's extraordinary. Like when my immersion happened a few days before I became an adult *bat mitzvah*, and I overcame my terror of chanting Hebrew in public by singing the *shehecheyanu* out loud, in the water. Or the month when my father was so sick, and I sobbed and sobbed into the *mikveh*, where I found comfort and hope.

But mostly, this month-to-month practice is about me and my husband. It's a secret we share with each other.

After all this time, you'd think he would remember and count the days, but he doesn't.

Now he asks, "Are you going tomorrow?"

We have little smiles on our faces when we talk about the logistics. He always does the dishes before I get home. And for one night, every month, from the time I walk into Mayyim Hayyim until I fall asleep, I focus exclusively on my love for my husband, my gratitude for our life together, and for the gift of some really great, holy love-making.

It truly does work that way. This is bigger than just the two of us making a personal choice. This comes from ancient wisdom.

This is, above all, a mitzvah.

Provenance: © The Mikveh Monologues © 2005, Anita Diamant, Janet Buchwald, and Mayyim Hayyim Community Mikveh and Education Center, Newton, Massachusetts.

It was about 1998 when I decided that I wanted a *mikveh*. Not my own personal *mikveh* in the backyard, but a community *mikveh* that I could call my own. Of course, there were *mikvaot* (pl) in the Boston area. I had been to one about ten years earlier. Once to accompany my fiancé for his conversion to Judaism, and once as a bride, where I felt odd and out of place as a Reform Jew.

But it was another conversion that made me understand precisely why that *mikveh* could never be "mine." I was there doing research for a book during the two hours set aside weekly for liberal conversions. A dozen men, women, and children were waiting at the door, the line spilling down the stairs and onto the walkway. In a way, it was inspiring to see so many people waiting, wanting to become Jews. But it was hot in the sun, and the *mikveh* is no place for a queue. The *mikveh* should be a place for reflection and celebration, but there was no time for any of those people to meditate or sing, no room where the assembled rabbis could offer a personal blessing or sing a song. And afterward, there was nothing to do but get back in the car—as if it was no big deal to transform your identity, alter your family constellation, and change the Jewish people forever. That was not the welcome those new Jews deserved.

And suddenly, I wanted a *mikveh* where converts could linger at the mirror before and after the blessings and immersions that symbolically transform them from not-Jewish to Jewish; a *mikveh* with a gracious room in which to give blessings and hugs, a room for raising a toast and bestowing books and candlesticks; a *mikveh* that provided both the space and time to savor a new beginning. That was the moment I started dreaming about what became Mayyim Hayyim in the spring of 2004.

Anita Diamant has written 12 books, including the international bestseller, *The Red Tent*. Her other novels include *Good Harbor*, *The Last Days of Dogtown* and *Day after Night*. Anita is a lecturer, award-winning journalist, and the author of six non-fiction guides to contemporary Jewish life, including *The New Jewish Wedding* and *Choosing a Jewish Life*. She is also founder and president of Mayyim Hayyim, Living Waters Community Mikveh and the Paula Brody & Family Education Center, in Newton, Massachusetts, a 21st century center for Jewish learning, ritual, community, and culture. (www.mayyimhayyim.org, www.anitadiamant.com)

The Bar Mitzvah – A Ghost Story
by Ed Feinstein

Rabbi Akiba traveled from town to town in Israel—teaching the Torah, judging cases, settling disputes, offering wisdom, and listening to the stories of his people. It happened that once as he made his way to a certain town, he stopped for a moment's rest beside an ancient cemetery. It was twilight, the moment between day and night, between light and darkness. It was twilight when the weary rabbi sat on the cemetery wall, between the living and the dead, between this world and the next. Suddenly a huge figure emerged from the darkness and rushed past, nearly knocking the rabbi over. In the gathering darkness, the rabbi made out the figure of a large man; on his back, a huge bundle of sticks. He was out of breath and panting hard as he hurried past the rabbi. The rabbi reached out and grabbed his thick coat.

"Wait, my brother," cried the rabbi. "Come and rest! You sound so tired. Come and catch your breath."

"Please sir, don't hinder me. I have no time to waste!" replied the man in his rush.

"Every man deserves a moment to rest. Come and sit with me, my brother," the rabbi offered.

"No, sir, you don't understand. My masters demand my every moment. I have not a second to waste. Please excuse me, but I must be off," the man panted, shaking off the rabbi's grasp.

"Your masters?" answered Rabbi Akiba. "Who would work a man so hard? If you are a laborer, I will pay for your time. And if you are a slave, I will redeem you. So come and tell me your story."

Terror began to fill the man's eyes. "Please, good sir, please let me be. I must be off!"

Now Akiba began to realize that this was no ordinary wood-gatherer and no ordinary hurry. "Tell me, brother, are you of the living or of the dead?"

"I am of the dead," declared the man. "It is my task, day and night, to gather wood and prepare charcoal. I have no permission to rest for even a moment!"

Akiba considered the man's plight—endless toil, work without rest.

"What did you do to deserve such a punishment?"

"I was the worst of sinners. I committed every conceivable offense. Every sin you can name I performed. My punishment is fair, for all the misery I brought to the world."

"And did your masters mention anything that might lighten your terrible load?" the rabbi inquired.

Once again, the man looked worried. "Please let me go. If my masters find that I've stopped, even for a moment, they will increase my suffering. Please let me go to my work. For I was told that there is no helping me. Nothing can ease this terrible burden. Except one thing—I was told that if I ever had a son who would stand before a holy community and offer praise to God...that, and only that, might lighten my terrible burden...But, sir, I don't know if I have a son. My wife was pregnant when I was taken. And if she gave birth to a son, who would want to teach him? And if someone taught him, would he rise to praise God, a boy cursed with a father like me?"

"What is the name of your city? What is the name of your wife?" asked the rabbi.

The man told him, "My town is Alduka. My wife's name is Susmida."

Some months later, Rabbi Akiba found himself in the town of Alduka. He inquired about the man's widow.

"That greedy, worthless crook! Do you know what he did to us? Let him rot wherever he is!" the townspeople screamed at the rabbi.

"And his evil witch of a wife! She was worse than him! Let her name be forgotten!"

Then the rabbi asked about their child.

"Yes, she gave birth to a son and died in childbirth," the townspeople told him. "He lives in the woods. He was raised by the beasts of the forest. No one would take him in."

Rabbi Akiba went looking for the boy, and soon found him. He had grown up in the forest. He was dressed in skins and smelled of the woods. He knew no words and acted more like an animal than a person.

Rabbi Akiba fasted for forty days, just as Moses spent forty days without food or water on the top of Mount Sinai receiving the Torah. Or like the forty days one fasts if someone accidentally drops a scroll of the Torah. Or like the forty days of repentance between the first of *elul* and *Yom Kippur*. He fasted until God Himself took notice. A voice from heaven called out, "Akiba, you fast for this boy?"

"Yes," cried Akiba. "For this abandoned child of Israel, I fast."

Then Rabbi Akiba took in the boy, bathed him, dressed him, and began to teach him the ways of human beings. And when he had mastered the ways of civilized human beings, Rabbi Akiba began to teach him what a Jew needs to know: the alphabet, then the grace after meals, the *shema* and the *amidah*.

After several months, Rabbi Akiba appeared in the synagogue. It was a *Shabbat* morning and the synagogue was crowded with worshippers. When the Torah was taken from the Ark, Rabbi Akiba stood and moved toward the *bimah*, where the Torah is read. Everyone in the synagogue rose to welcome the greatest rabbi and teacher of the generation. They anticipated a mighty sermon, words of teaching and wisdom. But the rabbi did not come that morning to offer teaching. He came to rescue a soul.

The rabbi nodded toward the door of the synagogue. Into the synagogue, fearfully and nervously, came a boy. At first, no one recognized him.

And then suddenly, someone shouted, "That's the devil's son! The child of our enemy!"

Ugly curses and words of contempt filled the synagogue. "After all they did to us, all the destruction and suffering his parents brought us, you would bring such a child among us?" they screamed.

Rabbi Akiba was undeterred. He waved his hand, and all in the synagogue fell silent. Then he gestured to the boy. The boy slowly made his way to the *bimah*, as if each step was test, a trial. Then, to the astonishment of the congregation, the boy took hold of the handles of the Torah scroll, and recited in Hebrew, "*Barchu et Adonai ha-mevorach*—Praise the Lord, Source of all blessing."

There was silence for a moment and another and yet another, as the congregation decided whether or not to answer the boy's prayer. And then, one by one, they joined together and chanted the response, "*Baruch Adonai ha-mevorach l'olam va'ed*—Praise God, Source of all blessing throughout time."

The boy completed his blessing and then read flawlessly from the Torah. Then the great Rabbi Akiba wrapped his arms about the boy and blessed him. And the community came forth and showered him with candies and sweets. The rabbi whispered, "My son, welcome home."

That night as he slept, Rabbi Akiba saw in his dreams the man he had met in the cemetery. The bundle of sticks on his back was much smaller, and the look on his face much brighter.

"Thank you, great rabbi," he said. "You have rescued my soul from the darkness. You have given me back hope."

Then Rabbi Akiba recited words from the Psalms:

O LORD, Your name endures forever,
Your fame, O LORD, through all generations;
for the LORD will champion His people,
and will have compassion on His servants. [Psalm 135]

Provenance: Based on the *Midrash Tehillim; Yalkut Sippurim, Parshat Vayeirah* 19:4; *Kala Rabati,* ch. 2.

Ed Feinstein is Senior Rabbi of Valley Beth Shalom in Encino, California. He teaches at the Ziegler Rabbinical School of the American Jewish University and the Wexner Heritage Foundation. His books, *Tough Questions Jews Ask: A Young Adult's Guide to Building a Jewish Life,* and *Jews and Judaism in the 21st Century,* were National Jewish Book Award finalists. His latest book, *Capturing the Moon,* retells the best of classic and modern Jewish folktales. Ed shares life with his wife, Nina, and three college-age kids. Every Friday afternoon, he bakes brownies from a recipe revealed to his ancestors at Mount Sinai.

The Eternal Hand
by Mark S. Golub

Once upon a time, a long, long time ago, in a far and distant land, there lived two children—a little girl and a little boy—who were the best of friends.

Every afternoon, sometime after the sun was highest in the sky, the girl would come down from her home on the hill, and the two would meet at the big rock, under the tree with the huge drooping arms, overlooking the babbling stream; and they would play all afternoon long.

They would catch frogs and laugh together as they watched the frogs jump back into the stream.

They would play hide and seek.

And they would see who could climb highest on the apple tree—or the cherry tree—and then they would sit on the ground and eat cherries for dessert together.

And when they were a little older, she taught him how to read and he showed her how to plant tulip bulbs.

And they shared secrets together.

And they made promises—which they never told another living soul.

And when they were a little older still and he was stung by a wasp, she ran up the hill and came back with a special cream that took the pain away.

And when her mother died, he sat with her on the big rock, under the tree with the huge drooping arms, overlooking the babbling stream while she wept all afternoon.

And he, too, wept inside for the pain of his friend.

And from then on, she didn't come down as often from her home on the hill; and then she didn't come at all.

And he would, from time to time, as a young man, go to stand on the rock under the tree with the drooping arms, overlooking the babbling stream—and he would think of his friend.

Then one spring morning, when young lads chase fair maidens round poles decorated with garlands, her father—the king—announced it was time to find a husband for his daughter; and that any worthy suitor could come to the castle and compete for the hand of the princess in marriage.

And the hand of the princess would go to the suitor who brought to the princess the most valuable gift of all—no simple feat for any man; for after all, what do you give a princess who already has everything?

And so two moons later, everyone gathered on the lawn of the palace to see who would win the hand of the princess.

Suitors came from miles around, bearing gifts of all kinds—wondrous gifts.

By the end of the day there were gifts everywhere on the lawn of the palace: treasure chests of fine jewelry; beautiful linens and embroidered gowns; sterling serving sets; a gold carriage pulled by a team of black Arabian stallions.

But the king—a good king and a caring father—saw that his daughter sat and nodded politely to each suitor presenting his gift, but was unmoved by all.

The king had been sure that one of the men, and one of the gifts, would stir his daughter's heart; but none did—even when the last gift had been presented.

And so the king turned to all his subjects who had gathered for this joyous occasion, and called aloud, "Is there anyone else who would compete for my daughter's hand in marriage? Is there anyone else who has a gift for the princess?"

For a moment, no one moved.

Then the gardener's son stepped forward.

He, too, had come up the hill for this great event.

And as the gardener's son advanced toward the seated princess, the king could see that his right hand was closed tight—held out in front of him.

What could he be holding?

What could he be bringing the princess?

Perhaps a precious jewel—a ruby or sapphire or diamond.

But how? Where would a gardener's son find such a prize?

The young man approached the princess, and the crowd grew silent. And when the young man stood before the princess, he opened his hand.

And behold, there was nothing in it!

All those assembled broke into laughter.

The princes and nobles jeered at the gardener's son; and the king bellowed in anger:

"How dare you mock my daughter, offering her nothing!"

And the crowd grew silent again, fearing the king's wrath.

But then the gardener's son spoke to the princess seated before him, saying:

"This *is* my gift. I give you my hand:

To help lift you up when you fall along the way;

To help carry your burden whenever it grows too heavy;
     To cradle your head in times of illness;
     To applaud your victories—large and small;
     To wash your tears when you weep from pain of loss;
     To caress your hair in evenings of love.

"And with this hand," said the gardener's son, "I will take your hand:

     To run with you through fields of joy;
     To splash through life's springs of laughter;
     To clasp your hand...in silent awe
     when we watch our children...
               grow and play
               and learn;
               and one day wed;
               and bear children of their own,
               our children's children.

"And to hold your hand tighter still

     when, at the twilight of our day,
     our sun does set;
     to feed you cherries upon your bed.

"Through this hand, I give you my heart, my being, and my undying love."

And with moistened eyes the princess arose and placed her hand in the hand of her friend.
     And the king smiled, and the people cheered, and ten days later the two friends wed—on the big rock, under the tree with the huge drooping arms, overlooking the babbling stream.

And in heaven it was written, on that summer's day: "No greater gift can one give another than an eternally loving hand."

Provenance: This story is one I have shared with my congregation on the first night of *Rosh Hashannah* to express the transcending mitzvah of life challenging us at the start of a New Year.

Mark S. Golub is the president and executive producer of Shalom TV, America's national Jewish television network. Recognized by *Newsweek* in 2009 as one of the 50 most influential rabbis, Mark lectures on *midrash* and Jewish thought to Jewish groups throughout America. Mark is also the founding rabbi of Chavurat Aytz Chayim in Stamford, Connecticut, and Chavurat Deevray Torah in Greenwich, Connecticut, which he has been serving since 1972. He also created the first Russian-language television channel in America (RTN) to serve the hundreds of thousands of Jews who have immigrated from the former Soviet Union. (www.shalomtv.com)

Men On Menses
by James Stone Goodman

My child was a precocious kid, a thinking sophisticate who was often overly confident about her life-wisdom. She had many challenges in her life, and met most of them with wisecracking wit; she was funny and confident. Some of her confidence was earned; some was not. She thought she knew more than she knew (I rarely challenged her). She was comfortable speaking to me about most everything, and it often was my place in the family to be the one on the scene for her. I was present when she began menstruating. It came to pass that it happened when her mother, my wife, was out of town.

After my daughter revealed to me her menstruating experience, I had a hard time sleeping that night. I was thinking I should make a ceremony out of her passage. I felt as if I we should mark it with ceremonies and songs, prescribed rituals to mark the transition, that we should find and perform a mitzvah associated with it, but what did I know about menstruation? My experience was limited; this is a woman's domain. And there really is no blessing for menstruation, no ritual that I was familiar with, only the obvious imagery—the moon. There must be some way I could share this with my daughter. She was amused by my efforts.

When I told her of my intentions, her face registered both a little girl look of disgust and a womanly look of expectation. The two expressions met at the boundary of her passing from girlhood to womanhood, a mask of girl–woman worn for these few days when she would be poised between the two—part girl, part woman—each tugging on the other, their proximity expressed in her face.

"OK," I said to her, "maybe we should go outside and do a menstrual dance under the moon."

"A menstrual dance?"

"Yeah, under the moon, a meeting of the cycles of the body—like the cycles of the moon.

So we went outside, and under the moon we did a goofy little dance that came off pretty well because it was dark. I sang a sacred Hebrew song normally sung during the New Moon ceremony, greeting the angels, greeting each other, and speaking the words with the proper intention: "O angels of peace, bless us with peace. Come in peace, bless us with peace, leave in peace." I sang a sinuous Sefardi melody that we both loved.

I picked her up and held her to my heart, her face bathed in moonlight. I'm not sure what I was doing but she was laughing, and inside the laughter was also a release into the moment.

"You know," she said in mock seriousness, "in the eyes of the Jewish people, I am now a woman."

The next morning she came out of the bathroom with another ambiguous expression on her face: horror and awe, girl and woman. She confided to me some of the particulars of bathroom hygiene and asked my advice. I answered, trusting again my intuition. She laughed.

She didn't have pads for school, and I insisted that we stop at Walgreens.

At Walgreens, I said, "I know where they are."

"How do you know?"

"Because it's Walgreens. I come here every day. I could be a guide for Walgreens."

We went to the pads aisle.

"I have no idea what to get."

"Here, get these," I said.

"How do you know?" she asked earnestly.

"Trust me. Get these."

She insisted that I carry them. Across the aisle were incontinence diapers. "One day you will carry these for me," I told her.

In the same aisle were baby diapers. "Yesterday I was carrying these for you," I said, the entire story of our lives together told in pads and diapers.

She asked me some questions about how to use the pads, which I answered to her continuing surprise, "Because it's, er, intuitive."

There has always been some gender-bending around our house. I had to learn to do things that were not natural for me, but I learned.

Later we rode in silence in the car. "There's a name for you," she said, laughing at her own joke before she said it out loud.

"Ok, what?"

"Lesbian. You're like a woman, who likes other women."

"Yeah, yeah, I get it. That's good."

In the car on the way to school, she opened the box of pads and put about a half a dozen in her backpack.

"How long do you plan to be away?" I asked.

"For today, and tomorrow, and the next day at school."

"OK."

"Daddy, what do I do, if you know. . .I have to. . .do I raise my hand and say, 'Miss Baker, I'm menstruating. Can I go to the bathroom?'"

"Exactly, except leave out the part about menstruating."

On the way to school, I stopped to give her lunch. Chinese Express. While we were eating, we played a game we always played, a variation on Twenty Questions but always about cartoon characters. We asked each other simple questions about the mystery character until we guessed it: male or female, Warner Brothers, Disney, animal, fish, etc.

"Cartoon character," she said.

"Menstruating or non-menstruating?" I asked.

Provenance: I grew up in a family without sisters. My first child was a son, so my knowledge of feminine things was somewhat theoretical and delayed until I was blessed with two daughters. I wrote this story in the way I write many stories, hoping I would remember the experience.

James Stone Goodman serves as rabbi of Congregation Neve Shalom and the Central Reform Congregation, in St. Louis, Missouri. He is a writer and musician who integrates story, poetry, and music in a performance art form. He has produced five CDs to date, the most recent *The Book of Splendor.* He recently finished an M.F.A. in creative writing at the University of Missouri–St. Louis. (www.stonegoodman.com, www.neveshalom.org)

Chayala, Give Me A Smile-a
by Eva Grayzel

It took me more than ten years to realize that my sixth grade teacher, Rabbi Reshevsky at Moriah Hebrew Day School, had had a memorable and positive influence on my life. One day when I was driving home from a storytelling performance, I was reveling in the warm feeling inside that came from my having involved in my storytelling program a young girl, supported by a walker, who had been sitting in the very last row of a large auditorium full of schoolchildren. Suddenly, my thoughts were interrupted by an image of Rabbi Reshevsky, with his peppered beard, *payes* tucked behind his ears, and *schmutz* here or there on his jacket. Why would I even entertain a thought about that school where I felt like such an outsider? Why Rabbi Reshevsky? Why now?

I remembered how I had always entered his classroom, disgruntled from my previous class in Prophets, or was it Gemara? I struggled through those classes taught in Hebrew. When we were short on time, my other Hebrew teachers would simply skip over me because I took so long. But when I entered Rabbi Reshevsky's class, he would open his arms saying, "*Chayala, Chayala,* give me a smile-a."

I liked the extra 'la' he added to my Hebrew name. He would motion for me to sit right next to his large wood desk covered with papers and old books. Then he would squeeze my cheek so hard. It hurt, but I never told him to stop.

Every year, Rabbi Reshevsky held a school-wide "Bracha Bee." It was like a spelling bee except you were asked to recite the blessings for different kinds of food. Just like everyone else, I wanted to win. There was a prize for the winners in the different classes. Although I studied the *brachas*, I felt I was at a disadvantage compared to my classmates because the only *brachas* I said outside of school were over the Sabbath candles, and even that wasn't every week.

In the first round of the Bracha Bee, when it was my turn, I stood up and Rabbi Reshevsky looked me in the eye with a confident smile and asked me,

"*Chayala,* what is the *bracha* for apple juice?"

Without hesitation, I answered, "*Baruch ata adoshem elokeinu*[20] *melech*

---

[20] To fulfill the practice of not taking God's name in vain, some Jews use *adoshem* and *elokeinu* and similar forms of substitution for the holy names used during prayer.

ha-olam..."

That part is easy. It's the same in most blessings. I slowed down a little, giving the last three critical words of this blessing... "*boray p'ri hagaf...*"

Before I finished the last syllable, the Rabbi asked, as he did with everyone, "Is that your final answer?" Most of my classmates were very confident with their first answer. I hesitated. Being given a moment to rethink the answer, I realized I was giving the *bracha* for wine. Juice was often substituted for wine; I had given the answer without really thinking it through.

Now, with a second chance, I said, "I mean, *borei p'ri ha-eytz.*"

Once again, my voice betrayed a lack of confidence. Even though I had studied, probably harder than most students. I didn't have regular opportunities outside of school to use these blessings.

Again, Rabbi Reshevsky asked, as he did with everyone, "Is that your final answer?"

I looked deep into his watery, glazed, gray eyes.

"Come on," a kid cried out. "She's always so slow," another whispered. From the end of the line, I heard, "Stupid."

Rabbi Reshevsky ignored the taunts, and I saw a warm sincerity and acceptance in his eyes. In that moment, it came to me. I had given the blessing for fruit from a tree, not for fruit juice.

For the third time, I gave my answer. I began slowly, feeling confidence well up in me,

"*Baruch ata adoshem, elokainu melech ha-olam, shehakol...*"

As that word left my lips, I saw his mustache widen. "*...niheye...*" The ends of his lips moved ever so slightly upwards. "*...bidvaro.*"

"Is that your final answer?"

I knew I was on the right track this time. "Yes."

Rabbi Reshevsky called out, "*Nachon, Chayala.* Next."

Believe it or not, I made it to the final round. After the first round, I didn't make any more stupid mistakes, I thought each question through before I answered.

Lo and behold, I won the Bracha Bee! The prize? A baseball game at Yankee Stadium. I was so excited. I had never seen a professional baseball game before.

On the appointed Sunday, Rabbi Reshevsky drove up in his blue Oldsmobile with a couple of other schoolmates in his car. I dressed in my usual attire: a long skirt, a long-sleeved T-shirt, and sneakers. Rabbi Reshevsky always looked the same in his black suit, his white shirt covered by his long-kinky, peppered beard.

The four other winners and I got out of his car and walked towards the stadium. I noticed a guy in the coolest faded jeans, which had a rip on one knee and below his back left pocket. I noticed a girl wearing faded Levi's, an over-sized jacket, and loose-fitting tie. How I wished I had a faded pair of jeans like hers. I wanted to feel "cool," too.

As he studied the signs to figure out which area and aisle our seats were located, Rabbi Reshevsky stroked his beard as he did while teaching *chumash*. "Section H," he said in his sing-songy voice, pointing his finger as he did as if he were teaching an important passage from the Five Books of Moses. After stroking his beard some more, he looked back at the ticket. In that same sing-songy voice, swooping his finger down, he said, "Aisle 12." We followed him to our seats.

I dropped to the back of the line, continuing to eye with envy the people around me, so comfortable in this environment. I think I was feeling uncomfortable standing too near Rabbi Reshevsky, all dressed in black. He really stuck out in the crowd. I found myself taking the furthest seat from Rabbi Reshevsky. My knees pointed in the other direction. I watched the family next to me more than I watched the game. I observed how they cheered together, at the same time as most people in the stadium; they enjoyed hot dogs and cotton candy along with so many others who bought food and drinks from the vendors who went up and down the aisle throughout the game. It was torture.

At some point someone passed me a bag of kosher potato chips and Sun-Maid raisins, which Rabbi Reshevsky had brought as snacks. Rabbi Reshevsky looked over at me and smiled.

"*Chayala*, give me a smile-a."

I tried hard to smile back, but could hardly manage a grin.

I left the stadium close to tears. I was so confused. When I got home, I threw myself down on my bed and cried my eyes out for a long time alone in my room, desperately trying to understand why I felt so confused and unhappy. Rabbi Reshevsky was my favorite teacher, the one who made me feel that I was important, that I counted. I always felt that I was not a good enough Jew because I was not raised in an Orthodox home like most of my classmates. Rabbi Reshevsky made me feel that I was good enough and that every little bit of goodness counted. Yet I didn't want to be seen near him in public. I wanted to feel like I was Orthodox and convert my family so I could feel a part of a larger community. But the truth was that I wasn't. I wanted to feel like those people around me in the stadium cheering and eating unkosher hot dogs, but I did not fit in with them, either.

Suddenly, I realized why I had thought of Rabbi Reshevsky in the car that day. I had always felt different, not quite fitting in. Today I had helped another misfit, a young disabled girl, appear more capable to the unconfident, negative teacher sitting beside her. That's what Rabbi Reshevsky taught me— that I was worth that extra time and effort, too.

Every child who spontaneously participates in my presentations has the opportunity to learn what Rabbi Reshevsky taught me: You are a star, just the way you are. That's what he made me feel when he would open his arms and say to me, "*Chayala, Chayala,* give me a smile-a."

Provenance: Eva attended Moriah Hebrew Day School in Englewood, NJ. She contacted Rabbi Reshevsky after writing the story to let him know how he impacted her life. She learned that he had been teaching at Yavneh Academy, but with over 15 years gone by, he did not remember Eva (aka Chaya). However, he was touched to know that he had made a difference.

Eva Grayzel is an expert on interactive storytelling, inviting as many as 50 audience members to spontaneously role-play stories emphasizing *derech eretz, tikkun olam,* and *tzedakah.* In addition to performing nationally, Eva teaches educators how to introduce Jewish concepts, Hebrew vocabulary, and history through interactive storytelling techniques. She offers a *bikkur cholim* workshop and a parent workshop on creating meaningful and memorable Jewish family rituals. Eva released an award-winning video, *The Secret In Bubbe's Attic;* two storytelling CD's, *Absolute Chanukah,* and *A Story A Day;* and authored *You Are Not Alone: Families Touched by Cancer.* (www.EvaGrayzel.com, www.SixstepScreening.org, www.Talk4Hope.com)

If My Wedding Dress Could Talk
by Bonnie Greenberg

"Something old, something new,
something borrowed, something blue."

Over the years as a wedding dress, I've been "ALL THAT."

When I was first fashioned, I was considered so beautiful that they featured me on the cover of *Bride's Magazine!* I was SO versatile. I gave the impression of a sheath dress, but the way I was draped three quarters around, there was plenty of room under my bustle for dancing with abandon and no fear of restrictions. My bride saw me on the magazine stands the day after she got engaged...it was love at first sight! She immediately placed a picture of her face on the model. By noon, she had mailed it to her parents! Her parents had a lovely ladies' shop and could order just about anything to wear!

Her note read: "Oh, Mom, Dad! Can you order this for me? I love it, and I know Larry will, too!"

Well, of course they could AND they did. My new life began within thirty days...shipping and handling included!

Not only was I a perfect fit, but we were a perfect match. August 22nd, the wedding day, arrived. The wedding music was played, and you could hear the guests gasp as the doors opened, and I had my "reveal!" My bride and her groom stood motionless. Eyes locked, they gazed at one another. As the strains of *Erev Shel Shoshanim* played, her parents walked her halfway down the aisle and kissed her. Her groom took her hand to lead her up to the *chuppah* on the *bimah.*

The rabbi began, "Larry, I don't know that there are words to describe the feelings that you felt as you looked upon your bride coming down the aisle to greet you."

Oh, there was not a dry eye in the room.

Well, you may well think that they locked their dreamy eyes and imagined their future in perfect harmony, but here's what I think:

Just one look at *me*, and he was transfixed! As they wrote in the newspaper, "The bride wore a formal, floor-length wedding gown of silk organza with embroidered mimosa. The sheath skirt extended into a full chapel train."

YES! Truly, I looked regal!

The last thing I remember about that evening is that after I was done swishing and sashaying non-stop around the dance floor for hours, the guests implored my bride to leave for her honeymoon before midnight!

She kept saying, "But I want to wear my wedding dress longer! It could be the last time."

You may think that's that. You may think I was hung out to dry after that, but you would be mistaken. Just a few years later, my bride donned me once again for a neighborhood "STILL MARRIED" party. Everyone dressed in their wedding gowns and went out to dinner! My bride and me? We were still a perfect match, but maybe not a perfect fit. I must admit my zipper strained a bit after years of sitting in the closet, but zip I did, and as a reward, I had another evening of dancing 'til the stars faded from view and the brilliant sun rose over the horizon. Johnny Mathis albums never get old.

Years passed. By now, I looked a little older. What had been dazzling white organza now was turning a little "antique white," shall we say? Yes, parts of me had gone south with age. Wrinkles appeared in places we won't mention. This is not to say I'd lost my glow...in fact, while not perfect, parts of me were excellent. My bride had again lovingly and reluctantly placed me back in the closet. How was she to know there would be a flood in that room? I did survive that flood, but I looked a little shabbier than before. Though my train had been bustled up, it still draped on the floor, and the floodwaters were not kind.

I remember the whole thing. At first, there was just a sprinkle of rain that didn't foretell the disaster that would ensue. I calmly comforted myself that a little water couldn't dampen my spirits or my savoir faire. As the waters rose, I wasn't so sure. At the end of the first flood, I was hung out to dry.

The room was repaired with a promise that no more floods would occur. No, I didn't see a rainbow exactly, but I felt secure that my bride would be careful about where I was placed. I've always been a relentless optimist! How could she know there would be a second flood...and a third. Both times, it was impossible to hustle my bustle quickly enough to avoid the near-ruinous damage.

Through all the years of married life, can one predict what floods will come? My bride was once madly in love with me! Would such a partnership last? Just one look at me would evoke memories for both of us of happier days. But flood after flood....

By now, I didn't think there was much of me to salvage. The part of me that once swished across the dance floor with fluid grace was now stiff with age and dried out floodwaters. You could hear me crackle as I was moved from the clothesline into the closet. Yes, I remained in the closet, but I wasn't sure I'd be dancing at any weddings any time soon.

Over the years, I watched other garments go in and out of the closet. Next to me was the tailored dress she wore to her husband's graduation from medical school. She never did part with the white suit she wore to court when the children were adopted. The somber black suit she wore to her father's funeral still had the torn ribbon on the collar. Don't repeat this, but when she and hubby renewed their wedding vows on their 25th anniversary, my train was used to make the lingerie for their repeat honeymoon!

In time, my bride became an adult *bat mitzvah* and she chose me... ME! once again to be her companion on life's journey. Well, the surgery I needed for that occasion wasn't all that pleasant. A nip here, a tuck there, tightening the loose places and adding a BLUE fringe here and there...and voila, a *tallis* I became! White organza with embroidered mimosa in all the right places. And...as a matching *kippah*, I was splendid. From there atop her head, I could see everything! I had never been that close to a Torah reader, and my bride could really belt out that trope! It was thrilling! And we were together again...on the *bimah* again...women crowded around us afterwards saying how proud and inspired they were to hear a woman read the Torah. At that time, it was not all that common like it is today! Tears flowed...just like at the wedding! I saw some of the same people there. I missed those who were no longer alive...and that was sad. Part of life's journey.

At *shul* as her *tallis*, we were inseparable. She held me, kissed me, prayed with me. Every time she put me on, she paused a moment for a special personal prayer under my protective veil. Many women wore their own *tallis*. Forgive me if I boast that I was the loveliest in the room.

For years, that's how it was. We had good times and bad...there were simchahs and funerals, holidays and regular *Shabbat*...times of unbearable sadness and inexplicable joy. Part of life's journey together.

Then, the unexpected!! For her recent birthday, my bride got a new *tallis*. I don't mind telling you I was enraged! I was jealous, hurt, mad!

"That's it!! I guess I'll be packed away by noon tomorrow!" I was inconsolable.

But wait, what's this? More nip and tuck? Oh my! Guess what? I'm to be the special handkerchiefs for her grandchildren's weddings. A *chasseneh*? More weddings?! Oh! I'll dance yet again!!

"Something old, something new, something borrowed, something blue."

I'm ALL THAT and more...the fabric of life's journey...and there's just enough of me left to make a story!

Provenance Note: In the New England floods of March 2010, my personal belongings took yet another hit. As I gently placed remnants of my wedding dress out to dry, I marveled that the fabric could reflect such beauty after all these years and three floods. Then, it occurred to me that this precious fabric had accompanied me through my life's journey through several cities and more than one continent. Maybe such a faithful companion deserved a voice. When the third flood ravaged our home, it was tempting to finally give up salvaging my beloved wedding dress. Then, I recalled a favorite Jewish folktale/song about the Tailor! I decided with a little snip here and a little snip there, I could fashion a story to preserve my wedding dress forever (while carrying on "TRADITION"!). Enjoy! It's all true!

Bonnie Greenberg, M.S., is an experienced educator/storyteller whose vibrant stories are rooted in her love of people, her Appalachian childhood, her life in Israel and her travels abroad. Replete with guitar, dumbek and song, her deep and dynamic approach to Jewish folktales and world folklore frame performances for all ages, including Holocaust Commemoration programs. Over the years, she's been a leader in the National Jewish Storytelling Network, the Jewish Storytelling Coalition, and the LANES Board. Bonnie's audio recordings, *From the Hearts of the People* and *The Wonder Child,* have won several awards, including a Parents' Choice and NAPPA Gold.

Floating Lovers
by Tina Grimberg

The waitress brought us two steaming cappuccinos, welcome heat to counter the snowy chill of a wintery New York City. My cousin took off her leather gloves and set her pack down on the seat next to us. The snowflakes fell gently outside our window. I joked lightly: "This weather reminds me of Kiev. You lucky goose—always on planes! And what do I get? A few stories and some pictures!" She laughed and reached for her bag. "You told me you missed something really grand in Paris on your last trip. It was too bad they were renovating at the time, because you really missed a masterpiece." From her worn leather knapsack, she pulled out a package. My hands held a colorful book filled with images of Marc *Chagall*'s ceiling in the Paris Opera House.

I flipped through the pages, marveling at the dreamy images that reminded me of my past. Suddenly, I stopped at one color plate that captured my attention. A city on a hill, a wise-looking playful calf, musicians and dancers challenging gravity, angels...and a couple of lovers floating over everything else. I said: "You devil, you! You got to see it before me...but you knew how much I would cherish this book." We sipped our coffees, enjoying the colorful pictures which shone from the pages. My eyes returned to the image of that couple in love. They were angelic, timeless and undisturbed by the earthly city below. Pointing to them, I commented: "This is what happens when you fall in love, right?" She laughed and replied: Well...that's what happened the last time...." We looked at each other knowingly. But a glance at my watch told me I was running late. "Oh, no...I need to run...I'm late for that appointment on the Upper West Side. Coffee's on me next time!" The book was quickly stashed in my briefcase, as I rushed out into the Russian winter clouding the streets of Manhattan.

The blue of her eyes reminded me of the color of a vast Russian sky. "I have been waiting for this my whole life," she said in Russian after she emerged, radiant, from the living waters of the small pool. I had been asked by a colleague to serve as a witness at this unique conversion, due to my ability to speak Ludmilla's mother tongue. The officiating rabbis needed an interpreter as well as a rabbi. I filled both criteria...

My new friend was seventy-nine years old. Born near Moscow to a Russian Christian family, she had witnessed the rise of communism, Stalin's purges, and World War II. As a young woman, Ludmilla had trained as a nurse, and at the beginning of the Second World War, she had been assigned to a Moscow hospital to treat and care for the numerous wounded soldiers who were brought in from the battlefields.

Yosief was raised in an Orthodox Jewish family in the Carpathian region. Later in his youth, he was drafted into the Soviet army. During the war, a bomb went off, killing several of his friends, but Yosief was lucky and was only wounded. The young Russian nurse Ludmilla had been assigned to his floor. His dark, inquisitive eyes melted into her blue, Russian gaze. And an unexplainable thing happened—two people from two different worlds looked at each other and heard the same music. The small piece of metal that made its way into Yosief's chest was not the only thing that settled near his heart for life. The love for Ludmilla and her cool, blue eyes also carved a place in his chest forever. She nursed him to wellness.

After the war, they married with joy, and Ludmilla followed Yosief to his home in the Carpathians and made it her home, too. They had children. Despite Soviet oppression, this brave woman pieced together a Jewish life for herself and her children. It was a dangerous period in Russian Jewish life. Rabbis were arrested and sent away, and synagogues and study houses were closed. Despite all the dangers, Ludmilla created Jewish life out of whispered blessings, a recipe or two, and a sigh.

Ludmilla was educated, and her Russian flowed with grace: "From Yosief's mother I learned to light *Shabbat* candles. My mother-in-law taught me what animals are permitted, and what is forbidden to a Jew. Together, Yosief and I skipped work on the Day of Atonement and fasted in secret. I held on to these little things with my life," she said. "They made me feel Jewish."

Accompanied by their children and grandchildren, Ludmilla and Yosief arrived in New York in the 1990's. And in this land of freedom, Jewish conversion became a reality for them. Because I was a rabbi who spoke Russian, I was asked to be on Ludmilla's conversion *beit din*, a conversion board, and I felt honored. We shared a culture and memories and love of Judaism. In our conversation, I asked her why she felt the need to convert after all this time, since I saw how she already felt Jewish and lived a Jewish life. Why was the ceremony so important to her? She was silent for a moment, then sighed and responded: "I chose Jewish destiny when I married my husband, and now that life is coming to a close, I want to be buried next to him as a Jew. This is the least I can do after the life we shared together."

I looked at them as they walked out on the street, leaving the West Side Mikvah behind. Yosief was leaning on his cane with one hand and holding the hand of his beloved with the other. Amidst the swirling

February snow, the two of them looked weightless, dancing in the sky... The scene reminded me of Marc Chagall's paintings. As if in a dream-like state, the two lovers were locked in a gentle embrace and floated high above the city skyline...moving to the inner rhythm of each other's hearts.

Provenance: This is a true story based on events that happened in New York City soon after my ordination from the Hebrew Union College. It is true not only because the events actually happened; its truth derives also from its timeless Jewish and universal lessons—love, courage and wisdom. Ludmilla and Yosief were wonderful teachers of such lessons. Their personal story reminded me that love often finds us at the most unexpected times, and that the warmth of a traditional Jewish family can model a life worth emulating.

Tina Grimberg grew up in the Ukrainian city of Kiev. She moved to North America with her family when she was sixteen. Tina initially trained and worked as a family therapist. She has her rabbinical degree from Hebrew Union College-JIR and presently serves Congregation Darchei Noam in Toronto. Her first book of memoirs, *Out of Line: Growing Up Soviet*, has won numerous awards.

The Lion of Yerushalayim
by Sharona Margolin Halickman

Here we go again: before the birth of each of my children, I bite off the *pitom* of the *etrog* on *Hoshannah Rabbah*. There's a *midrash* that says that the fruit that Adam and Chava ate in the Garden of Eden against God's wishes was an *etrog*, not an apple. Chava's punishment was that she, and the women who would come after her, would have a difficult childbirth. I have waited patiently throughout the holiday of *Sukkot*, until *Hoshannah Rabbah* to taste the *etrog*, so there can be a *tikkun*, and instead of having a difficult childbirth, I should have an easy one.

This *Hoshannah Rabbah* is different, as the birth of my third child will take place in the land of Israel, while the birth of my other two sons took place in the Bronx, New York. The *etrog* smells so good; and I can see why Chava would have felt that it was seductive. I can see why she couldn't wait, but I hold off for a week. There is no way that I will eat this $25 fruit (a bargain compared to the $50+ that it would have cost me in the US) before the end of the holiday. I have had difficult births with my first son, Dov, and my second son, Moshe. I'm hoping that this time, two months from today, I will give birth to a healthy baby boy here in Jerusalem without very much pain.

After I bite off this *pitom*, I will say a *techinah* prayer found in *seder techinos u'vakashos* that Jewish women have said throughout the ages: "Lord of the world, because Chava ate of the *etrog* all of us women must suffer such great pangs as to die. Had I been in the Garden of Eden, I would not have had any enjoyment from the fruit. Just so, I have not wanted to render the *etrog* unfit during the whole seven days when it was used for a mitzvah. But now, on *Hoshannah Rabbah*, the mitzvah is no longer applicable, but I am still not in a hurry to eat it. And just as little enjoyment as I get from the stem of the *etrog*, would I have gotten from the *etrog* that you forbade." These words, along with the biting off of the *pitom*, will hopefully be the key to an easy and quick birth.

I can't believe that I'm due in a week. I'm so excited about my Jerusalem, *sabra* baby. I just happened to see this great ad for a doula, a young woman finishing her training who will come to assist at my birth at no charge! In America, people pay hundreds of dollars to have these women come in and help them relax during labor, and I don't have to pay a single *agora*! My pregnant friends in America would be so jealous right now if they found out.

"Hi, Sarah, I read an ad that you would like to help assisting at births in order to finish your degree. I'm due next week, at the end of *Hanukkah*. Are you free to come help out? OK, wonderful, tomorrow is great. Let's meet so we'll know a little bit about each other before we get there."

Sarah sounds lovely, and I can't wait to meet her. But in the meantime, I'm going to go check out the Hadassah Hospital on Mt. Scopus and make sure that I want to give birth there.

This hospital is gorgeous, and everything is so clean. There is a certain friendly atmosphere at an Israeli hospital, as opposed to the Bronx where they told me to "take a seat" and didn't care that I was waiting to get checked out. How does a woman who is in labor for four days and having contractions "take a seat"? In the Bronx they tore up my paperwork on *Shabbat* when they said that it was too early to admit me! There I felt no love or respect. Here in Jerusalem, everyone is excited that I'm giving birth to another Israeli. This place is so nice; this is where I want to give birth. I'm going to tell Sarah, my doula, that I'm registering here.

The *meyaldot* (midwives) seem really great. In Israel they don't even use doctors at births. They are very progressive here. The *meyaldot* spend their days assisting at births, and doctors are only called in an emergency. In Jerusalem, between the Arabs and *haredim*, who have between 8 to 12 children per family, a lot of the mothers come in as pros already!

"Bubbie and Zaydie should be arriving from the airport any minute! Let's get all of the *latkes* ready so that as soon as they get here, we can light the sixth *Hanukkah* candle together and eat all of the *Hanukkah* treats," I tell my children as they run around our home with excitement in their eyes.

These *latkes* smell so good! I have been on my feet preparing them for the last two hours. Now I am ready to eat them all. If Josh and his parents don't get here in two minutes, I will eat them all myself. As I set the table, and am about to bring out the *latkes*, the doorbell buzzes and my in-laws, Bubbie and Zaydie, Myrna and Mel, come in from the airport with Josh. They are shocked to see how many *latkes* I have on the plate and how many we have already devoured. After some hugs and smiles, we light the *Hanukkah* candles and sit down to eat.

"Sharona, you look fantastic, and I can't believe we haven't seen you since before you were expecting. I can't believe you made all these incredible *latkes*, given the circumstances," my mother-in-law says. "You look like you worked really hard, so tomorrow we'll treat you to Chinese food so you don't have to do any more work, and you can just relax."

Chinese food, with all of those spices, may actually push my labor along. I then smile ecstatically. "I can't argue with that. After all, I remember how those spices from the Chinese cooking class I took before Moshe's birth got him moving. If that's going to help me and I won't have to cook or clean up, then that sounds great."

The beef and broccoli, flaky spring rolls, wonton soup, sweet and sour chicken, fried rice, and garlic fried vegetables are virtually all gone. It didn't take much time for us to eat everything we had on the table.

I think we've all had enough to eat, and the boys need to go to bed. I'm not feeling great, but I need to finish my *d'var Torah* that I send out each week over e-mail. My in-laws help put my children to bed while Josh and I clear the table. I sit at the dining room table in front of the laptop computer since my in-laws are already sleeping in the room with the computer. I am hoping to finish this *d'var Torah* as soon as possible.

I'm almost done with it, and I think I just felt a contraction. I can't stop typing until I finish, because if this is it, I won't have a chance to finish before *Shabbat*. I am typing as fast as I can. Oh, no! Another contraction! I just need to send it out to everyone on the email list. OK, it has been sent. Time to go to the hospital! I need to wake up Josh, call the doula, and let my in-laws know that we are off to the hospital.

I'll wake up Josh first. As I open the door to our bedroom without knocking, Josh springs up and asks, "What's going on?" His voice is filled with fear.

"Get up and get dressed. I'm calling Sarah, the doula, and we're going to the hospital," in a hurried voice. "It's time!" As Josh gets ready to leave, I throw on a loose, purple dress and rush down the hall to where my in-laws are sleeping. I knock on the door and am answered with a muffled, "Come in..."

I open the door, and in a voice just above a whisper, tell my in-laws, "I'm in labor, and we are going to the hospital."

All of a sudden, they are awake, and Josh's father asks, "Really? Are you sure?"

I respond, "Yes! It's 2 a.m. I wouldn't have woken you up otherwise!"

As we call the cab, a sharp pain shoots through me; another contraction is happening. The cab comes to a quick stop in front of us, and we get in. It's so surprising to me to see how busy the streets of Jerusalem are at this time on a Thursday night as we drive to Hadassah Hospital.

I see Sarah standing at the curb waiting for me to arrive. The nurse examines me. I am happy to see I am already three centimeters dilated, which back in America would have gotten me admitted to the hospital. However, the nurse politely points out that here in Israel I need to be four centimeters to be admitted. I will now be spending my time walking around Hadassah Hospital to encourage the dilation. It's great to have Sarah walk the halls with me, and Josh is able to relax a little and read the newspaper, building up energy to help with the birth. All night long, we spend walking the corridors, reading the plaques with names of all of the generous people throughout the world who made the hospital possible.

The sun is up, and I am finally at four centimeters. To my relief, they admit me into the hospital, and they're taking me to a labor room. The clock reads 7 a.m., and the nurses are switching shifts as they squabble over which room to give me. I am thrilled to find out that due to all my walking, I am worthy of a room that has a huge window with a breathtaking view overlooking all of Jerusalem. I have yet to fall asleep, and don't expect to any time soon. Josh is relieved to find that we have an English-speaking *meyaledet* from Boston, Massachusetts, who will be delivering the baby. Gail is her name, and she couldn't be more perfect for us at this time.

Sarah is such a wonderful help. Gail is rotating between the other women, and Sarah stays at my side. Since I'm not making much progress right now, Josh quietly takes his *tefillin* and leaves to go downstairs to find a quiet place to *daven shacharit*. He tells Sarah to look for him if we need anything. Josh doesn't return for a while. What was supposed to be a few minutes has now turned into an hour. Where is he already? I start to get nervous, and I'm not sure why he is delayed. Why is it taking so long to *daven*? What if he misses the birth? I could send Sarah to look for him, but I really don't want to be left alone. Sarah puts music on and soothes me with her positive comments and helpful remarks as we focus on the priceless view from our window of the old and new cities of Jerusalem.

Now things are moving fast, and the pregnancy is accelerating. Josh hurries in and explains that he ended up finding the *shul* downstairs and *davened* with a *minyan*. The service ended up lasting longer than usual, since it is *Rosh Chodesh* and *Hanukkah*, one of the longest weekday services of the year. Since they were *davening* Carlebach style, they sang the entire service out loud. As it turned out, the man leading the service was someone that we knew from Riverdale. Now that I know who was leading the service, a major Carlebach follower who dresses like a shepherd, wearing a white robe with long *payes*, long hair and a large *kippah*, I understand why it took so long!

I am glad that Josh is back and in such a good mood after having the chance to attend such a spiritual service. This was very different from the births of my other two sons. Before Dov's birth, we were in such a rush to get to the hospital that Josh hadn't been able to grab his *tefillin* before we left. The day of Dov's birth was the only day that Josh missed putting on *tefillin* since before his *bar mitzvah*. For Moshe's birth, we had Josh's *tefillin* packed a week before, but in the end, Moshe was born early on a *Shabbat* morning, a day when *tefillin* are not worn. I knew it had been difficult and stressful for him not to have been able to put on *tefillin* during Dov and Moshe's births, so this was a good change for him.

Finally, it's really time.

As my new son emerges, Gail, the *meyaledet*, asks me if she can do *negelvasser*, to wash his hands ritually as traditional Jews do when they wake up in the morning, something that definitely wouldn't have happened back in the Bronx! I, of course, agree, and she begins to discuss the significance of our new son being born on the seventh candle of *Hanukkah*. Against the background of the holiest city in the world, it is so spiritually uplifting seeing my new child perform his first mitzvah.

Just as I am about to hold the baby for the first time, Sarah's phone rings. Another expectant mom has just gone into labor and asks Sarah to meet her at Shaarei Zedek Hospital on the other side of Jerusalem so that she can check in and get settled before *Shabbat*. We thank Sarah for all of her help and promise to keep in touch.

They move me into a very small room in which I will be staying until Sunday, and I am introduced to my new roommates, one of whom is *Chassidic* and the other, *Haredi*. I am sure this *Shabbat* will be spent discussing the numerous differences between our ways of life.

Josh comes in the room to tell me that on his way home, he is going to *daven minchah* at the *kotel*. He will then pick up our older children, Dov and Moshe, as well as Bubbie and Zaydie, and drive them to the hospital to meet the new baby. They will then have to rush home. (Since it is the shortest Friday of the year, they will need enough time to light the candles for the eighth day of *Hanukkah* before they light the *Shabbat* candles.) A friend of ours has graciously agreed to wait in our home while the *Shabbat* food cooks so that everything will be ready in time. The older brothers and grandparents are excited to meet the baby during their brief visit. They know that on Sunday, they will have more time to spend with us.

The room I am in is very different than the ones that I stayed in during my previous births in the Bronx. It is much smaller, and I am not bothered with people asking if I would like to rent a television or buy formula and diapers. Over *Shabbat*, everything is quiet, and there are no photographers trying to sell us pictures, or magazines begging us to subscribe. It is so different from the US, with not a mention of the Christmas season. Rather, there is excitement in the hospital for all of the newborns who were born on the Festival of Lights.

In Israel, after the women give birth, they don't lie in bed all day. They are expected to pick up their babies from the nursery at 6:00 a.m. and eat all of their meals in a cafeteria. There are no worries about the food being kosher (at least for me—the *Chassidic* and *Haredi* ladies had their own food brought in). Each meal is served buffet-style, with a range of choices, and the breakfast could rival any of the five-star hotels!

As *Shabbat* and *Hanukkah* come to an end, all of the moms and babies are invited into the hallway to hear *havdalah*. Soon after, all of the fathers begin to arrive to see how their wives and babies have managed over *Shabbat*.

When Josh arrives, we immediately begin discussing the *bris*. The head *mohel* from Shaarei Tzedek Hospital has said he would be available to us at 7 a.m. on Friday morning. In a strange turn of events, maybe you could call it *hashgachah pratit* [personal providence], Rabbi Avi Weiss, our rabbi from Riverdale who was at our wedding in Montreal as well as at our son Dov's *bris* in NY, happens to be in Jerusalem at the same time. To our delight, he says that he will be able to attend the *bris* as well. It was as though everything we had expected out of this experience is truly happening, and that God has blessed us with a relatively easy time. Maybe the *etrog* had something to do with this after all!

At the *bris*, which is a longer service in Israel than *chutz la'aretz* (outside of the land of Israel), we speak in English, a surprise to Rabbi Weiss, who would have assumed it would all be in Hebrew, seeing as we are in Israel. We announce the name of our third child as "Yehuda Maccabi," named after Judah Maccabee in the story of *Hanukkah* as well as in honor of the tribe of Judah, which is highlighted in the Torah reading that week. The Biblical Yehuda's symbol is the Lion of Jerusalem, which we encounter on every park bench, not to mention the random statues of lions, which are spread out throughout Jerusalem. *Maccabi* is also an acronym for the prayer that is recited each morning and evening, the first verse of which is: *mi chamocha ba'eilim Hashem*, "Who is like God among the heavenly powers?" In addition, it doesn't hurt that many of the sports teams throughout Israel are called "Maccabi," including the most famous, Maccabi Tel Aviv basketball team, a great treat for Josh, a big sports fan.

At the end of the meal, we begin packing up the leftover food. All of a sudden, we magically find ourselves in a story told by Peninnah Schram. A beggar whom we have never seen before comes into the *shul* and asks if he can take the leftovers home for *Shabbat*. This, too, is something we had never experienced back in Riverdale, yet we readily agree to participate in this mitzvah of *tzedakah*.

On Friday afternoon, after the *bris*, we go to the *mohel's* house near Mea Shearim to have Yehuda Maccabi checked out and to make sure that he is healing properly. Driving through Jerusalem before *Shabbat*, we feel a new kind of peace come over us as the streets empty and as everyone is preparing for candle-lighting and *davening*. As we drive home, we are not only delighted to be blessed with another child, but to have had a *sabra* in the city of Jerusalem.

Whenever people ask us his name, we say, "Yehuda Maccabi." Israelis are so surprised to hear this—as if they had never heard of the name before! Many Israelis choose shorter names with no middle name. Every time, their response is: *"b'emet*—really?" There is such an excitement in their eyes as we tell the story of the first native Israeli in our family and of his birth in Jerusalem on *Hanukkah*. A miracle child full of light, Yehuda Maccabi, the Lion of *Yerushalayim*.

Sharona Margolin Halickman founded and directs *Torat Reva Yerushalayim*, Torah study for women with young children, and for elders and disabled persons. She is also founder and director of Midreshet Devora, for young North American women who want to live, learn and experience the love of Israel. A graduate of Stern College and Azrieli Graduate School of Jewish Education and Administration, Sharona was the first Congregational Intern at the Hebrew Institute of Riverdale and the Hebrew Institute's first *Madricha Ruchanit*. She has been a visiting teacher in Jewish communities across North America and Israel. Sharona resides in Jerusalem with her husband, Josh, and their children Dov, Moshe and Yehuda. (www.toratreva.org and www.midreshetdevora.org)

A Teacher
by Syd Lieberman

By the time I graduated from Harvard, I was sick of school, but I needed a reason to stick around Cambridge. Adrienne, now my wife, was a year behind me at Radcliffe. So I looked for a program that was a year long and found the Master of Arts in Teaching (MAT) Program at the Harvard Graduate School. It was perfect. Not only was it a year long; it only had one semester of classes. The other semester was for student teaching.

I applied and got in, though I really didn't think I would become a teacher. To me, applying was an act of love. Little did I know that I would wind up teaching for thirty years. One reason was my Master Teacher and what he did for me.

The MAT program began with a summer school session in Milton, Massachusetts, where we taught seventh and eighth graders. Each Master Teacher was assigned four students to supervise. Ducharme was mine. He would help each of us plan our lessons, watch us teach them, and critique the results.

The situation was intimidating enough, but on top of that, Ducharme really was a master. He would teach now and then to illustrate what he was talking about. His questioning was so good that he could take a class wherever he wanted them to go without uttering a declarative sentence. I remember him standing in front of the desk with one foot up on a chair, calmly asking question after question that led the class down the road to his main point. Those lessons were worthy of applause. The other Master Teachers knew it. Whenever he taught, they would come and watch, quietly standing in the back.

Each of his four students took turns teaching. I was the last. My three colleagues weren't very good (how could they be the first time out?), and during the critiquing session Ducharme presented them with a long list of problems. Our MT was blunt but fair, and he provided solutions for each problem. But it was hard to watch a fellow student teacher sit there and sink under the weight of all he had done wrong.

I watched this three times, so you can imagine how I felt when I got up to teach for the first time. I began to wonder whether Adrienne was worth it. Yes, I liked books, and, yes, I liked talking about them, but I hadn't thought about what it would be like to talk about them with twenty seventh graders.

I knew my lesson. I knew the questions I wanted to ask. Then I got up in front of them and forgot most everything. I'm not sure if you know what it is like to stand up in front of twenty seventh graders. Some were smiling cherubs ready to listen to my words, but most looked like imps. I could see them smirking to one another: here comes fresh meat.

I fell apart. The structure of the lesson I had planned quickly collapsed, metamorphosed into a snake and slithered away. In my panic, I began to ask random questions. Discipline became a problem. Everything seemed out of control. I stopped caring about the lesson. All I wanted was for those forty minutes to pass. I was devastated when they did.

Needless to say, I wasn't looking forward to the critiquing session. I had performed far worse than my colleagues. I couldn't imagine how bad the critique was going to be. I stalled, going out in the hall to get some water, but my wish that my MT Ducharme and my fellow student teachers would just disappear didn't come true. They were there when I returned, my three fellow student teachers looking at me sadly, as if I were arriving at my hanging. My MT Ducharme watched me, too, but his face didn't disclose what he was feeling.

We sat down, and he, Ducharme, asked how I thought it went.

"Terrible," I replied.

"You're right," he said, "but I don't want to talk about it now."

"The session's over. See you tomorrow."

And then he left. I was stunned. So were my fellow student teachers. If misery loves company, they were hoping for a new friend.

Four days later I was up again. Once again I was horrible. Once again we sat down, and once again Ducharme asked how I thought it went.

"Just horrible," I replied.

"You're right," he said, "but I don't want to talk about it now. The session is over. See you tomorrow."

My fellow student teachers gave me angry looks. It seemed as if I were teacher's pet. If they had to suffer the barrage of comments, why didn't I?

Things changed the fourth time I taught. I actually did a little better. Not good, but a little better than awful. We sat down, and Ducharme asked what I thought, and I said, "It was a little bit better today.'

You're right," he said. "We have a lot to talk about."

And we did, during the critiquing session and throughout the afternoon. He had been saving all of his comments about the problems he saw and ideas of what I could do about them.

I asked him a few weeks later why he had done that with me. He replied that he could see that I was really beating myself up.

"I didn't want to add to that," he said. "I knew that you would need some success before you would be able to hear me."

He was right, but how did he know that? Well, he just did. It's one of the things that made him a great teacher. He could read who you were and know what you needed. He did a tremendous mitzvah for me. Not only had he given me what I needed without my asking, but he also gave me what I needed without my even knowing I needed it.

Syd Lieberman is an award-winning storyteller, teacher and author. Many of his best-loved stories deal with growing up and raising a family in a Jewish neighborhood in Chicago. Syd is also known for his original historical pieces and signature versions of Jewish folktales. He has taught storytelling internationally and at the Kennedy Center and Disney World, among many prominent US venues. Syd is the recipient of numerous commissions, including those from NASA and the Smithsonian Institution. Currently, he is creating stories for the US Capitol Visitors Center and teaching their docents and volunteers how to tell stories.

Permission to Leave
by Melvin Metelits

Sadly, we would not be expecting Howie M. for High Holy Day services at *P'nai Or* this year. We had grown accustomed to greeting Howie and his wife Sheela every *Rosh Hashannah* that God sent. They were an unmistakable pair. Sheela, with her striking white hair, would take her place with our holy musicians, playing a soft flute and occasionally providing an appropriate percussive beat. Howie was equally recognizable. He had a sweet, round face with eyes at once intelligent and compassionate. His trademark was a white shirt with pants held up by suspenders.

This year was different. Howie had an inoperable and terminal brain tumor. Most of us heard about it when he was already in the midst of his final passage. Sheela had invited Rabbi Marcia Prager to their home to minister to Howie and to consult about final arrangements. Reb Marcia asked me to accompany her. For me, it was an opportunity to fulfill the mitzvah of visiting the infirm, but I was completely awed by the mitzvah, which I was about to witness.

I was prepared to see Howie firmly planted in bed and immobile. I was mistaken. He was dressed comfortably in shorts and a T-shirt, lying on his back on a cot in the living room. Sheela informed him that the rabbi and I were present. There was no perceptible acknowledgement. I was asked to keep vigil while Sheela and Reb Marcia consulted in another room. Suddenly Howie jumped up and walked to the other side of the cot and lay down in reverse. He lay quietly for a few moments and then unexpectedly called out in a normal and completely lucid voice,

"Is the rabbi here? I want to talk to the rabbi."

I summoned Reb Marcia and Sheela.

"Yes, Howie," Reb Marcia said softly, "I'm here. What do you need?"

"I have a question," said Howie. "I have a question."

"Yes, Howie," Reb Marcia replied calmly. "Ask me whatever you need to."

"Is it all right to go? Is it all right to leave?"

I was taken aback by the directness of the question, but Reb Marcia was not.

"Yes, Howie," she answered firmly. "It is absolutely OK to leave."

Howie was not yet satisfied. "How will I know when it's OK to leave?"

Without a moment's hesitation Reb Marcia stated, "The soul has a way of letting the body know."

Howie spoke no more after that. Howie's noble soul left his body peacefully sometime within the next 24 hours.

I had witnessed a miracle of tender mercy and compassion.

Provenance: I was present at the home of Howie and Sheela M. when Rabbi Marcia Prager, who had previously said the *shema* with Howie, transformed a poignant moment in the end-life of a human body into a transcendent soul experience.

Melvin Metelits returned to Jewish life in 1994, following a long, satisfying career as a Philadelphia public school teacher. After retiring, Melvin studied with Rabbis Marcia Prager and Kevin Hale. Torah captivated his imagination, and he soon began teaching Torah in his community as well as for pre-confirmation classes at Or Hadash, a Reconstructionist congregation. He trained with *Maggid* Yitzhak Buxbaum, receiving his *smichah* as a *maggid* in 2006. Since then, he has developed a teaching style that integrates sacred stories with Torah learning and has helped to organize Torah study groups in various parts of North America.

A Kiss Divine
by Steve Nathan

And Moses, the servant of the Eternal, died there in Moab, by the mouth of God (*al pi YHWH*). God buried him in Moab ... but to this day, no one knows where his grave is. Moses was a hundred and twenty years old when he died, yet his eyes were not weak, nor his strength gone.

—Deuteronomy 34:5-7

Moses stood at the top of Mount Nebo and surveyed all that was before him.

"So, this is the land of promise," he said, "the end of my journey."

Moses was 120 years old, and yet up to that moment, his eyes had remained as bright and clear as when they first beheld the burning bush more than forty years earlier. His eyes had the same inner intensity that Pharaoh had seen when Moses first approached to demand the people's freedom. Aaron and the people saw it, too, when he smashed the tablets in front of the Golden Calf. Now, as he prepared for death, the intensity of his eyes began to dim. In its place, a kind of sadness could be seen. That is, had anyone been there to see it. At this moment, he was alone.

"Promise," Moses muttered to himself. "I should have known better than to put my faith in a promise, even from God. This land, the promise of my ancestors, was never to be my promise, was it?"

Unexpectedly, no answer came. In the past, every time he had spoken to God, especially from mountaintops, God always responded to the questions Moses asked. Was God...preoccupied? Perhaps God was pondering the question and trying to formulate exactly the right response for God's beloved servant. So, Moses waited...and waited... and waited. Still, there came no response.

Finally, Moses inquired of God once again, "Was the land ever truly to be my promise? Did you know even before I struck the rock that I would never enter? Was my rash act merely an excuse for you to decree again what had been decreed from the start? Did you lead me to believe you, just so I would do your bidding all those years?"

Again, no response.

Moses's sadness began to turn to anger as he cried out, "God, why do you hide your face from me? Why don't you respond? Why are you leaving me to die alone?"

The only response Moses received was the echo of his words floating over the mountain. Moses sank to the ground and simply let out a sigh.

Then a familiar voice spoke softly to him, "You are not alone."

Moses listened closely. He recognized the voice immediately, but it was not the usual mountaintop voice he knew so well. He turned around and saw Gershom, his eldest son, standing there with tears streaming down his face. Gershom sank to his knees and embraced his father tightly. Moses did not know what to do or say.

This was new. He could not remember the last time he and his son had embraced. Moses rested his head on top of his son's, and he, too, began to weep. He wept as never before. He wept for those now dead who had raised him as a prince in Egypt. He wept for Yocheved, Amram, Miriam, and Aaron, his family whom he himself had buried in the desert, but had been too busy leading the people to mourn.

He also wept for those slaughtered, at his command, after the Golden Calf incident. He wept for each person who had died during the forty years of wandering. But most of all, he wept for himself. He wept for the sons whom he had never really known. Moses's and Gershom's tears fell onto the sandy earth and formed a river of tears.

After some time had passed, Moses spoke, "Gershom, I am glad that you are here. But...what made you come? I never..."

After a pause, Gershom replied, "Nor did I...But I could not let my own father die without honoring him with my presence. I knew I must come to see you one last time."

"And your brother?" Moses asked rather tentatively.

"I don't know where Eliezer is. I haven't seen him for days. I wouldn't expect him to come. Then again, I wouldn't have expected me to come, either. When you were on a mountaintop with God, there was never any room for me."

Gershom could see a look of pain and sorrow in his father's eyes as the old man began to speak.

"I am sorry. There are so many things I wish I had done differently. But I cannot undo the past. This moment is what we have. It is really the first time that we are together, and I am actually here. This is truly a blessing."

Moses continued, "Before I die, there is something I must tell you, my son." He paused. "Though I may not have always seemed to pay attention, I could see for years how you watched every move I made, assuming some day you would assume my role. I know you have been angry with me and with God because Joshua is to take my place as leader. I ask you not to be angry. I did what I did because I love you and because I wanted your life to be different from mine."

Seeing that Moses was struggling to find the right words, Gershom interrupted, wanting to ease his father's pain.

"I know," said Gershom. "That is why I am here now. I finally understand everything. I want to thank you for what you did for me. It took a great deal of love and courage to make an agreement like that with God."

Moses did not know what to say. For all these years, he had carried this secret, this burden. Not even Gershom's mother knew of the promise he had extracted from God. Yet somehow Gershom had found out! There was only one way he could have known.

"God spoke with you?" Moses asked in a whisper, both amazed and confused that God would have spoken to his son after all these years.

"I'm not sure," Gershom replied. "It happened in a dream, but it seemed so real. I know that the voice was God's voice, and I know that the words I heard were the truth."

Moses breathed a sigh of relief. After all, he knew the burden that accompanied direct communication with God. He also felt relieved, because, though he was ashamed to admit it, he had felt some pain thinking that God might have spoken to his son when God had clearly stopped speaking to him.

Gershom continued, " By telling me the true story, God enabled me to let go of my anger and see that I needed to be here. I realize now that Joshua is your successor not because you thought me undeserving, but because you didn't want me or my brother to feel isolated and lonely as you have felt so much of your life."

"Gershom, my son, in many ways I feel blessed to have been chosen to lead the people. Yet this blessing was also a curse. I have prepared the people well to enter the Promised Land, but I am afraid that I have not prepared you or your brother very well. It's not only that you are not succeeding me as leader, but also I have left you no legacy. I am leaving you in death without ever having been with you in life. I regret this more than anything else."

Gershom held his father tight, as again their tears flowed, mingling together and soaking into the sand beneath them. After a long silence, Gershom responded, "Father, I know that what I thought was your indifference was really your pain. I wish I had seen that then, but I am glad that I can see it now. I wish my brother were able to see it as well."

At that moment, Gershom heard footsteps behind him. He turned, hoping to see his brother Eliezer standing there. Instead, he saw Joshua, the man whom he had hated until a few minutes ago.

"Gershom," Joshua said, "it is time to go. God has instructed that your father must be alone at the moment of his death."

"No," said Gershom emphatically, "God has been with my father every step of the way. I have never sought to be there when it was not my place. But I will not leave my father at the moment of his death. I deserve to be with him and to accompany him; he deserves to have his son there."

Joshua could only stare at him. The look in Gershom's eyes was so similar to the look in Moses' eyes when he had first glimpsed the Golden Calf. Joshua knew that Gershom could not be moved, but God's instruction had been clear.

Moses spoke, "Joshua, please leave us. I need to speak with Gershom. If God wants me to be alone when I die, then I will receive the message directly from God, as I always have."

Knowing better than to argue, Joshua looked into Moses's eyes one more time as he departed.

Moses rose and put his hands on Gershom's shoulders. "My son, earlier today I placed my hands upon Joshua's head and anointed him as leader. I then spoke to all of the tribes and blessed them. Before I die, I wish to offer you a blessing as well. I know it is no substitute for the years when I was not there for you, but I hope it will allow us at least to treasure our last moments with each other."

With these words, Gershom bowed down, and Moses placed his hands on the head of his eldest son.

And Moses spoke to Gershom, saying, "My beloved son, may God bless you with the strength to be a leader, not of a nation, but of yourself and your family. May your soul lead your feet to walk a path of righteousness, justice, kindness, and compassion."

"May you never be lonely, even when you choose to be alone. May the One who blessed me by showing me the Divine Glory on Mount Sinai show you the Divine Glory that dwells within you and within everyone. May that glory always shine through your eyes, illuminating the hearts and souls of all whose lives you touch. May you, your family, and all the people be blessed with peace, joy, love, and compassion. May this be God's will."

Moses then tenderly kissed his son's head, something that he had not done since Gershom was a little boy.

"Now go," said Moses. "God told Joshua I must be alone."

"But Father..." Gershom cried.

"Please," Moses interrupted, "the fact that you are here and that I can bless you is more than I could have hoped for. If your brother ever asks about this moment, please tell him that I am not angry. I send him the same blessing that I have given you. Now go."

They embraced one last time. Gershom then turned and began to descend the mountain.

As he was descending, he suddenly sensed a warm breeze blowing across the mountaintop. He then heard a soft, deep sigh, but not from any human being. He turned around and looked toward the place he had left his father. He saw an iridescent cloud envelop Moses. Without taking time to think, he ran back towards his father. When he reached the cloud, he did not stop. The moment he entered the cloud felt unlike anything he had ever experienced before. The cloud at once surrounded and embraced him while also propelling him back, away from Moses and the mountaintop. Gershom persisted, and, struggling, reached his arms into the cloud until he held the warmth of his father's shoulders. Blindly in the mist, he pulled his father close to him. Through the shroud of fog, he could still see the clear light shining in his father's eyes. Gershom pulled the old man closer and kissed his father on the lips for the first and last time. At the moment their lips parted, Gershom felt a rush of breath leave his father's mouth, and Moses fell lifeless into Gershom's arms.

Gershom called his father's name, and from out of the cloud, a voice answered. It sounded like his father's voice. It sounded like his own. But it was neither.

"Gershom, let go. Your father is now with me. He is at peace. He is home."

Tears once again flowed down Gershom's face.

Then God spoke again, "Gershom, look down."

Gershom did so and saw a sapling sprouting miraculously out of the desert sand. An almond tree grew before his eyes and blossomed with the most beautiful flowers he had ever seen.

"Gershom, here your tears and your father's tears flowed together. This is the spot where I will bury my most faithful servant in gratitude for all that he has done for me and because it is a symbol of the love you shared and the honor you gave him in the last moments of his life. The tree before you will always bloom, even in winter, so you can always find the spot where your father is buried. No one will know this place, except for me...and you."

"This is my gift and my blessing to you, for I know that what I asked of your father kept him away from you in life. May you carry this blessing with you along with the blessing you received from him. Now, return to your family and to your people. Fulfill your father's blessing. Enter the land and live in it."

Gershom then did as God asked of him and returned to his family, and the people prepared to enter the Promised Land.

Years later, as Gershom neared 120, the age of his father at the time of his death, he heard a young girl outside his tent reading aloud the last verses of the story of the people's forty-year journey through the desert. Lying there in his tent he closed his eyes and listened to the voices outside. As the girl read the closing words of the Torah, the words penetrated his soul, even though he had heard them numerous times before:

"For there never arose another prophet like Moses who knew God face to face."

He smiled and said to himself, "and who, at the end of his life, finally came to know his son face to face."

The young girl continued, "So Moses, God's servant, died there in the land of Moab by the mouth of God."

He then heard the girl say, "My mother told me that this means that Moses died with a kiss from God. Is that true?"

Gershom did not hear the response to the girl's question. His eyes still closed, he continued to smile and he murmured,

"Yes. God's kiss. Perhaps."

He remembered the moment, his father, the kiss, and felt the memory so strongly on his own lips. But this was not only a memory. He opened his eyes and saw his beloved son Shevu'el looking down at him, stroking his hair and smiling. In that instant Gershom's life breath left his body and returned to its source. Shevu'el sat there, still smiling as he wept, for he knew that finally Gershom was reunited with his father and that someday he would join them both.

Provenance Note: I wrote one of my first midrashic stories when studying with Peninnah Schram at the Institute for Contemporary Midrash at Elat Chayyim in 1998. The story focused on Gershom, the eldest son of Moses and Zipporah. The story, "A Stranger No More," takes place as Moses is preparing to transfer the mantle of leadership before his death to Joshua. At first, Gershom is angry with his father and with God for not choosing him as a successor. Through a dream or vision, Gershom discovers that he was not chosen to succeed his father because when Gershom was born, Moses had extracted a promise from God not to choose him. Moses told God that he did not want his son to be a stranger to his own family and his people as Moses had been due to the burden of leadership. That is why he named his son "Gershom," meaning "a stranger there." The *midrash* ends with Gershom running to find his father before he dies. This story begins just after Moses has transferred the mantle of leadership to Joshua and as he is preparing for his death.

Steve Nathan is a rabbinic graduate of the Reconstructionist Rabbinical College, the Institute for Contemporary Midrash, and the Meditation Leadership Training Program at Elat Chayyim Retreat Center. His classes and scholar-in-residencies for congregations are enriched by his singing, drumming, chanting, and contemplative prayer. A blogger and podcaster, Steve writes and performs original essays, *midrash*, and poetry based on the weekly Torah portion, Psalms, and other texts. Steve has served various congregations and communal settings, most recently for Hampshire College and Colgate University. He is the proud father of three children, Shira, Eitana and Noah.
(www.mindfulTorah.blogspot.com & www.mindfulTorah.podbean.com)

Why I Volunteer
by Caren Neile

It was a Wednesday. This is important, because Wednesday was the busiest day of the week for my husband and me at that period of our lives. We had a home-based public relations business, and every Wednesday we had to get out a newsletter, press releases, and a flood of faxes and calls. As if that wasn't enough, that particular night I was performing a story at a local school.

But I had promised Jeannie, the patient care volunteer coordinator at our local hospice, that on this particular Wednesday, I would go to visit a hospice patient at her home. This was my volunteer work: I visited patients while their caregivers took off a couple of hours to do errands, see friends, or just decompress.

Today my assignment was to stay with a woman—let's call her Kay, to preserve her privacy—with terminal lung cancer. Actually, in hospice we don't use the word *terminal*. We describe our mission as providing services to patients and families facing a life-limiting illness. I saw from my assignment sheet that Kay's "life-limiting illness" caused her to sleep most of the day, so I figured I could get some work done during her naps. No problem.

That afternoon I threw my laptop, some books, and a couple of files into the car and set off for Kay's condo community, about 10 miles north. I hadn't gone more than 100 feet when my cell phone rang. While I was talking, call waiting alerted me to another. And while I was on that one...It was that kind of a day. As I say, a Wednesday.

Kay's community was one of those gated villages in South Florida where every street looks the same and every building looks the same. I followed my directions until I reached her door, which looked, predictably, the same as every other. Before getting out of the car, I finished my last call and turned off the phone. Then I pulled out my laptop, my books, and my files and approached the door.

The man who answered my knock could have been an aging forties movie star. He was tall with thick, wavy white hair and luminous blue eyes. A real William Holden type, fifty years after *Sunset Boulevard*. I introduced myself, and he held out a meaty hand.

He invited me in. The room was decorated in what I think of as late American hospice: a hospital bed in the small living room, flanked by a recliner, and behind that, a ventilator, its soft *whirr* an accompaniment to our conversation. On the wall above the ventilator was the glaring orange and black sign: DO NOT RESUSCITATE.

"This is Kay," he said, beckoning to the wan-looking woman in the recliner. "Kay, this is Caren. She's from hospice."

Kay looked to be in her seventies. Her cap of dark hair was cut close to her pale face. In contrast to those of her husband, her eyes were black as coal. She smiled warmly and raised a thin hand in greeting.

"Please, come in," she said. "Sit down."

Kay's husband said his good-byes and left. Typical of this couple, he had requested a respite visit because he had to take a neighbor with cancer to the doctor.

After he was gone, Kay turned back to me and said, "So, what shall we do?"

I proceeded to ask her the question I put to every patient I visited: "Could you tell me a little about yourself?"

Kay's answer astounded me. It seemed that she had been born in New York City's Greenwich Village, the bohemian section of town. In a neighborhood of painters, musicians and writers, her father was a pipe cleaner.

"Do you know what that means?" she asked.

I shrugged. "He did something with plumbing?"

She shook her head. "No, he took those nubby wires and cleaned out the pipes people smoked."

Well, she continued, you can imagine that when the Depression came, pipe cleaners were the first to lose their jobs. To make matters worse, Kay's father and mother were deaf-mute. They couldn't find work, so she and her brother were sent off to an orphanage in New Jersey.

I shook my head. "What a story!" Then a thought occurred to me. "You must know sign language, huh?" She nodded. "I've always wanted to learn that. Could you teach me a little?"

"What would you like to know?"

"Umm, how about some letters?" So she taught me *a, b, c, d, e, f* and *g.*

When I had sort of mastered the signs, I asked if she could teach me to say something.

Again she asked, "What would you like to know?"

I considered a moment. "I'd like to know how to say, 'I love you.'"

Once more I caught the generous smile with which she had greeted me. She pointed her thumb to her breastbone, with her three middle fingers pressed against the palm. "I." Then she folded her arms across her chest. "Love." Finally she pointed at me. "You. I...love...you."

When the lesson was over, she asked the one question no hospice patient has ever asked me, before or since. "Will you tell me about yourself?" I have found that people facing death are usually too involved in their own issues to be open to anyone new.

I said, "How about if I tell you a story? I have to rehearse it for tonight, when I'm performing it. It's about the time my husband and I found a crab in our bedroom."

The performance starts with my standing on a chair. I took off my shoes, pulled out a chair from under the tiny Formica table, and hopped up. I had not gotten very far when her eyes began to flutter. I hesitated.

At the silence, her eyes flew open. "Oh, I was just resting my eyes," she assured me. "Keep going, please."

When I finished the story a few minutes later, she applauded weakly. For our next activity, I offered to read her the paper. Before I finished the first story, however, her eyelids lowered, lowered, lowered. She was asleep.

Great! I jumped up, grabbed my laptop and phone, my books and files, turned everything on and plugged everything in, and set to work typing, dialing, talking, reading.

About twenty minutes later, I was finished. I looked up at Kay. She was still sleeping. Briefly I wondered about the ethics of waking a hospice patient in order to chat. But I decided it probably wasn't such a great idea.

It was the first time since my arrival that I noticed the whirr whirr of the ventilator, filling the silent room.

At last her eyes opened, and we resumed our conversation. She told me that her son had died years before. She talked about her collection of tiny pewter statues in the kitchen, and she asked me to hand a few to her so she could examine them.

It wasn't long before I noticed something strange: she had started to breathe heavily, to suck up oxygen as though she couldn't get enough. The coal black eyes began to cloud slightly. My heart pounded.

"I think you need to reset the machine," she said, waving in the direction of the ventilator.

I told her I had no idea what to do with the machine. But I did know the number to phone hospice. I called, was put through to purchasing, and was told how to recalibrate the unit. In about a minute, she was breathing normally. It took a while longer for my breath to settle back to its former rate.

We talked some more after that, and then she did the thing that all storytellers appreciate: she asked me to tell the story again. I was back on the chair in an instant. I had gone through maybe the first five or ten lines before I heard the key in the door. Kay's husband was home.

He asked us how everything had gone. Kay said I'd told a wonderful story about finding a lobster in my bedroom. I didn't correct her.

Then he looked at me. "Well, there was a slight problem with the ventilator," I said. "But we called hospice, and everything is under control."

He held out that huge hand again, and I took it and squeezed. "Thank you for coming," he said.

And because I had been a guest in his house, I said, "Thank you for having me."

Then I turned to Kay and smiled. I pointed my thumb to my breastbone, with my three middle fingers pressed against the palm. I. Then I folded my arms across my chest. *Love*. Finally I pointed at her. *You. I love you.*

She smiled and signed the words back to me. Then I picked up my laptop, my phone, my books, and my files, and I headed out for the car. As soon as I put the key in the ignition, the phone rang. I didn't open it to see who was calling. Instead, I threw it in the back seat.

And I sang all the way home.

Provenance: As a professional storyteller, "Why I Volunteer" is my signature personal story. It's one of those few narratives that happened nearly exactly the way it is told—except for the last two lines, which are the concrete manifestation of abstract emotion that is essential to the storyteller's art. I consider this my signature story because it is the best way I know to answer the question, "Who are you?

Caren S. Neile, Ph.D., MFA, directs the South Florida Storytelling Project at Florida Atlantic University, where she is faculty in Storytelling Studies for the School of Communication & Multimedia Studies. A graduate of The Jewish Theological Seminary and a former Peace Corps volunteer, she has performed, lectured, and published throughout the US and abroad, including as a Fulbright Senior Specialist at Hebrew University. She is also former chair of the National Storytelling Network and a co-founding editor of the academic journal *Storytelling, Self, Society*. Caren co-hosts and produces *The Public Storyteller*, a weekly segment on South Florida public radio. (www.publicstoryteller.com and www.thepublicstoryteller.org)

Every One Is a Story
by Yoel Perez

I consider myself as a 'not bad at all' storyteller (some of my friends say that I'm quite good), but this invitation—I did not like it—not to say I hated it—from the very first moment: an official invitation to perform at the local Rotary Club. I don't like places of this sort; they are nice people, even generous, when it comes to money, but somehow not sensitive enough, too closed. But work is work, and I needed the money, so I accepted the invitation.

I came just on time, that is to say, ten minutes before the performance. The doorman was very polite. He took my coat, offered me a cup of tea—but he did not smile even once; for me this was a sign of what lay in store for me. And sure enough, like a self-fulfilling prophecy, they were a difficult audience. They were silent. Too silent. They sat there with their poker faces, and I felt some sort of panic.

So I steeled myself, I mustered all my charm and my storytelling skills, and began my performance.

"Look, gentlemen," I told them, "I'm going to take you on an enchanted journey: a journey to places that are not written on any map, to times long forgotten, with an extraordinary vehicle—a flying carpet. As a good guide, I must open with a warning: our travel agency takes no responsibility for incautious travelers who fall off the edge of the carpet (no banister), or cannot answer the riddles of cruel princesses, or who fall prey to blood-thirsty dragons—I'm warning you! But the more serious warning is that whoever joins me in this journey does not come back the same person he was before. Something happens to him on the way—good or bad; it depends on you and what you are."

I noticed a shadow of a smile on the faces of one or two of them, but that's all. So I went on. I used my best stories, all my magic.

Nada! Gurnisht! Nothing! Such a heavy silence! Am I repeating myself? It was the silence of a graveyard.

And then, at a certain point, I said to them: "You know, people, everyone has a story, everyone is a story. You should just open your hearts and be attentive."

And once more, I looked at their faces: Yes, we know that phrase. We've already heard it. So what?

So I said to myself: I'm going to show them. I'm going to jump into the water.

I looked around. The doorman sat at the edge of the first line. He didn't smile even once, even though he seemed to be interested and listened to every word.

I turned to him: "Sir, I would like to ask you a question."

He nodded with his head.

"Tell me, then," I said. "I looked at you during my performance. I got the impression that you like my stories, but still—you did not smile even one time. Please tell me why this is so?"

There was a long heavy moment of silence. One could cut it with a knife.

"My goodness!" I thought. "What did I do? Where is all my political correctness?"

And then he raised his head, looked around, stared at me—still no smile—and said slowly:

"I'm glad that you ask me this question. You see—some years ago I was in a car accident. I was injured in my face. My face nerve was cut, and I lost the capability to control my facial expression. I cannot smile. And you know," he continued, "it hurts me so much. I work here in this club. I like the people and my job. I like to greet them when they come. I want to smile at them, to show them my appreciation, but I cannot. And now you have given me the chance to tell it. Thank you so much..."

I continued my performance. The atmosphere was different—I cannot put my finger and say what exactly, but it was not the same. I felt that my opening words had come true: one does not come back from this journey the same as he was before. Neither do I. Next time they meet the doorman at the club door, neither he nor they will be the same.

Provenance note: This is a true story, which happened to one of my storyteller colleagues, Mrs. Talia Mitelman, from Tel-Aviv. I share it with her permission, having only changed the name of the club and added some descriptions based on my own experience as a storyteller.

Yoel Perez was born in Jerusalem in November 1945 to a Sefaradic-Jewish family that has lived for seven generations in Israel. He studied biology at the Hebrew University and the Sorbonne (1966-1970). A member of *moshav* Yodfat in the western Galilee, he worked for many years as a farmer in the flower fields of the village and later became a systems analyst and a manager of a software house. He has four children (three daughters and one son) from his first wife, Gila. After her death, he married Nurit and now they live in Haifa. In 2005 he got his PhD. in Folklore from Ben Gurion University in Beer-Sheva; he now teaches folklore there. Yoel is a professional writer and professional storyteller.

Serach bat Asher —
A Midrashic Monologue
retold by Peninnah Schram

My grandfather Jacob prayed for me to have a never-ending life, and God granted that request. God also gave me a long memory, and I have always used it with wisdom throughout the centuries to make peace, to resolve dilemmas, and to tell the stories of the Jewish people. You may think an old woman doesn't remember many things—but I recall everything that I witnessed happening to my people. I've become the holder of stories of the Jewish people. You know why? Because my grandfather always told me stories when I was a young girl. I would even ask for some of the same stories over and over again. Then I would go to my favorite place and compose a song on my harp. I still love to sing. Something like that never leaves you.

Having such a sharp memory can also be unbearable at times. It means that when I hear someone saying something that is not completely true or not right, I must interrupt and correct the record. Since I travel all over the world, I get to hear a lot of teachings and comments that are not the full story. Of course, I also learn a lot from great teachers and their students discussing the lessons.

Listen to what happened just a few years ago—well, maybe it was a bit longer than just a few years. While I remember events and conversations exactly, I lose track of the centuries and exact dates. I remember that it was some time in the second half of the third century C.E. that I was listening to the great *amora* Rabbi Yohanan ben Nappaha, who lived in Tiberias. He was teaching in his academy, interpreting the lessons of the rabbis of the *Mishna*. Some of the most gifted students of that generation came to study with this brilliant teacher.

One day, Rabbi Yohanan and his students were discussing the crossing of the Sea of Reeds and how the water formed a wall to the right and left of the Israelites walking through. He was explaining that the wall of water looked like a lattice. Suddenly, a voice from the back of the classroom—my voice!—interrupted the rabbi. You know, as I get older, I get bolder even to the point of daring to interrupt a great rabbi. Everyone in the class turned around, surprised to see an older woman standing there.

"Well, not exactly," I said. "It was like a lattice, but the open work of the lattice looked like shining glass reflecting the sun. I know this because I was there.[21] It was a wondrous sight!

"When we first came to the sea, we were all so frightened. How could we leave our homes and go to a strange land? We didn't know where we were going. How could we go across such high, raging waters? After all, we had children with us along with some of our things that we packed quickly. Suddenly, that young, brave Nachshon ben Amminadav, who had such faith in God, pushed his way to the edge. Then he just jumped into the sea up to his nose. Some people said that he was pushed. It doesn't matter, because when he did that, the miracle happened, and the waters parted.

"As we marched through this dry path, some of the children began to cry—perhaps from fear, perhaps from hunger. What did the mothers do? They reached out to those shining windows and plucked an apple or a pomegranate that soothed the children.[22] And as we reached the other side, Moses and Miriam, playing her tambourine, began to sing and dance, with all of us joining them. I'll never forget this crossing. We were already feeling like a people."

At this point, all of Rabbi Yohanan's students had gathered around me, listening to my account of the crossing of the Reed Sea. Some were crying as though they had come with me through the sea; some were cuffing their pants so as not to get them muddy; some were laughing because they had experienced the joy that they had only imagined before; some were praying. Soon, everyone was asking me questions. The rabbi rapped on the desk in order to quiet everyone down. Then he thoughtfully asked me if I was perhaps too tired to answer questions. I thanked him for his thoughtfulness and agreed to answer all their questions if they asked them one by one.

One of the youngest students stood up and asked, "The Israelites had promised Joseph to take his bones with them out of Egypt. But four hundred years had passed! The Torah says, 'There arose a pharaoh who knew not Joseph.'[23] So maybe the Israelites also forgot about their promise?"

I smiled at this question and said, "You are right. Joseph was one hundred and ten years old, near death, when he asked the Israelites to promise him that they would take his bones with them when they

---

[21]   Pesikta d'Rav Kahana 10:117

[22]   In Shemot Rabba 21:10 it says that it was as though they were "upon the dry ground," finding everything there.

[23]   Exodus 1:8

left Egypt someday.[24] Joseph didn't want to be left behind in Egypt. He knew that someday the Israelites would leave for the Promised Land. And after hundreds of years, when they were finally able to leave with Moses as their leader, the Israelites did remember their promise to Joseph, but they had forgotten one important detail. They no longer remembered where Joseph had been buried. How could they then take his bones with them to fulfill their sacred promise? You understand what happens to memory and promises, even with the best intentions, right? But as it turned out, all was not lost.

"Moses knew about me, that I had lived at the time of Joseph. Somehow, Moses found me and asked, 'Do you happen to know where Joseph is buried?'

"As I've already told you, I have a great memory. I replied, 'Of course! I remember exactly how the Egyptians made a metal coffin and brought it to the Nile River to sink it deep into the waters so that the Nile would be blessed. But I also recall that the sorcerers and magicians told the Pharaoh, "If you want this people never to leave your land, then bury Joseph so the Israelites will never find him, because they will never leave without him." I remember where Joseph was buried. Come with me to the edge of the Nile, and I will show you where Joseph's coffin was lowered.'"[25] And I brought Moses to that specific place.

"Moses stood by the banks of the Nile and called out, 'Joseph! Joseph! The time of our redemption has come. We want to take you with us, as you made us promise you. Now we will fulfill that promise and take your bones with us out of Egypt. We are leaving now. If you don't come, then we shall be released from the oath you asked us to take.'

"As soon as Moses said those words, the ark-like coffin rose from the riverbed. Moses and some other men took the coffin out of the water and carried it with them across the Reed Sea. And forty years later, Joseph's bones were finally laid to rest in a plot of land that Jacob had bought in Shechem. I was there in Shechem, too."

For years afterwards, I visited Rabbi Yohanan's class from time to time, always answering his students' questions. I especially liked to talk with the younger students, who were inquisitive and always showed me such kindness. They also seemed to have more time to listen to my stories, whereas the older students were always busy and rushing around.

---

[24]   Genesis 50:24-25

[25]   Mechilta Beshalach Pesikta

Maybe they were rushing to find a bride. Who knows?

At the rabbinical academy, I met a student who liked to compose songs, as I used to do. We would sit in the garden and talk, or he would sing his songs to me. One day, he asked me a question no one had ever asked me before: "What song of yours changed someone's life?" I was startled by that question and began to think through my long life. I went back years, centuries, to the time when I was a young girl. Then I remembered, as vividly as if it were yesterday, the song that had changed someone's life. It was the song I had sung for my grandfather Jacob on one particular day.

My father Asher had eleven brothers. One of his youngest brothers, Joseph, was a dreamer, who had astronomical dreams of grandeur.[26] As soon as he dreamed one of these dreams, he couldn't wait to share them with his brothers and parents. I don't know what he was thinking in doing that—that they would love him more after hearing how he visualized them bowing down to their young brother? How foolish of him! But despite his self-importance, I loved Joseph because of the stories he told.

To make matters worse, Jacob gave Joseph, elder son of his beloved Rachel, a wonderful coat of many colors. No wonder my uncles became jealous and angry. Benjamin was still too young to understand what was going on. So they ambushed Joseph one day and stripped him of his precious tunic. Then they sold him into slavery. But how could they explain Joseph's disappearance to my grandfather? So they came up with a plan to fake his death: they dipped his coat in goat's blood as 'proof' that Joseph had been killed by a wild animal. When Jacob heard their made-up tale, he wept and grieved for his most beloved son, Joseph.[27]

Years later, when my uncles went down to Egypt to buy food during the great famine, they learned that the conceited younger brother they had sold into slavery had become viceroy of Egypt! The brothers were stunned by this revelation, never dreaming that Joseph was still alive and had reached such powerful heights. Joseph asked them to bring their old father Jacob to Egypt but cautioned them that they were not to tell him the truth of Joseph's survival too abruptly. He understood that the shock might give Jacob a heart attack.[28]

---

[26] Genesis 37:1-11

[27] Genesis 37:18-35

[28] Genesis 40-45

Joseph also feared that Jacob might not believe his brothers since they had already lied to him about his "death." You know that once caught in a lie, people tend not to believe you ever after.

To convince Jacob that he was indeed still alive, Joseph told his brothers, "Tell our father that before I left home the day that I disappeared, he and I had been studying the law of the heifer whose neck is broken in the valley.[29] That will convince him that you are telling the truth."

On the way home to Canaan, the brothers debated how to tell their old father that Joseph was still alive. They feared for his fragile health. As they approached the house, they saw me playing my small harp, which gave them an idea.

"Serach, take your harp and sing to Jacob that Joseph is alive in Egypt. Go immediately and do what we ask!"

But I was a wise and compassionate young girl with an understanding heart. I agreed to do what they had asked, but I insisted on waiting until Jacob was standing in prayer. Then I sat down in a corner of the room and began to play my harp quietly and sing:

Joseph, my uncle, Joseph, your son, lives!
Isn't he in Egypt where it is food he gives?
Born on his knees are his sons, Manasseh and Ephraim,
These two grandsons of yours live in Egypt, l'chaim.
Joseph, your beloved son, is still alive.
Sing 'Hallelujah,' for Joseph did survive.[30]

At first, my singing was almost inaudible, a soft background to his prayers. Slowly, my words and rhythm began to weave in between the words of the prayers—almost in counterpoint. Then, as though discerning through a thinning fog, my grandfather began to understand the words I had been singing. Slowly, slowly, as if emerging from a deep sleep. Was this true? Could it be true? He asked me to repeat the song over and over. At that moment, he saw his sons arriving, bearing magnificent gifts from Joseph. Then he noticed the many wagons that would transport them all to Egypt.

---

[29] BT Sota 46b

[30] Midrash Ha-Gadol, Vayigash, Genesis 45:26 - in Hebrew: Yosef be-mitzrayim / Yuldu lo al bir-kayim / Menasheh ve-Ephrayim. This English version of the song is adapted/expanded by Peninnah Schram.

Jacob's heart revived. He felt happy for the first time in many years. He turned to me and said through tears of joy, "Because your words brought me such happy news, Granddaughter, my spirit is revived. I bless you, my dear Serach bat Asher, that death should never have power over you and that you may merit to live forever."[31]

And so it came to pass, because of my grandfather Jacob's blessing, that I entered Paradise alive, escorted by 600,000 angels[32] with great ceremony and celebration. But my story doesn't end there. I can never sit still for long—so I often set out to roam the world, always ready to set the record right.

Peninnah Schram, storyteller, teacher, author and recording artist, is Professor of Speech and Drama at Stern College of Yeshiva University. She is the author of ten books of Jewish folktales, including *Jewish Stories One Generation Tells Another* and *The Hungry Clothes and Other Jewish Folktales,* and has also recorded a CD, *The Minstrel and the Storyteller,* with singer/guitarist Gerard Edery. Peninnah is a recipient of the prestigious Covenant Award for Outstanding Jewish Educator (1995) awarded by The Covenant Foundation. She has been awarded the National Storytelling Network's 2003 Lifetime Achievement Award, "For sustained and exemplary contributions to storytelling in America."

---

[31]   Midrash Ha-Gadol, Vayigash, Genesis 30:12-13, 45:26

[32]   Targum Yonathan

Chutzpah Awakening
by Carla Vogel

I just turned 48 years old. I am a storyteller and a chaplain intern. I am single, never married, and have no children. Lately, I have been waking up in the middle of the night, worrying, asking myself: could I have lived my life differently? In my search for answers, I find myself surprised by the lessons I have learned from my friends, the elders at the Jewish nursing home.

It's Tuesday, and it is my first day as chaplain intern at the nursing home. My first assignment is to lead the Jewish learning hour. I peek into the second floor dining room and take inventory. There are a handful of elders scattered around the room; some sit in chairs, others in metal, clunky wheelchairs, facing the television set. I make a decision to create a circle, where the elders can hear and see each other.

I step into the dining room and shout enthusiastically, *"Shalom aleichem!* I am Carla Vogel, the new chaplain intern. Let's make a circle!"

I watch their heads slowly rise like turtles coming out of their shells. As I push the dining room table off to the side, I accidentally fall into the lap of a woman sitting in her wheelchair.

"I am so sorry," I say, and as I unlock her wheels to move her forward, she is adamant that she stay in the back. Suddenly, the only man in the room pounds his fist on a table, lifts his head, leans forward, and shouts, "Where is the rabbi?" setting off his wheelchair alarm, which sends in a nursing assistant to his aid. I feel overwhelmed in this chaos as I try to remember some of the lessons I learned in my chaplaincy training. I step back, take a deep breath as a warm hand grabs mine and pulls me into the chair next to her. Her name is Goldie.

"Hop nisht der luchschen far di fish!" she shouts in Yiddish. This translates to "Don't grab the noodles before the fish,"meaning—chill out!

Feeling calmer, I take another deep breath, look around at each elder, and begin again. *"Shalom aleichem.* My name is Carla Vogel, and I am the new chaplain intern. My Hebrew name is Chaya, and I am named after my great-grandmother, Chaya, who was born in Kynszyn, Poland. Tell me about yourself."

Goldie begins to share. "My name is Goldie. I am named after my Great-Aunt Goldie. She taught me how to laugh in spite of the hardships of her life. See these lines on my face—they are laugh lines. You know, I will be 98 next week." After the other elders share stories from their lives, Goldie takes my hand in hers and says, "*Chayala*, don't forget it's a mitzvah to make a hundred blessings a day." I look around at this colorful crew of elders and thank them for sharing their stories. Suddenly, I feel empowered, as I realize that their stories are blessings for me, and to receive these blessings is a mitzvah!

As I prepare for the next Tuesday's Jewish learning hour, I realize it is the Jewish holiday of *Tu b'Av*, the Jewish day of love. This ancient holiday served as a matchmaking day for unmarried Jewish women. In ancient times, the young women, dressed in white, would dance in the vineyards in hopes of meeting their beloved. That night I have a dream. I am back in the nursing home, sitting in the dining room. I look up and see two older women coming through the doorway. One is carrying a large shopping bag. These women are my two grandmothers, Minnie and Tessie, who were foes on earth, but are now compatriots in the heavenly realm. They both bend down and carefully pull out of the shopping bag a large, red cloth banner with bold, black letters. Together they unfurl it. It reads: NU, CARLA, WHEN ARE YOU GETTING MARRIED? I wake up the next morning with that familiar anxious feeling and ask myself: could I have lived my life differently?

The next afternoon the group of elders is sitting around the dining room table, sipping coffee in Styrofoam cups—ready for the Jewish learning hour.

As I begin to tell them about *Tu b'Av*, Goldie interrupts me, "*Chayala*, tell us about your husband and your children."

I say hesitantly, "I'm not married, and I have no children."

"Not married, no children, what happened?" Ruth another member of the group asks.

What happened, I ask myself. Suddenly, it is as if I hear two large, crashing cymbals, then the voice of a Greek chorus: "No children, no children, not married, not married"; then the crescendo: "What happened, what happened?"

What do I tell them? Do I give them the whole *megillah*—that my parents got a divorce when I was fifteen, and then when I was nineteen, I became an anarchist, marching to the beat of Emma Goldman—no marriage, free love!

I take a deep breath, smile, and slowly look around the circle, and divert their attention by saying, "Tell me how you met your husbands."

It is as though I have opened up a magical door. Each woman blushes as she shares her story.

"I met my husband dancing," Goldie muses.

She pushes herself up from her walker and leans against the table, and shimmies her hips as the other women laugh and cheer. Sitting down, Goldie leans forward, lifts her hand and lightly touches my upper lip.

"*Chayala*, do you know why you have this indentation? There is a story that before you were born, the Angel Laila whispered to your soul. She told you many secrets. What were the secrets? She told you about your life and what was to come. When you took your first breath, she kissed you right here and you forgot everything she told you. *Chayala*, you have your whole life to live these secrets. Nu, so you meet your soulmate a little later in life. It's never too late to find love. Have faith, *Chayala*, don't regret the past, celebrate your life now, laugh, dance! All you need is a little *mazel*, lots of *chutzpah*, and—a touch of lipstick."

The following Sunday, I tell my friend Shari about my new position as chaplain intern. She gasps, "Carla, I feel it. You're going to meet a man, the one, at the Jewish nursing home. I just know it!"

The following Saturday, I am co-leading *Shabbat* services with the rabbi. *Shabbat* services at this Jewish nursing home are very holy. I escort the elderly men into the chapel, place their yarmulkes on their heads, and gently cover their shoulders with their prayer shawls. Then as I stand on tiptoe singing the kedushah prayer, "*kadosh, kadosh, kadosh,*" I glance over at the entry of the chapel, and, suddenly, in walks a man, the one! He is around 50, curly hair, a little nebbishy, but really cute. I can't believe it! This is the man Shari was talking about. I know it. He gives me a big smile, a really big smile, and sits down. I smile back. He must feel it, too, I'm sure. I immediately fly off the *bimah*, hand him a prayer book, and excuse myself to the rabbi, as I slip into the bathroom to put on a touch of lipstick.

I can barely get through the Torah portion and concluding prayers as I glance over at him often. After *hamotzi*, I rush off the *bimah* with my grandmothers' banner waving behind me and introduce myself.

"Hello, my name is Carla Vogel—I am the new chaplain intern."

He smiles and tells me he is visiting from New York and is staying in an apartment downtown.

"I love downtown!" I gush. And I can just see it now: we are sitting in a coffee shop, our hands sliding across the table, slowly touching. Suddenly, I hear a shout. It is Shmuel, a resident, coming towards us in his walker.

"*Oy, gevalt*, it's you, the famous Hollywood director. *Mazel* tov on your academy award! It's nice that you are visiting family here."

I freeze. Deflated, embarrassed, and *mazel*-less, I look again at the one. The famous one, the famous, unattainable, married one. The one so-famous-I-can't-even-mention-his-name-in-this-story one. Why didn't I recognize him?

As my grandmothers put the banner back into the bag, I walk over to Goldie and help her with her walker. She looks into my eyes and sees my sad face and whispers, "*Tanz, tanz, tanz!*" Dance, dance, dance!

It is one year later. I am still single, still working at the Jewish nursing home and my dear friend, Goldie, has passed away. I am at a salon, getting my eyebrows waxed, when something wonderful happens. Dwight the beautician looks at my upper lip and says, "Carla, it's time." He puts the hot wax on my upper lip, adds the sticky strip of tape, waits a moment, and then rips it off.

"Ouch!" I shout, and immediately rub my upper lip to ease the pain. Suddenly, I feel Angel Laila's kiss on my upper lip and hear Goldie's words, her blessing to me,

"Have faith, *Chayala*, it's never too late to find love. Don't regret the past. Celebrate your life now, laugh, dance. All you need is a little *mazel*, lots of *chutzpah* and—a touch of lipstick." And then, in a magical moment, I have a *chutzpah*-awakening. I realize that I am exactly where I am supposed to be.

This *chutzpah*-awakening became an invitation for me to relax into my life as a single woman, surrounded by a loving circle of friends. Feeling Goldie's presence, it was also an invitation for my heart to open fully to the possibilities of love. When *Tu b'Av* came around, my friend Sara shared with me how she met her husband. She met him shortly after she sent a prayer request to "Western Wall Prayers—40 Days For You," an organization in Israel. She wrote down the website and said, "What do you have to lose, Carla?"

Ninety dollars. I was reluctant at first. Then, after a cosmic nudge from Goldie, I took a leap of faith and sent my ninety dollars in with my prayer request to meet a spiritual, abundant, and joyful man. Three weeks later, I received an email from my friend Michael, who, in the subject line, wrote: "Possible fella for you." I took a deep breath and opened the email, wondering if the prayer had really worked.

Well, to make a long story short, this possible fella has blossomed into a loving, joyful relationship, one that I could never have imagined. I smile now, thinking of my two grandmothers, their hearts bursting as they once again pull out the large, red cloth banner with the words: NU, CARLA, WHEN ARE YOU GETTING MARRIED?

Provenance: As a chaplain intern in a Jewish nursing home, I found myself surrounded by elderly women who had a lot of advice for me. As a single, Jewish woman in her forties, I welcomed their stories about love and courtship. Each story they shared was filled with blessings and life lessons. Their guidance became fodder for my life and for this story.

Carla Vogel is a writer, storyteller, and community artist residing in Minneapolis. As a storyteller, Carla reaches into the past, drawing on her own Eastern European ancestry and family folklore, to bring a colorful world of Jewish characters to audiences of all ages. She is an associate artist and dancer with Kairos Dance Theater's Dancing Heart Program—Vital Elders Engaging in Community. She is a Certified Legacy Facilitator, assisting individuals and communities in writing their spiritual and ethical wills; and she also serves as a chaplaincy intern. (www.carlavogel.com)

V

Finding Holiness & Happiness
Mitzvot of Serving & Experiencing God

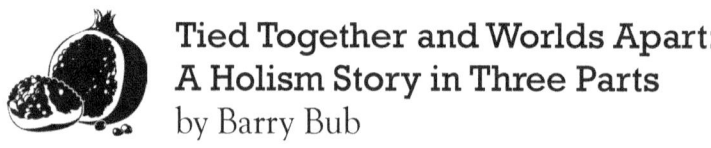

Tied Together and Worlds Apart:
A Holism Story in Three Parts
by Barry Bub

Scene 1. Philadelphia, USA

Subject line: "What is holiness?"
Body of email: "There can be no doubt, holiness is all about separation- Israel from the nations, *Shabbos* from workweek, sacred from profane, kosher from *treif*, milk from meat. The list is endless."

So began the long *drash* (teaching) from my Orthodox friend in his email to me. I read and reread his email.

Yes, it makes sense but surely he is missing a vital component of holiness, I thought to myself. What about the other aspect of holiness—the healing that occurs when that which is separated or split apart or broken is brought together to create a whole?

I researched the derivation of the words, "holy and whole," and found that *Merriam–Webster's Dictionary On–line* lists the derivation of both as emerging from the Old English, *hāl*, meaning "healthy, unhurt, entire."

After further reflection, I crafted a response, being careful to cite an Orthodox source:

"Is it not possible," I wrote, "that holiness includes both separation and connection? On the face of it, the word "cleave" makes no sense at all, since it means both "to sharply divide" as well as "to adhere tightly." If you think about it, however, there cannot be separation without connection—the one is dependent upon the other. Perhaps this explains Rabbi Joseph Soloveitchik's quote that 'sanctity is not a paradise but a paradox.' Perhaps holiness really is a paradox. What do you think?"

His email response arrived within a few minutes. It said just one word: "No."

Scene 2. Venice, Italy

After touring yet another desolate, ruined Jewish site in Europe, it came as a relief to see a living, breathing Jew in Venice. With his black hat, black suit, open-necked white shirt, and his flailing *tzitzit*, he was unmistakably Jewish.

"Are you Jewish?" he asked, by way of greeting.
"Yes," I replied.

He didn't mince his words: "Did you lay *tefillin* this morning?"

"Bed 6 needs a bedpan! Jew on Calle dell'Aseo needs tefillin!" He is no more interested in me, the person who is a Jew, than the nurse is in the person who is the patient occupying bed 6. I, my beliefs, and practices are all invisible to him.

I left that encounter feeling disappointed, annoyed, and firmly resolved: *No more tefillin ambushes; next time I'll be prepared.*

Scene 3. Tzefat, Israel

It was a bright, sunny Friday afternoon, and we were in Tzefat, Israel. Since *Shabbat* dinner would be fairly late, I stopped at the outdoor stand in the little square to stock up on a last-chance falafel sandwich.

Standing a few feet away from my table were three young men, schmoozing. Backpacks and books on an adjacent table suggested that they might be *yeshiva bochers*, though they were not dressed in regulation black. From time to time, one young man snuck a look at me from under his Andy Capp flat cap. Eventually he sauntered over.

"Did you lay *tefillin* this morning?" he asked.

"No" I replied, calmly.

"Why not? You are Jewish, yes?"

"Yes."

"It's a great mitzvah to put on *tefillin*."

"So they say."

"And tonight is *Shabbos* so it's a very wonderful thing to do."

"Yes."

"So, here are my *tefillin*. Let me help you put them on."

"No."

"How can it be that you do not do this important mitzvah if you are Jewish?"

Nice and slow, that's the way to reel him in.

"I do other things that connect me to my Judaism. Things that are very important to me."

"Like what—what is more important than doing the mitzvah of laying *tefillin*?"

"I counsel and teach," I respond, "and I use Jewish practices, teachings, quotes, and books. For example, have you read Viktor Frankl's book, *Man's Search for Meaning*?"

"Everything I need to know is here," he says, slapping his Tanakh.

"Frankl's book is perhaps one of the greatest books on suffering published in the twentieth century," I explain. "Studying this helps us more fully understand the books of Psalms, Lamentations, Job."

Pause. Let it soak in.

"So you have not read Frankl, Buber, or any of the great Jewish philosophers?" I ask.

He now seems puzzled, uneasy; he hadn't signed up for this.

"No, but let's get back to the *tefillin*. It's a great mitzvah."

"Perhaps they are both great mitzvahs," I counter.

Now to make my move:

"Here's a thought. If I agree to lay *tefillin*, will you agree to read *Man's Search for Meaning?*"

He frowns.

"But I don't have money to buy the book."

"No problem. Every library carries it."

"But it's *Shabbos*. The libraries are all closed."

"That's ok. You can read the book next week. Just promise me you will do it."

He asks his friend to check out this Frankl fellow with the *rebbe*. A few minutes later, his friend returns and nods his head affirmatively. It's a deal; we shake hands.

Mission accomplished.

Ever so gently, and lovingly, the young man opens the little, navy blue bag and unwraps the *tefillin*. His face positively glows with anticipation of the mitzvah about to be performed. Now it is my turn to be surprised. With distant but vivid memories of a mindless, primitive ritual, something thrust on an innocent and confused pre-*bar mitzvah* boy, I feel totally unprepared for this man's passion and commitment and unprepared as well for the degree to which I myself feel touched and awed. I read the prayers, and in ten minutes, it is over. Just as carefully, he rewinds and returns the *tefillin* to its bag. We say goodbye, he to join his friends and me to continue my journey into the mystical experience that is *Shabbat* in Tzefat.

Separated by age, nationality, priorities, beliefs, and religious affiliation, two strangers had encountered each other, connected, and been transformed.

Holiness had happened.

Provenance: This is a true story.

Barry Bub, MD, a native of South Africa, creates and tells stories that highlight communication opportunities within relationships. Physician, gestalt psychotherapist, author, and educator, Barry's stimulating talks and experiential workshops are offered to wide-ranging audiences. Author of *Communication Skills that Heal: A Practical Approach to a New Professionalism in Medicine,* he serves on the adjunct faculty of Temple University Medical School. He is also the innovator of Confidential Litigation Stress Management, a program in which he mentors physicians experiencing litigation stress and trauma. His passions include art, photography, travel, and his wife/muse, Rabbi Goldie Milgram, with whom he delights in 5 children and 9 grandchildren. (www.processmedicine.com)

The Kabbalah of Laundry
by Dan Gordon

Traveling can be stressful, especially when trying to "hurry up and relax." When I rush the preparations for a trip, sometimes I imagine how our Israelite ancestors must have felt when they embarked on their journey through the wilderness, which would be filled with such mystery. I didn't predict the curious adventure that would happen when I planned a week's vacation prior to attending a summer conference. Three of us were traveling together to what was then called the Conference for the Advancement of Jewish Education (CAJE), and two of us had the additional burden of preparing presentations for the conference. I talked my friends into sharing a condo in Vail, Colorado, thinking we could all escape the world for a short while. But even atop a 10,000-foot high mountain, reality found us. During a hike, two women who were also going to CAJE recognized us and started a conversation about the upcoming workshops.

The night before leaving the condo, with the conference registration just a few hours away, we decided to keep it simple—make dinner, do laundry and spend some quiet time putting the finishing touches on our presentations. As we were making our grocery list for dinner, we heard a loud noise coming from the laundry room. The dryer had broken, leaving the clothes in it still soaking wet.

We quickly created "plan B" for the evening. In the phonebook, we found a laundromat next to a grocery store. While one of us babysat the clothes, the other two would go shopping for dinner. The two guys took on the grocery task, leaving our female friend to tackle the laundry alone. At the store, the two of us walked slowly through the aisles, talking about what was coming up in the near future and how our vacation time had been less than relaxing.

When we finally got back to the laundromat, we were justifiably greeted with, "What took you so long?" As we sorted through the clean, dry laundry, it became clear that some clothes were missing. We retraced our actions. We got all the dirty clothes from the laundry bags, right? And all the wet clothes from the broken dryer, right? What about any wet clothes still in the washer?

Oops. We looked at each other without verbalizing the question that was on our minds: Which of us was so STUPID as to forget to look in the washer? We all had, of course.

Was anyone up for Plan C?

In silence we drove the rental car back to the condo to retrieve the wet clothes. New plan: The one who had already done most of the laundry was exempt from any more tasks, and could stay back to finish her presentation. The guys would take it from here. I would finish the laundry while my friend would take the rental car and go pick up a pizza—forget about cooking.

As soon as we got in the car, we started to giggle like college students, acknowledging that we had screwed up. I especially felt responsible and embarrassed; I had wanted everything to be perfect during our stay, and it certainly wasn't.

At the laundromat, I was alone in blessed solitude for the first time all week. I started to put the wet clothes in several different dryers to allow them to dry quickly. I wasn't alone for long. Four people walked in: the two women we had met atop the mountain and their husbands. I was not in the mood to make conversation but tried to be polite.

"Oh, look who's here!" the women chortled. "Aren't you excited? CAJE is starting tomorrow already! I can't wait! Have you ever met my husband? He's a rabbi, too, you know."

I smiled and made pleasantries, and then, desiring privacy, focused my attention on the dryers.

A moment later, I felt my space crowded and heard a quiet, "Excuse me."

I smelled the man's presence—a familiar blend of sweat, alcohol, and urine—before I turned to see him: A young man with torn clothes and a scraggly beard.

He said again, "Excuse me. Did I hear them say you were a rabbi?"

I'm a pretty friendly person, usually. But this night, I found myself decidedly disinterested in conversing.

"Sort of," I answered. At the time, I was leading a synagogue but had not yet finished my rabbinic studies, so the title "rabbi" was only partially accurate.

"I need you to come with me," the man said, very seriously.

I looked at him for only a second before replying coldly, "I'm doing my laundry right now."

Turning my attention back to the dryer, I reached to put another quarter in the machine.

He offered his own quarter and said, "Let me take care of that. I need you to come with me."

I took a look around the room, wondering where my CAJE friends were now. They were now dispersed to the four corners of the laundromat, seemingly unaware of my situation. "Please. I need you to come with me," the man repeated.

In my mind, I heard my mother's voice saying, "Don't EVER go with strangers!"

But I was also remembering the words of Leviticus, Chapter 19, which teach, "Treat the stranger as one of your own, for you were strangers in the land of Egypt."

I let the man put his quarter in my machine and followed him.

We didn't go far—just to a little room next to the laundromat.

We sat down on plastic folding chairs, and he said, "I need you to give me a blessing."

I asked him why, and he proceeded to tell me his story. He told me his name and that he was an alcoholic. I asked some questions and learned that he had been raised a Baptist but had not been to church in a long time. He had a daughter he had not seen in a long time. He wanted to change and wanted me to bless him. I thought about what kind of blessing I could possibly offer.

"Chris," I began, "you can beat this addiction. And you will. When you do, you will realize it was the hardest thing you've ever done, and you will feel the greatest sense of accomplishment possible. It may take a long time, but when you succeed—because you can and you will—you'll feel like you can do anything."

Just the right words of inspiration, I thought to myself. Now I can move on with what I need to do.

I looked in his red, tearful eyes as he said, "Please. Will you give me a blessing?" I thought I just had. Obviously, he wanted something more formal. So I tried again. I held his hands in mine and said:

"Long ago, my people had a struggle. They were enslaved by other human beings, like you're enslaved by alcohol. When they were finally freed from their bondage, they embarked on a journey through the wilderness. That journey was long and difficult, and they didn't know when it would end. But they hoped and prayed that at the end of the journey, they would reach a place called, 'the Promised Land.' And you know what? When they finally got to the Promised Land, there were struggles there, too. Throughout the journey, they had to be reminded they would make it. So in the middle of the journey, in the middle of the wilderness, they got a blessing. That blessing helped them find the strength to continue. Moses and his brother Aaron offered them a blessing that reminded them that they were not alone on the journey because God was with them. Well, Chris, God is with you on your journey. So I'm going to give you that same blessing."

I put my hands on his head and said:

"*Yih-va-reh-cheh-cha Adonai v'yish-m'recha.*
May God bless you and watch over you.
Ya-eir Adonai panav eilecha v'yi-chu-nekka.
May God's face shine upon you and be gracious to you.
Yi-sa Adonai panav eleicha, v'ya-seim l'cha shalom.
May God's presence be with you and grant you peace. Amen."

After a moment of quiet weeping, Chris hugged me for a long time. He then said, "God bless you," and left. As he walked away, I knew I would never see him again. I wondered if my blessing was the one he needed and whether it would make a difference. He disappeared into the night, and I sat in silence for a few moments, thinking about my own journeys and the blessings I sought. And then I went back into the laundry room.

Again, I looked around for the CAJE participants. I didn't know how long I'd been gone, but the four of them were intently working on their laundry, seemingly oblivious that anything unusual had happened. I stood alone by my own dryer, expecting they would ask me a question or two. They had no questions, but I did. Suddenly, I had four questions:

1. Why on this night, did the dryer break?
2. Why on this night, was I the one chosen to finish the laundry rather than get a pizza?
3. Why on this night did Chris approach me instead of the other person in the room who was identified as a rabbi? And...
4. Why do we wait until *Pesach* to open our doors and our hearts?

Provenance: I first told this story just a few days after it happened: August, 2001, at the Conference for the Advancement of Jewish Education (CAJE) in Fort Collins, Colorado. I was scheduled to present a workshop on "Creating Personal *Midrashim*: Turning the Text of Our Lives into Sacred Stories." I had prepared the activities for the workshop, but was struggling with which personal story I was going to use as an example. The night before the conference began, I experienced this unforgettable encounter. It became the introduction to that workshop, and I've found several other occasions to share it. While it's been heard by many in both synagogues and churches, the occasion of this volume inspired me to put it on paper and publish it for the first time.

Dan Gordon has served Temple Beth Torah of Humble, Texas, since 1998, and was also part-time rabbi for Jackson Hole, Wyoming. A professional storyteller since 1993, Dan is a former camp director, religious school principal, and youth director. Dan co-chaired CAJE's National Jewish Storytelling Network. He is a leader with interfaith communities, and volunteers as a prison chaplain. Also known as "Dante, teller of tales," he collaborates with Young Audiences, Houston, teaching public school teachers about incorporating storytelling into curriculum. He was previously published in *What's Jewish About America's Favorite National Pastime*, edited by Rabbi Judith Abrams. (www.rabbidangordon.com)

The Taxi
by Dan Grossman

When Abraham welcomed the three travelers into his tent, as he sat in the midday sun at Mamre, he taught us the mitzvah of welcoming strangers into our homes. Sometimes, a home is a tent, a house, or even a taxi.

I entered this story in July of 1971, in the holy city of Jerusalem. But as you will hear, this story began many years before that. Let's start in Jerusalem. It was my first trip to Israel, and I was preparing to stay for a year of college. I landed in Israel on a Sunday. As our bus rolled down the long road leading into Jerusalem, not the super-highway of today, many of the first-time tourists made plans to drop off their bags at Mount Scopus and make their way to the *kotel*, the Wall. Although I had been planning this trip for two years, I wanted to wait till *erev Shabbat*, Friday at sundown, to approach the Wall for the first time.

Each day during that first week, I thought, "Maybe today I should go to the *kotel*. Why wait?"

Yet each day I waited in anticipation, the image of the Wall steadily growing in appearance and importance. Finally, late Friday afternoon, I set out from my dorm on Mount Scopus to walk down the hillside, through the Arab neighborhoods of East Jerusalem, and up to the plateau of the Temple Mount, the *kotel*. In 1971, the hope for peace was in the air. Jews and Arabs were dreaming of some sort of a peace agreement. We could walk through neighborhoods then that we would not even think of entering today. I went on my way with another student, a young woman, also going to the *kotel* for the first time.

As we moved down the hillside, through these Arab villages, I nicknamed the route, "Gasoline Alley." The houses were various shades of light blue, green, and white with flat roofs and small yards. Children were playing anywhere and everywhere. I called the area, "Gasoline Alley," because there seemed to be cars, trucks, and old WW II motorcycles in every yard in various stages of repair, or disrepair. Wherever I looked, I saw cars up on cinder blocks, radiators and parts strewn about in the yards. This was the "Gasoline Alley" of my childhood, only in blue and green and Arabic instead of blacktop, red brick, and Italian.

As we crossed the road, a large, old Mercedes taxi pulled in front of us to block our way. The taxi was various shades of green with fringes hanging around the back and side windows and various talismans hanging from the mirror. The driver was ruddy and mustachioed, wearing a white shirt open to the belly. He and his cab were the stereotypes of a 1970's Arab taxi and driver.

He waved for both of us to get into the cab. "*Bo, yallah*–Come, I give you a good ride!"

I waved him on. It was almost *Shabbat*, and I carried no money. Besides, we had planned a good sixty-minute walk to the *kotel*. Once again, he pulled in front of us to block our way.

"Come, come–I know, I know, *Shabbat, kippah,* no money–*bo, yallah!*"

You are nineteen, in a new country and walking in a strange village. You don't think: "This could be dangerous." You think: "This is an adventure–this could be very interesting!"

So together we got into the green Mercedes taxi with the fringes, the hamsas, and the open shirt. After a few hundred yards, our driver turned to look at us in the back seat, and he said, "I need something from you."

For a moment, we looked at each other with concern. The driver continued, "No, no money, I see your *kippah*–I know. I need for you to hear my story."

And so he continued, "My name is Mahmud. I live in Jerusalem all my life. My father, grandfather, great-grandfather, all Jerusalem for generations. Listen–my grandfather, Akim, made his living moving things in his wagon. Furniture, dry goods, people, anything. He was a wagon man, a taxi, a moving man. Anyway, one day in 1937, an old man, a rabbi, came to him with a job. The rabbi said, 'I am too old to walk from my home to the Wall back and forth each Friday at sunset. If, however, you drive me in your wagon to the Wall, God willing, I will find the strength to walk back home.' They agreed on a price, and so it began. A regular job, one way from the rabbi's home to the Wall each and every Friday week after week, rain or shine. In the beginning, they said nothing to each other. On the wagon, off the wagon, a few coins–silence. Then one day, the rabbi said, 'And your name is?' And so it began. Two men talking. What did they speak of ? Their wives, their children, their aches and pains. They talked and talked. Once a week, one way, they talked. Weeks became months, months became years. A sick child, a marriage of an older child, complaining wives and relatives, they talked. They spoke as men of families and of concerns. Successes– all their hard work. Failures–always someone else's foolishness. In the summer, sharing a jug of cool water, and in the winter, hot tea with mint. Perhaps on occasion, some cakes from a local bakery, kosher always, and they talked.

"Then it happened, after more than ten years. 1948. Israel becomes your nation, and Jerusalem is divided. Just like that, one Friday came and Grandfather could not see his rabbi. The rabbi could not see his wagon, or his Wall, or his old friend. For nineteen years, not a word. They might have called on the phone, but that was not their way. The wagon, the route, the Wall, was not the same as a phone. Time passed as it always does, then in 1967, Jerusalem, again one city. By this time, the wagon is gone; the horse gone to pasture, and now my father drives this very taxi.

"It was Friday, July 14, 1967, when Grandfather told my father and me to wash the taxi and prepare to drive him to the rabbi's home. The three of us drove to the same address, just as it had begun in 1937. When we got to the address, I went to the door and rang the bell. A man much younger than I imagined opened the door.

"'Are you Rabbi Roth?'

"'Yes, and you are?'

"'The grandson of the man who used to take you in his wagon to the Wall!'

"'Oh, oh, I understand, not me, but my father, Rabbi Roth. You must be Akim's grandson.'

"'Yes, yes, and your father—is he here?'

"'No, my father of blessed memory died some years ago.'

"'I see. I will tell my grandfather.'

"The rabbi stepped from his house and waved at my grandfather in our taxi, who smiled back. And so it ends.

"But not so. I thought about this story for a long time. For now, for five years, each Friday I take my father's taxi, and I drive the streets of Jerusalem, and I look for a Jew going maybe in the direction of the Wall. Where else could you two be going in this neighborhood on a late Friday afternoon? Anyway, I pick you up just as I have picked up others, no charge, just to hear the story of two men, friends in Jerusalem. An Arab and a Jew. Into this taxi, our home, our city, you are welcome. *Saalam aleikum.*

"Here we are. I'll pull up to the curb; just walk straight through the Dung Gate. Then you will see your Wall. Remember me, remember this story."

With that, my friend and I began to get out of the taxi. I paused, shook Mahmud's hand, and promised him that I would remember not only his story, but also that my true welcome to Israel began in his taxi.

Provenance: This is a true story, which describes my first week in Israel during my junior year of college, July 1971. I first told this story at a CAJE conference in Columbus, Ohio. As we were preparing for *Shabbat*, Peninnah Schram asked if anyone wanted to share a story. Although I had spoken of this incident on many occasions, I had never before told it as a full story.

Daniel Grossman serves as Rabbi of Adath Israel Congregation, Lawrenceville, New Jersey. His focus is Jewish Special Needs within a normative congregation. Dan co-wrote and participated in the video *Someone Is Listening*, the story of a young deaf Jew and his search for fulfillment. Dan and his wife, Elayne, perform *Siman Tov*, an educational entertainment program which uses sign language, mime, music, and storytelling to bring audiences closer to the world of the Jewish deaf. He is very proud to share a place in this volume with his daughter, Miriam, and to recognize the wonderful artistic talents of his son, Sam.

These Are Your Laws
by Miriam Grossman

We drove over shadowed hills, and I watched the land roll, arching and curving like an animal waking. It was springtime, my junior year of college, and I was interning at a Tribal Historic Preservation Office (THPO) on Standing Rock Reservation in North Dakota. THPOs are tribal-run agencies that safeguard Native sacred sites. They protect cultural artifacts and indigenous graveyards against looters, collectors, power plants, oil pipelines, and apathetic federal agents, who will sign away holy land in an outgoing stack of mail.

As my boss, Tim, drove his wife's sedan over narrow highway strips, we told stories of our people–his, Dakota and Lakota; mine, Ashkenazi Jewish. Riding through towns with no signs and highways with barely any lights, I felt my heart stretch open. Tim drove with no stops. I watched the sky change. We drove for hours, past deer, horses, and buffalo grazing frosted grass. He told me what it means for the sun to chase the moon, for thunder to wake the earth. He told me stories of what white settlers had done to his family, stories of his youth in boarding school, stories I do not have the right to tell. He told me we were stepping into a fight.

We drove to a small Lakota community, hours from the reservation. Many smaller bands like these still do not have a THPO to protect their legal land rights, so well-established THPO's will often step in to support them, as Tim and I were doing today. In the case of this particular community, members of the tribe were fighting efforts by the Department of the Interior to build an elementary school on top of a known Lakota burial mound. When we arrived, tribal leaders explained to us that government agencies had initially forged the necessary papers to get the ball rolling. No authentic survey of the site had ever taken place.

The meeting was packed with THPO leaders, elders, and families. When I entered the room, each person, from grandmothers to children just out of diapers, reached out and shook my hand. I took a seat in a middle row, holding a yellow legal pad on my lap.

"Take notes," Tim said. "We'll need them later."

The elders began the meeting in a spirit of humility. First, Lakota blessings and songs were offered. Then an elder brought out an offering, a spirit plate, to feed the ancestors. We, the living, would soon eat the same meal. Everyone had a role.

The first to speak was an elder, "These are my relatives!"

A grandfather shouted in a cracked voice, "My great-grandmother and grandmother are buried there. I know it as a fact. But what do you want? You won't be happy unless we dig up bones."

A woman my mother's age spoke next. She spoke in Lakota, then repeated her last sentences in English. Her stories were meant first for her own people.

"Education matters,"she said. "But what are we teaching our children? To disturb their ancestors? To disrespect the dead? It isn't worth it."

"If we don't stop this," an uncle said, "if we don't believe this matters, is it all for show? The spirit plate? The prayers? Everything we do here?"

For Lakota families, bones are sacred. A person's spirit is free and safe when their bones are at rest. To disturb the dead is much more than just a sentimental discomfort. When a person's spirit or bones are dishonored or disrupted, their spirit feels that pain.

"My God," I thought, "their ancestors are feeling real physical pain."

I shuddered, thinking of the elders in my line, the ones before me, the ones who had died after long, honorable, happy lives, the ones lost in genocide and strife. What would I do if I believed that they were in pain? What would I do if the Torah taught me ways to protect them but a mid-level bureaucrat in a car more expensive than my house signed away their eternal rest? In front of unsympathetic officials who would soon write off sacred stories as folklore and fantasy, these people were bearing witness to their oral Torah.

One of the THPO leaders stood up and addressed the crowd. He, too, spoke first in Lakota, comforting his people before confronting the federal agents.

"There is a legal process you have failed to comply with," he said, "spelled out by the National Historic Preservation Act, the National Environmental Protection Act, and the Native American Graves Protection and Repatriation Act. You are breaking your own laws, the very ones you forced upon us. But there is still natural law for you to answer to."

Unfolding here in this gathering, I recognized the same battles of assimilation and tradition I had witnessed countless times in my own community.

"Let go of all that," some Lakota families were now saying. "It's time for progress."

The federal agents looked at the gathering, at the community divided, at the families who were seeking recognition and justice.

"Love is never having to say you're sorry," one of the agents, wearing a starched white linen shirt, stuttered. "I think *this* is a lot like that. If you have to say you're sorry, then you just shouldn't have done it."

The crowd murmured, trying to understand what he meant.

"And hey, listen, you know, my wife...my wife has breast cancer. So, you know, I'm not some evil, heartless jerk."

True, he wasn't without heart, but he was perhaps without understanding.

By the end of the meeting, nothing had been resolved. Some families were afraid to send their children to the new school. Others thought that an honor ceremony might set things right. Still others sat in small family groups, whispering,

"What has been done can never be made right."

I left to wash my face in the bathroom. I stared at the wet, white skin in my reflection. After all those years learning American history in Jewish day school, I had self-righteously washed off the blood of Native peoples, claiming, "My family wasn't yet here when those injustices were perpetrated. We were busy in our shtetls, suffering pogroms of our own."

But right where I stood, Native land, bones, even blood was still being taken in the country that my family has called home for two, nearly three, generations.

I shook the water off my *hamsa*, afraid it might drip down my shirt, and, holding the delicate silver piece between my fingers, opened the bathroom door.

"Protect me from hate," I prayed under my breath, holding tight the *hamsa*, which symbolically protects travelers from giving or receiving the evil eye. As I stepped out of the bathroom, I caught sight of the federal agent who had last spoken, approaching Tim a few feet away.

"Listen, I know a family that does this thing with hides and skins. Maybe that could...make a little peace here?" He was sweating as he spoke.

It was too much. The history of federal agents offering cheap trades, hides or leather, beads, whiskey, or horses, for holy, holy, holy land. I felt the openhearted space that had been dug clear through me in the country ride to this rural community, a space that mirrored the empty horizon of the plains. I watched and felt that space inside me fill, brim, and bubble over with hate.

Without prompting, Tim reached out his hand. "We'll see."

I knew that Tim wouldn't decline a gift offered in good faith. But I also knew that it wasn't an apology Tim was accepting from the sweating agent, who was standing in front of him, riddled with guilt.

"We have a lot of talking to do," Tim said. Then he looked the agent in the eye and wished his wife good health.

I remained standing by the bathroom door with my hands in my pockets until Tim called me to the car. On the drive back to Standing Rock, I was silent for a good while.

"Well, that was something, wasn't it?" Tim said. He laughed and rolled down the window by his side.

"How did you do it? How did you shake his hand like that?" I asked.

"Come on now, he's a person like anybody else."

Would my great-grandmother, whose legs were, until the day she died, mangled and scarred from a violent pogrom, let the son of a Cossack into her house? Would she wish his wife well, knowing that his father might have killed her own brother? Would she shake his hand?

I sat looking out the window, letting North Dakota wash over me, until the grassy dunes of the prairie reminded me of another story from another time. When I was a child, my teachers had always vilified Esau, the older twin son of the patriarch Jacob. Esau was wicked, they had taught me, not to be sympathized with or trusted. But my father had taught me otherwise.

"Esau was misunderstood," he would say. "If you read the text, it isn't right or fair to call him evil. He was just a man like anyone else. Esau was Issac's favorite son, simple and brutish, but not evil."

In the end, Jacob and Esau had stood face to face with their camps behind them, both capable of destruction and vengeance, both harboring venomous memories of a war they had fought since the womb. What did they do, standing face to face, when after years of scheming and running they finally met again?

The Torah tells us, "And Esau ran to meet (Jacob), and embraced him, and fell on his neck, and kissed him: and they wept" [Genesis 33:4]. The brothers had held one another. But they had not journeyed on together.

I know that Tim will never accept a handshake or a hide as the final word in the fight for tribal sovereignty. But I also now understand that he lost nothing in accepting another person's humanity.

Perhaps, at the end of the day, my great-grandmother would have let her enemy in the door. Perhaps not. Maybe such forgiveness is too much to ask. Thinking about the embracing twins, the scars on my great-grandmother's legs, and the out-stretched hands of a confused government agent and a confident tribal leader, I imagined what it would take for my heart to turn from revenge, for my eyes to see more than snapshots of hands and bodies and wrongdoings, but rather a vast honest terrain of stories and whole, imperfect lives.

Provenance: This is a true story, which took place while I was living on a Lakota reservation in 2008. I write this story with a heart full of love and gratitude for the friends, tribal activists, and teachers I was blessed to meet.

Miriam Grossman is deeply passionate about social justice and the power of story. She is currently the Educational Programs Coordinator at the Jewish Council on Urban Affairs and the publishing intern at Reclaiming Judaism Press. Miriam is also a recipient of the Jewish Educators Assembly's 20/20 Award for twenty emerging Jewish community leaders in their twenties and an alumnus of AVODAH, the Jewish Service Corps. She is continually inspired by the spiritual vibrancy and call to social action that exists within the Jewish tradition.

 # Working Together
by Fred Guttman

The date: 1983. The place: Israel. The main character: a young, Jewish man from Nashville who had recently made *aliyah* with his wife. The goal: to survive the Israeli army's basic training.

Before I went into the army, I was scared to death that I was not in good enough shape. At that time, I was 30 pounds lighter than I am now. My fear motivated me to start a training regimen in which I ran ten miles and swam five each week. As a result, when I went into the Israeli Army, I was in the best shape of my life. I felt pretty good about myself.

But my newfound confidence was put to the test on the second or third day at the base, when the army decided to test our physical ability. We all lined up and in the distance could see our target: a nineteen-year-old female corporal stood on the road a kilometer away from us. The task for the 63 of us in that unit was to run to the female corporal, circle around her and run back to the starting point.

"Go!" yelled the sergeant, and we all took off. I was in full army gear and was not used to running in heavy boots, so I decided that a slow and steady jog was the way to complete this two-kilometer run. To my abject terror, everyone took off running much faster than I.

"How could it be," I asked myself, "that after getting in such fantastic shape all of these other people could be in so much better shape? How could that be?"

At that moment, fear crept in again, and I wondered whether or not I could make it through basic training in the Israeli Army. If the expectations of the army were so much greater than what I was able to achieve myself, how could I survive?

But then something happened. After the first three hundred meters, I began to pass people, one by one!

I ran past most of the unit as I neared the corporal, with one notable exception. Fourteen newly arrived Ethiopian immigrants ran in front of us all like gazelles, laughing and joking, seemingly without a care in the world. For them, this was not a race, but an opportunity to run together and have a good time! Eventually, the Ethiopians passed the finish line together as a group, ahead of us. I was the second non-Ethiopian to finish!

At the end of the run, I asked the Ethiopian soldiers which of them had "won" the race. Their response was that in Ethiopia, in the Gundar region, running was not a competitive activity, but a group effort. It made no difference to them who crossed the finish line first, as long as they all finished the race together as a group!

One of the hardest moments of basic training yet one of the most important lessons occurred a week later. At this time, twenty-one of us had to do a five-kilometer stretcher drill. In this drill, the unit would practice what to do if one of our soldiers was injured. Unfortunately, our make-believe "injured" was a rather beefy 220-pound Russian immigrant who was strapped onto a stretcher and had to be carried by the twenty-one of us five kilometers. Because he was supposed to be injured, we had to run with him and make sure that we didn't drop and really injure him. Four men at a time would carry the stretchers on their shoulders. Every twenty seconds, the two men at the back of the stretcher moved to the front and were replaced by two men in the line behind them. The men carrying the front of the stretcher then went to the back of the line. Thus each person carried the stretcher for forty-second intervals, then went to the back of the line and worked his way up for another turn.

Never in my life have I felt so physically exhausted. This was the closest thing to hell on earth. As we were running, the little nineteen-year old woman corporal shouted at us,

"*Mah yiheyeh?* What's going to happen? What will be? Is he going to live? It's up to you!" Needless to say, at that moment we all hated that woman.

To make matters worse, when we returned to the base, the young woman would not allow us to put the stretcher down until we had thrown it up three times, saying, "Up, up, up!" But despite our fatigue, we managed to successfully return our "injured" soldier to the base!

After we put him down, the Israeli Army threw a party for us at which they broke out beer and shish-ka-bob. Only in the Israeli army!

We learned very valuable lessons about life from both experiences. The previous week, we had learned that we all have different abilities and capabilities. This week we learned that the most important thing was not that we were different, but that if we worked together, we could save a life. Together, we could make a difference.

Provenance: This story is autobiographical; in 1983 as a thirty-three year old new immigrant, I entered the Israeli army for basic training. I learned many life lessons from that experience, two of which are recounted in the story. The new immigrants in basic training were from all over the world, including the Soviet Union, various European countries, South Africa, the United States, and Ethiopia. All of us were part of what was then called *Shalav Bet*, a special section for new immigrants from the ages of 24 to 39. The story shows the uniqueness of the IDF as a Jewish and Israeli army.

Fred Guttman has served as Rabbi of Temple Emanuel in Greensboro, North Carolina, from 1995 to the present. He is known for his telling of stories from the pulpit, many of which are autobiographical. He was ordained by Hebrew Union College in 1979. From 1979 to 1991, Fred lived in Israel. While there, he also served as a reserve soldier in a combat artillery brigade, extensively in the administered territories. Since returning to the United States, he has led numerous trips to Israel, including the March of the Living, family trips, and in 2008, an interfaith clergy trip.

The Escort
by Benji Levene

In the summer of 1970, I was studying in a *yeshiva* in Jerusalem. My parents had come back to Israel after living in the States for thirty years. My father was serving as the rabbi of a town called Pardes Hanna, near the Coastal Road, not far from Caesaria.

One Friday morning as I got on the bus in Jerusalem to spend the *Shabbat* with my family, someone called to me, "Hey, Benji! Did you see the *Yediot* newspaper today? There are wonderful stories about your grandfather."

My grandfather, Reb Aryeh Levin, was known as the "Tzaddik of Jerusalem." He was one of modern Israel's most saintly and beloved icons, known for his great acts of kindness as he tended to prisoners, lepers, the meek and the downtrodden. He passed away in Jerusalem in 1969—a legend in his time.

When I changed buses in Tel Aviv, I bought a copy of the weekend newspaper and read the article about my grandfather. There were stories of how he would always escort people on the streets of Jerusalem. Many famous people spoke about their visits with him in his simple, little room in downtown Jerusalem, on the street that today bears his name. They all mentioned how he would escort them to the main road when they took leave of him, quoting to them from Maimonides on the importance of this mitzvah.

Later at the *Shabbat* meal at my parents' house, I asked my father, "Where did your father, Reb Aryeh, learn to fulfill this mitzvah?"

"Well," my father said, "Reb Aryeh was a great scholar in his own right, and he knew of this mitzvah, but there is a story attached to it."

Reb Aryeh was known throughout Israel as "The Father of the Prisoners," because he tended to young men and women who were incarcerated or were fighting to free Palestine from British rule and declare an independent Jewish state. Many of these young boys who were sentenced to the gallows asked for him to be with them at their last moments.

"One Friday morning," my father said, "Reb Aryeh visited a prison outside of Jerusalem. There in a cell sat a man imprisoned for a daring raid against the British. This man had heard that Reb Aryeh was visiting the prison and asked to speak to the rabbi. Even the British had great respect for Reb Aryeh and granted the prisoner's request.

"The man said to Reb Aryeh, 'My wife and I both lost our families in the Holocaust. We met in Cyprus on our way to Israel. We married and had a child, and now we live in Jerusalem. My friends in the underground are afraid to visit my wife because they fear they may be caught by the British. Rabbi, please visit my wife and tell her you saw me. Tell her I'm OK.'

"Reb Aryeh took the address and promised to relay the message, if at all possible.

"He went back to Jerusalem and set out to find the prisoner's wife. It was getting close to *Shabbat*, and he couldn't find the address. People were in their homes preparing for *Shabbat*. As he walked by a small street, Reb Aryeh saw a woman in a window preparing the *Shabbat* meal. He asked her if she knew the place he was seeking.

"She said, 'Please wait a moment.'

"She took off her apron, walked outside, and said, 'Please follow me.'

"She led him through the street to a small house and said, 'This is the place!'

"'Why did you have to come all this way?' asked Reb Aryeh. 'You must be in a hurry before *Shabbat*. You could have simply given me directions.'

"'Oh, I thought about doing that,' she said, 'but then I remembered that this is my special mitzvah.'

"'What do you mean?' asked Reb Aryeh.

"'My father was a very pious man,' she said. 'Before he passed away, he called me and my siblings to his bedside and said, "What do people take with them when they leave this world? Their honor, money, position, status? No! The only thing they take with them are the good deeds they performed during their lifetime."'

"'My father said to each of us, "Of all the mitzvahs you perform, choose one mitzvah and make it your special one. Whenever the opportunity comes along to perform this mitzvah, however difficult it may be, do it in its entirety." My father then helped me choose my mitzvah of escorting a person on their way.

"'When you approached me today I said, "This is my special mizvah I'm going to perform it in its entirety."'

"Reb Aryeh thanked the young woman. He visited the prisoner's wife and brought her regards from her husband in jail. When Reb Aryeh came home just before candle lighting he wrote in his little notebook: 'Today I learned from a young woman the importance of fulfilling this commandment, and from today on, I'm going to be careful to always perform this mitzvah.'"

When I heard this story, I said, "Wow! What a beautiful mitzvah." There and then I decided to make this mitzvah mine as well. Saturday night I went back to Jerusalem. Two days later, on Monday night, I was walking in the street in the early evening when I noticed an elderly man across the road, walking back and forth as if he had lost something.

I crossed the street and said, "Excuse me. I couldn't help noticing you walking back and forth. Did you lose something?"

"Well, actually," he said, "I got a little confused here in the dark. I'm looking for Portzim Street."

I said to myself, "God, I promised two days ago to make this mitzvah of escorting another person mine. God, are you testing me already?"

"Come," I said to the old man. "Let me perform the mitzvah of escorting you."

I brought him to the street—to the house he sought—and said: "Here it is! Shalom!"

"Just a minute," he said. "Why did you stop and ask me if I'm looking for something? Why did you escort me? Young people don't do these things today."

"Well, I probably wouldn't have done this," I said, "but my grandfather used to do this."

"Who was your grandfather?"

"Oh, you wouldn't know," I said.

"What was his name?"

"Levin," I said.

"Which Levin?"

"Aryeh Levin."

"The famous *tzaddik*, Reb Aryeh Levin?" he asked.

"Yes," I replied.

The old man took hold of the lapels on my jacket and started to cry. I saw the tears roll down his cheeks, and I was at a total loss of what to do.

I waited.

Finally, he looked up at me and said: "Do you know who I am?"

"No," I replied, "I never had the pleasure."

"My name is Menachem Ro-iy," he said. "I am a reporter for *Yediot*. Last week I wrote a number of stories about how your grandfather would escort people on the streets of Jerusalem. And here a few days later, I lose my way and who escorts me? None other than Reb Aryeh's own grandson."

I looked at the old man and said, "And do you know why? Because Reb Aryeh's grandson read your stories and learned how important and beautiful it is to escort another person on his or her way."

Provenance Note: This is a true story that happened to me regarding this mitzvah in the summer of 1970, in Jerusalem.

Benji Levene is a Yeshiva University graduate. His rabbinical ordination is from the Chief Rabbi of Israel. After serving as advisor to the Chairman of the Aliya Department, Jewish Agency for Israel, he began to offer Seminars in Tzefat for the Gesher organization, dedicated to bridging the gap between religious and secular Jews. Best known for his show, "The Four Faces of Israel," Benji is one of Israel's foremost educators and storytellers. Benji walks in the footsteps of his legendary grandfather, the Tzaddik of Jerusalem, Rabbi Aryeh Levin, known for his love and tolerance of all Jews.

Playing Monopoly with Melvin
by Herb Levine

Our synagogue participates with local churches in a project of offering hospitality to homeless families for two or three weeks at a time. Members of the synagogue volunteer to spend time with the families while they are in our building—serving dinner, playing with the children, sleeping over. One Sunday afternoon about twenty years ago, most of the families were out of the building, but one family had nowhere else to go, so it was our responsibility as hosts to keep them company. That family consisted of a father, Melvin, and a ten- or eleven-year-old boy, Robert, about the same age as my daughter Sarah. I had signed up for that shift and brought Sarah with me. I also brought along a bag of board games.

Melvin chose Monopoly, and we all started to play. Robert had never played the game before and had a hard time learning the rules. He became frustrated and dropped out within the first fifteen minutes. While the two adults and Sarah continued the game, he amused himself riding little kids' bikes around the big, empty room.

Sarah, who had been playing Monopoly for about three years, played her usual careful game. She'd already learned that buying the lower-priced purple, brown, red, orange, and yellow properties in the first couple of rounds put you at a disadvantage, depriving you of the cash you'd need to afford the more expensive green and blue properties at the far side of the board. So she bided her time and bought greens and blues as she landed on them. Eventually, she acquired Boardwalk and Park Place, built hotels on them, and claimed huge rents.

Given that Sarah had chosen what our family had deemed the best strategy for winning the game, I had to pick another, so when I landed on railroads and utilities, I bought them, building up monopolies of those properties. Even if I wasn't going to build lots of houses and hotels, I could frustrate the other players by getting large infusions of cash each time they landed on my properties. Perhaps, if I had enough money, I could even break Sarah's monopoly.

Melvin, meanwhile, bought whatever property he landed on. He bought Arctic and Mediterranean and St. James Place—a smattering of purples, oranges and even a more expensive red or yellow, if he happened to have enough cash. Whenever he landed on one of my utilities or one of Sarah's high-rent properties, he had to fork over cash, sometimes very large sums. When he had no money left in his kitty, he simply mortgaged a property and borrowed from the bank so he could pay. As the game went on, he had to mortgage more and more of his holdings, for Sarah's rents continued to rise as she gained monopolies and built hotels. Melvin also had some good luck. When he picked a Community Chest card that got him some cash, he inevitably bought back his properties from the bank.

At one point, I turned to Melvin and asked him why he continued to buy every property he landed on, since it didn't appear that he was ever going to get a monopoly and win.

"All I want to do," he said, "is to stay in the game."

Melvin's answer was like a banner headline bearing the message: "Notice this. It will change how you think about the world."

At that moment, Melvin became my teacher. His answer put into bold relief for me how a person who had never been encouraged to succeed might end up homeless, whereas a person brought up in a family like mine absorbs so many strategies for winning, not just at Monopoly, but at life. At age ten, my daughter could make a choice about a course of action, invest resources in that course, patiently defer gratification, and succeed in her goal of winning the game.

Melvin's goal was simply to stay in the game. That was his way of winning. I often think about him and hope that he's still at it.

Herb Levine is the Executive Director of the Mercer Alliance to End Homelessness, based in Lawrenceville, NJ. He is also the author of *Sing Unto God a New Song: A Contemporary Reading of the Psalms* and *Yeats's Daimonic Renewal*. His poems, essays and *divrei Torah* have appeared in *Tikkun, Kerem* and *The Reconstructionist*. He is a past chair of the National Havurah Committee.

The God of Curried Fish
by Goldie Milgram

It's a little too close to dark. I'm driving through a dicey neighborhood. Five hours on the road and didn't stop yet to eat. On the right
just ahead, a neon sign declares, "Hallal Jamaican Restaurant," and
drawing closer, I can see under it is written on a white board: "Today's
special: Curried fish, fried sweet plantains." Perfect.

Inside, the take-out line is short, but growing. Only one customer
sits at the old diner-style, cruise-ship blue, Formica tables, a large,
powerful-looking man in a fire engine red T-shirt with tall white letters
screaming on it: "Did I give you permission to talk? Shut the ____ up!"

The woman at the counter is wearing a bright white, immaculately
clean apron over a boxy, navy dress suit, with matching stockings and
pumps. Her swollen ankles seem crowbarred-in beyond bearability. I
lose this trend of observation while lurching and ducking in concern at
a sudden bellowing from behind:

"Where the hell is my refill#@!"

Almost simultaneously, the much-stained chef emerges from the
kitchen, and the counterwoman turns to receive a steaming, savory-
scented bowl of oxtail soup.

"Excuse, please," she speaks softly to our take-out pick-up line.

Bowl carried firmly in two hands, without hurry or slosh, she
aims straight for the big customer, sets it down, blowing strongly on
superheated fingers.

"Reggie, it's so nice to see you again. Let me know should you want
anything more."

Reggie responds kindly, "Thanks, Alinda. Thanks."

Alinda returns to the counter. I can see down the line that I'm not
the only one whose shoulders relax at Reggie's polite response.

Several orders, including mine, are taken and turfed back to the chef
on scraps of old, paper placemat. The eat-in tables are filling rapidly.
Alinda is hustling as best she can. The early-bird take-out crowd, we're
leaning against the walls covered in jazz, gospel, library, social service
and Bible study announcements. No one seems to read them, though
they are surprisingly current.

Hmmm, wonder if the gentleman five people behind me might be a
minister, in his shiny black suit and polished shoes, short-cropped hair,
and request to post a gospel poster upon arrival. Or, my shadow side
considers, maybe he's a recovering addict; he keeps fingering a pack of

cigarettes nervously. Maybe he's both. A wiry fellow hosting a huge head of dreadlocks spits loudly onto the floor without missing a beat of full body sway to whatever is coming through his headphones. No one gives him a glance, save for Alinda who uses her same kind voice:

"Sir, please don't do that in here, not sanitary." He gives no indication of listening or hearing.

Two young ones, maybe age seven at best, hair in corn rolls with beads and bows that bounce, and dressed in impeccable Sunday-best, start to whine in boredom and get smacked real good. I flinch, and the mom gives me an I-dare-you-to-say-something glare. We all start reading the wall posters. Alinda comes to the rescue, fumbling in her apron pocket while balancing two platters of what looks like chicken, rice, and red beans on her wrist and palm:

"Crayyyonnns, come'n get 'em! Show us what you two young artists can do."

Twenty minutes further, I'm debating leaving without my order. It's getting quite dark out. Suddenly, from behind, I feel a light shove. It's Reggie, pushing past all of us, holding up a ten-dollar bill. The chef, Jamaican by accent, has just brought out a bowl of what appears to be lamb curry, passes it to Alinda, and then pauses to take the payment. Instead of handing it over, Reggie balls the bill up in his hand, lifts his thick, muscular arms on high, and then smashes both his fists down on the counter. Being closest to him, I can't help but jump and gasp along with the chef and many others. Reggie turns and flashes me a maniacal smile of bright, white, bulbous teeth, punctuated by gaping spaces with a touch of a gold partial bracket showing on the lower right canine. He then vibrates the air into palpable waves with a passionate declaration: "I am so worn out, defeated, and lost. I would rather be dead."

Everyone backs up about three paces. The fellow to my right fingers what might well be a gun tucked into his pants under his African pattern shirt. Big Reggie looks at me, and I become conscious of my paling face, mint green, huge-brimmed sun hat, bright yellow silk designer top, and sun-resistant mesh-vented hiking pants. Reggie re-bellows with head slightly lowered, eyes fixed on mine,

"Sister, did you hear me?! I'd rather be dead, girl, dead."

Considering the situation, the many church store-fronts in the neighborhood, and that he is directly addressing me, I respond softly,

"Have you...have you asked God to help you?"

Deafening silence with a few strong nods, and then one fairly feeble, "You said it, sister," from a table near the back.

Reggie glares but responds in a voice slightly less deafening, "I'm so tired of that bullshit...(pause)." His eyes are closed, he looks beyond weary, his shoulders are somewhat lower, but his fists are still balled up.

"I've been a Christian all my life, and I've discovered it's all complete bullshit."

So much for my projections. I note the chef's hands are now under the counter and wonder if he's surreptitiously reaching for an alarm. I respond as I would to any congregant, slowly, clearly: "You are suffering and lost, worn out and defeated."

Pause...shoulders a bit less down. "Lady, do you believe in God? In any of the types of god being peddled these days?"

Pheww, he's hurting. My old social worker instincts tell me he's not so dangerous now that he's reached out and seems to feel heard. I take a step closer to him, tilt my head to one side with a neutral yet present look, and venture an educated summary: "You feel betrayed by God."

"Yup, all that prayin' and believin' and nothin' comin' of it...Lady, you didn't answer my question: you believe in God?"

Need something to give him a further toehold on sanity. Has to be honest because body language tells all. Seems this is no time for the "G" word.

"Reggie, I'm for sure amazed by creation and live in awe. It's incredible what we've got here. Not so impressed by what we do with it lately."

Reggie just continues, "You believe in life after death?"

Oh, whoa! Might he be considering checking-out on life, as in suicide, or committing a crime to get what he needs and contemplating the eternal consequences?

"Reggie, my daddy taught me it's a mystery, and we'll find out one way or the other when we die."

"Mystery, that I can do! Makes sense, treat'n it as a mystery. I don't believe all that crap about going to hell and burning. And it is awesome, just awesome sometimes." Everything in the restaurant has come to a standstill. "Halleuyah, brother!" echoes from various tables.

I come back with: "Anyone who tells me they know the answer for sure, I kinda tend to avoid."

Reggie appreciates that: "Yeah, how could they know? They brainwashed."

He gestures at a table that just opened up. We both sit down. No one argues that it's really their turn to sit down.

"Reggie, what happened that's got you so low?"

Reggie places his warm, thick hand over my small fingers, where great-grandmother Goldie's three-diamond engagement ring lives. A ring that survived the Cossacks and serves for me as an enduring reminder of her courage and ability to protect her girls and use all of herself to survive when they rampaged through her cottage in Russia. I consciously bid my hands not to tense up.

Folks turn back to their meals, as Reggie lowers his voice to conversation level.

"Thing is, lady, I'm a simple man, and I lost my job twice this year to companies downsizing. See, I'm a simple man. You tell me 'pick that heavy thing up,' I can do that. You tell me, 'put it over there,' I can do that. You want me to figure a good or right place to put down what you told me to pick up, I can't do that, I'm no good at that. I can't boss others, I can't make a schedule. I can pick up what you tell me and put it down just right. I need a job, a simple job. I bartered my good old Pontiac car this week for money to live. If I miss my next rent payment, I live on the street. God don't deliver. God don't care."

"Goldie, curried fish and plantains!"

I rise reflexively and Reggie does, too. Index finger raised in the language of "hang on a sec" to the man at the counter, I return to Reggie: "You are a simple man, and you want a simple job, and God does not provide."

He looks into my eyes the way you know you've got a friend for life and says, "Are you some kind of Christian?"

"Actually," I reply softly, "I'm a rabbi."

"A rabbi?! No shit." He looks around as though expecting a surprise TV crew to pop out. Then Reggie claims both my hands in his and passionately pleads: "Rabbi, what am I to do? I'm scared. It's too tough now out there to make it. I know lotsa folks got no job. I'm two minutes from sleeping on the street."

Indeed, that's the 30 billion dollar question. I do the only thing left inside, in a strong, firm voice everyone in the shop can hear: "Holy One of Blessing, this man needs a job. Right now."

Folks turn and stare at me. I'm aware of the pattern of whites of eyes in variously dark, surprised, but not frightened faces. I'm aware of feeling angry—at God, at government, of a glowering impotence that just isn't acceptable. The prayer, my clear petition, pours through again, louder, toward Heaven: "Holy One of Blessing, this man needs a job. Right now." The silence is complete; even the two children fold their hands in prayer.

The chef clears his throat. "Ma'am, your order's getting cold. $11.50, please." No one moves. Reggie lets go of my hands in an incredibly tender way, the whites of his huge brown eyes are red-lined and brimming with tears that don't fall.

As I shift to my purse, trying to focus on securing $11.50, the chef's voice turns thoughtful:

"One more thing. Reggie. You can work for me. I've got a bad back these days. You pick it up; I'll tell you where to put it. Every morning be outside at seven am for deliveries. You can also push a broom and bus tables 'cause Alinda can't cope since Orly quit yesterday. You can work a full day. But—and it's a big but—you have to keep it together, stay on your meds, and treat folks respectfully. Get rid of that damn T-shirt for starters." He tosses a sky blue shirt with the restaurant's name and logo on it to Reggie. "Put this one on. Free meals, minimum wage."

Both of us gape at the proprietor.

Reggie pumps my hand, "Thank you, Ma'am! I mean, thank you, Rabbi! Jews surely are the Lord's chosen people; the Lord was listen' to your prayer! Thank you, Ma'am, thank you, thank you."

I stutter out, "Ddddon't thank me, thank the proprietor. He's the one who's giving you a..."

The chef interrupts me, "Don't thank me. Seems I gotta check out what you Jews got goin'. Sure does work on a man's soul."

I shake his hand. "Thank you, sir, thank you for giving Reggie a job. You see, what you've just done, it's so very holy. It's what in my tradition we call a mitzvah, a wonderful, huge mitzvah."

One of the little boys jumps up and down, shouting, "Chef Ali, you a *bar mitzvah*. How about that?! Here's a present, Chef Ali, the picture I drew, and Sammy's, too. OK, Sammy? Good. Chef, here. Looks like I made you your first *bar mitzvah* present."

A raw, sharp sound pulls our jubilation up short. What is that noise?

Reggie's laughing! Awesome, glorious, full-bodied laughing, which triggers me laughing, and now everyone's laughing. Curried cold fish, coming right up, hope hubby will understand the delay. No, the holy chef's already on it. "Rabbi Lady, can I warm that up for you?"

Provenance: A therapist once said my life would be turned down as a plot for a soap opera. This true story is a good example.

Goldie Milgram, Editor-in-Chief of Reclaiming Judaism Press, Executive Vice-President of Reclaiming Judaism, is a Covenant Award finalist and was named American Cancer Society Most Distinguished Citizen for creating and anchoring television's first health interview series, "Health Watch" (NBC TV40). "Reb Goldie" serves internationally as a vibrant, experiential teacher of Torah and Jewish spiritual practices. An RRC graduate, Goldie has also been honored with Rabbi Zalman Schachter-Shalomi's *smichah* as rabbi, *maggid, schaliach* and *mashpiah.* Among her many published works are her widely-utilized *Mitzvah Cards* and also her Jewish Lights Reclaiming Judaism trilogy which includes *Meaning & Mitzvah: Daily Practices for Reclaiming Judaism through Prayer, God, Torah, Hebrew, Mitzvot & Peoplehood. (www.reclaimingjudaism.org)*

Being a Wrestler with God
by Peter Pitzele

After the encounter between Jacob and the angel, the angel returns to heaven for a de-briefing with God.

Angel (sullen): Well, I did what you said.

God: And?

Angel: Why ask? You know everything. You set it up. You saw it.

God: Don't be so sure about me. I am a lot more complicated than even you can imagine. And you're one of the brighter stars in the heavens.

Angel: Well, he beat me.

God: Yes.

Angel: He didn't exactly beat me. You could say it was a draw.

God: Yes.

Angel: Still, he is only a man, an ordinary guy.

God: And what did you find out about this "ordinary guy"?

Angel: He was tough. He wouldn't let go. You know, like stubborn.

God: I believe the right word is "tenacious."

Angel: If you say so. If that means he held on, like for dear life.

God: Yes.

Angel: Of course, I don't understand this thing about "dear life." Being immortal. But what I couldn't figure was that he really didn't want to beat me. He just didn't want to get beat.

God: Yes! (Pause) Something else surprised you?

Angel: Yeah. Pain. When I...when I broke free and twisted him, something flashed through me like light. It came from him. But what flashed through him was heat. And he screamed. I never heard that sound before.

God: Humans are different from the Heavenly Host. It would be hard for you to understand.

Angel: Death, pain, and darkness. I mean they don't seem to have a clue as to where they're going. Human life—well, forgive me for saying this—but is it a curse?

God: Sometimes I wonder if...(breaks off)

Angel: What?

God: Never mind. It's more than you need to know. (Pause) Something else?

Angel: Yes. He wanted a blessing. (Pause) From me. Well, really, he wanted a blessing from you, but like through me.

God: And you gave it to him. You did just fine.

Angel: Did I? I thought, you know, I thought I was supposed to put him in his place.

God: But that's exactly what you did.

Angel: I don't understand. I thought you sent me down to wipe the floor with the guy.

God: No, I sent you down to contend with him. To exercise him. To prepare him.

Angel: "Prepare him"? For what?

God: To become Israel. It means: "the one who wrestles with God."

Angel: My Hebrew isn't too good.

God: Well, that's what it means. Israel is the God-wrestler.

Angel: No kidding. There's no percentage in that. Nobody wrestles with you and wins.

God: You'd be surprised.

Angel: But why?

God: Because it's what I want in the world.

Angel: You want someone to fight with?

God: (Pause) I miss Abraham.

Angel: You miss Abraham?

God: I do.

Angel: Funny to think of you missing anybody. What do you miss about Abraham?

God: You probably don't remember this, but there was a moment...I was getting ready to smash Sodom and Gomorrah, and Abraham wrestled with me.

Angel: Oh, yeah. Sure. I remember. That was the talk up here. What balls, I mean. Sorry, Boss. No way to talk. But going toe to toe with you...We thought, for sure, you'd turn him to salt.

God: On the contrary. It was his finest moment. His sense of justice—so limited, so human, but so noble—contending with my sense of justice—so impersonal, so vast, so unknowable. I never loved him more.

Angel: No kidding. I didn't know.

God: It's true. And then I made this huge mistake of asking him to sacrifice his son.

Angel: But you weren't ever going to take the sacrifice. We all knew that.

God: I knew. Of course. But he didn't know. I wanted him to protest, to argue. To question. But he submitted.

Angel: And you had to send me down to stop the whole thing.

God: Yes.

Angel: And get the ram.

God: Yes. Anyway, it was not his finest moment, and it was not mine. And since then, I have been afraid that human beings would think Abraham's obedience was what I wanted from them, and not Abraham's resistance.

Angel: And you think Jacob can do this resistance thing?

God: I'm not sure. Free will keeps me guessing.

Angel: If you ask me, Esau would have made the better wrestler. But Jacob was pretty good.

God: I have other things in mind for Esau. (Pause) Anything else?

Angel: No. Well...I don't know how to ask this but...

God: There is something. Something you want from me.

Angel: Yeah. You know what it is.

God: Tell me. In your own words.

Angel: I uh. I...want a blessing. Nah, that's stupid. I am blessed. I'm an angel, for God's sake...sorry. But I want a new name. That's what I want.

God: Ah. Yes. And what name would you like to be called?

Angel: Well, I don't know. But maybe like, you know, the other side of the coin. If Israel is the man who wrestles with God, then I'm the angel who wrestles with man. Yeah. Something like that. Would that be possible, Boss?

God: I think that can be arranged. We shall call you "Ishrael." Ish is the word for man. You'll be the man-wrestler.

Angel: I like the sound of that. Ishrael. Thanks, Boss. (Gets up to leave. Then stops.)

God: Something else?

Angel: Yeah. I was wondering what's going to happen to this Israel?

God: Ahhh...well, you know human freedom turns prediction into a guessing game. But some things I see. This Israel will become more than a family, more than a tribe, it will become a nation among the nations. It will wrestle the world for its rightful place. It will wrestle with its own demons and desires. It will learn the humbling lesson all nations learn. It will endure, limping and yet noble, tenacious for life, and able to wrestle with me for justice and for mercy.

Angel: Sounds like I'm gonna have a lot of work to do.

God: You have no idea.

Provenance: This short two-person play, first performed at a *shabbaton*, has often been used by rabbis as a substitute for a sermon. I have always been interested in what I call "participatory narratives," and a play such as this one is designed to generate discussion and interaction.

Peter Pitzele, PhD, is trained in the improvisational methodology of psychodrama, which he applies to Biblical narratives under the name Bibliodrama. Peter also writes plays designed for a reader's theater format rather than for professional actors in a theatrical context. These plays have been widely performed in synagogues and educational settings and especially geriatric communities. Peter is also working as a visual artist, making use of torn paper *midrash* to illuminate the Bible. (www.bibliodrama.com and www.biblioartist.com)

Whitewater
by Zalman Schachter-Shalomi

I want to tell you a story about a river.

One day Reb Sholem came to see Reb Nachum. He had just been thinking about the problem of divine providence and freedom of choice. No matter how he looked at it, there was no way that a human being could solve this conundrum of believing in both at the same time. If there was such a thing as divine providence, how could human beings have freedom of choice, and if there was freedom of choice, then how could divine providence exist?

He simply couldn't find any peace. So Reb Nachum said to Reb Sholem, "Go and bring me Wojtek the ferryman."

When he came, Reb Nachum said to him, "A good day to you, Wojtek. Let me know what you want to take me, and my friends, in your boat and I will pay you well. I am sure we will come to an agreement."

A price was agreed upon. Reb Nachum said, "Let's load the boat onto the wagon." So they lifted the boat on to the wagon and moved on. In a short while, they came to a quiet pond. Reb Nachum asked Reb Sholem to take the oar and row. So Reb Sholem rowed to the right and rowed to the left, and rowed wherever he wished.

The whole time, Reb Nachum didn't say a word. Then they rowed back to the wagon, loaded the boat on the wagon again, and journeyed on until they came to a small waterfall.

Reb Nachum then asked Wojtek if he would take the boat down the waterfall.

Wojtek said, "Are you God-forsaken Jews crazy? It may not be a big waterfall, but the boat will break into pieces and break every bone in my body. I refuse to do this! I'm not going over that waterfall, which would surely destroy me and any man foolish enough to do this."

Reb Nachum said to Wojtek, "One of the tributaries of the River Bug, the Bialtchik, has a wild, flowing current, and it isn't too far from here. I'd like you to take me and Reb Sholem, along with Reb Chayim Elyah, down the rapids."

Wojteck looked at them and said, "I don't understand. This is something that the wild boys are doing. I used to do it in my youth and I still know the rapids quite well, but I can't understand why you would want to do this."

Reb Nachum said to him, "How much do you get paid these days?"

Wojteck said, "It's not a matter of money. I'm prepared to take you."

Reb Nachum said, "Then what are you talking about? So take us."

So they traveled and came to the river. As they sat in the boat, Wojtek asked them, "Can you swim?"

They looked at Reb Nachum and asked, "Can we really swim?"

Reb Nachum said to them, "Can you swim across the ocean?"

And they said, "No."

"Could you swim across the sea?"

They said, "No."

"Could you swim across a lake?"

They said, "No."

"Could you swim across a pond?"

And they said, "*Efshar,* maybe."

So he said, "O.K. Let's go."

They then tied themselves by their *gartels* (cloth belts) to the gunwale of the boat. Wojtek took his place at the helm, and asked Reb Nachum to sit up in the front, and he handed him an oar. He himself sat in the back with the other oar. As for Reb Sholem and Reb Chayim Elyah, they sat in the middle.

Then Wojtek steered the boat into the current, which carried them toward the rapids with big boulders in it. The whole time the Jews prayed *t'filat yam,* the prayer for traveling on water. They said it at the beginning when they started out...and afterwards, they repeated it whenever they became frightened. Every time that they drew near to the boulders, it looked like the end, but Wojtek always seemed to know what to do. He would give a push in one direction, and then a push in the other direction. Sometimes Reb Nachum paddled hard with his oar on one side, and then on the other side. And each time they managed to avoid the big boulders.

The water was white and foaming, and then the river seemed to take a turn, rushing on even more rapidly, faster than they were willing to go. Reb Sholem's face started turning white. Reb Chayim Elyah tried to pull himself together, telling himself that the boat was going to be OK, but something in his stomach didn't believe him.

At one point, Reb Nachum had to push the oar very strongly against a boulder so they could avoid hitting it. From the back, Wojtek shouted, "*Dobzhe, Dobzhe.*" Polish for "good." He did this each time Reb Nachum did something skillfully with his oar. So they made their way safely through the rapids and finally came to the place where the Bialtchik issues into the Bug River. There Reb Nachum said to Wojtek, "Now it's OK. We can go."

Meanwhile, the wagon that had first taken them to their starting point arrived, while they were still settling their stomachs and drying their clothes, which had gotten soaked from the river. Soon Reb Nachum said, "Let's load the boat now on the wagon." They lifted the boat on the wagon and made their way back.

As for Reb Nachum, he continued to keep his own counsel. They arrived back at the house of study, the *beis medrash*. They paid Wojtek and gave him a stiff schnapps for a *l'chaim* (a toast), and then they all drank a *l'chaim*. Then they discussed whether they should *bentsch gomel* (recite a prayer thanking God for having kept one safe from harm). After all, wasn't it written in Psalm 106 that people who were sick or in prison had to thank God for their deliverance? And didn't that also apply to those who went down to the sea in ships, toiling in the mighty waters?

Then Reb Nachum asked them, "Well, what do you think? Do we need to *bentsch gomel?*"

They said, "Yes, we do, absolutely!"

So he asked them, "Why do you think so?"

And they answered, "Because it was so dangerous. We could really have gotten killed! But we still don't understand why you took us to that place and had us risk our lives in the boat."

Reb Nachum replied, "Have patience a little while longer. Let's now spend some time in prayer and meditation and afterwards *bentsch gomel.*"

And they did.

Then he asked them, "What is it that makes us responsible for exercising free choice?"

He asked, but still didn't answer the question.

The following *Shabbos*, when they were sitting at *s'udah sh'lishit* (the third Sabbath meal) and singing the contemplative psalm, "The Lord is my shepherd; I shall not want. He leads me beside the still waters," Reb Nachum suddenly banged on the table and said, "I want to interrupt you for a moment and sing to you the song from *Yom Kippur* night that goes, 'We are as clay in the potter's hand.'"

He began to sing, and all the *chassidim* joined him in song.

KI HINEI KA-CHOMER

We are as clay in potter's hand.
He does contract, he does expand.
So we are Yours to shape at will.
We yield to You—our passions still.
Like mason shaping rough-hewn stone,
We are Your stuff in flesh and bone.

You deal with us in death, in life.
We yield to You–Please heal our strife.
The smith can shape a blade of steel,
Shape the edge and bend the heel.
So in life's furnace You temper us.
We yield to You–Surrender us.

When they came to the verse–

A boat is steered by helmsman's might.
He turns to left, he turns to right.
As long as You keep straight our keel
We yield to You–Please make us feel.

Rabbi Nachum turned to Reb Sholem and said, "He leads me beside the still waters–and on the rough waters as well. At what point do I have a choice, and at what point is everything preordained?"

Reb Sholem's eyes lit up, and he became very excited. He turned to the *chassidim* around the table and said, "I know, I know, I know why you did it! Now I know!"

Reb Nachum asked him, "What is it that you know?"

Reb Sholem answered, "Some people think that their freedom of choice is like the still waters: whichever way I want to row–to the right or to the left– I can row. But as it says here in the *Yom Kippur* liturgy, 'We are like the rudder in the hand of the sailor: whichever way he wants to go, he turns to the right, he turns to the left.'"

Without comment, Reb Nachum resumed singing, joined by the others. When they finished the song, Reb Nachum asked Reb Sholem again, "Sing that stanza again–

A boat is steered by helmsman's might.
He turns to left, he turns to right.
As long as You keep straight our keel
We yield to You–Please make us feel.

So they sang it again, ending with the words, "As long as You keep straight our keel, we yield to You–please make us feel."

Then Reb Nachum said to Reb Sholem, "Now think back to the whole experience. What is it that you know? What is it that you see?"

Reb Sholem lit up again because he now understood perfectly. He understood that when the philosophers argued that God's Divine Providence was active in everything happening in the world, they were talking about the waterfall. When God decides to take you, there's nothing you can do. When you're tumbling down the waterfall, you can't steer. But on the quiet lake, on the pond where the water is calm, there you can steer in any direction where you wish to go. However, most of life is neither the waterfall nor the calm pool, but is more like the Bialtchik River, brisk with whitewater, which is to say, that life is a stream which flows down from a high place to a low place but leaves some room for us to do some steering.

Reb Nachum continued, "*David hamelekh*, King David, is saying that throughout my life, God leads me beside the still waters, granting me the greatest amount of free choice. But even at those moments when I walk through the valley of the shadow of death, gam ki elech b'gey tsalmoves—those moments, which are like a waterfall, I fear no evil, for Thou art with me. Because who makes the waterfall in the first place? It's You, God, Who brings me to the waterfall in the first place. It's all You."

"And finally," concluded Reb Nachum, "the holy Izhbitzer, Reb Mord'chai Yossef, teaches, 'When everything is over, at the end, when we look back, we will realize that everything was the hand of Divine Providence; even our 'free choices' were in fact decreed.'"

Reb Chayyim Elyah asked, "So why is it that we experience such trouble, such travail, such effort when we have to make choices?"

Reb Nachum said, "That, too, the holy Izhbitzer explains: God so loves us that even though he decrees everything that is to happen to us, He lets us feel as though we are acting freely. This subjective experience is what gives meaning to our lives. This is the way God invites us into partnership. It's not that we can steer our life by ourselves, or that we can even navigate it at all, but by giving us the illusion that we are in control of our own boat, God empowers us to act in the drama of our own choice.'"

When Reb Chayim Elyah came home from his whitewater journey on the Bialtchik, Tzillah, his wife, wondered why his clothes were all wet. As he was changing, he was telling her about Reb Sholem's question to the *rebbe* and the way in which the *rebbe* proceeded to answer it by engaging Wojtek to take them in his fishing boat.

When he explained what the question was, Tzillah, his wise, talented, and artistic wife, asked him to come with her into the shack in which she was doing her artwork. There, she had the room in which she did exquisite *tallis* weaving. Someone had requested that she design curtains for the sacred ark that would be like a tapestry, in which certain special symbolic motifs were embedded.

She asked her husband to watch what she was doing, and she took the shuttle with a purple thread and sent it across the loom as she was working the heddle. The warp also had various colors, and it was always very important to make sure which of the threads of the heddle were up and which were down.

She then showed him a similarly designed Torah mantle that she had completed, in which she had also embroidered symbols with gold thread. She smiled at him and said, "I could have given you this answer and perhaps that would've made sense without your getting wet."

He looked at the loom that he had seen and was familiar with, but still he did not see—until Tzillah pointed out—that the warp was threaded, stretched, and wound to prepare the loom. And when she began to weave, there was little more she could do than pass the shuttle while watching which threads to lift and which not to lift. She had full choice over the colors of the threads that went into the shuttle. When she showed him the Torah mantle, she further pointed out to him how with great *kavannah* and intention, she had embroidered the symbols with gold thread, and she said: "Don't you see that Divine Providence is like the warp? It is for us to choose which threads we put into the shuttle with which God weaves the tapestry. What we add is our love and intention and care."

After a long sigh of insight, Reb Chayim Elyah continued the *Yom Kippur* hymn with the lines:

> As tapestry is formed, thread by thread,
> And color is to texture wed,
> Our life is woven on Your loom.
> We yield to You—save us from doom.

The next day he invited his friends to his home for a *l'chaim* in Tzillah's shack, and after they downed a few glasses, they were also able to see the answer to their question.

Provenance: This new story is told in a classic *chassidishe* way. Many people find themselves in a dilemma between their belief in Divine Providence and their belief in the freedom of choice. This story was given as a response to that dilemma.

Zalman Schachter-Shalomi was born in Zholkiew, Poland, in 1924. His family fled the Nazi oppression in 1938 and arrived in New York City in 1941. He was ordained as a rabbi by HaBaD-Lubavitch in 1947, and earned his MA in psychology from Boston University and a DHL from Hebrew Union College in 1968. Professor emeritus at both Temple University and Naropa University, he is primarily known as the father of Jewish Renewal. His many published works include *Jewish with Feeling: Guide to a Meaningful Jewish Practice* and, as co-author, *A Heart Afire: Stories and Teachings of the Early Hasidic Masters.* (www.rzlp.org)

The Dead Sea
by Howard Schwartz

He decided to go there, even though he had stayed up all night. Before he fell asleep on the bus, he noticed that the young man beside him was reading a book about angels.

When he opened his eyes, he saw he had missed his stop. He got off anyway, where the beach was covered with signs warning of danger: the Dead Sea drying up, and the beach full of sinkholes. He spent the afternoon sleeping in the sun.

It was already evening when he woke up. He could barely see in the dark and stumbled into a deep pit. He shouted, but no one heard him. There was no way to climb out. Would he die there? He cried out to God for help. Peering out, he saw a heart-shaped rock embedded in the mud beyond the rim of the pit. He grabbed on to it, and little by little pulled himself out.

When he caught the bus going back, he saw the same young man with the book about angels and told him about his escape. The young man smiled and said, "I know."

Howard Schwartz, a three-time winner of the National Jewish Book Award, is the editor of four important collections of Jewish folklore: *Elijah's Violin & Other Jewish Fairy Tales, Miriam's Tambourine: Jewish Folktales from Around the World, Lilith's Cave: Jewish Tales of the Supernatural* and *Gabriel's Palace: Jewish Mystical Tales. Tree of Souls: The Mythology of Judaism* won the National Jewish Book Award in 2005. His most recent book is *Leaves from the Garden of Eden: One Hundred Classic Jewish Tales. Gathering Sparks*, a children's book, won the 2011 Sydney Taylor Book Award.

The Surprising Ones
by Rami Shapiro

The sages were summoned to the highest heaven to meet with God, and to answer a question that the Holy One, Blessed Be, wished to put to them. Not just any question, the summoning angels explained, but the question of our time; and not all the sages, but only the dead; and not all of the dead but only those few who managed to surprise God while alive.

There were not many, but how many I am not at liberty to say, though if I said there was a *minyan*, I would be lying. Thousands of years, tens of thousands of rabbis, and only a few surprises; it is hard to be God and not become bored out of your mind. That is why God loves the Surprising Ones. That's what He calls them, the Surprising Ones. They are, He once told me, mutations.

"Most of what I create replicates itself," God said to me once—though I cannot say if this was long ago, far in the future, or just at this very moment, since we live outside time and space. "If you know one cow, you know them all. That's why Adam had only to name the first. The same is true of oak trees and salamanders. Know one; know them all. I thought it would be the same with people, which is why I made only two. I was wrong about that. People don't just replicate, they variate. Variation is more interesting than replication, but still not truly surprising. Fat, tall, thin, short, pink, yellow, brown, red, black, or some hybrid shade—these are just variations. The same is true with their ideas and their actions—replication mostly, with an odd variation tossed in now and then.

"Mutations, though, they are something else, literally. That's what makes them fun, interesting, surprising. Mutations can lift the entire human drama to a new level of insight and hope. But they are so very rare.

"Yet that's what keeps Me awake. David said—or will someday say, I'm not sure which—that I neither sleep nor slumber. Psalm 121, verse 4, if I'm not mistaken, and I'm never mistaken; which is another curse I foisted upon Myself. Anyway, the reason I don't sleep is for fear of missing the birth of a mutation, and the thrill of being surprised.

"This is the only emotion I have left. Well, maybe not; maybe there's a bit of sadness left in Me. But it is surprise that I live for."

Now I don't have to be God to know what you're thinking: how can the Almighty, All-Knowing Creator of Heaven and Earth be surprised?

And I admit it is quite confusing even to me, and I've ministered to Him since, well, forever. This is how it works: God knows the plan from the start. It's like He's read the screenplay before the show is produced. He knows what the actors are going to say and do before they say and do anything. Still, it is interesting to see how each actor gets into her role and plays out her part in the story; interesting, but not fun. Fun comes from not knowing; fun comes from being surprised. I mean just like you can't get into a horror film if you know exactly when the monster is going to jump on screen, so you can't really give yourself over to the drama of life when you know each twist and turn in advance.

I've suggested to God that He not read the scripts in advance, but He says it isn't like that. He just knows them. They're in His head. But every once in a while, someone goes off script. This is what He lives for: the dead rock that suddenly oozes a bit of life; the dumb ooze that suddenly has a creative thought; that kind of thing. It might take billions of years for something like that to happen, but He doesn't care. Time is irrelevant to God.

But, you might wonder, if time is irrelevant, doesn't God know the mutations in advance as well? Actually, no. You see, He and I see everything as now—past, present, and future; it's all now. So if someone or something goes off script, it is happening now, so He is surprised. Don't try to make too much sense out of it. God's thoughts aren't your thoughts, after all. See Isaiah 55:6-9, if you doubt me.

Of course, He's not the only one who's surprised. Everybody's surprised, especially the mutant herself. I say "herself" because the first mutant was the first woman, and we honor her by naming all mutants after her kind. She had her script: Don't eat from the Tree of Knowledge of Good and Evil. Not all that difficult. Even when the snake read his lines, we knew she'd stay on task. So when she saw the fruit was good for eating, and yet she didn't eat it, we sighed. And when she noticed how beautiful it was, and yet she still didn't eat it, we shrugged. But when she saw that it would make her wise, and then plucked and ate the damn thing—that was unexpected! We danced and clapped and cried with joy at the gift of surprise. This was going to be a great show!

Except it wasn't. It turned out that surprise is very rare, and wisdom even rarer. Most humans haven't got a clue what wisdom is, and are petrified of variation, let alone actual mutation and surprise. So they cling desperately to their scripts: hating who they're supposed to hate, loving who they're supposed to love, doing what we tell them even if that means violating what we told them. It is all part of the game. And the game gets old. So God waits for the mutants, the jazz players, the improvisers, the daring few who make things up as they go along, the Surprising Ones.

At least, that is what He used to do. Then all of a sudden—but everything here is all of a sudden—He decides to call the Surprising Ones to council. Surprising even them, I suspect.

They gathered in a nice seminar room created just for the occasion. Everything was new—oval oak conference table, plush red leather seats with brass upholstery studs. Bottled water at each place-setting with a nice piece of *shmurah matzah* baked by Zipporah herself. When everyone settled in, God took His place.

Now I know what you're thinking—God has no shape or form, so how can He take His place? Can you fit God into a chair? Actually, you can. Why can't the One Who Can Do Anything not manifest as one of those who can't do most things? So He took on human form and sat Herself in a chair set between two of the Surprising Ones.

The sages made to rise as She entered, but She shook Her head and bade them stay seated. "Do you know why you're here?" She asked. The sages hadn't a clue. "Of course not," She said. "Do you know how close humanity is to destroying itself and the world?"

Again, the sages were silent. "Of course not," She said. "Do you know what is ultimately going to destroy them?" Again, nothing. "No more mutants!" She said, and even though She did Her best to keep Her voice down, two planets in the Alpha Centauri quadrant suddenly turned to dust.

"No more mutants," She said again softly. "No more surprises. Everyone is just copying everyone else. They've all gone mad with imitation, and yet each insists that his or her imitation is in fact the original that everyone else is copying. So they are killing themselves over faux-originality, when in fact they are replicating insanity."

"This is not the first time such a situation has arisen," Rabbi Kerov said. "And each time it does, a mutant arises with a new insight that saves the day. Like Hillel and Luria over here." Rabbi Kerov bowed vaguely in the direction of Hillel and Luria, and they nodded modestly.

"Yes," said God, "that is what I thought as well. So I waited and I waited, but no one goes off script. They are running out of time, and something drastic has to be done."

"Something drastic?" Rabbi Yarovski asked worriedly. "When You do drastic, lots of people die."

"Not that kind of drastic. Besides, they are going to kill themselves off anyway if we don't act."

"We?" Rabbi Bat Sack Sack said. "Why 'we' and not simply 'Thee?'"

"Listen," God said, "I am going to send one of you back to earth, to bring surprise to the people, and perhaps save them."

"Which one?" Bat Sack Sack asked.

"That is what we are here to determine," God said. "You are My Surprising Ones. Each of you brought something surprising to the story, something unanticipated. I want you to surprise Me, and the one who does, gets to go to earth and bring surprise to the people."

Now the Surprising Ones were surprised, and waited for God to elaborate.

"I am about to ask you all a question. A question to which I have lots of answers. What I want is to learn an answer I do not have. Whoever can offer Me this will bring it to earth and perhaps save the planet."

The sages were silent, most staring at their hands, a few staring at God.

"I want to simplify My teaching. I want to offer a single commandment that will bring peace and harmony to the earth. One commandment. No commentary. No offense, Rabbi," She said looking at Hillel, "but don't pull a Hillel and tag on 'all the rest is commentary, now go and study it,' because nobody is going to go and study it. One line. No extras. A tweet, if you will."

Hillel frowned. Several sages snickered.

"What, you think I don't Twitter? I do. I just don't use My real Name. So that's it: one law for all humankind, 140 characters or less. Now write!"

Suddenly, a legal pad of white, lined paper and a new Mont Blanc pen with the white Star of David on the cap appeared before each sage, except for two who still preferred quill and parchment.

How long the exercise took, I can't say. It seemed over before it had begun. God collected the papers and read them silently to Herself. If She had blood in Her face, it would have drained. She seemed almost translucent.

"This? This is it? This is the best you can do? *Keep the seventh day and make it holy? Seek peace and pursue peace? Love your neighbor? Love the stranger? Love the Lord?!* What do you think this is—The Best of Torah? Give me something fresh!"

A mocking, female voice came from a shadowy corner of the room, "They can't."

"Let there be light!" God said, and there was light, and the light was good enough to allow all of us to see who was standing in the former shadows.

"You!" God said a bit too loudly and another planet turned to ash. "You."

"Of course, me. Well, not really, of course, because if it was truly a matter of course, You would have expected it, and hence there would be no surprise. So I just thought that at an assembly of the Surprising Ones, there ought to be some modicum of surprise."

God did Her best to scowl, but She loved this one too much, and a smile danced at the corners of Her mouth. After all, this was Her first-born, Sophia.

"Mutations happen only once," Sophia said. "Then, if they are lucky, they replicate. The replications may in time allow for variations, but the mutation itself is done. These mutant geniuses, these Surprising Ones, are all one-song wonders. They can't offer You anything new."

"And you can?" said Rabbi Mindle Mendle ben Mendle Mindle. "You can do what we cannot?"

"Yes, she can," God said, "All right, surprise Me."

"Surprise us," the sages said with one voice.

"Yes, surprise us," God said, "what is the one commandment for this time and this place?"

"*You shall blot out the remembrance of Amalek.*"

The sages stared and were silent. God, too, said nothing.

"It's Deuteronomy 25:19," Sophia said helpfully.

"Yes, but so what?" shouted Rabbi Povich the Moor. "Your commandment demands murder and destruction. The people need peace, not more violence!"

"And they need love, not hate!" shouted Rabbi Hilda the Hooverite.

"And they need peace, not more violence!" shouted Rabbi Hoover the Hildite.

"I just said that," shouted Rabbi Povich the Chassid.

"Oh," said Rabbi Hoover the Hildite, "damn replication!"

"And how will this commandment save the people?" asked God.

"Look, humanity is drowning in love. Every religion claims to be a religion of love, and by doing so, it excuses hatred in the name of love. As long as they can pretend that true love requires the destruction of one's enemies, there is no hope. So I say, let's command them to hate, to murder, to destroy mercilessly. Because this is so absurd, the people will reject it, and when they reject it, they will reject us, and when they reject us, they will reject You, and at last they will be free to think for themselves. And when they think for themselves..."

"They will tear each other limb from limb!" hissed Rabbi Chayyim ben Shiloh, the Tzaddik of Borsht.

"Perhaps, but that will be their choice. And besides they are doing that already."

"Think for themselves? Choice?" asked God.

"Yes," Sophia said almost in a whisper. "Think for themselves; choose for themselves."

"Most will choose slaughter," God said.

"True," Sophia said, "But some…"

"Some may surprise us."

"And surprise is what You live for."

God glanced down at the table, and thought for a moment, and when She looked up, Sophia was already gone, and a new religion of death had already appeared on the earth, and while most of humanity thought it wise, there were a few who thought it mad, and with these lies the salvation of the world.

"Stay and see what happens," God said to the Surprising Ones. "We'll order in."

Note: Don't be surprised if you don't recognize the names of the Surprising Ones. With very few exceptions, they are forgotten as soon as their mutation takes hold so as to allow you humans the illusion of steady state replication.

Rami Shapiro, Ph.D., is a rabbi and award-winning author, poet, essayist, and educator, adjunct Professor of Religion and Director of The Writers' Loft at Middle Tennessee State University, and the Director of Wisdom House, a center for interfaith study, dialogue, and contemplative practice at the Scarritt-Bennett Center in Nashville. Author of over twenty books on religion and spirituality, Rami also writes a regular column for *Spirituality and Health* magazine called "Roadside Assistance for the Spiritual Traveler," and blogs at www.rabbirami.blogspot.com. His most recent books are *Recovery: The Sacred Art* and *Ecclesiastes: Annotated and Explained.*

The Elevator that Wouldn't Go
by Shohama Harris Wiener

It was quite a long time ago. I think it must have been 1987. I had arranged for Rabbi Zalman Schachter-Shalomi to teach at the rabbinic seminary in New York City I was heading as Executive Dean, a non-denominational seminary called The Academy for Jewish Religion (AJR). This was the first time I had brought in such a powerful spiritual leader. Reb Zalman, as he likes to be called, had come all the way from Philadelphia to teach about prayer and spirituality. I was somewhat nervous awaiting his safe arrival, and praying that the class would be as extraordinary as those I had experienced with him. In those days, Reb Zalman was still a controversial figure.

The AJR was then meeting at a synagogue in New York City named Ansche Chesed, whose venerable old building was still serviced by its original elevator. This elevator was the kind that used to be run by a uniformed, old elevator man, wearing white gloves. The elevator had beautiful, dark wood, a very high ceiling, and lots of buttons. If you pushed the button for the floor you wanted, it would begin to sing a moaning song, and move ever so slowly toward your destination. In the elevator door was a window, so that it was possible to see the walls of the elevator shaft as well the corridors of the various floors that it reached. This elevator no longer had an operator—it had been transformed into a self-service model—but it still had its character from a prior and elegant era.

I had come downstairs to greet Reb Zalman and escort him up in the elevator to the second floor, where his class was being held. A couple of the students had arrived at the same time, and joined us.

We stepped into the elevator, and I pushed the button marked "Close." The door shut. Then I pushed the button that was marked with a number 2. The elevator began to move, ever so slowly, as was its way. It groaned upwards for about thirty seconds, and then—it stopped. We could see the walls of the elevator shaft; we were stopped in between the first and second floor.

I pushed the number 2 button again. Nothing happened. Then I pushed the number 1 button, hoping it would go back downstairs. Nothing happened. We were stuck in between the floors, with no way to go up or go down. No way to get out. No way to move.

Just as my heart began to sink, I spied a bright red button, the Emergency button, and pushed it. It activated an intercom.

"Hello, hello," I said. "The elevator seems to be stuck."

"Stuck, did you say?" said the voice on the other end.

"Yes, stuck. Between the first floor and the second floor." My voice rose with my anxiety. "Can you send the maintenance man to help us?"

"Well, I could if he were here, but he's not. He won't be back for at least an hour," said the voice on the other end.

"Oh, no," I said. "We can't wait that long. We have a distinguished visiting rabbi who has come to teach the prayer class that starts in just a few minutes."

"I'm sorry," was the reply. "There's nothing else I can do to help you right now. Even if I called the elevator maintenance company, they wouldn't send anyone right away. You might be there for hours."

Oy! This was not good news. We were stuck in a broken elevator with no way to move and no way to get out. By the time the elevator would likely be fixed, the class time would be over and students would be heading back out to their jobs.

Then I turned to Reb Zalman. "I'm so sorry, Reb Zalman, I don't know what to do. Perhaps you have an idea."

Reb Zalman looked up and said, in his resonant voice, *"Ya'aleh v'yavo!"* (May it rise and come [up]).[33]

The echo of Reb Zalman's booming voice had hardly finished reverberating through the elevator shaft when the elevator began to make sounds, and to move ever-so-slowly. We all held our breath. Moaning and groaning, it rose to the second floor and stopped. We sighed a deep breath of relief as I opened the door, and we walked out into the corridor.

We were safe, and the prayer class could begin on time.

Epilogue: The class itself I don't remember. But the introduction— ahhh. God gave us living proof of the power of a heartfelt prayer to bring help to any situation, even that of an elevator that wouldn't go.

---

[33] A prayer said only on *Rosh Chodesh* and *Chol Ha-Moed,* eight words in essence meaning may our prayers rise up and incur God's favor for us.

Provenance: This story gives an example of an "arrow prayer."

Shohama Harris Wiener, D.Min., serves as *Rosh Hashpa'ah,* Director of Spiritual Guidance and Development for ReclaimingJudaism.org and for the ALEPH Ordination Programs, www.aleph.org. Shohama was the first woman to be president of a Jewish seminary, The Academy for Jewish Religion. She is also founding director of HASHPA'AH, ALEPH: Alliance for Jewish Renewal's training for Jewish clergy to receive ordination as Spiritual Director/Mashpia; and she serves as Rabbi of Temple Beth-El of City Island, NY. (www.yourshulbythesea.org)

Glossary

a. All non-English terms translated below are Hebrew, unless otherwise noted.
b. Transliterations may at times vary from typical forms, since in *Mitzvah Stories*, the authors may have adapted them to reflect regional accents.
c. Transliterations of Hebrew terms are given first in Sefardi, then Ashkenazi, and where appropriate, in plural forms.
d. CH=kh, guttural sound
e. Most Hebrew terms, other than Adonai, *Hashem* and Jewish holidays, are italicized and in lower case.

abdallek (ahb-dah-lk): Iraqi-Jewish term of affection, half Hebrew— half Arabic, meaning "may I be your sacrifice," or "I would die for you," expressing a mother's absolute love of her offspring.

Abraham (Av-rah-hahm in Hebrew): Jewish Biblical patriarch in the book of Genesis. Known as the father of the three monotheistic (Abrahamic) religions—Judaism, Islam, and Christianity, and for creating a lasting covenant between God and the Jewish people.

ad lo yada (ahd lo yah-dah): "Until you do not know." The tradition of becoming so intoxicated on *Purim* that one curses the name of the hero, Mordechai, and praises the name of the villain, Haman, in order to celebrate the surprising twists and role reversals in the *Purim* story. While some groups advocate drinking alcohol, many advocate achieving such intoxication through pure joy of connection and spirit.

Adonai (ah-doh-nai): Lord, from the Hebrew root, *adon*, or from *eh-den*, threshold. A sanctified name for God. Outside of the context of prayer, religious Jews will say *adoshem*, or another of the many other substitute names for God to avoid invoking God's name in vain.

agora (a-gor-a): 1/100th of a shekel, Israeli coin.

Akiba (ah-kee-ba): A foundational and innovative rabbinic sage from Palestine in the early second century C.E. who taught Torah despite stringent prohibitions and threats of violence from the Roman conquerors. After defying Roman rule by teaching Torah and becoming active in the anti-Roman rebellion, Rabbi Akiba was murdered by the Roman government.

aliyah (ah-li-ah): To "ascend," to have an honor and be called to recite a blessing at the Torah during religious services. To "make *aliyah*" is the mitzvah of moving to Israel and taking up citizenship.

amidah (ah-mee-dah): Peak point of a Jewish service, prayer recited while standing. Each prayer in this section serves as a springboard to finding and expressing the prayer of one's heart.

amora, ah-mora'im (ah-mo-rah, ah-mo-rah-im pl): Early rabbinic scholars who commented on the *Mishna* and then codified the commentaries into the Gemara, from 200-500 C.E. in Babylon and ancient Israel. *Mishna* and Gemara are the two foundational sections of the Talmud.

Ashkenazi (ahsh-k'nah-zi): Jews of Central and Northern European descent. Jewish traditions can vary by region.

ba'alabatim (bal-a-bah-tim pl): Leaders of a congregation or organization, from the word ba'al, as in masters of, e.g. *baalabus* is Yiddish for a woman who excels at heading her household.

Baal Shem Tov: (1698-1760) Israel ben Eliezer. Founder of the *Chassidic* movement in Eastern Europe.

bar and bat mitzvah (bar/baht mitz-vah): Rite of passage for adolescent Jewish males and females admitting them into empowered Jewish young adulthood; now a rite also undertaken by Jews from adolescence upward who wish to deepen their Jewish learning and practice in meaningful ways and celebrate this as a life transition with family and community.

beis medrash (Yiddish, base med-ra-sh; *beit midrash* in Hebrew) House of study, or space designated for study of Torah and other sacred Jewish texts.

beit din (bayt dihn): Literally meaning "house of judgment," this form of Jewish court presides over Jewish ethical and ritual arbitrations such as conversions, business, divorce and child custody disputes between Jews.

bentsch gomel (bench go-mel): Blessing after surviving an operation, physical trauma, childbirth, dangerous journey, or any other serious danger.

bikkur cholim (bee-cor kholim): The mitzvah of visiting the sick.

bimah (bee-mah): Pulpit. The platform from which the Torah is read during a Jewish prayer service.

bisl (Yiddish, biss'l): A little bit.

bracha, brucha, brachot (brah-kha, bruh-kha, bra-khot pl): Blessing(s).

brit milah, bris milah (breet mee-lah, bris mee-lah): A Jewish circumcision. Covenantal rite performed on the eighth day of a male baby's life; later, if health issues prevent the traditional timing.

bubbe (Yiddish, bub-uh, also affectionately, bubbie): Grandmother.

bubbe mayse (Yiddish, bub-eh my-seh): Lit. "A Grandma's story/tale." Colloquial term for a tall tale, folktale, or something more fabricated than truthful.

burga (Iraqi Arabic, bur-ga): A caul. A thin portion of the amniotic sac covering an infant's face after birth, regarded as a wondrous occurrence and blessing in many ancient cultures.

chag, chagim (khag, kha-gim pl): Holiday(s), holy day(s).

challah (kha-luh): Braided egg bread blessed and eaten on the Sabbath and festivals (but not on Passover since it is made with leavening). First mentioned in Temple rituals in the Torah.

charoset (kha-ro-set): A mixture of chopped fruits, nuts, and wine representing the cement or mortar used by the Hebrew slaves to build the Egyptian pyramids as described in the book of Exodus. Among Sefardi Jews, the recipe may include additional ingredients such as honey, dates, and other sweets. Eaten during the Passover meal as a Gestalt-like experience to remind us of the bitterness of slavery.

chasseneh (Yiddish, kha-sen-eh): Wedding.

chassid, chassidim (kha-sid/kha-seed, kha-see-dim pl): Members of a Jewish mystical folk movement begun in the 18th century by the Baal Shem Tov; some sects continue to this day.

chazak, chazak, v'nit'chazek (khah-zahk, khah-zahk, v'neet-khah-zek) "Be strong, be strong and let us be strengthened." Chanted at Torah service upon completing each book of Torah.

cheder (hey-der): Hebrew school.

chessed (kheh-sed): Lovingkindness, mercy.

chevra kaddisha (khev-ruh kah-dee-shah): Volunteer group that ritually prepares a Jewish person's body for burial.

Chofetz Chayim (khofetz khah-yim): Yisroel Meir Kagan, (1838-1933), influential Eastern European rabbi.

chol ha-moed (khol ha-moe-ed): Intermediate days of Jewish festivals.

chumash (khu-mahsh): Torah. An alternative name for the Five Books of Moses.

chuppah (khuh-puh, khu-pah): Jewish wedding canopy.

chutzpah (Yiddish, khuts-pah): Audacity. Can be used with positive connotations, suggesting "guts" or "gall," or with negative connotations, suggesting "insolence." Adjective form: chutzpadik.

Conference for the Advancement of Jewish Education: Founded in 1976 as the Coalition for Alternatives in Jewish Education), a national organization for Jewish educators. Also known as CAJE. After closing, renewed in 2009 under the name NewCAJE.

daven (Yiddish, dah-vehn): To pray, especially with focused intent and feeling.

Deuteronomy: The fifth book of the Torah, devarim in Hebrew, meaning "things" or "words."

doula (ancient Greek, doo-lah): A healer who provides emotional and spiritual support to a woman during childbirth; in some countries the term means a midwife.

drash (dra-sh): A teaching, homily, or story that explicates verses of Torah or other Jewish sacred texts.

dreidl (drey-dl): A spinning top used on *Hanukkah* in a game of chance, possibly used to divert attention from Torah study during the original times of *Hanukkah* when Jewish practice was forbidden by edict.

echt (German, Yiddish, ehkht): Genuine, true, bona fide.

efshar (ef-shar): "Maybe," possibly, or "is it possible to..."

Elijah (ee-lie-zhuh, eh-lee-yah-hu in Hebrew): Prophet and Jewish folk hero. In Elijah stories, the prophet aids or imparts wisdom to Jewish people, often in disguise as a beggar or traveler. In Jewish scripture, the prophet Elijah never died but ascended to heaven in a fiery chariot.

Elimelech of Lizhensk: *Chassidic rebbe*, (1717-1787), founder of *Chassidism* in Poland-Galicia. A follower of Dov Ber. Author of Noam Elimelech.

elul (eh-lul): The month of reflection and *teshuvah*, contemplating errors, admitting and healing relationships with those wronged, leading up to the Jewish High Holy Days of selichot, *Rosh Hashannah*, and *Yom Kippur. Elul* is the twelfth and final month in the Jewish calendar year.

Ephraim (Ef-rye-im): The patriarch Joseph's second son and forefather of the Tribe of Ephraim, one of the twelve tribes of Israel.

erev (eh-rev): Evening.

erev shel shoshanim (eh-rev shel sho-shanim): Lit., the "evening of roses," a popular Israeli folk song and phrase from the Song of Songs.

etrog (eht-rowg): A fragrant, yellow citrus fruit used during the holiday of *Sukkot* to celebrate the harvest season. The stem is called the *pitom*, and must be intact for the fruit to be kosher for the *Sukkot* rituals.

evil eye (ayin ha-ra in Hebrew): The belief that a negative influence can curse your good fortune if you draw attention to it. The evil eye is sometimes personified in stories.

gartel (Yiddish, gahr-tl): A cloth belt that a *chassid* wraps around his abdomen during prayer to separate the upper spiritual realms from the lower physical realms.

Gerer Chassidim: Hungarian *Chassidic* group.

g'millut chassadim (g'mee-lute kha-sah-dim): Deeds of lovingkindness.

golem (go-lem): An animated clay figure in Ashkenazi Jewish folklore, typically associated with the protection of the Jews of medieval Prague.

grogger (groh-gr): Noisemaker used on *Purim* to help drown out the name of Haman, the villain.

groschen (German, grow-shen): Name of a small silver coin formerly used in Austria and Germany.

gut vokh (Yiddish, *gut vokh*): "Good week," typically said after *Shabbat* ends.

haggadah (ha-gah-dah): Booklet containing the Passover *seder* rituals and story.

halachah (ha-la-kha): Jewish law, from the root word for "walk" or "pathway."

hamelech (ha-meh-lekh): The king; ofen appears as a metaphor for God; also refers to kings such as David "*hamelech*."

hamotzi (ha-moe-tsee): Lit. "Who brings forth." Refers to the blessing over bread.

hamsa (kham-sa): A hand-shaped symbol that holds deep symbolic meaning in both Jewish and Muslim Middle Eastern cultures. They are traditionally worn or displayed to ward off the Evil Eye and more recently as forms of identification with Middle Eastern traditions and practices.

Hanukkah (kha-new-kah): The Jewish Festival of Lights, an eight-day festival commemorating the victory of the rebel Maccabee group in defeating the Syrian-Greek army in the second century BCE and rededicating the holy Temple in Jerusalem, which had been desecrated by the Syrian-Greek occupation. The word *Hanukkah* means "dedication" in Hebrew.

Har Hazeitim (har ha-zei-tim): The Mount of Olives. Mountain ridge which rings the city of Jerusalem upon which is set a huge Jewish cemetery.

haredi, haredim (hah-ray-dee, hah-ray-dim pl): Lit., "those who tremble before God," referring to the most separatist *Chassidic* sects.

Hashem (hah-shem): The Name. One of one hundred and five names of God found within Jewish texts. This one is typically used in conversation or in written form so as not to invoke the Tetragrammaton (YHVH, the most holy name of God) outside of prayer.

hashgachah (hash-gah-hah): Destiny, providence. *Hashgachah pratit* refers to the belief in personal providence at work in an individual's life.

havdalah (hav-dah-la): Lit., "separation. " This ceremony of prayer over wine, spices, and a braided candle marks the the end of the Sabbath Day and the begining of the secular week. Jews traditionally conclude *Shabbat* when there are three stars visible in the sky on Saturday night.

havurah (hah-vu-rah, havurot pl): A small group of like-minded Jews who gather for religious occasions, services and/or study. Smaller than a congregation, sometimes independent, and sometimes existing within synagogues, havurot are generally lay-led and highly participatory.

hiddur mitzvah (hee-door mitz-vah): To embellish a mitzvah with beautiful ritual items or new melodies or elaborations to enhance the beauty of the experience.

High Holidays: Also known as the High Holy Days or Days of Awe, yamin nora'im in Hebrew, these days occur in the fall and consist of *Rosh Hashannah* and *Yom Kippur*.

Holocaust: The systematic Nazi genocide of over six million European Jews. May also refer to the murders of another five to eleven million Romani; Soviet prisoners of war; Polish and Soviet civilians; lesbian, gay, bisexual and transgender people; people with disabilities; Jehovah's Witnesses; and other political and religious opponents from 1938-1945.

Hoshannah Rabbah (ho-shah-nah rah-bah): The seventh day of the holiday of *Sukkot*. On this day, willow branches are often beaten on the ground, and hoshannot, supplicatory prayers, are offered. Friends are greeted in Aramaic, "*piska tava*," "may there be a 'good note' inscribed in your book of life," since the Gates of Repentance are believed to remain open until this day.

ima (Ee-ma): Mother.

Jewish Day School: Jewish parochial school.

jinn (Arabic, jihn): A trickster spirit popular in the folklore of Arabic-language lands and Muslim theology.

Judah Maccabee: Jewish leader of the revolution against the Syrian-Greeks in the second century BCE, which is celebrated on *Hanukkah*.

Kabbalah, Kabbalists (ka-bah-lah): Lit., "receiving." Refers to the Jewish mystical traditions, texts, and Jewish mystics.

kaddish (kah-dish, kadeesh): Holy, sanctified. In a Jewish prayer service, various forms of the *kaddish* prayer are recited, all centered on appreciating the awesomeness of God. The Mourner's Kaddish is a variation during which the mourner rises and says the prayer in honor of the deceased. There are several other forms of *kaddish* for other purposes and occasions.

kadosh (ka-do-sh): Holy.

kavannah (ka-va-nah): Intention or focus.

kayna hora or kinahora (Yiddish, kin-ah-ho-rah): From *k'neged ayin ha-rah*, lit., "against the evil eye." Incantation to avert the evil eye. Often said after something positive happens to ward off negative consequences.

keva (keh-vah): Fixed, as in the fixed form, structure, or routine of a prayer in the Jewish liturgy.

ki hineh ka-homer (key he-nay ka-kho-mer): "We are like clay." A hymn found in the High Holiday liturgy, comparing God to human artisans, and human beings to raw materials being shaped.

kippah (kee-pah): Scullcap worn to indicate pious intent to live a mitzvah-centered life.

kishkes (Yiddish, kish-kehs): A person's guts, instinct, or intuition. Also a meat dish made with intestines.

kosher (koe-sher): Jewish dietary laws and practices. *Kasher* in Hebew.

kotel (Koe-tell): Also known as the Wailing Wall or Western Wall. A remnant of the outer wall surrounding the ancient Jewish Temple in Jerusalem. Supremely sacred to the Jewish people. To this day, Jews from around the world make pilgrimages there to pray and make petitions there to God.

lamed vavnik (la-med vav-nick): One of the thirty-six righteous and humble souls believed to appear in every generation. While humankind does not realize the identities of these people, their righteousness is believed to transform our lives continuously.

latkes (lat-kehs, also affectionately lat-keys): Fried potato pancakes, eaten to commemorate the *Hanukkah* tradition of one day's oil lasting for eight in the ancient Jerusalem Temple *menorah*.

l'chaim (l'kha-yim): "To life." Traditional Jewish toast.

l'dor va'dor (l'door va-door): From generation to generation.

maggid, maggidah, maggidim (f.) (mah-geed, mah-gee-dah, mah-gee-dim pl): Jewish storyteller. Traditionally, an itinerant Jewish preacher. Also, a section of the *hagaddah* devoted to telling the Exodus story.

Maggid HaMakom (mah-geed ha-mah-comb): "Storyteller of the place," the official storyteller of an area or community.

Maimonides: Twelfth century rabbi, philosopher, and physician. Famous for writing the Mishna Torah, The Guide to the Perplexed, and other major Jewish works. His full name was Moses Ben Maimon, also known as the Rambam.

Mamela (Yiddish, mah-meh-la): Little mother, Mama, term of endearment.

Mamre (mom-rey): The grove of trees where Abraham learned of Sarah's pregnancy. An important mercantile fair site during his time, now a region of fields and vineyards.

Marc Chagall: Prominent twentieth century French-Russian Jewish artist, known for his paintings, tapestries, ballet sets, and a set of stained glass windows in Hadassah Hospital depicting Jewish lore and *shtetl* life.

Mattathias: Father of Judah Maccabee, who launched the revolution against the Syrian-Greeks, whose victory we celebrate on *Hanukkah*.

matzah (mah-tzah): Unleavened bread eaten on Passover to mark the quick departure from Egypt and to recall the poverty of slavery.

mazel (maz'l, *mazl tove*, mazelle tov): Lit., "constellation." Good luck. An expression from astrology meaning: 'may the star under which your event occurs be auspicious for good outcomes.'

Meah Shearim (may-ah-sh'ah-reem): Lit., "100 gates," a *Haredi* neighborhood in Jerusalem.

mechitzah (m'khee-tsah): A physical room divider or balcony separating men and women during an Orthodox prayer service.

megillah (m'gi-lah, m'gee-lah): "Scroll." Typically referring to the Book of Esther. The Jewish canon has five *megillot* (pl): Esther, Ruth, Lamentations, Ecclesiastes, and Song of Songs.

Menashe (Mena-sheh): Manasseh in English. The patriarch Joseph's older son and forefather of the Tribe of Manasseh, one of the twelve tribes of Israel.

menorah (men-o-rah, alt. *hanukkiah, menorot* pl): A term used to describe both the seven-branched candelabrum which sat in the ancient Temple of Jerusalem and the nine-branched canelabra used today to celebrate *Hanukkah.*

mentsch (Yiddish, men-ch): A good man or person.

Methuselah: The oldest figure in the Bible, living until age 969. Mentioned in Genesis.

meyaledet, meyaldot (m'yal-leh-det, m'yal-dote pl): Midwife, midwives.

midrash (*midrashim*, plural) A method of interpreting scripture to bring out lessons through stories or homilies; a particular genre of rabbinic literature. A *midrash*, sometimes in the form of a story or folktale, explains or "fills in the spaces between the words" of Torah text.

Midrash Tehillim (mid-rah-sh t'hih-lim): Ancient rabbinic legends about the Psalms.

mikveh (mik-vuh, mikva'ot pl): A Jewish ritual bath in which Jews immerse to mark the monthly cessation of menstruation, to prepare for a holy day, or to mark a significant soul-level transition in a person's life, such as conversion, marriage, or recovery from a major illness. *Mikveh* waters must include "living water." This means that most natural bodies of water can serve as a *mikveh*, and that indoor facilities must filter in specific amounts of rainwater.

minchah (min-cha): The second of the three Jewish daily prayer services, occurring in the afternoon.

minhag (min-hog): Matters of custom.

minyan (min-yahn): A quorum of ten Jews above *bar* or *bat mitzvah* age needed to hold a prayer service or to recite certain public prayers. In most Orthodox communities, only men are counted for a *minyan*; some now count ten men and ten women before starting. In Conservative, Reform, Reconstructionsist, and Renewal communities, Jews of all genders are counted. The decision as to what constitutes a *minyan* is unique to every synagogue or prayer group.

Mishna (mish-nah): The first major compilation of emerging Jewish practice and law produced after the exilic period, documenting laws, practices, stories, and rabbinic debates from 70-200 CE.

mishpacha (mish-pah-cha, mish-puh-kheh): Family.

mitzrayim (mitz-rah-yim): Lit., "narrow place or birth canal, or strait." Biblical name for Egypt.

mitzvah (meetz-vah, mitz-vuh): A traditional Jewish guideline for ethical relational and ritual living. A commandment.

mohel (moyl): A Jewish person trained to perform circumcisions.

moshav (moe-shahv): A socialist Israeli community with no individual ownership of property, originally agrarian. Some also do manufacturing and offer services such as web design as well.

Mount Sinai: The mountain where the Jewish people received the revelation of the Ten Commandments and the Torah, recounted in the book of Exodus and Deuteronomy. Mount Sinai is considered the birthplace of the Jewish nation, the place where the relationship among all Jews and between God and the Jewish people was sanctified.

Nachman of Breslov: (1772-1810) Founder of the Breslov *Chassidic* movement. Reb Nachman was the grandson of the Baal Shem Tov (the founder of *Chassidic* Judaism) and a widely followed mystic, who taught Jews to seek a personal relationship with nature and God.

nachon (Nah-khown): Correct.

negelvasser (Yiddish, neh-gl-vasser): Jewish ritual washing in the form of full body immersion, *mikveh*, or hand washing, *netilat yadayim*.

neshamah, neshamot (neh-shah-mah, n'shuh-muh, nish-ah-moat pl): Soul, one of five Hebrew terms for different levels of soul.

niddah (nee-dah, nee-duh): A woman who is menstruating or having another reproductive blood-related event.

niggun (Yiddish, nih-gin): A wordless melody or a Jewish song that is sung or hummed without lyrics, intended to raise the spiritual level of an individual or gathering.

nusach (new-sakh): Melody, style, or mode of Jewish prayer.

olam habah (oh-lahm ha-ba): The World to Come; life after death.

oy gevalt (Yiddish, oy g'valt): Exclamation of concern.

parasha (par-ah-sha, parshiyot or parashot pl): A designated portion or section of the Torah. Around the world, Jews read the same *parasha* on a weekly schedule throughout the Jewish calendar year. Also known as *parshat ha-shavua*.

payot, payes (pay-ot, *payes*): Lit., "corner." Side-locks. Orthodox Jewish men often leave the hair at their temples uncut as a reminder of the mitzvah that the Torah commands for Jewish people to leave the corners of their fields unharvested for the poor.

Pesach (peh-sakh, pay-sakh): Lit., "pass over." Hebrew name for the holiday of Passover, which commemorates the Exodus of the Hebrew slaves from Egypt and the national birth process of the Jewish people. Passover is a holiday of spiritual, communal, and political liberation, marked by eight days of refraining from eating leavened bread and two feasts during which the *seder* rituals are enacted.

pitom (pee-tome): The stem of an *etrog*, the citron fruit used to celebrate the holiday of *Sukkot*. The *pitom* must be intact for the *etrog* to be ritually kosher.

Purim (pu-rim, pu-reem): Spring holiday commemorating the story recounted in the Book of Esther. A rite of reversal, this holiday calls for adults and youth to dress up as characters and to hear the public recitation of the Book of Esther, the *megillah*, which celebrates the heroism of Queen Esther and Mordechai who averted the near destruction of the Persian Jewish people.

pushke (Yiddish, push-keh, push-kee): Container kept in one's home to collect donations for those in need.

rabbi or rebbe (English, rah-bye; Yiddish, reb-uh, reh-bee): An ordained Jewish clergyperson. "The *rebbe*," head of a *Chassidic* sect.

Rosh Hashannah (roesh ha-sha-nah): The Jewish New Year.

saalam aleikum (Arabic, sah-lahm ah-lay-kum): A greeting meaning, "Peace be with you." The traditional response is "*aleikum saalam.*" The Hebrew equivalent is "*shalom aleichem*" with the response of "*aleichem shalom.*"

sabra (sab-ra): Prickly pear. An Israeli cactus fruit with a rough exterior and soft interior. Term also used as a metaphor to describe native-born Israelis.

s'chach (s'khakh): Organic material used to cover the roof of a *sukkah.*

schmaltz (Yiddish, shmal-tz): Chicken fat. Also used to describe sentimentality or heavily laid-on humor.

schmutz (Yiddish, shmuh-ts): Dirt.

seder (say-dr): Lit., "order." This is the ritual feast of Passover, celebrated on the first (and in some diaspora communities, second) night of the holiday. Consisting of a uniquely ordered set of prayers and customs to mark the liberation of the Israelite slaves from Egypt and inspire appreciation for freedom and peoplehood.

Sefardi (seh-far-dik): Jewish culture that originated in Spanish and Portuguese communities before the 15th century explusions.

sephirot, sephiros (s'fee-rote, s'feer-us): The ten mystical realms through which God manifests within creation, as describe in Kabbalistic literature. According to the Jewish mystics, humans can strive to cultivate seven of these forms as well.

Shabbat, Shabbos (shah-bat, shah-bs): Meaning "rest," *Shabbat* is the seventh day of the Jewish week, a day of sanctity and rest for resouling, study, prayer, and nurturing of love, relationships, families and communities. Some Jews refrain from all work and productive activities from candle-lighting at sundown on Friday evening until Saturday night when three stars appear in the sky.

Shabbaton (shah-bah-tohn): Weekend retreat for Jewish study, prayer, and community building.

shacharit, shacharis (sha-kha-rit, shah-kha-ris): Morning service. The first of the three daily Jewish prayer services.

shamash (shah-mahsh): The "helper" candle used to light all other candles on a *Hanukkah menorah*. Also, the caretaker of a synagogue.

Shavuot, Shavuos (shah-vu-ot or shah-vu-os): Holy day that commemorates the Jewish people's receiving the Torah at Mount Sinai in a revelatory experience.

shehecheyanu (she-heh-kheh-ya-nu): Lit., "who has kept us alive." A prayer of gratitude for reaching a particular season of life. Recited the first time something occurs within a year cycle, something such as wearing new clothes or tasting a fruit.

Shechinah (sheh-khi-nah): Lit., "dwelling" or "presence." The term refers to our sense of the immanence of God in the physical world. Became a feminine name for God as its use evolved, especially in the Jewish mystical tradition.

shema (sh'mah): "Listen," with understanding. A major prayer in daily Jewish services, taken from Deuteronomy, and recited in daily services, upon going to sleep, and on the threshold of death.

shmurah matzah (shmor-uh mat-zah): Lit., "guarded *matzah*." Unleavened bread for Passover which has been watched to ensure that it has not baked past eighteen minutes; usually round in shape.

shofar (sho- far): A ram's horn blown during the High Holy Days and during the prior Hebrew month of *elul*.

shteibel (Yiddish, shtee-bl): Term for a small Eastern European synagogue.

shtetl (Yiddish, shteh-til): Small 19th century Jewish village, inhabited by Jews throughout Central and Eastern Europe. Until the Holocaust, shtetls were cultural hubs of Ashkenazi Jewish life and Yiddish culture.

shul (Yiddish, shool): Synagogue.

simchah (sim-khuh, seem-kha): Celebration of a major life cycle event or accomplishment; from Hebrew for "happiness."

Simchat Torah, Simchas Torah (sim-khat toe-rah, sim-khas toe-rah): Final day of *Sukkot* festival cycle. Celebrated by rejoicing in and dancing with the Torah at services as the final chapter of the Torah is reached in the yearly cycle, and the reading is begun again from the scroll's beginning.

s'udah sh'lishit (s'oo-dah sh'lee-sheet; Yiddish, shalos shudes): Third meal of the sabbath, generally accompanied by slow pace of music and a desire to delay the end of *Shabbat*.

sukkah (sue-kah, sue-kote pl): Fragile booth built outside one's home and synagogues for eight days during the holiday of *Sukkot* to commemorate the temporary dwellings of the Israelites during their wilderness journey. The *sukkah* symbolizes the fragility of life and inspires *yirat Hashem*, divine awe.

Sukkot, Sukkos (su-kote, suh-kus): An eight-day harvest holiday following four days after *Yom Kippur*.

synagogue: A Jewish house of worship, also called *beit knesset* (house of gathering) in Hebrew or *shul* inYiddish.

tallit, tallis (tah-leet, tah-lis): A ritual prayer shawl worn by Jews after their bar or *bat mitzvah*, with knotted fringes on the four corners to remind the wearer and those who see the fringes to live a mitzvah-centered life. Generally worn during morning prayers and not during the evening, except by service leaders, with the exception of *Yom Kippur*, and for Ashkenazi Jews, not until the afternoon service on *Tisha B'av*.

Talmud (Tal-mud): Comprised of the *Mishna*, the first compilation of rabbinic law, and its commentary, the Gemara. The Talmud is a record of centuries of rabbinic discussion concerning civil law, ritual law, and ethics. It also contains many sacred stories, known as *aggadah*, often referenced or created to anchor important decisions about Jewish practice at that time. Subsequent generations have built upon the Talmud as they, too, evolve Jewish practice in relation to changing times.

Tanach (tah-nahkh): An acronym for "Torah, *Nevi'im*—prophets and *Ketuvim*—other canonized sacred writings contained in the Hebrew Bible." The TaNaKh is the full canon of the Jewish Bible.

techinah: (t'khee-nuh, techines, techinot pl): Prayer(s), usually in Yiddish, written for, and sometimes, by women, found in special prayerbooks for Jewish women.

tefillin (t'-fill-in, t'fee-leen): Phylacteries. Small boxes, usually made of leather, with straps to wrap around the arm and between the eyes. Inside the boxes are parchments that contain sections written by scribes from the Torah. *Tefillin* are aids to contemplation worn during daily morning prayer, except on *Shabbat* and by *Ashkenazim*, not until the afternoon service on *Tisha B'av*.

t'filat yam (ti-fee-lat yam): "Prayer of the Sea," also known as "Miriam's Song," found in the Book of Exodus 15:1-8, recounting the crossing of the Sea of Reeds/the Red Sea.

tikkun (tee-coon): Healing or repair, as in *tikkun olam*, care for the environment, social justice matters, and working for peace.

Tisha B'av (tee-shah b'av): Day of mourning on the ninth day in the summer month of Av, commemorating the destruction of the Jerusalem Temple and many other tragedies that befell Jewish communities at the hands of oppressors.

Torah (toh-rah, toh-ruh): The Five Books of Moses, hand-written on a parchment scroll by a scribe trained in special Hebrew calligraphy. It is the primary basis for Jewish ethical and legal precedents and the holiest of all Jewish scriptures. Torah is also sometimes used to refer to all Jewish study, as in "engaging in Torah study," or to refer to the totality of Jewish learning.

treif (trey-f): Non-kosher food. Food that is unacceptable under the prescribed laws and traditions of Jewish food preparation and consumption. Now also applied by some to foods where the workers, land, or animals aren't being treated ethically.

Tu b'Av (too b'-av): The Jewish holiday of love, on the fifteenth day of the summer month of Av, on which contemporary programs focus on helping individuals find a beloved with whom to establish a family. Sometimes referred to as the Jewish "Sadie Hawkins Day."

tzaddik (tza-deek): A righteous person.

tzitzit, tzitzis (tseat-tseat, tsit-sis): Special knotted fringes attached to a *tallit* (prayer shawl), representing the 613 *mitzvot*. *Tzitzit* can also refer to a *tallit* katan (little prayer shawl), which is a simple four-cornered garment with the knotted fringes, which is worn underneath one's clothing.

vidui (vee-doo-ee): Confessional prayer said before the final *shema* at the end of life. There are versions also for high holidays and other service times.

Yaakov, Yaakob: Hebrew and Arabic name for the patriarch Jacob, son of Issac and father of the twelve tribes of Israel, who wrestled with an angel and won the new name, *Yisrael*, "One who wrestles with God."

yahrzeit (yor-tzayt, yar-tzayt): Jewish mourning ritual marking a *yar*, a year, of *tzeit*, the time since a person's death. On the anniversary of a loved one's death, family members light a *yahrzeit* candle, which burns for twenty-four hours, and also go to synagogue to say the *kaddish* prayer in their memory.

yamim noraim (yah-meem noe-rah-eem): Lit., "days of awe." See "High Holy Days."

Yediot Achronot (y'dee-ot ach-roe-noht): A modern Israeli daily newspaper.

yerushalayim shel zahav (yeru-sha-layim shel za-hav): "Jerusalem of Gold." A phrase used to describe Jerusalem's beauty; turned into a popular song by Naomi Shemer immediately before the Six Day War and the reunification of Jerusalem.

yeshiva bokher (Yiddish, y'shee-vah buh-kher): A student/bachelor attending a private *yeshiva* religious school.

Yom Kippur (yom key-pour): The Jewish Day of Atonement. A prayer and fast day during which Jews review ethical marks missed in relationship, repent, and commit to spiritual reconnection in the new year. Also called *Yom ha-Kippurim.*

yallah (Arabic, yah-lah): Colloquial term for "Let's go!" or "Come on!"

zaydie (zay-dee, Yiddish): Grandpa.

zechut: (z'khut): Merit.

zemirot (zmi-rot): Songs sung at Sabbath meals.

Recommended for Further Study

Artson, Bradley Shavit. *It's a Mitzvah: Step-by-Step to Jewish Living.* West Orange, NJ: Behrman House, 1995.

Artson, Bradley Shavit and Gila Gevirtz. *Making a Difference: Putting Jewish Spirituality into Action, One Mitzvah at a Time.* Springfield, NJ: Behrman House, 2001.

Chasin, Esther G. *Mitzvot as Spiritual Practices: A Jewish Guidebook for the Soul.* Northvale, NJ: Jason Aronson, 1997.

Chill, Abraham. *The Mitzvot: The Commandments and Their Rationale.* Brooklyn, NY: Urim Publications, 2009.

Dorff, Elliot and Avram Kogen, Editors. *Mitzvah Means Commandment.* New York: United Synagogue of America Department of Youth Activities, 1989.

Golub, Jane Ellen and Joel Lurie Grishaver. *Zot Ha-Torah: This is the Torah – A Guided Exploration of the Mitzvot Found in the Weekly Torah Portion.* Los Angeles: Torah Aura, 1994.

Ha-Levi of Barcelona (Venice 1523), Aaron (ascribed to). *Sefer Ha-Hinnukh.* Jerusalem: Feldheim, 1978.

Isaacs, Ronald. *Mitzvot: A Sourcebook for the 613 Commandments.* Northvale, NJ: Jason Aaronson, 1996.

Landesman, David (trans.), Ze'ev Greenwald (arranger). *Taharas Halashon: A Guide to the Laws of Lashon Hara and Rechilus.* Spring Valley, NY, 1994.

Maimonides. *Sefer ha-Mitzot –Book of Commandments, Volume I – Positive; Volume II –Negative.* New York: Soncino Press, 1976.

Milgram, Goldie. *Meaning & Mitzvah: Daily Practices for Reclaiming Judaism through Prayer, God, Hebrew, Mitzvot & Peoplehood.* Woodstock, VT: Jewish Lights Publishing, 2005.

Milgram, Goldie. *MITZVAH CARDS: One Mitzvah Leads to Another.* New Rochelle, NY: Reclaiming Judaism Press, 2011. [A deck of 52]

Wengrov, Charles. *The Concise Book of Mitzvot: The Commandments Which Can Be Observed Today, compiled by The Chafetz Chayim.* Nanuet, NY: Feldheim Publishers, 1990.

Index

N.B. For a story theme index, visit ReclaimingJudaism.org.

engagement, 187.

environment, 9, 196, 316. See also *derech ha-teva*.

environmentalism, 256.

Esau, 259, 279.

escorting guests, 252, 264. See also *hachnassat orchim* (hospitality, care for the stranger).

ethical will, 34.

ethics
b'shem omro, 24.

Ethiopian Jews, 261.

etrog, 205, 210, 305, 312.

etrogim, 205.

Europe, 42, 59, 79, 86, 89, 92, 146, 148, 162, 243, 301, 315.

evil eye, 59, 60, 258, 305, 308.

fables, 103, 119, 139, 163, 187.

families, 109, 122, 167, 175, 183, 198, 205.

family purity laws. See also *niddah*, menstrual ritual.

fate, 74, 104, 281.

fathers, viii, 7, 40, 41, 42, 43, 45, 46, 47, 48, 55, 56, 66, 67, 69, 73, 74, 75, 83, 87, 104, 113, 114, 115, 120, 122, 123, 144, 159, 175, 176, 177, 178, 179, 181, 183, 184, 187, 188, 191, 200, 207, 210, 217, 218, 219, 220, 221, 222, 223, 225, 233, 234, 253, 254, 259, 264, 265, 268, 287, 300, 317.

feeding the hungry. See *maachil re'evim* (feeding the hungry).

fertility, 163.

floods, 198.

food, 13, 34, 50, 51, 55, 56, 64, 67, 77, 78, 81, 82, 95, 109, 122, 123, 125, 155, 178, 184, 194, 196, 207, 209, 210, 211, 233, 234, 317.

Frankl, Viktor, 3, 244.

freedom, 12, 103, 146, 167, 170, 171, 203, 217, 280, 281, 284, 287, 313.

free will, 293.

friendship, 187.

full moon, 139.

GBLTQ inclusion, 130.

geneivat da'at (intellectual property theft), 103. See also truth.

Germany, 4, 57, 96, 113, 146, 147, 148, 305.

Gershom, 217, 218, 219, 220, 221, 222, 223.

gezeirah, 4.

girls, 6, 80, 88, 97, 115, 132, 167, 170, 194, 272.

giving a blessing, 95.

g'millut chassadim. See deeds of loving kindness (*g'millut chassadim*).

God, i, ii, iii, 3, 6, 10, 16, 25, 40, 41, 42, 46, 52, 81, 82, 86, 92, 95, 110, 115, 117, 119, 134, 135, 139, 142, 143, 146, 148, 153, 160, 161, 168, 172, 173, 180, 181, 184, 185, 187, 194, 205, 210, 211, 215, 217, 218, 219, 220, 221, 222, 223, 230, 231, 242, 249, 250, 253, 257, 266, 269, 270, 271, 272, 273, 274, 275, 276, 277, 278, 279, 280, 281, 283, 284, 285, 286, 288, 289, 290, 291, 292, 293, 294, 296, 300, 305, 306, 307, 308, 311, 314, 317, 319.
Adonai, 88, 185, 250, 300.

golem, 58, 176, 305.

gomel. See *bentsch gomel*.

graduation, 200.

grandchildren, 82, 83, 89, 91, 165, 172, 176, 200, 203, 246.

grandfathers, 28, 45, 83, 110, 146, 147, 151, 153, 175, 176, 230, 233, 234, 235, 253, 254, 257, 264, 266, 267.

grandmothers, 151.

grandparents, 35, 46, 109, 147, 161, 164, 165, 209.

grandsons, 264.

granparenting, 109.

gratitude (*hakarat ha-tov*), ii, viii, x, xi, 9, 10, 14, 32, 175, 181, 221, 260, 314.

groggers, 156.

hachnassat orchim (hospitality, care for the stranger), 10, 73, 92, 163, 264, 268.

hadlakat neirot. See candle lighting (*hadlakat neirot*).

haggadah, 66, 305.

haggadot, 147, 148.

Western Wall, 239, 308. See also *kotel.*
widow, ii, 85, 132, 184.
women, ix, 6, 39, 40, 41, 64, 92, 93, 94,
  95, 115, 122, 129, 140, 142, 143, 153,
  167, 169, 170, 172, 173, 182, 192, 200,
  205, 208, 210, 211, 230, 237, 238, 240,
  247, 248, 264, 309, 311, 316.
World to Come, 312. See also *olam haba.*
yahrzeit, 179, 317. See death. See also *kaddish.*
yamim noraim. See High Holidays.
Yediot Ahronot, 264, 266, 318.
Yerushalayim shel zahav, 88.
yeshivah bochers, 144.

yiras Hashem, yirat Hashem (fear of heaven), 6, 8, 315.
Yom Kippur, 113, 154, 184, 281, 283,
  284, 286, 304, 307, 315, 316, 318. See
  also High Holidays.
zachor (remember), 12.
zeicher litziyat mitzrayim (remembering the
  Exodus), 109, 167.
zemirot, 86, 318.
Zionism, 153, 261. See also *ahavas tzion,*
  ahavat tzion (love of the land of Israel).
  See also Israel. See also Palestine.
Zipporah, 223, 291.

www.ingramcontent.com/pod-product-compliance
Lightning Source LLC
Chambersburg PA
CBHW080859020726

47502CB00008B/2282